BAD SEEDS

JASSY MACKENZIE

Published by
Soho Press, Inc.
853 Broadway
New York, NY 10003

Library of Congress Cataloging-in-Publication Data

Mackenzie, Jassy
Bad seeds / Jassy Mackenzie.
ISBN 978-1-61695-794-0
eISBN 978-1-61695-795-7
1. De Jong, Jade (Fictitious character)—Fiction.
2. Women private investigators—Fiction. 3. Murder—Investigation—Fiction.
4. South Africa—Fiction. I. Title
PR9369.4.M335 B33 2017   823'.92—dc23   2016042635

Printed in the United States of America

10 9 8 7 6 5 4 3 2 1

For Barry and Rosalie de Jong

Author's note

Inkomfe Nuclear Research Center is a fictional place, based on the Pelindaba Nuclear Research Center, which is located in the same area of South Africa. The Robinson Dam referred to in the book is a fictional version of the Robinson Lake, which is also in western Johannesburg and affected by the same problem of acid mine water.

Chapter One

THIS IS HOW you hide a body.

We're not talking a scenario where you've had weeks to plan, to scope out the area, to assess the terrain. This is a rush job. Risky and dangerous, but a job nonetheless, and you are a professional.

First, the killing. Up close and personal is easy with the help of your accomplice, who provides a distraction at the right moment. The method you use is quiet. You've done it before. It's also quick, bloodless and effective, but it requires skill and resolve.

You have both.

You maneuver the body into the car and drive the short distance to your destination, where you go about moving it to its permanent resting place.

"Where do you think he's . . . ?"

Your accomplice speaks the words, and you mutter, "Shut up." Voices can be overheard. You need to work, as much as possible, in silence. Sulkily, your accomplice refuses to help you any further, meaning that the job now rests on your shoulders alone.

The clock is ticking, and you need to get the body out of the car. You lean across the backseat, push the handle from the inside. At the same time, you breathe in, relieved that your nose can pick up no smell of urine or shit, which would have complicated things.

"Where do you think he's . . . ?"

You find yourself repeating your accomplice's nonsense words in your mind as you climb out of the car, stepping carefully over the uneven ground in the darkness, bending through the open door.

Lifting a dead person out of a car is difficult. Dead bodies are heavy, limp, awkward to handle. Limbs flop, creating a weight imbalance that can send the corpse slumping out of your grasp. It's easier if you turn the person into a package first.

You truss the wrists and ankles firmly together, pulling as tight as possible, using thin nylon rope that will grip and will not slip.

Then you crouch down and get yourself underneath, pushing your head and shoulders through the loop that the trussed limbs have made and grabbing onto the arm with both your hands. This is an up-close-and-personal business, where you smell the trace of deodorant and stronger hint of sweat from the corpse's underarms, and you feel hair tickling your face. This butterfly caress reminds you of a lover's hair, a comparison you'd rather not have thought about and now wish you hadn't.

You need to distance yourself; it's easier that way. Think of it not as a corpse, but rather a heavy sack. Even so, this is not for the faint of heart, nor for the weak, because heaving yourself forward so that the body is pulled from the car seat and staggering into a standing position with this weight around your shoulders is a challenge.

You stand, limbs quaking, hearing your breath coming fast, puffing from your lungs. But you've found your balance, and you're carrying the burden. Your feet scrunch over twigs as you stagger forward, and you have a nasty moment where the corpse's shirt catches on an overhanging branch, yanking you both backward in a wild rustling of leaves.

Now you're out of the woods, so to speak, limping onward with your load toward the bridge that crosses the dam. A hidden ditch nearly claims you both—you stumble into it and lurch out, your ankle twisting in agony as you save yourself. Your heart is racing now, your breath harsh as you gulp in the cool air, your progress marked by the startled caws of night birds you can't see.

"Where do you think he's . . . ?"

The words are bothering you, although logically they shouldn't. But perhaps it's that you're focusing on the one thing that doesn't matter to distract yourself from the grim reality of all the things that do.

You reach the top of the incline. At last you're where you need to be. The whiff of poisoned water taints the air, and some light—the fat maggot of a quarter moon—casts faint shadows but does not glimmer off the dam's fouled surface. Now you can drop to your knees, tilt your shoulders and allow the burden you have carried to slide off so that it flops down near the edge of the dam wall.

Sweat crawls down your cheek, and you shake it away. You stride back toward the car and then veer left, hoping the supplies you brought here yesterday are still undisturbed. You brush aside the covering of leaves and branches that offered a rough camouflage, and there they are. Two heavy concrete blocks, each twelve inches in diameter, with holes drilled through their centers, and a longer length of coiled nylon rope.

The easiest way to carry the blocks is with the handles you've already made by threading a piece of rope through each center hole and tying it. You sling the coiled rope around your neck and pick up a concrete block in each hand. The rope bites into your palms. They are heavy, but the load is more balanced than your previous one, so it is easier.

Another minute, and you're at the top of the hill, smelling the sour air, placing the concrete blocks next to the body and crouching down to do what you need to do.

Now your weighted load is ready for transfer. You loop the rope through it and anchor one end to the trunk of the nearest tree. You hold the other end tightly, and with your foot, you nudge and push the body, scraping it over the earthen bank until it reaches the point of no return and topples over the edge down to the brackish water below.

You fling your weight back as the rope burns your palm, hauling on it, trying to slow the fall of your victim, because an almighty splash you do not want. Inch by painful inch, you ease out the rope. The trickle of sweat has become a stream, tension and exertion combined, but your efforts are rewarded by the almost soundless plop as the corpse meets the water with barely a ripple spreading across its surface.

Now you can play out the rope faster, letting it slide through your hands as your victim completes the downward plunge, through water twice as deep as you are tall, to rest at last on the dam's beslimed floor.

You let go of the rope, untie it from the tree and pull it out of the dam, coiling as you go, the length slipping through your fingers, first cool and dry, then slick and wet and stinking.

Then you stand up again, exhausted from your efforts, resting your hands on your knees for a moment. And it is then that you see it.

Even in the muted light of that ungenerous moon, the shape is unmistakable. A human figure, facing you, dark jacketed, standing near the edge of the trees.

You draw a sharp breath, preparing to give chase, but before you can sprint closer, the man turns and swiftly melts into the cover of the bushes.

Now, suddenly, the half-finished comment your accomplice offered makes sense. *"Where do you think he's going?"*

It was an observation; your accomplice had noticed that man.

Your job was not done in secret.

Somebody was watching; somebody saw.

Somebody knows.

Chapter Two

JADE DE JONG saw the accident happen as if in slow motion. She was driving her rented Mazda into the forecourt of the Best Western motel, Randfontein, in the full fury of an evening thunderstorm. The windscreen wipers were whining back and forth on their fastest setting, and the rain was drumming down.

Through the storm's chaos, she saw the silver SUV reverse out of the parking space outside one of the units and head at high speed toward the gate. She just had time to think, *In the rain, they haven't seen the pole.* And then she watched as the truck slammed head-on into the sturdy, gray-painted metal post that supported the motel's sign high above. Jade guessed that the sign was usually brightly lit, but the area was being load shed. This was the term given to the infamous rolling blackouts that had been implemented a few years ago by Eskom, the embattled national electricity supplier, and were now becoming more frequent.

The matte gray pole must have been invisible in the downpour. The truck's grille folded into a deep V shape, the bonnet buckled upward and the vehicle slewed heavily to one side before rocking to a stop with its bumper still buried in the metal.

Jade drove into the parking lot and stopped a short distance from the truck's ruined bonnet. She looked more closely but couldn't see any movement from inside. Perhaps somebody was slumped unconscious over the steering wheel.

Best to take a look. Offer some help. She took her umbrella off the backseat and scrambled out. Rain hammered onto its black canopy as she splashed over to the other vehicle. "Do you—" she began.

She gasped as a bloodied palm slammed hard against the window from the inside.

It left a five-fingered crimson stain that oozed slowly down over the glass.

Jade grabbed the door handle and yanked it open. Inside, as she'd expected, the smell and powdery bulk of a half-deflated air bag. And a woman. A petite woman with blonde hair and blue eyes. She was breathing hard—sobbing, in fact. Her eyes were streaming, and her hand was clamped over a nose that was spouting blood.

"Tip your head back," Jade advised. She glanced into the car. No convenient box of tissues.

She hurried back to her own car, flinching as lightning bathed the courtyard and a deafening clap of thunder split the air.

The rental company that supplied her rides always put a pack of Kleenex in the glove compartment. She took it out, ran to the SUV and wedged the umbrella between the car's roof and the open door. She tore the packet open and passed a handful to the injured woman.

Smears of blood on the deployed air bag, on the window glass, on the woman's face. She wasn't wearing a seat belt. The air bag must have hit her like a giant fist. It could have broken her nose.

"Try putting your head down slowly," Jade advised.

The woman did so. She lowered the bloodstained tissue. The flow had abated, although her nose looked swollen and her eyes were red.

"You want me to get you some ice?" Jade asked, glancing at the motel room door—number twelve—from which the woman had been driving away.

"Uh-uh," she said. Her voice was croaky and uneven, her breathing still rapid, but the tone emphatic.

"You sure?"

"I'm fine." And then, in a desperate-sounding tone, "Go *away!*"

Jade wasn't a busybody. Hell, she wasn't even a very good Samaritan. If the woman wanted to sit here and bleed on her own for a while, Jade wasn't going to stop her.

"All right, then," she said. "Take care."

The inner voice she'd learned long ago to trust was telling her something was wrong here—very wrong. But there was no time to worry about this. She wasn't here to help strangers. She was on a surveillance job.

She turned away, splashed back to her car, climbed in and pulled the wet umbrella in after her. Carlos Botha, the man she was following, had driven around to the motel's reception area as she'd pulled into the parking lot. When she eased her own car around the corner, she saw his white Porsche parked outside the office door.

Jade stopped in the farthest corner of the lot and waited until she saw him drive across the lot to room number nineteen. She saw the door slam shut, and then he was inside.

He'd booked into such an out-of-the-way motel. Why, she had no idea. But for now, she might as well check in, too.

The Best Western motel in Randfontein had seen better days, that was for sure. The lobby must have been redecorated in the eighties, and the receptionist looked like she was about to audition for the *Rocky Horror Picture Show*. Thanks to the load shedding, it was also steeped in gloom. The only light came from the screen of the receptionist's laptop, and from three candles burning on the counter. The candles added to the eighties effect. The 1880s, Jade decided.

"Power's due back on at seven," the receptionist told her, handing over a room key.

When Jade unlocked her room, the first thing she saw in the beam of her phone's flashlight was a large cockroach in the middle of the gray-tiled floor, staring back at her, unafraid.

"Roaches are actually clean creatures," she remembered a restaurant manager telling her long ago. "They preen themselves often."

That fact didn't give her much comfort right then. She marched over to the roach, ready to stomp it, but as she brought her foot down, it scuttled to safety under a baseboard.

"Show your ugly face in this room again, and you're history," Jade warned the roach. Reflexively, she curled up her toes in her drenched shoes. She put her bag on the chair, deciding it would be safer not to unpack. What other creatures were hiding out in this motel? Moths in the cupboard? Bedbugs in the mattress? She opened the curtains to let in what little light there was. The added illumination did nothing to improve the décor, but through the window, she could see Carlos Botha's Porsche parked outside the door to room nineteen.

She needed to get hold of a spare key for that room.

The door locks here were simple enough. In the words of a locksmith she'd known, they would have been a joy to pick. Security here, like the décor, was also from the eighties. Lock picking wasn't her specialty, though. She hoped getting a key would be quicker and easier. Angling her umbrella to shield herself from the gusting rain, she ran back to reception.

The receptionist looked bored and tired as she stared at

her computer screen with her chin in her hand before swiv-eling her gaze in Jade's direction. Her eyeliner had smudged, and her big sprayed style had started to wilt.

"I wonder if you can help me," Jade asked, shaking out her umbrella and closing it up. "I have a small problem."

"Sure." The woman sighed, pushed her chair back and glanced longingly at her screen again in a way that con-vinced Jade she'd been playing a game. Solitaire, if she had to put money on a retro-themed guess.

"The door hinges in my bathroom are squeaky. Is there any chance you could oil them for me?"

The receptionist checked her watch before shaking her head. "It's after five. Handyman's gone home. I can put it on the list for tomorrow."

Jade needed to get her out from behind that desk, so if one way hadn't worked, she'd have to try another. "Also, I'd like an extra blanket."

Looking resigned, the receptionist heaved herself to her feet.

Once she'd gone, Jade checked to make sure nobody else was coming. She propped her umbrella against the wall, moved the candles to one side and scrambled over the wooden counter that separated reception from the back office.

Working fast and quietly, she opened the steel cupboard where she had seen the room keys were kept. There were two spare keys for every room, hanging on numbered hooks. Her phone's flashlight helped her identify number nine-teen. To her annoyance, there was only one spare key on room nineteen's hook. Jade hoped the receptionist wouldn't notice the gap. She didn't seem to be the noticing type. Jade took the key and pocketed it.

Then she did everything in reverse. Lock cupboard, close

drawer. She looked at the computer screen when she turned around to see that the game had indeed been solitaire. Pity she hadn't put any money on that bet.

She was back over the desk and waiting innocently when the receptionist returned five minutes later, carrying a thread-bare blanket.

With the blanket, Jade walked out into the gusty, blowing darkness. The storm had passed over, leaving behind a spattering residue. The silver SUV was still where she'd seen it, its bumper buried in the steel post.

The driver's door was still open. The car was empty, its upholstery and bloodied air bag now sodden with rain.

It was an expensive vehicle, and the damage could probably be repaired. Had the woman gone back to her room? If so, why hadn't she closed the door? Why was the rain being allowed to blow in, saturating the carpets and ruining the plush leather seat?

It made no sense at all. Jade's instinct was telling her something was amiss, prickling her spine with chilly fingers. She decided to check just to set her mind at rest. She turned away from the car and headed toward the closed door of number twelve.

Chapter Three

WARRANT OFFICER THOKOZA Mweli, Acting Station Commander of the Randfontein South African Police Service division, got the call at twenty to seven in the evening.

"It's a murder. It looks bad. You need to get here fast."

"I'm on my way," she said.

It was turning into a bad week for murders. Last Tuesday, one of the construction workers from the new industrial complex had sidled into the police station and muttered something about taking a shortcut home and seeing somebody dumping a body at night, up near the Robinson Dam. After questioning him, Mweli had decided that there was sufficient proof to get a dredging operation authorized. She'd just been finalizing the logistics of this with the dredging company and coroner. But already there was another serious crisis to attend to.

She grabbed her car keys, hitched up the belt of her too-tight pants, ran a hand over her short, curly hair and strode purposefully to the door.

Five minutes later, siren blaring, she was on her way to the Best Western motel. Traffic was terrible. None of the lights were working, thanks to the power cuts, and even with the siren it was difficult to make headway through the gridlock.

Eventually she reached the place. The motel's neon sign flickered into life as she pulled into the parking lot. It was five past seven, and power had just been restored to this part of the city.

A small crowd of onlookers was gathered outside one of the rooms. The crime scene, presumably. Checking her rearview mirror, she saw her junior detective Phiri arriving in his beige unmarked car.

Puffing from the exertion, Mweli marched toward the motel room. Phiri followed, carrying the large bag with the equipment, cameras and protective footwear. The forensics van, thankfully, was already there.

Mweli gave a puzzled glance at the silver SUV that had collided with the motel's signpost. Was this related to the crime? Drugs, alcohol—had they contributed to the crash? Had the perpetrator been attempting to escape?

She was distracted by the manager hurrying over to meet her, her face drawn with anxiety.

"Has anybody been inside?" Mweli asked. "Who discovered this?"

"That lady over there in the beige top. She said she opened the door and saw the bodies, but didn't go in."

Bodies? A multiple murder?

Mweli turned to the slender, brown-haired woman standing near the door. She was wearing a body-hugging beige shirt under a black jacket and a pair of black cargo pants.

"Wait here, please, ma'am. I must interview you," Mweli told her.

The woman tightened her lips, as if she was going to argue that she couldn't wait. But then she simply said, "Okay." Her voice was calm, like her eyes. Too calm for a civilian who'd just stumbled upon a grisly murder scene? Mweli would need to look into that.

A camera flash blinded her. Already the press was here, if only the journalist from the local gazette. How did they always know?

"No photos, please, not yet," Mweli said in an authoritative tone, holding up a palm in his direction. "Move away from the door, people. We need room to work. Phiri, if you could tape off the area—yes, from that pole there. Give us some space."

She stretched a pair of gloves over her hands and, with some difficulty, bent down and eased on a pair of foot covers.

Then she pushed the door open and switched on the light. The bulb flickered into life, and Mweli's eyes narrowed. The floor was a scarlet lake. She could smell the coppery taint of the blood. And in the center of the lake lay two bodies.

This wasn't just blood.

Over the swish of tires and the babble of voices outside, the sound of running water was audible.

"Crap," Mweli muttered. She bent again and rolled her trouser legs up a few turns, exposing the faded pink socks she wore beneath.

Taking a deep breath, she splashed her way carefully over the flooded floor, stepping around the bodies of the man and the woman and noticing as she did so the bloodied baseball bat that lay on the bed.

She took another step, and her foot skidded forward. Her arms pinwheeled as her toe made abrupt, painful contact with the side of the bed, sending a splash of reddened water onto the off-white sheets. Breathing hard, she grabbed the edge of the bedside table for support. The floor was as slippery, as if it had been greased. In fact, she could smell the thick aroma of oil over the stink of blood.

The foot covers were unnecessary; this scene was contaminated beyond any hope of salvaging.

Treading more warily, determined not to slip and fall into this oily, bloody mess, she maneuvered into the bathroom.

The smell of the oil was stronger here. The bath was over-flowing as the tap released a deluge of lukewarm water into the tub.

Swearing under her breath, Mweli leaned over and turned it off.

Chapter Four

THE COOL NIGHT air smelled fresh after the stink of the bloodied motel room. With her back against the building's brick wall, Jade waited as Warrant Officer Mweli jotted down her name and occupation in her notebook.

"Yes," Jade responded. "The driver of the silver Toyota Land Cruiser was the same woman I saw dead in the motel room."

"Had you seen her before?"

"Only after the collision. She had a bloody nose. I gave her tissues, but she didn't want any further help."

"Did you notice anything in the vehicle?"

"There was a black leather purse on the passenger seat."

Now that Jade recalled the purse, she realized she hadn't seen it in the motel room. Where had it gone?

A pause as Mweli scribbled down her statement. Then she asked, "Can you please, in your own words, tell me exactly what occurred from the time you arrived at the Best Western Randfontein?"

At that moment, Jade heard the growl of the Porsche's engine. Glancing to her right, she saw its white bonnet appear around the building. Botha was going out. So soon after he'd checked in? She couldn't follow him now, but it would give her the chance she needed to get into his room.

Per Mweli's request, Jade described the accident. "The silver Toyota SUV left the parking spot outside room number twelve and sped toward the exit. It was raining heavily, and the car collided with that signpost."

As she was describing the bloodied air bag to the detective, she glanced toward the gate and saw that the Porsche
hadn't yet left. Botha had stopped. His window was rolled
down, and he was staring across the forecourt at the blue
flashing lights of the police cars, the crime scene tape, the
crowd of curious onlookers.

Watching Jade as she spoke to the overweight detective.

"Coming out of the lobby later, I saw that the SUV's door
was still open," Jade continued, turning her back to Botha.
It was crucial that he didn't notice her. Rule number one of
surveillance: Don't let your target know who you are.

"I knocked on the door to room twelve, and when there
was no answer, I tried the doorknob. It was unlocked. I took
a look at the scene. Then I closed the door and called the
manager and the police."

"Thank you, Ms. de Jong. I'll need your contact
information."

Jade gave the detective her phone number and email
address. When she looked around again, Botha's car was gone.

From inside the motel room, she heard the whine of an
industrial vacuum cleaner as the forensics crew struggled to
clean up the slick, bloodied water flooding their crime scene.

"Guy's got an ID," she heard one of the detectives say.
"South African driver's license in the name of Wouter Loodts.
No ID for the woman. No bag, either."

"Hell," Mweli muttered, overhearing this. Jade could
imagine her blood pressure spiking in response to this new
complication. The detective turned back to the scene, and
Jade took the stolen room key out of her bag and hurried
around to the south wing of the motel, hoping she'd be able
to do her work before Botha came back.

———

JADE HAD BEEN briefed on the job a week ago when she'd met with her employer, Ryan Gillespie. She hadn't known anything about the assignment before the meeting, which he'd arranged at a coffee shop in a casino complex between Randfontein and the Cradle of Humankind.

Jo'burg was a large, sprawling city, and the casino was located on its outskirts, where the concrete footprints of development were beginning to trample the area. Nobody had planned the growth. She guessed it was Jo'burg's usual style—a mishmash of industries that had been started up by whoever had money and the ambition to make lots more. *Construction permits? Who cares! The city needs to grow. Municipalities can be bribed. Build now, apologize later.*

The casino was located in a small mall that fronted a nature preserve amid rural suburbia. Across the road from it was a large industrial and warehousing center that looked brand-new. Talk about a clash of cultures.

Jade had thought the coffee shop would be tacky, but in fact, it turned out to be upmarket. Its name was Origins of Life, and someone had poured a lot of money into the décor. There was an exhibition in the hallway with framed images of the excavations in the nearby Cradle of Humankind, and of the *Homo naledi* fossils that had recently been discovered. A skull with half its jawbone crushed stared out at her from one of the black-and-white canvases.

She glanced into the large copper-framed mirror on the opposite wall. Chestnut-brown hair tied back in a ponytail, sunglasses pushed up onto her head, green eyes.

The image of the skull lingered in her head. It reminded her of the fragility of human life. She touched her cheek, feeling the hard outline of bone under flesh. In a hundred years, everyone here would be scattered to dust, but it didn't stop any of them from worrying about the here and now. It was why she was a successful private investigator. She made her money from people's problems.

The waiter showed her out onto a big wooden deck overlooking the nature preserve. Beyond it was another concrete shore of squat buildings and a set of tall cooling towers. Birds fluttered overhead, and an animal moved through the bushes—some sort of buck. She supposed she should know what type it was, but she didn't. You didn't have to know something's name to appreciate it. That's what her father, a police detective, had always said.

"Animals don't commit crimes," he'd grumbled after a much younger Jade had told him it wasn't a goose swimming in the park's dam, as he'd said, but a duck. "There's no need to get personally acquainted. Just enjoy them for what they are. Instead, take a closer look at that guy over there, loitering behind the lady with the stroller. He looks like he's checking out her purse. I'd like to know more about him, not that swan."

"Duck!" Jade had repeated, and although she'd been laughing by then, she recognized the logic in his statement.

Now, waiting to meet her new employer, she sat out on the deck, and a minute later a tall, good-looking man in a charcoal business suit strode out to meet her, setting a Mercedes key ring down on the table so that he could shake her hand as he introduced himself as Ryan Gillespie.

He had sandy-gold hair and blue eyes; his hands were soft, immaculately manicured. A corporate warrior, but his grasp was firm and his smile charismatic. Jade guessed he was in his mid-thirties.

"Thank you for coming out this way so early," he told her. "I schedule most of my business meetings here, because it's fairly close to the research center, but without visitors having to go through all the security checks."

"The research center?" Jade asked.

"I'm the Director of Security Operations at the Inkomfe Nuclear Research Station, which is over there." Gillespie pointed to the concrete cooling towers Jade had noticed earlier beyond the trees. "Inkomfe owns a lot of the surrounding land as well. In fact, they've just built a big industrial center across the street from here, including warehousing and a gas station so warehouse vehicles can refuel close to base."

"I noticed it on my way in. Impressive," Jade said, keeping her expression deadpan.

"Now I'll tell you why I want to hire you, but first you'll need some background."

"Of course; please explain," Jade said as the waiter arrived with coffee.

"Inkomfe has a fascinating history," Gillespie began. "It was originally built as a nuclear weapons plant during apartheid days, but it was decommissioned in the 1970s, and the weapons were dismantled. The reactor has been used since then for nuclear science purposes. It's a massive property. The security-fenced perimeter covers a thousand acres, and there are thirty-three separate buildings of different sizes. Some of these are no longer in use. A few are permanently locked for safety reasons—mostly high levels of radioactivity."

"Must be a challenge to secure it," Jade observed.

Gillespie smiled ruefully. "It's difficult at the best of times, but I've run into serious problems recently, and that's where I hope you can help me."

"What kinds of problems?"

He lowered his voice and leaned toward her. "Very early on Friday morning, Inkomfe was a target for attempted sabotage. Armed intruders broke into the complex and managed to get as far as the backup control room before the alarm was sounded and they fled."

"How did that happen?" Jade asked.

Gillespie nodded. "My question exactly."

"Did you come up with an answer?"

"I did, Jade. More coffee?" He poured for her. She noticed he wore a gold Rolex on his left wrist, and no wedding ring on his finger. "I can't help but think this is related to the recent government decision to introduce nuclear power in this country."

"I've heard about that," Jade said. South Africa's secretary of energy had recently entered into a "strategic partnership" with Russia to build nuclear power stations in South Africa. The flaws in the agreement, and the scope for potential disaster, had sparked major media outcry.

"It's a double-edged sword. People only see the risks. But the existing power stations simply aren't meeting the country's need, as you know." Gillespie leaned forward, his elbows on the leather-covered menu. "The increase in demand should have been planned for decades ago, and it wasn't. Blame and accusations are flying around from Eskom to the government, but the bottom line is that we do need an effective medium- to long-term solution, and nuclear power can safely provide that, if it's done right."

Jade wasn't sure about the "safely" part of that statement, based on what she'd read, but she nodded nevertheless.

"I don't know whether the sabotage was environmental activism or an act of plain terrorism. Either way, the sad truth is, there are people who are willing to gamble with the lives of thousands of people just to prove a point—and they nearly hit the jackpot on Friday night."

"Why target Inkomfe?" Jade asked.

Gillespie spread his hands and let out a frustrated sigh. "Sabotaging the offices of the decision makers would have been more logical, but I guess logic doesn't come into it. It's all about doing damage in order to get a message across. Inkomfe is one of only two centers in South Africa that use nuclear technology, and I believe that has made it a target. And if the worst were to happen, and saboteurs managed to seriously damage the reactor building, there could indeed be a radioactive leak."

"That's scary," Jade agreed. She guessed that the other location Gillespie was referring to was the Koeberg nuclear power station in the Western Cape, which had produced power safely and reliably for decades. Maybe Gillespie was right about nuclear power being a solution if it was done right.

"The intruders had insider knowledge of our systems," Gillespie said. "Whoever broke in knew how our security worked, the timing of the alarms and door locks and the lay-out of the entire plant. They were very familiar with Inkomfe. In fact, the ace up their sleeve was that they knew about a short section of the fence that wasn't electrified because we were replacing one of the cables. They gained access at that point, when no scheduled patrols were in the area."

"That does point to insiders," Jade allowed.

"I have spent the past four days—when I haven't been in emergency meetings and sourcing backup security personnel—trying to figure out who had the knowledge to do this as well as a possible motive. And I came up with a name."

"Who?"

Gillespie set his empty cup down. "I took over as director of security in June this year and replaced the previous director, Lisa Marais. There had been issues with Lisa's work performance . . . It was an acrimonious parting of ways. She joined an environmental activism group called Earthforce."

"From nuclear research to environmental activism?" Jade asked, surprised.

"I know. I should have looked into Lisa's decision more seriously at the time, but . . ." He shrugged apologetically. "There were a lot of other urgent issues to handle. I didn't believe it was important. Now I'm starting to think differently."

Jade added Lisa's name to the list of notes in her notebook as Gillespie continued.

"Shortly before she left, Lisa hired a consultant to manage the upgrade of key security areas, computer systems and other aspects. The consultant she personally chose—and *she* hired, and *she* background-checked—is a guy named Carlos Botha."

"Carlos Botha," Jade repeated. His name went into her book below Lisa's.

"Botha has gone AWOL. The last time he signed in was Thursday, the day before the attempted sabotage. He hasn't come in since then, hasn't answered his cell phone, hasn't reported sick."

Car accident? Emergency hospitalization? The possible scenarios raced through Jade's mind.

"We have established that he is not in jail nor in a private hospital," Gillespie said, as if reading her mind. "I even drove around to his home address—he lives in an eco-estate in Alberton—and asked the guards at the gate if they'd seen him. They said the last time he swiped his card was Friday morning, a few hours after the sabotage took place."

"That's worrying."

"Jade, I really need your help here. I'm a security director. Tracking missing people is outside my field of expertise. But the matter is extremely urgent. Whoever these criminals are, the odds are good that they're going to come back for another attempt." Gillespie spoke calmly, but Jade noticed he was gripping his key ring with his left hand. The metal logo dug into his palm.

"Can you find him?" he asked. "I need to know where Botha is now, and more importantly, what the hell he's up to."

"I'll do my best," Jade promised.

"I'll give you all the paperwork this afternoon," Gillespie told her. "In fact, I'm hosting a press briefing at two P.M. You can join if you like. It will give you some background on Ink-omfe and show you the size and scale of our facility."

"I'll be there."

Gillespie handed her an official-looking laminated press invitation before standing up and shaking her hand. His palm felt warm, but the grasp was surprisingly tight, reminding her of the way he'd crushed the key ring in his hand. The grip belied his relaxed demeanor and likable confidence. It hinted at the tension simmering below the surface.

Chapter Five

Knowing she'd have to drive out this way again in a few hours, Jade decided to find the gas station Gillespie had mentioned and fill up her rental car. Since there was no sign of it near the casino mall, she guessed it was on the opposite end of the industrial complex, closer to Inkomfe itself.

Taking a shortcut through the complex didn't save her much time. The place was so freshly built she could almost smell the concrete drying, and it looked to be unoccupied apart from one huge warehouse near the far side. Here the entire road was blocked by a large blue-and-yellow delivery truck with GOLD CITY GAMING — EQUIPMENT & SUPPLIES in large letters on its side.

The truck's back doors were open, and a delivery of slot machines was—very slowly—being unloaded. Jade watched, first with interest and then with impatience, as groups of workers hoisted the heavy-looking machines one by one onto carts and rolled them carefully down a ramp. She wondered whether the slot machines were being warehoused before being installed in the casino nearby. Perhaps it was expanding, and needed to store these goods in the meantime. Or maybe the existing slots had already worn out, their buttons faded and tired after millions of hopeful presses.

The truck didn't look like it would be moving anytime soon, so Jade turned her car and drove the other way around the large warehouse.

On the opposite side, one of its massive doors was open,

and she heard the screech of a grinder and the sizzling of welding machines at work. Glancing in, she saw to her surprise that the machines were being worked on by two black-clad technicians. One of the slot machines had its backing removed, and the technicians appeared to be welding something inside. Another machine stood next to it, also with its innards stripped away.

She slowed to take a better look. The way the men were hunched closely together in the poorly lit warehouse, blocking the open back of the machine, suggested a clandestine operation. This was reaffirmed when one of them glanced around and noticed Jade's car. He lifted his helmet and abandoned his job to hurry over and shut the big steel door, scowling at her as he did so.

Amused, Jade drove on. The things that happened in Jo'burg. She wondered for whose benefit the tampering was being done. Was the casino doing this to maximize profits, or was it private enterprise, hoping to get a better payout? Would three rows of cherries come up more often, or never? Was tampering with slots even possible? She had no idea, and in any case, it wasn't her business to find out; she had a nuclear research site to visit.

UP CLOSE, INKOMFE was like a prison. A three-meter-high chain-link fence set in concrete and topped with strands of electric wire protected it from the world. Inside that was a second fence, which also hummed with an electric current. The fences stretched for what seemed like miles, a steely double barrier punctuated by a series of gates. The visitors' center where Jade had been directed was through gate three. Only when the guards on duty had scanned her ID and driver's license, inspected her invitation and issued her an entrance pass and visitor's card were the gates opened for her to drive through.

The place was a paved concrete jungle, dominated by the cooling towers. The road Jade was on led directly to an enclosed parking lot on the far right-hand side, outside a large building.

The inside of the visitors' center was friendlier than she'd expected. A team of receptionists and security guards were on duty behind a long, dazzlingly white console. On the walls, official-looking safety notices were displayed in silver frames. A row of tables with starched white cloths had been set up at the far end of the room with drinks and snacks for the guests.

One of the journalists asked Jade who she worked for. She told him she was a freelance journalist, and received a sympathetic grimace in response. He poured her a Diet Coke, which she drank while waiting for the manager to arrive and start the tour. Not inclined to socialize with the others and inadvertently display her lack of a track record in the freelance world, she stood in the corner and thought about Inkomfe's security.

Everything looked good so far. The guards had been attentive and thorough, and certainly this visitors section was properly enclosed. But perhaps she hadn't been thinking like a criminal would. Could you secure a massive nuclear power station well enough to guarantee intruders would never break in?

"Humans are like rats. You can't keep them out of anywhere they really want to be."

Words she'd always remembered, spat contemptuously by somebody who'd proven them true many times over. Somebody she didn't want to think about, but whose presence was now in her head.

Robbie, the criminal-for-hire she'd worked with closely in the past.

Long ago, he had helped her take revenge on her father's murderer, but only after making it clear that she would pay in kind for the favor by helping him with other jobs.

Soon after they'd met, Robbie had tried to force himself into intimacy with her. She'd fought him off, and to her surprise, he hadn't fought back but grudgingly respected her boundaries. Since then, their relationship had been purely business, a business way outside the law. Memories of Robbie always brought with them a wave of fear and shame. She hadn't seen him in over a year, and yet his face was as clear in her mind's eye as if he were there in the room. His hard eyes; the small scar above his lip; his hair, which varied in length, style and color according to his dubious fashion sense. The last time she'd seen him, he'd sported short red-tinted dreads, an improvement on the bleached catastrophe of the time before.

"A beanie covers all styles anyway, baby. Wear it, and that's all people will remember. Take it off, and you're suddenly the guy with the crazy hairdo. Not the criminal they think they saw."

And Robbie's wisdom when it came to breaking in.

"You know something? That chain-link fencing is just a big climbing wall. Find the right spot, and you're in. Doesn't matter how many guards are waiting at the gate. You might think a place is a fortress, but fortresses can be infiltrated, too. Pay the people inside. Leave a Trojan horse outside for them to bring in. Crawl through the sewers. Do whatever it takes."

Jade's thoughts were interrupted by a voice she recognized. Turning, she saw that Gillespie had arrived and was standing near the main doorway.

"Good afternoon, ladies and gentlemen, and thank you for

coming here today. My name is Ryan Gillespie, and I head security and operations here at Inkomfe. As you know, we've been holding these press meetings throughout the year to help the general public understand more about nuclear technology via your skilled pens and keyboards."

He smiled at the waiting journalists as a ripple of laughter went around the room.

"Today's event will also include a visit to the reactor room in the classified security area known as the red zone. However, due to upgraded security measures, this will be the last time our media friends will able to access the red zone. We'll be taking you to the reactor's viewing deck two by two after the main presentation. In the meantime, we're glad to welcome you here. Now there's been a lot of bad press about the proposed nuclear power stations to be built in South Africa, so I thought I'd start by giving you a balanced picture of the role that nuclear technology plays, and why it might not be the monster everyone's making it out to be."

In fact, he began by breaking off his speech as a late arrival hurried in: a sallow-faced journalist with a hunted expression, dressed in an unflattering gray pantsuit. After the embarrassed woman had joined the group, Gillespie continued.

"People are afraid of nuclear technology because they don't understand it. But we at Inkomfe are far more worried about what's happening to this planet as a result of fossil fuels. Pollution, environmental degradation, global warming. Has anyone noticed how hot this summer has been? And precious little rain so far." He paused, scanning the room, letting his words sink in before continuing. "Coal-fueled plants don't only emit greenhouse gases, although they're very efficient at doing that. They release over two pounds of carbon dioxide into the atmosphere for every kilowatt hour of electricity they create."

There was a murmur of surprise from the crowd.

"Wind turbines have their place, but they're not suitable for all locations. They're extremely noisy, a major threat to wildlife and not very efficient. At the moment, solar power is costly, and the panels, which, incidentally, contain toxic metals including mercury, don't have a long life span or high efficiency. Solar technology is still in the early phases of development. Nuclear technology is already here. Yes, it has its challenges, but it's by far the best answer at the present moment, so we're in favor of the decision to build more nuclear power stations. We work with the technology every day; we understand it."

A couple of nods greeted this statement.

"The reactor here at Inkomfe has operated safely for decades, starting with the manufacture of nuclear weaponry, then moving on to the more peaceful process of constructing medical isotopes. You don't need to worry—the bombs were all dismantled decades ago." More laughter filled the room. "In fact, South Africa was the first country in the world to voluntarily dismantle its nuclear weapons, a fact that we're very proud of here. Please follow me inside and have a look around the visitors' center. The reactor tours will start in half an hour."

Jade followed the group into a spacious, high-ceilinged hall where informative posters and displays were arranged.

Inkomfe was built in the early apartheid days for the sole purpose of creating nuclear bombs, she read on the first poster. *The plant was originally named Mamba, after the poisonous snake—a fitting name for an establishment dedicated to the manufacture of lethal weaponry. But when nuclear disarmament became an international priority in the late 1980s, the plant was decommissioned, and the weapons were dismantled. At that point, the plant was renamed.*

The second poster told her about the weapons themselves. From the 1960s to the 1980s, South Africa had researched weapons of mass destruction and built seven bombs. Getting hold of the necessary materials hadn't been easy, with sanctions that became increasingly stringent during the apartheid days. However, the country's natural resources included ample uranium, which South African scientists learned how to enrich. This was used for the warheads.

In order to prevent nuclear catastrophe, Jade read, the weapons were worked on by only a few carefully chosen technologists. The weapons themselves could only be released from their top-security bomb storage lockers once a security code had been keyed into the strong room door.

While our bombs have been dismantled, we place the same emphasis on security, and certain areas of the plant still require codes that are known to only a few trustworthy individuals, the poster informed her.

Jade wondered who held the codes, and for which sections they were needed.

Moving on to a different part of the room, she was surprised to see a poster featuring an attractive tuber with dark green sprouting leaves, a bright yellow flower and dark, glossy seeds. This was Inkomfe, the plant after which the nuclear facility had been renamed. Reading the caption, she learned that the African potato plant had once grown wild in the surrounding area, but had been nearly wiped out in the rapid urbanization that had taken place.

In its raw state, the African potato, or Inkomfe as it is known in Zulu, is poisonous. However, when correctly prepared, its medicinal properties are well documented. It boosts the immune system and protects against carcinogens. It is also one of the traditional remedies for treating HIV. With the nuclear facility's focus

shifting to the manufacture of medical isotopes for cancer treat-
ment and other forms of valuable research, it was decided in 1990
that it would be fitting to rename the place after the healing powers
of this indigenous shrub.

"Jade?"

She turned to see Gillespie approaching her.

"Come with me. You want to see the reactor, don't you?
I'll take you on your own, ahead of the others."

Pleased that her questions about the place would be
answered without her having to blow her cover, Jade followed
Gillespie out of the center to a custom-made blue-and-white
golf cart, where a security guard was waiting at the wheel.

Chapter Six

THE CAR HEADED out of the visitors' parking, turned right, and joined up with a main thoroughfare. In the opposite direction, Jade saw a large van approaching. It had the international radioactivity symbol displayed on its side, a black trefoil on a bright yellow background. Below that, in black on yellow, was the lettering WARNING: RADIOACTIVE MATERIAL IN TRANSIT.

"What's in there?" Jade asked.

"It's our low- and intermediate-level waste," Gillespie said. "Lab coats, consumables, contaminated machinery. It's sealed in containers and loaded into the vans, which leave the complex late at night, then travel through the night while the roads are quieter, for added safety. The waste is transported to a place called Vaalputs, on the Northern Cape, and buried there. It's a safe way of disposing of it. The nearest town is more than one hundred kilometers away, and the area is not seismically active."

"What about the high-level waste?" Jade asked.

"High-level waste is not transported. It is securely stored here on-site," Gillespie told her. "Such waste has potential to be reused in the future."

Glancing to the right, Jade saw a large, empty parking lot surrounded by floodlights.

"We sometimes get large-scale deliveries of dangerous and flammable materials coming in at night," Gillespie told her. "Now they're off-loaded in this fully lit area for better

security. Of course, all trucks and their contents are checked
at the gate before being allowed through in the first place."

They turned off the thoroughfare, rattled over pavement,
then joined another road. They wove between huge buildings punctuated by occasional tall, narrow chimneys on a
route that led them into the shadow of the cooling towers.

The car approached the double doorway of a massive
building whose gate swung open when the guard pressed
a button on the dashboard. They stopped inside, and the
guard accompanied Jade and Gillespie to an industrial-sized
elevator that took them down a level. A reception console
opposite the elevator was manned by two staff members, busy
on calls. They hardly even glanced up as the doors closed.

The parking lot had been unpleasantly warm and the
reception area cool; as the doors opened into the underground heart of the building, the temperature dropped to
freezing.

They walked out into chilly, brightly lit silence, insulated
by silver-white walls. Their footsteps were hushed, cushioned by the rubberized tiles. Jade had the impression that
megatons of concrete surrounded the labyrinth of corridors.
She wouldn't have liked to work here, she decided. It felt too
much like being buried underground.

Gillespie didn't share her unease. Seemingly in an upbeat
mood this afternoon, he began talking animatedly as they set
off down what proved to be a long passage. "Do you live in
the West Rand, Jade?"

"No. I'm in the northern suburbs, near the Kyalami race-
track. In a furnished garden cottage."

She hoped whoever had furnished it would one day end up
in some sort of upholstery hell as punishment for their over-
use of the color pink and the plethora of scatter cushions that

adorned every soft surface. Jade could have sworn there were more of those cushions now than there had been when she first arrived. She was scared to lock them away in cupboards, in case that was their breeding ground.

"That's nice. Good to have somewhere quiet and private to live. I came back earlier this year from an overseas assignment, so I'm renting in a nearby townhouse estate. My bonus is coming through soon, and I'm going to buy a home when it does. In Dainfern golf estate, maybe. You know where that is? Just down the road from Montecasino?"

"Yes, I've been there a few times on jobs for clients." Mostly women. In her experience, Dainfern was the city's epicenter of cheating husbands.

"I recently looked at a lovely four-bedroom house there. The other place I like is Blair Atholl, although that's a bit farther out of town."

Expensive properties. Right at the top of the scale. Jade guessed Gillespie's bonus was going to be substantial.

"And I've got my eye on an investment apartment in Sea Point, Cape Town. Just a small place, but beautiful, and so close to the beach you could throw ice cubes into the ocean."

The probable size of Gillespie's bonus doubled itself in Jade's mind.

"But that's in the future. My dreams for tomorrow. Normally I live for today—I'm a big believer in making the most of the here and now, but until these security challenges are resolved, I'm afraid I've turned into a survive-for-today kind of man."

"I adhere to the same philosophy. Of living for today, I mean," Jade said. "There's no guarantee of tomorrow, so why have regrets?"

"My feelings exactly." Gillespie grinned at Jade, the

expression warming his face and bringing a sparkle to his deep blue eyes. Jade smiled back. The conversation had taken her mind off the gloomy chill of the corridor. Perhaps that was why Gillespie had started it, to put her at ease.

They turned a corner, and sheets of thick glass on the right-hand side showcased a brightly lit office that looked to be an admin hub. The far wall made Jade think of the flight console for a spacecraft, formed from contoured metal with computer screens set into it at intervals. Two white-coated technicians were at work, monitoring the machines intently. They didn't turn around.

"This is where they broke in early Friday morning," Gillespie told her. "The door has already been repaired and reinforced."

"What's inside?"

"It's our ancillary operations area, which contains backup systems for the main operations center. That room is far bigger; it has screens, counters and calibrators that monitor every part of the nuclear processor, from the heat of its rods to the radiation levels it's producing."

Jade nodded. It made sense: put the backup machines out of action, then head for the main room.

They stopped at a large locked door ahead with a CAUTION sign and the now-familiar trefoil below it. The door had a keypad on its right-hand side. His body blocking Jade's view of the numbers, Gillespie typed in a code, and the door unlocked.

It opened into a wider corridor, where two men in red overalls and protective gear were pushing a cart loaded with large containers. Jade wondered if this was low-level waste, heading to the transport trucks.

Another elevator took them up a level, and Gillespie headed to a narrow, curving ramp with a rubberized floor.

"The reactor is housed in an extremely thick concrete shell. It's a safety precaution so that any radioactivity can be contained, should there be an incident."

The idea gave Jade chills, or maybe that was just the cold air trapped between these dense concrete walls. She was relieved when the narrow tunnel ended. Stepping out, she caught her breath. She was standing on a suspended walkway that ran all the way around this circular space. Thick metal balustrades protected her from the two-story drop below. She looked down in fascination.

"This is as close as a member of the public can get to a nuclear reactor anywhere in the world," Gillespie said. "You're just eleven meters away."

The reactor itself was under the surface of a pool of water, and it glowed a brilliant neon blue. She hadn't expected the color to be so unusual or beautiful. She could hardly tear her gaze away from its eerie luminosity, but when she did, it was to stare at the structures nearby. On the back wall, a large screen displayed the continuously blinking words REACTOR IN OPERATION.

The screen was flanked on each side by ranks of computers and other huge steel machines whose functions she couldn't guess at. Ladders and scaffolding lined the walls. She looked down onto a multitude of pipes and rods in shiny polished chrome that crisscrossed the area above. She'd imagined the reactor doing its work in solitary splendor, but every inch of floor space was occupied, leaving barely enough room for walkways that looked only a little wider than the one she was standing on. Though when she saw two white-coated workers striding purposefully along the closest walkway, she realized they were wider, and she'd simply underestimated the sheer scale of the place.

Both the workers carried small yellow devices in their hands, which they glanced at every so often.

"Geiger counters to measure radioactivity levels," Gillespie told her. "Every technician who works in the reactor room has to carry one with them at all times. They are compulsory equipment."

The area was strangely quiet. Nuclear energy seemed to be produced in silence. All she could hear was background noise, the soft humming of pumps at work, not much louder than white noise. She could even hear the tread of footsteps on the floor below.

"Why is the reactor such a bright blue color?" she asked.

"It's an effect of the radiation. Cherenkov radiation, they call it," Gillespie explained.

"It looks incredible," Jade said. "Otherworldly."

Gillespie smiled again, the expression softening his eyes. "It does."

They stood there a few moments more before he asked, "Are you ready to go?"

"Yes," Jade said.

With the security guard following, they retraced their steps back to the transport vehicle that had carried them there.

They didn't speak again until they arrived back at the visitors' center. The security guard had already climbed out of the car when Gillespie took a brown envelope out of his briefcase. Handing it to Jade, he said in a low voice, "I've put together all the employee information I could find on Carlos Botha. You can start immediately."

"Will do." Jade tried to take the envelope from him, but Gillespie held on.

"I was in two minds over whether to hire you for this. I don't want to put you in danger. I don't want to gamble with anyone's life. It's a question of the balance of odds, I suppose. Many more innocent lives might be at risk if the worst happens."

"I understand the risks," Jade said. She was taken aback by the intensity in his eyes.

"I don't know if you do," Gillespie said. "I don't think anybody does, until tragedy strikes. I've had it happen to me. I wouldn't wish it on anybody else. Please, Jade, be careful."

With that, he climbed out of the car and strode away.

Chapter Seven

JADE HAD EXPECTED that even with the information Gillespie had given her, it would take her a few days to get results. In fact, she got lucky the very next day while checking up on Botha's home address.

She'd been parked across the road, ready to climb out and ask the gate guards at the estate some questions, when a Porsche had pulled up at the entrance boom and sped off, heading west. It was white, and although she hadn't had time to see the whole plate, it had started with a D, like Botha's.

Jade had sprinted back to her car, jumped in and followed. She'd never have caught up with him if it hadn't been for rush-hour congestion combined with load shedding, reducing the westbound traffic to a standstill. Crawling along in the jam, she'd been able to get the white Porsche's taillights in her sight again, check the plate and confirm that this was in fact Botha's car. She'd kept up with him even when the sky had darkened and a heavy thunderstorm had descended. In the pouring rain, she'd been a few cars behind him when he'd driven through the Best Western motel's entrance, checked in and then sped around the corner to a room in the southern wing.

Jade had no idea why he'd been in such a hurry to get to this out-of-the-way place. As she drove in behind him, the woman in the silver SUV had been leaving, and she'd watched the car collide with the pole.

NOW JADE TURNED her back on the crime scene in room number twelve and hurried around to the motel's eastern wing. Her hands felt cold as she approached Carlos Botha's motel room.

She was going to use her stolen key to access it and plant a bug there.

Number nineteen was in darkness. Tiptoeing inside, Jade switched on the light. The layout was simple and basic, a mirror image of her own room. A double bed with a beige coverlet, worn in places. A single bedside table and a wooden desk. A small wall-mounted television.

Botha's black canvas gym bag was at the foot of the bed. It was empty, and a few garments were folded neatly in the cupboard. Presumably this room was cockroach free. There was a toiletry bag in the bathroom. No toothbrush. Perhaps he had gone out to buy one.

When he came back, where might Carlos Botha do his talking?

In the end, she planted the small listening device on the underside of the desk. It was easy to apply and would be quick to remove. The tiny battery would last for a maximum of twenty-four hours, so she might need to sneak in again and replace it.

She switched on the recorder, and the whine of feedback told her everything was working as it should. She snapped the recorder off again. Time to go—and not a moment too soon. Wherever he'd been, Botha was already back. As she was locking the door behind her, she heard the growl of the Porsche's engine.

Jade ran to the other side of the parking lot and pulled her jacket's hood up just as the Porsche rounded the building. Turning her head away from him, she hurried toward the motel's west wing. A few more steps, and she'd be out of his sight. In the meantime, she was a nobody. A dark-clad figure in a hooded jacket. He wouldn't look at her twice.

Behind her, she heard the car stop, the door slam. And then she heard him call out. "Hello?"

She tensed. There was nobody else in sight. He had to be calling to her.

Reluctantly, she turned to see Carlos Botha striding purposefully toward her.

He was shorter than she'd supposed—maybe five-eight, five-nine, but powerfully built. Deep brown eyes, olive skin, dark hair razored so short it was no more than a shadow over his scalp. He wore a khaki T-shirt with a black logo on the front, faded blue jeans, sturdy lace-up shoes. As he approached, she saw he was sizing her up in exactly the same way she'd done with him. His face looked hard, as if it wasn't used to smiling. She found herself suddenly thinking of Gillespie's easy grin.

"I wanted to ask you . . ." Speaking in a low voice, Botha glanced in the direction of number twelve. "I saw you talking to the police earlier. Do you know what happened over there?"

"I don't know what happened, but I saw two dead bodies in the room. A man and a woman," she said.

He frowned. "Serious? A man and a woman?"

"Yes."

"Do the police know how they died?"

"I've got no idea," she told him. It was weird speaking to a person she'd been paid to follow. It felt dangerous and forbidden, a conversation that was breaking all her rules. It made her uncomfortable to think that she'd just planted a listening device in his room.

"Could it have been random crime? Like a robbery gone wrong?" He sounded almost hopeful, as if he wanted it to be a robbery.

"It didn't look like that," she said.

He was quiet for a minute, taking in that information before saying, "Well, thanks."

At that moment, her cell phone buzzed inside her bag—finally, and too late, giving her an excuse to turn away.

It was Gillespie on the line. She punched the button to send it through to voice mail. She couldn't take that call right then. Not when Botha might overhear. And not when her face felt hot and her heart was still pounding from the shock of the mistake she'd made.

She couldn't fix this situation now. Botha was clearly rattled by the murder, and she couldn't blame him. If he decided that the Best Western motel was too dangerous, there was no way she could follow him somewhere else.

He'd noticed her already, and had spoken to her. He would recognize her again.

BACK IN HER room, Jade tuned in to her listening device. Botha was moving around in his room. She heard the bathroom door close and open again. The bug picked up a rapid clicking sound, which must be him typing on his keyboard. That gave her a chance to call Gillespie back.

"Do you have any news?" he asked. The tension was audible in his voice.

"I've found Botha."

"You have? Good work. Where is he?"

"The Best Western motel in Randfontein. He's checked into room number nineteen. But there are complications."

"What's happened?" Gillespie asked, sounding concerned. "Why do you say that?"

"There's been a murder at the motel. Botha just asked me about it. He knows who I am now. I can't tail him discreetly anymore, and I can't follow him if he moves. There's too much risk of him recognizing me."

Jade pushed aside the image of that room, the sickly fragrance of oil overlaying the copper stink of blood, the bodies lying there, pale limbs in a crimson-stained sea.

Another silence.

"I think we can work something out," Gillespie said after a pause.

"How do you mean?"

"We can do this another way, which might get even better results. With your agreement, of course."

"What do you suggest?"

"Engage with Botha. You've already spoken to him once; do so again. Try to get friendly, and find out some background. He doesn't know why you're at this motel. Make up a reason. Maybe he'll share some information with you."

Befriend a man who was clearly on the run? After a murder in the motel? For sure, Botha would be suspicious of everyone now, herself included.

"I'll try," she said reluctantly.

"I should warn you, though, that the police came around to Inkomfe today, looking for Botha."

"Why?"

"He has had a charge laid against him of malicious damage to property."

"What did he do?"

"He smashed up a bar early Friday morning. A place called Lorenzo's in Sandton. The owner told the police that he wanted to lay a charge of assault as well, but the lady involved wouldn't press charges."

"Thanks for telling me." Great. So she was now supposed to become friendly with a man who showed a propensity for violent behavior. "Gillespie, are you sure you want me to do this?"

"As long as you are willing. I'll put another payment into your account if you feel that the risk merits it."

"I haven't had the first one yet," she told him.

"What do you mean?"

"I looked at my bank account this morning. There's nothing from you there."

There was a pause.

"I must apologize," Gillespie said. "I'll check what happened on my side. This isn't the first time I've had a payment mysteriously disappear. It's happened twice in the last week, and I must admit it's making me slightly paranoid."

"I would be, too," Jade agreed.

"I need to take an urgent look at my online security." He sighed. "But I haven't had the time to do it. Anyway, I'll arrange to give you cash in full as soon as possible."

"I'd appreciate that."

They disconnected, leaving her wondering what she should do next. How was she supposed to engage with Botha? Knock on his door and ask to borrow some sugar while hoping he didn't go berserk and try to assault her?

But even as she pocketed her phone, her recording device crackled into life again.

She heard footsteps, then the sound of the door opening and closing. The key turned in the lock.

Botha was heading out.

She'd have to follow. Maybe she could find a reason for

bumping into him again. She shoved her bag into the cupboard and threw the bug's recorder onto the pillow. Then,
car keys in hand, she opened the door and waited to hear the
Porsche start up.

But instead, all she saw was a dark-clad figure walking out
of the motel and across the road.

Craning her neck, Jade saw that there was a run-down restaurant on the other side of the road. It was open, although it
didn't look busy. Like the motel, it seemed quiet and forgotten. But it was where Botha was heading. There was nowhere
else to eat nearby, in which case it would seem innocent if
she ended up there, too.

When she left her room, she saw that the police were still
working in number twelve, with portable lights set up outside. The coroner's van was parked nearby, ready to transport
the bodies. The crowd had dispersed, although a few people
were still watching from a respectful distance.

Jade let out a frustrated breath as she turned away. It was
stupid to blame herself for the murder, but she couldn't help
feeling guilty that she hadn't done enough.

How could she have changed things? Would the out-
come have been any different if Jade had ignored the blonde
woman's desperate plea for her to go away? What if she had
insisted on walking back with her to the motel room?

Would the woman be alive now?

Or might there be three bodies on that flooded floor?

She headed across the road to the restaurant and walked
inside. The tables were weathered and mostly empty. She
saw Botha immediately. He was sitting at a corner table
with his back to the wall, drinking what looked like whiskey. Although his laptop was open, she saw his head jerk up,
instantly clocking her arrival.

The only other customers were a middle-aged couple conversing quietly at one of the window tables, and an elderly man sitting near the bar, reading the newspaper over a glass of beer.

The waiter was dividing his time between WhatsApping on his phone and watching the soccer game on the television above the bar. He took a break from these activities to bring Jade a glass of wine and hand her the food menu. Despite the tense knot in her stomach, she knew she needed to eat. She'd been watching for Botha since early morning, and all she'd had was a muesli bar. She scanned the menu quickly and ordered a toasted cheese sandwich and a salad.

Ignoring Botha's stare, she took a seat at the bar and feigned fascination with soccer. Perhaps he would make the next move. Her job would be so much easier if he believed he had approached her.

In the meantime, she'd have to be an unwilling football spectator. She'd never been able to muster much enthusiasm for the game. Perhaps she lacked appreciation for its finesse and could only stare, puzzled, at the spectacle of grown men writhing on well-tended grass while trying to convince the referee they were about to die.

She'd seen two Oscar-worthy performances and one consolation-prize winner by the time her food arrived.

"Do you have any Tabasco?" she asked the barman, and waited while he got her a bottle.

"Hot sauce improves most things."

The voice was Botha's.

She turned to see he'd packed up his computer and was standing behind her. His whiskey glass was still half full. He'd been nursing it. Not a habitually heavy drinker, it seemed, but she'd have to watch him carefully. Why else would he have lost control, assaulted a woman and smashed up a bar's worth of furniture?

"You're right," Jade agreed with a smile. Then she let herself look at him more carefully, frowning slightly as if trying to place who he was. "We spoke at the motel, right?"

"Yes. I asked you what was happening in room twelve. You said there'd been a double murder." Botha glanced around the almost-empty pub as if that fact might go some way toward explaining its lack of business.

"Two dead bodies. Not necessarily a murder." Jade shook salt over her fries.

"How do you mean?" Botha asked. He wasn't sitting down. Instead, he was standing near the counter, at an angle that gave him a view of the other patrons as well as the door. Then he added, "I'm being rude. I haven't introduced myself. Carlos Botha."

His voice was deep, with little accent.

"Jade de Jong," she replied.

He held out his hand, and Jade leaned over and shook it. His grasp was cool and firm, and his skin felt hard. In the past, Jade had shaken the hand of a black belt karate champion, ninth *dan*, who specialized in smashing concrete blocks with his limbs. His palm had felt like a piece of concrete—rough and callused. Carlos Botha's hand wasn't quite as tough, but it wasn't far off, either.

She wondered if he ever smiled.

"Do you want another drink?" he asked.

"Thanks. White wine, please."

He ordered wine for her and a ginger ale for himself.

Snapping open the soft drink can, he asked, "Did you know either of the victims?"

"No," she said.

"Why were the police talking to you, then?"

"I saw the woman crash her car when she was trying to leave. And I was the first to discover the bodies."

"What did you see?" Botha asked, his voice sharp. "How do you think it happened?"

Jade dunked the corner of her sandwich in a pool of hot sauce. She hadn't expected Botha to be so interested in the murders. "There was a baseball bat on the bed. It's possible he might have assaulted her with it and then slipped on the floor and hit his head."

Jade watched carefully to see if Botha would react to the mention of assault, but he didn't blink, simply listened intently. "He was an older man—in his sixties or seventies. She was much younger. The room was flooded with oily water. It was bizarre."

"You sure that's what happened?" Botha asked after a minute's pause.

"If I'd been working the crime scene, I would have kept that scenario in mind," Jade said carefully. "Sometimes the simplest explanation is the correct one." She speared a slice of tomato and stabbed her fork into a crisp lettuce leaf.

"And how would you know that?" he asked.

He didn't sound suspicious, just curious. At any rate, it was time to offer up the start of a cover story and see if he swallowed the bait.

"I do investigation jobs from time to time," she said. "I work with the police. I've seen crime scenes before."

Now his gaze held hers like a magnet. "Is that why you're here now? On a job?"

Jade offered him a reluctant half-smile. "If I were working, I wouldn't be drinking," she said. "I was supposed to meet a friend here tonight. A detective." She took another, larger sip of wine.

Mirroring her actions, Botha drank some more ginger ale. She wondered if he was going to eat at all. The only item in his wastepaper basket had been a water bottle.

"What brings you here?" she asked, deliberately changing the subject as if she didn't want to talk about herself.

"Business meeting," he replied. He glanced around the bar again.

"What line of work are you in?" She didn't necessarily expect the truth, but it would be interesting to see what response he gave.

"Security."

Honest, then, but no embellishment. Botha didn't want to talk about himself. Jade barely had time to draw breath before he continued. "So tell me about your detective friend."

"He's married," Jade said. "Unhappily. But he won't leave his wife."

In the past, she'd met Superintendent David Patel at places like the Best Western motel when he was on the way back from crime scenes. In shabby hotels and motels in decaying suburbs where rentals by the hour were more common than by the night. She'd waited for him in rooms with damp on the walls and threadbare sheets and cloudy window glass, the better to hide their actions from the outside world.

Not places she or David would have wanted to spend the night—but usually, they'd been done within the hour.

"Is he handling this investigation?" Botha's gaze flicked in the direction of the motel.

"No. He's a different division. Organized Crime."

"And he stood you up?" The observation was more of a question.

She shrugged. "He couldn't make it. Maybe tomorrow, he said. Maybe not. It goes with the territory."

"What does?"

"Disappointment."

And that was true, too.

Botha nodded but said nothing. She thought he believed her cover story, grounded in truth as it was. He shifted position, leaning back against the bar counter. He hadn't stopped watching the room.

Jade had the sense that their conversation, such as it was, was over. Staying longer would send the wrong message and might make him even more suspicious. It was time to go back to her room and start listening in for his return. Tomorrow morning she would find a reason to knock on his door. "I guess I'd better get some sleep. Thank you for the drink."

He raised his glass to her. "Nice meeting you."

As she left, he called after her. "Jade!"

"Yes?"

"What room are you staying in?"

"Two."

It was a sign he wanted to stay in touch. Perhaps tomorrow morning *he'd* be knocking on *her* door.

Crossing the road to the motel, Jade had the feeling he was watching her.

She let herself into her room, locked the door and undressed, folding her clothes over the back of the chair.

She stepped under the shower and turned it to its hottest setting, which was lukewarm, as she had expected. Life was full of disappointments.

And surprises.

Ten minutes later, she slid between the cool sheets of her

bed and reached for the listening device on her pillow, planning to leave it on the table for the night.

But to her puzzlement, the light was flashing.

Botha wasn't in his room. How was it possible that the bug had picked up sounds?

Her pulse quickening, she pressed PLAY.

With the volume turned up as high as it could go, Jade listened to the rattle and crack of the lock, footsteps and muttered conversation that intruders had left on her listening device while breaking into Carlos Botha's motel room.

Chapter Eight

SUPERINTENDENT DAVID PATEL felt as if his head was going to explode. Taking a break from the relentless glare of his computer screen, which had recently developed a migraine-inducing flicker, he rested his forehead in his hands and massaged his temples with his thumbs.

It wasn't just the screen that was giving him brain-bleed. It was the thought of his massive caseload. There were innumerable crises clamoring for his attention. He'd had one of those days where the phone hadn't stopped ringing, with some high-level government official on the other end lambasting him and his team for not having done what was (usually) the official's job.

Another two rhinos had been killed and dehorned. The public was frothing about it. One woman had taken it upon herself that afternoon to personally picket the front entrance of the police station, waving a banner with illegible lettering scrawled in red paint, together with a hand-drawn picture of what looked like a dog with a sausage sticking out of its forehead.

David was as sorry for the rhinos as anybody, but for Christ's sake, Organized Crime couldn't allocate a personal guard for each and every one of them. They were doing their job, they had suspects behind bars, dockets prepared by sleepless officers at the end of double shifts . . . It wasn't their fault that new, different poachers had slaughtered two more of the poor animals the previous day. Give the police a break!

And now there was the outcry over the nuclear deal with Russia that President Zuma had announced. Six new power stations providing electricity the country desperately needed, but in a form the population really didn't want. Everybody knew about Chernobyl. Even people who couldn't find Russia on a map were suddenly experts on it. And an incident of sabotage at Inkomfe had just been reported. The docket hadn't been handed over to his department . . . yet. He was waiting for somebody to decide this was, in fact, organized crime.

Meanwhile, the police were battling to do their jobs, thanks to the rolling blackouts crippling the country as outdated equipment, inefficiently maintained for the past twenty years, finally stopped working. Coal silos were collapsing. Transformers were giving up the ghost.

The building where David worked had one generator, which was often out of fuel and only big enough to power the emergency lights and the central database server. Everyone else had to sit in semidarkness staring at their blank screens, or go the old-fashioned route and do some paperwork.

Never had David's filing been so up-to-date, but filing alone didn't solve crime. They needed to be fully powered up at all times. He needed some power, any power. He didn't really care what kind it was. Coal, solar, wind, nuclear . . . just having the lights on consistently, the computers working and being able to boil a kettle would be a good start.

His attention was brought back to the present by a knock on his door.

Turning, he saw with surprise that it was Commander Ward, his immediate superior who headed up the Organized Crime unit.

"Commander," he said, hastily unfolding himself from his chair and striding across the room.

"Patel," the commander replied. "I have a serious problem on my hands. There's something I need your team to investigate urgently."

"Of course," David said, feeling his blood pressure rise as he thought of his impossible caseload. "What is it?"

"I've received a heads-up from my contact in the FBI."

"Yes?" Oh, God, this involved the FBI? David could visualize all his available time being sucked into the vortex this new case would create.

"As you're aware, there is a list of known terrorist sympathizers they keep tabs on."

"Yes, Commander."

"We've been warned that one of these sympathizers may have traveled to South Africa recently, or be arriving here in the very near future."

David stood up straighter, looking down at the shiny, balding pate of his superior as he took a folder from his briefcase. "Who is he?"

"His real name is Rashid Hamdan. He's based in the Middle East, mainly in the Emirates and Iraq, according to their intel. He owns a string of casinos and other businesses, and is suspected of laundering money for certain extremist groups, including ISIS. He was banned from entering the United States a few years ago, and his name is on our watch list as well, but he is known to have multiple passports in other names and nationalities. There's a description of him in the folder. He's forty-eight years old. May have had facial surgery in the past few years. Brown eyes, dark hair, though he has been known to dye it other colors or shave it. He's five-nine, average build."

"So we're looking for a guy with brown eyes, basically?" David asked.

The commander frowned, as if he suspected David was being facetious. "There are some old photographs of him in the file, and on this USB device."

"Any idea when he arrived here?"

"He's either traveled here in the last week, or is planning to arrive within the next day or two. He is flying, or has flown, from the Middle East."

Guy with brown eyes, who may or may not have landed from one of over fifty possible flights. Great. "Do you know why he's traveling here? Who he was going to meet?"

"Superintendent, all the information we have is in the folder."

The very slim folder.

"Read through it and put a task team together as a matter of urgency," the commander continued. "I would start by circulating the photograph to all border control officials, and to the major hotels as well. This man is on the FBI's wanted list. We need to be seen to be taking positive action here."

"Understood, Commander," David said.

Perhaps the only hint that his commander had given as to the futility of the exercise lay in the words "be seen to be taking." Well, David would do his bit. He'd be seen putting a task force together, and be seen circulating the photo as the commander asked. And if the FBI's reliable contact came back with any real information, David might even be seen as striking a blow against terrorism by actually arresting the man.

He could only hope.

Chapter Nine

INTRUDERS HAD BROKEN into Carlos Botha's motel room.

Sitting bolt upright in her bed, Jade watched the recorder in the same way she supposed a wary horse might watch a flapping piece of plastic. Her body tensed, her gaze fixed on the device as if, by looking hard enough, she might be able to see who was trespassing in his room and why.

Had Gillespie hired a second investigator without telling her? If that was so, she didn't mind. But the longer she listened, the more she began to think this theory was wrong.

She had heard the intruders entering.

But no matter how hard she listened, she could not hear them leave.

The lock had been forced open, and the hinges had creaked when they arrived. She'd heard the door close. Then she had heard movement and low voices.

Then silence.

No sounds of anybody searching the room. No squeak to tell her the door had been opened again.

Five minutes passed, then ten.

Only one possible explanation—they were still there, waiting for him.

Jade eased herself off the bed and got dressed again. She left her room quietly, locking the door behind her. Then she followed the path to the southern wing of the building.

From the outside, room number nineteen looked peaceful.

Door closed, no lights on that she could see. Botha's Porsche was where he'd left it, with no other cars nearby. She made her way carefully over to it. Was somebody hiding in or under it?

She bent down to look.

Nobody underneath. Just an acrid smell that was tickling her nostrils.

Probably Botha needed to get his Porsche serviced.

Jade walked around to the back of the building. Her feet trod on blacktop, then concrete paving, then over gravel half-smothered by grass. She saw peeling plaster and smelled a whiff of drains. This was the ugly back view of a building whose front was not exactly beautiful to start with.

The windows of number nineteen had the curtains drawn, and there was no light behind them. A legitimate visitor would surely have turned a light on.

Jade let out a slow breath, biting her lip in indecision. She was hired to investigate, not to interfere.

And yet you couldn't question a dead man.

Okay, then. Plan-making time. Somehow she needed to warn Botha about this.

But when she walked back the way she had come, she saw that the neon Heineken sign in the pub's window was switched off, and its door was shut.

Closing time had come and gone.

Where was Botha? Had he gone to reception for some reason? She jogged to the office, only to find that it, too, was locked up tight.

She had no idea where he'd disappeared to. His car was still parked outside. She'd have to go back to her own room and watch for him through the window.

Jade walked back. She was unlocking her door when she

sensed movement in the shadows nearby. She froze, listening, and then jumped when she heard a voice, hard and deep.

"Jade."

She spun around, her heart pounding.

Botha was standing in the shadows. He must have been waiting for her.

"What do you want?" she said. Her voice was high. She couldn't stop thinking about what Gillespie had said, about the malicious damage and Botha assaulting a woman.

He moved closer, as if her words had given him permission. "I want to speak to you."

"About what?" She could see he'd picked up on her tension, that he realized how off-balance he'd thrown her.

"I thought you were in your room. I knocked a minute ago, and I didn't know if you'd heard me," he said.

"I went to the office to see if they had cockroach spray, but it was shut," she lied. She turned away from him, unlocked the room, switched the light on.

He followed her in, and she closed the door behind them.

In the uncompromising harshness of the room's light, she thought Botha looked not just tired but deeply exhausted. Shadows underscored his eyes, and the frown lines between his eyebrows spoke of sleeplessness and stress. He looked older than she'd first thought. She guessed he must be in his early forties.

First thing: the listening device. It was on her bedside table with the volume turned up. She desperately needed to mute it and hide it away without Botha noticing.

"Could you put the kettle on?" she asked, and while he busied himself with filling the small plastic kettle, she turned the device to silent and slipped it under the pillow. Then she tipped a sachet of instant coffee into each of the two small mugs.

"Have a seat," she told him, indicating the single chair. She handed him his mug before perching on the edge of the bed. Now that they were locked in her room, she felt more composed and in control.

"What do you want?" she said again, taking a sip of the steaming brew. Cheap coffee, bitter. It begged for sugar, but the motel had not provided any.

"I want to hire you," he said, and Jade nearly choked on her mouthful.

She swallowed hard. "Hire me?"

"You said you're an investigator."

"I am."

"If you're available, I could use your services."

Jade hesitated. This request had caught her off guard. The safest answer would be no. But saying yes would allow her into Botha's world.

"Why do you need my services?" she asked eventually.

"I came here today for a meeting," he said.

Once again, she found herself surprised by his response. "And?"

"The man I was supposed to meet is dead," he said, and Jade felt her skin prickle into gooseflesh. "His name was Mr. Wouter Loodts, and he was staying in room number twelve."

Chapter Ten

WARRANT OFFICER MWELI had hoped to get an early night. To drive back to her single-story house with the leaky roof in a backwater suburb of Randfontein, close to the edge of nowhere. After the storm, there might be water to mop up and buckets—placed permanently below the two main leaks—to empty.

She wanted to settle down in front of the TV with a family-sized bucket of drive-through chicken and a can of Coke. To eat and drink her way mechanically through both while watching *Gold Rush* and *Deadliest Catch* recordings. She adored reality TV shows, especially *Deadliest Catch*. Captain Sig Hansen of the *Northwestern* was a hero in her eyes. He was her secret crush, in fact. Decisive, quiet, with wicked humor, steely integrity and a sharp edge to his personality that she loved. Damn, the man ran a tight ship—tough but fair, navigating safely despite everything the elements threw at him.

But thanks to the murder, Mweli's fast food and viewing schedule would have to wait.

"Double murder. Or one murder, one accidental death?" she muttered, swinging her battered Isuzu into its allotted parking space at the back of the station. The faded white lines that demarcated the bay were too close together to accommodate her vehicle's bulk, in just the same way that Mweli's office chair was too damned narrow to accommodate her butt.

She wedged herself into it nonetheless, hearing the customary creak as the chair accepted her weight.

Wouter Loodts. Gray-haired and plump. Wearing a white dress shirt and a charcoal suit. Blood-spattered as they were, his shoes looked expensive, and so did his briefcase . . . and the BMW 7 Series parked outside the motel room door was last year's model. A wealthy man with a much younger woman in a dilapidated motel. The story was beginning to offer up a possible explanation. But unfortunately, only five rooms in the motel were occupied, and none in the same row as number twelve. There were no ear-witnesses who might have heard raised voices or the sound of an argument turning violent.

Time to discover who Wouter Loodts was.

Mweli started up her computer and scribbled the beginnings of a list on her notepad.

1. Notify next of kin about death.

The only spark of light on an otherwise bleak horizon was that this could well be a case of domestic violence. She hoped the pathologist's report would confirm what the detectives had hypothesized from the time they had spent on the scene.

Mweli added to her list:

2. Who is the woman? Is she his wife, girlfriend, hired entertainment?

There had been no ID for her, and none of her possessions were in the room. But Mweli was trying hard not to worry about that particular problem. The ID and luggage had probably been in the trunk of the car.

The way Mweli saw it, they'd argued, it had turned violent, and the woman had made a run for it. She hadn't seen the metal post and had sent the car careening into it. Damaged it so it was no longer drivable.

And then she'd done the worst possible thing.

She had gone back inside. Gone back to him.

Perhaps she'd started to feel sorry for him. But he'd been furious. He'd armed himself with the bat, and he was waiting for her.

And then what?

Had he slipped on the tiles and fallen, hit his head on the corner of the desk, been unlucky? Or in the heat of the moment, perhaps he had suffered a heart attack or a stroke. This was a possibility that felt all too personal to Mweli most days, when she climbed up the short flight of stairs that led from her garage to her front door and felt her heart laboring in her chest in a way that told her if she didn't make some lifestyle changes soon, they were going to be made for her.

Diet and exercise sounded like foreign words. South Africa might have eleven official languages, but this was a twelfth, and she was reluctant to learn it.

And as for the car . . .

Mweli huffed out another frustrated breath as she wrote:

3. *Find out where the silver Land Cruiser came from. And where the hell it is now.*

The car hadn't had any numbered plates, and things had gone from bad to worse when it had been towed while they'd been trying to vacuum up the flooded crime scene, before she'd had the chance to note down the particulars on the license sticker.

"I didn't know it was evidence!" the motel manager told Mweli defensively after she'd stepped out of the musty-smelling room for some air and realized to her dismay that there was only an empty space in front of the solid pole, which had survived the impact with barely a scratch. "It was obstructing the entrance, and a tow truck driver offered to remove it."

"What driver? Where did he tow it to?"

The manager handed over a business card. "I don't know who he was, but he said he'd take it to Ashveer's Auto. It's down the road." She gestured in the direction of the main road, which, as Mweli recalled, was long and flanked by innumerable mom-and-pop motor businesses, crammed shoulder to shoulder beyond the litter-strewn sidewalks.

An unidentified car, now missing. An unidentified murdered woman with no ID and no luggage. An older man, whose cause of death still had to be determined, but whose name they knew.

Wouter Loodts. It was a common enough Afrikaans name. Perhaps that was why Mweli had thought it sounded familiar, and why it had taken her so long to make the connection.

"Oh, hell," she muttered, staring in consternation at the results on the screen as her mind raced.

Wouter Loodts.

He wasn't a John Doe. Mweli had indeed heard of him.

Mr. Wouter Johannes Eugene Loodts, age seventy, was an ex-government minister. He had been the Minister of Science and Technology under President F. W. de Klerk, and had retained his portfolio for another term under the new African National Congress government. He had been on the management committee of the Mamba nuclear plant while it was manufacturing bombs in the 1980s and had overseen South Africa's nuclear weapon disarmament process in 1989. Loodts was still on the board of the Nuclear Industry Association after having recently stepped down as chairman, and played an active role in the management of the Inkomfe Nuclear Research Center.

"Hell," Mweli said again.

Loodts's closest surviving next of kin were two sons who

had immigrated to Australia and a brother who lived in Tucson, Arizona.

She'd need to contact the embassies of those countries to track them down.

There was no way she was going to be able to contain this news for long. The media would home in on it, and she and her department would be in the glare of their spotlight. Questions would be asked . . . and she desperately needed to have the answers. She might only be the acting station commander, but the responsibility still fell on her shoulders.

She reached for the phone and dialed hurriedly. "Phiri?" she barked out. "Get hold of the pathology lab. We need to fast-track those autopsies and find out what the hell's happened here."

Chapter Eleven

JADE SAT ON the bed, facing Botha, trying not to let her face betray her frantic thoughts.

She'd thought Loodts's death might have been accidental. But Loodts had been going to meet with Botha, who'd gone AWOL from work after a sabotage incident and had unknown intruders waiting for him in his room. Now accidental death was looking like a big coincidence.

Botha drank his coffee. She noticed his hands were steady. He looked extremely serious, but he didn't look rattled. He remained composed.

She, on the other hand, was feeling uncharacteristically jumpy. Everything about this assignment seemed to be catching her on the back foot. She needed to follow Botha's example and draw on her own reserves of calm.

"Why were you meeting with Mr. Loodts?" she asked him.

"If you take the job, I'll tell you."

He could have played poker for his country; his face gave nothing away.

Jade sipped at her coffee. "Who's the woman?"

"She shouldn't have been there. Nobody else should have. I was supposed to meet Loodts alone. I have no idea who she was."

Jade watched him for a few moments. "Why do you need me?" she asked. "What needs investigating?"

"I'll tell you if you agree to work with me," he said.

This was an impossible situation. Ethically she was in a

very gray area. She desperately needed more information, but she wasn't about to get it. "I can't work with you," she said.

"Why?"

"It's too risky."

"I know," he said. "I can't deny that."

"You need to be careful, Botha."

"I'm trying."

"Not hard enough."

"Why do you say that?" He leaned toward her, his gaze unfaltering.

"Because people have broken into your motel room. They're still in there, waiting for you."

Cracks finally began to show in Botha's controlled façade. The changes were subtle, but Jade was looking for them. His lips tightened, his eyes narrowed, his posture tensed. "How do you know?"

"I saw them through the window when I came back from the pub. Two men, I think, but there might have been three," Jade said. It was a lie, because she hadn't seen them arrive, just heard the sounds. "I thought it was odd because you weren't there. And I didn't see them turn any lights on."

"You serious?"

Jade nodded. "You want to check for yourself?"

"I—no, of course not, it's just that . . ." He looked helplessly from side to side. "Are you sure? People went into *my* room?"

"Yes. I'm positive. They jimmied the lock somehow and got in. It made a noise. Your room's not locked anymore. If you go and try that door now, it will swing straight open."

Botha swallowed.

"You need to decide what to do," Jade said. "If they get

impatient, they may start looking for you. And if they're clever and observant, they'll be here soon."

Botha glanced at the door with its flimsy bolt. "If you're right, I'm in trouble," he said.

"You are. You should get out of here."

"What about you? You said that if they were clever, they'd be here soon. That means you could be in danger, too."

"Don't worry about me," Jade said.

Botha's frown deepened. "I am worried about you. I can't leave here knowing they might come looking for you. What if they try to force you to tell them where I am? No, Jade. I'm not going to let that happen."

Jade hadn't expected Botha to be so concerned about her—he seemed to feel as responsible for her predicament as his own. Surprising as this was, it was also helpful. It would be easy for her to follow Gillespie's instructions and stay close to him.

"We both need to go," she said. "I'll follow you in my car."

"Does this mean you'll work with me?"

"We can talk about it later, when we're somewhere safe."

Botha shrugged. "Where's safe?"

She guessed he didn't expect an answer, which was good, because she didn't have one. "We need to set a rendezvous point in case we lose each other."

He thought for a minute. "There's a Sasol gas station three blocks north of here on Randfontein Main Road. If we get separated, we meet there within the next hour."

Jade checked her watch. It was exactly half past ten.

"Okay," she said. "Let's go."

She let him out and grabbed her bag, leaving the door key in the lock. Checking out, Best Western motel–style. Then she climbed into her car.

The scent of pine air freshener masked the mustiness of the upholstery. She found herself remembering the odd smell she'd breathed in when checking under Botha's car. That sharp, acrid odor had reminded her of a gun after it had been fired.

The realization hit her like a fist to the face. The intruders had rigged it, turned it from a luxury ride into a death trap. Shit, shit, she'd been too slow to realize, preoccupied and distracted, and now he would pay the price.

She started up the Mazda, but before she could reverse, she heard the roar of the Porsche making its getaway.

Gravel sprayed from under its wheels, and its headlights blazed as Botha rounded the corner. Maybe she was wrong; the car hadn't blown up on ignition. But there was no way she could warn him it was potentially booby-trapped. She had visions of Botha stamping on his brake pedal, only to go flying into oncoming traffic. She flung her Mazda into gear and followed.

Botha accelerated onto the road, going at high speed. If they'd sabotaged his brakes, he was history. He would crash head-on into the first obstacle that crossed his path. Behind him, she flashed her high beams frantically, hoping that he would glean her message from them.

His brake lights glowed red. They were working. He slowed, waiting for her.

But she didn't reach him.

A massive blast shook the air. The Porsche lifted off the tarmac and slewed sideways as if a giant hand had smacked it from underneath. The shock wave rocked Jade's car a moment later. She flung her hand in front of her face. The Mazda skidded as debris ricocheted into the windshield.

When she opened her eyes again, she saw the Porsche spinning across the tarmac, tires screaming.

Jade jumped out and sprinted over to the ruined vehicle as it decelerated. Smoke billowed from the wreck, stinging her eyes. Was Botha still inside? Had he survived the blast?

She heard a shout. Turning around, Jade saw two men at the motel's exit gate. They were heading toward her at a run.

Chapter Twelve

NINE FORTY-FIVE P.M. Mweli heaved herself out of her chair. Her to-do list had been completed, tasks assigned, fellow detectives briefed and the embassies contacted. On her desk lay a cardboard folder on which she'd written *Loodts, Wouter* and the official case number in neat lettering. One dog-eared case folder—the item officially marking the end of a man's life and the start of the investigation into his death.

What the hell had happened to this highly regarded ex-government minister, for his body to be found in such sordid surroundings?

Wouter Loodts had lived in a secure gated housing estate in Glen Lauriston, Centurion. Why had he died in a downtrodden motel seventy kilometers away? Mweli's team would have to find answers without any leads. This former politician's fame made the case critical. She could not risk compromising it through the mishandling of evidence or other police bungling.

She might be fifty pounds overweight and addicted to junk food and cable TV, but Mweli had always done her best to run a tight ship. Every case she handled had been properly presented, and if the evidence let her down when it came to court, it was not because she or her team had done a shoddy job.

This was one of the reasons she'd heard whispers—just whispers, but still—that if the station commander didn't come back to work soon, she might be promoted to replace him. Grobler, the commander who was currently on extended sick leave for a heart condition, had in Mweli's opinion left the precinct in rather a mess. He blamed his health problems for his recent lack of performance. She preferred to blame the bottles of brandy stashed in his desk drawer.

A promotion would mean more responsibility and the power to set things right. And, of course, more money. It would allow her to get her roof fixed, help send her nieces to university, maybe even put down a deposit on a new truck.

There were so many changes, so many opportunities a salary hike could bring that it was sometimes better not to think about it at all, because hope was dangerous and disappointment cruel.

She let out a sigh. There was nothing more she could do here tonight. Sitting at her desk into the early morning wouldn't move this case forward. She needed to get some supper and rest. She'd stop by Pizza Express on the way home and order her favorite, the tandoori chicken special.

Or . . .

On her way to work this morning, she'd heard two radio DJs discussing Meat-Free Monday. For one's health, and to save the animals. Meat-Free Monday had been yesterday, when she'd pigged out on ribs. The DJs had made her feel guilty about that. So maybe she could have her very own Meat-Free Tuesday. There were all sorts of good reasons to go vegetarian a couple of days a week. It might even help her lose some weight. Perhaps a Quattro Formaggio—mozzarella, cheddar, feta and gorgonzola—would be the best bet.

As she locked her office's security door, Mweli heard her personal landline ring.

She paused for a second, torn between the twin forces of

duty and dinner, knowing that she would probably miss the call even if she decided to unlock again.

Her potential promotion won the day. She jammed the key back into the door, swung it open, lumbered over to the desk and stretched for the receiver. She caught the call on the eighth ring. "Mweli speaking."

No answer. The line sounded open, but nobody was saying a word.

"Mweli speaking," she said again.

Still only silence.

Running out of patience, she slammed the receiver down again. Her pizza was calling, and it wouldn't wait forever. As she locked the security door, she heard the faint sound of the telephone ringing again. This time, she ignored it.

Twenty minutes later, Mweli was heading home with the pizza on the passenger's seat. She'd chosen the Quattro Formaggio, but in order to avoid hunger after this vegetarian main dish, she'd added a small portion of crispy potato wedges to the order.

The smell of melted cheese and fried potato permeated the truck. Driving one-handedly, she prized open the lid of the box and removed a slice. Strings of warm cheese stretched and snapped. She folded the slice over and took a large bite.

Gooey topping, crispy crust, a hint of flavor from the tomato-and-herb base. An excellent choice.

Turning onto the road that led to home, Mweli checked her mirrors before reaching into the box for another slice. She'd been sure that the road behind her would be clear, and was surprised to see twin beams in her view.

She eased the slice out of the box, slowing down while she munched on it. She'd expected that the other car would pass, allowing her to enjoy her starters in peace, but to her annoyance, it remained behind hers.

In her mind, alarm bells started to sound—faint but persistent.

The strangeness of this case. The phone call she'd taken before leaving the station. And now this.

It was probably nothing to worry about, but it was better to be sure.

Instead of heading straight down the road, which became gravel after a steep dip, Mweli turned right at the only crossroad.

The car behind her turned, too.

Her hunger forgotten, Mweli carefully wiped her fingers on the napkin wedged into the corner of the box. Then, putting both hands on the wheel, she sped up, driving purposefully down the dark road and checking behind her as she went. Still she could see the headlights there.

What was interesting about this street was that it looped back onto itself and joined the main road again farther up. In fact, it would have been quicker and easier for any local going home to have taken the first turnoff, which they had passed earlier on.

Now she reached the main road and, once again, indicated right.

She eased off on the accelerator, and in due course saw the other driver's lights appear at the intersection. This time, whoever it was turned the other way, back toward town.

Had somebody been following her?

Or was she just becoming paranoid?

Hoping neither was true, Mweli reached into the paper bag and snagged a potato wedge before turning her full attention to the road home.

Chapter Thirteen

"BOTHA!" JADE YELLED. She ran over to his Porsche, which had rocked to a stop and was wedged against the curb. Smoke seethed from its undercarriage, and her feet crunched over shards of shattered glass. For the second time that day, she was treading on glass at the scene of an accident. The fact spun unwanted through her mind.

No time to worry about whether there might be another blast still to come. She grabbed the door handle, even as it was pushed open. "Are you okay?"

Botha was alive but dazed. He was breathing hard, and his face was bloodied from a gash on his eyebrow. The interior of the car wasn't badly damaged. She guessed the blast had been directed downward. He was able to nod in response to her shouted question. She grasped his shoulder and helped him scramble out. None of his bones seemed to be broken, thankfully.

"Come on," she urged, leaning back in to grab his laptop bag. Then she helped him stumble over to her car. They climbed inside, and she burned rubber on their getaway as two gunshots split the air behind them.

"Get down," she ordered, but he refused to listen, instead craning around to look through the rear window.

"They're following us," he said, and her heart sank. She checked her mirror and saw headlights in pursuit, dazzlingly bright. There wouldn't have been time for the two men on foot to go back and get their car. That meant there must have been a third waiting behind the wheel.

"Go left," Botha gasped. He face was covered in blood, and he had one hand pressed to his forehead, trying to stem the bleeding with his sleeve.

Jade complied, swinging the car onto the side street. "You know this area?" she asked through a clenched jaw, flicking her high beams on as she sped down the narrow road.

"No. I don't have a clue."

"Why the hell did you tell me to go left, then?"

"Because that car was gaining on you. It would have caught up. Now it's getting closer again." He twisted around, peering behind him as the headlights flared once more in her mirrors.

"If you don't know the area," Jade snapped, "you should be careful where you turn. Minor roads like this are dangerous. Next thing you get trapped in a cul-de-sac."

"Okay. Sorry. 'Scuse me for trying to get us away from guys who just blew up my car!"

Jade gritted her teeth in lieu of a response and focused on steering.

"You need to drive faster," Botha implored, panic in his voice.

What part of "I'm already going as fast as I goddamned can" was he not understanding? Jade wrenched the wheel right again at the next crossroad. Behind her, the wailing of tires told her that the heavier car following wasn't as nippy through the turns.

Nothing for it but to carry on zigzagging and pray she didn't get unlucky with a dead end.

"Go left again," Botha yelled over the howl of the engine.

Jade barely made the turn, hearing tires scream, feeling the car fishtail as it lost traction on the bend. She couldn't keep this up; she wasn't a race car driver. They desperately needed a lucky break. To have the other driver lose control.

Or to find help—a security vehicle, a traffic light turning red with cars waiting at the cross street.

She saw the signpost out of the corner of her eye at exactly the same moment Botha shouted, "Go right! There's a police station down this way."

"I'm on it." She swung the wheel sharply to avoid a deep, gaping pothole near the side of the road, hating the glare of the blinding headlights they couldn't outrun.

She squinted ahead, only to see the sign she'd feared the most.

The road she was on was a dead end.

"Where the hell is this cop shop?" The road looked devoid of police stations. Perhaps the sign was outdated, and they were hurtling into a trap. She needed a new plan. Out of the car might be better than in. They could split up, run in opposite directions . . .

"Careful of this turn," Botha warned.

She hadn't even noticed the chevrons ahead indicating the sharp bend in the road.

"We're not going to make it," Jade gasped. No time for a hard brake; it would send them spinning off. Every muscle in her body felt as taut as steel while she steered the speeding car around the curve.

Just stay on the road, she silently begged the sedan. What irony it would be if they crashed now. She felt everything start to slide. The tires wailed, and sweat made her palms slick as she forced herself to keep her foot down and power it through the skid and into the straight section ahead.

"Here it is! On the left!" Botha said.

She would have missed it. In the dark, it was not clearly marked. Only as she ripped the wheel around and sent the car skidding into the driveway did she see the modest sign on the gatepost which informed the public that this was the Rand-fontein branch of the South African Police Service.

The headlights were no longer in her rearview mirror, blinding her. In fact, she couldn't recall the driver following her around the bend.

Perhaps he hadn't made it. Or maybe he, too, had seen the signpost and guessed where they were heading.

At any rate, they'd bought some time. She released her death grip on the wheel at the same time Botha leaned away from the dashboard.

He touched a hand to his forehead, and it came away wet with blood.

"Let me see that cut," she said.

It was bleeding freely, but it didn't look too deep. He'd been incredibly lucky. Lucky that the Porsche was a tough, strong car, and that he hadn't been going too fast when the explosion occurred.

She grabbed the last packet of tissues from the glove compartment, ripped it open and handed a wad to Botha. Her hands were shaking badly. When he took the tissues, she saw that his were, too.

There was still no sign of the car that had been following them, and Jade started to wonder whether the driver had turned back to get reinforcements.

She wanted to walk with Botha into the safety of the police station. But the longer they spent there, the better their chances would be of getting ambushed when they left.

She started the car again.

"We're not going inside?" Botha sounded incredulous.

"They'll be expecting us to."

"So we leave now?"

"Before the three of them come back and trap us here."

She reversed, swung the wheel left and headed for the gate once again.

"You're crazy," Botha hissed. "That driver's waiting on the other side of the bend."

"He's not. He's gone back to get the others." Jade tried to sound sure of herself, even though her legs were quivering so badly that she worried she might stall the car.

She drove cautiously around the bend. Headlights blinded them, and they both flinched, but the passing car was only a small truck with a security logo on its side.

Jade breathed out again. The road ahead was clear.

"Now we go the other way," she said as they exited the cul-de-sac.

She drove carefully, spending as much time watching her mirrors as she did looking ahead. In twenty minutes, they were on the N1 highway, heading back toward Johannesburg.

The closer they drove toward the city, the safer she felt. Traffic was her friend. On busier roads, in the dazzle of headlights and taillights, it would be much more difficult to single out any one vehicle.

She remembered that there was a late-night pharmacy in Woodmead, so they switched highways, took the next exit and a few minutes later had stopped and bought disinfectant, gauze and dressing.

Jade took care of Botha's face right there in the car. She switched on the light, drenched the gauze in disinfectant and dabbed it on the cut, carefully removing the crusted blood before taking a better look at the injury.

The damage wasn't as bad as she had feared. Head wounds always bled more. She tried to be gentle, but she knew it must be stinging like hell. Even so, Botha did not move a muscle or even catch his breath. He simply sat, eyes closed, face still.

She cut a strip of gauze, pressed it onto the cut, taped it down with narrow pieces of sticking plaster and finally placed a white dressing on top of that. It looked neat, and she thought it should heal well. Assuming Botha stayed alive long enough.

Then she handed more disinfectant-soaked gauze to Botha so that he could rub the blood off his hands and face.

"Thank you," he said in a low voice when she'd finished.

"No worries." Jade cleared her throat. For a moment, she'd thought of Botha as a friend . . . an ally. But he was her surveillance target, charged with malicious damage to property and possibly involved in a serious incident of sabotage. And now she'd fled with him from a crime scene after helping him survive a hit.

She had no idea how far the reach of their pursuers was. They'd escaped immediate danger, but Jade was sure the gunmen wouldn't be giving up.

She pulled into a gas station near the pharmacy. While she filled the car up, Botha went into the twenty-four-hour convenience store and bought some bottles of water and fruit juice, dried fruit bars, packets of chocolate and nuts. When you were on the run, you needed supplies.

The roads were quieter at this hour, but there was still traffic heading toward Sandton. Safety in numbers. The Central Business District would be a good place to spend what remained of the night. She merged onto the highway, driving cautiously and frequently checking her mirrors.

"Why were you meeting Wouter Loodts?" she asked Botha. "He's an ex-government minister, right?"

"He is—was. He was also my boss. And I wanted to discuss something urgent with him."

"I need more information," she insisted.

"Okay. I'll tell you more." Shifting in his seat, Botha gently touched his forehead with his fingertips. She guessed that, with his adrenaline ebbing, the wound must be throbbing painfully now. "I've been working on contract at Inkomfe Nuclear Research Center, helping with security upgrades."

"Okay," Jade said.

"Loodts used to be in charge of Inkomfe, and he's still a decision maker there. I called him yesterday, hoping to discuss a very serious and confidential matter."

"What was this matter, exactly?"

"Long story. Probably too long for this drive."

They were passing the Marlboro Road turnoff—Sandton was five minutes away. He was right. No time for a long story at the moment.

Jade noticed a pair of headlights that had been close behind her for a while. It was starting to make her jumpy. She slowed down and waited for the car to pass. "Why did you meet Loodts at that motel? It's really out of the way. Is it close to where either of you live?"

The car was passing them now. She glimpsed the driver, an elderly man frowning ahead as he gripped the wheel. He must've been following her taillights because they offered security in the darkness. She silently wished him a safe journey as he headed onward into the night.

"I suggested meeting in Sandton, at the Da Vinci Hotel lounge. Then, just before I left, I got a text message from him saying the venue had changed to the Best Western," Botha said. "I thought it was strange, but I didn't argue. I was grateful he'd agreed to meet me at all."

Jade wondered whether Loodts had really sent that message himself.

"Traffic was a nightmare with the load shedding," Botha

continued. "It took me an hour and a half just to get across town. I tried calling him when I was close to the motel, but his phone was turned off."

Jade glanced at Botha, but he was staring straight ahead. "So you checked in to wait for him?"

"I thought I'd stay there awhile and see if he called me back. Then I saw the police outside that room and knew something had happened. I called reception and asked them to put me through to Mr. Loodts, and they said they couldn't, because the police were investigating a crime scene in that room."

"So you went across the road to the pub?"

"I needed a drink, and to try and think things over. I probably should have left straight away." She sensed, rather than saw, his shrug. "Coulda, woulda, shoulda. As it turned out, I'd already stayed too long."

"I see," Jade said. If Botha was telling her the truth, his actions seemed reasonable. But she had little reason to trust him, even if they had narrowly escaped a set of killers together.

Botha could have gone to number twelve after he arrived and murdered Loodts and the blonde himself. She wasn't going to view anything as truth until she had hard evidence to back it up.

Chapter Fourteen

ELEVEN P.M. WARRANT Officer Mweli was comfortably installed on her corduroy couch. The pizza and wedges were a memory now, their packaging folded and crammed into the trash can. The nearby chair was occupied by Chakalaka, the ugly tabby cat who'd adopted her three years ago, soon after her husband's fatal heart attack. She'd tried to chase him out at first, because he'd broken glasses on the drying rack while jumping through the kitchen window to steal her bread, but he was thin and young and pitiful, and eventually she'd found herself in the pet food aisle of the supermarket, loading up bags of the best stuff she could find. Chakalaka had showed his gratitude a few days later by scratching her arm bone-deep while she'd struggled to get him into a basket and off to the vet to get all the necessary done.

Now he was grooming himself in a focused way, so noisily that Mweli was forced to turn up the sound on the television. *Deadliest Catch* was playing on the DVR, and Mweli was watching Sig Hansen haul in pots that were crawling with Alaskan king crab.

"He's a magician," she muttered to herself, her eyes glued to the screen as giant waves crashed into the boat's iced-over hull.

Then she and Chakalaka both jumped as her cell phone started to ring.

It was Constable Theron, who was on night duty at the station. "Evening, ma'am," he said.

"What's up, Constable?" Mweli stabbed at the DVR's MUTE button and then, after a moment's thought, the PAUSE button. She needed her full attention for this conversation, but more importantly, she would need it for Hansen's haul.

"Someone called in a report of a one-car accident on West Street, near the Best Western motel. A white Porsche. Metro police have just arrived on the scene."

"Mm-hmm?" Mweli supposed this was going somewhere. Theron wouldn't have contacted her for a bumper bashing. And the mention of the Best Western had her instincts prickling. She'd barely heard of West Street before today, but it sure was making a lot of paperwork for them now.

"Cops called it in because it looks like something in the car's undercarriage exploded."

"Accidental? Or an explosive device?" Mweli sat bolt upright, causing the couch to creak in protest and Chakalaka to stare at her inquiringly.

"Looks like an explosive device. The vehicle's undercarriage is severely damaged."

"Casualties? Survivors?" Mweli was wondering exactly when her precinct had turned into the Wild West. A bomb? In Randfontein? That was as unlikely as—as South Africa winning the 2018 World Cup.

"Nobody on the scene at all, ma'am. No driver, no casualties. The vehicle's abandoned."

"Tell the team not to move it till I get there. And not under *any* circumstances to have it towed. I'm on my way now, and you can call the bomb squad and ask them to meet me."

Placing her palm on the arm of the couch, Mweli heaved herself to her feet and followed the worn path in the beige carpet that led from the couch to the living room door.

Twenty minutes later, she arrived at the scene. Metro

Police had followed instructions. They'd cordoned off a safe distance around the vehicle and blocked the entire road with traffic cones. Occasional passing cars were detoured through the side streets. As soon as she climbed out of the car, two young Metro cops, both wearing excited expressions and carrying heavy-duty flashlights, hurried over to her, offered a quick greeting and escorted her to the damaged sports car.

Or rather, not all the way there. They stopped a safe distance away and regarded it cautiously. Grabbing a flashlight from the nearest cop, Mweli made the last few steps of the journey on her own, picking her way through chunks of metal, her feet crunching on broken glass.

It would be more accurate to say this car had once been a Porsche. It was expensive, new and irreparable. She shined the flashlight onto the car's undercarriage and drew in a sharp breath as she saw a gaping, ragged crater.

Metro Police had not exaggerated. This, with little doubt, was the work of explosives. Where one had detonated, there might be more, which she assumed was the reason for the cautious attitude of the young constables.

She moved carefully around the vehicle, assessing, breathing in the lingering smell of metal and plastic that had torn and burned. The trunk was empty, as were the seats, which were relatively undamaged by the blast. She narrowed her eyes and shined the light carefully on a smear of blood on the pale leather upholstery. Only a smear.

She guessed that the driver had been alone, and he'd certainly been lucky. He hadn't waited around, for which Mweli couldn't exactly blame him.

So who was he, and where had he come from?

Thankfully, this car had an undamaged rear license plate, whose number Mweli jotted down. Then, training the flashlight beam on the faded tarmac, she trudged down the road in the direction of the motel.

A few steps later, her guess was rewarded when the beam picked up two thick, parallel stripes on the road.

This explosion hadn't come from nowhere. The driver had not been unaware. He'd been speeding off, racing away. Why? Had someone been chasing him? Had he known something had been about to go wrong?

Keeping her light carefully focused on the dark tire marks, Mweli walked down the street, step by deliberate step. A minute later, a sense of inevitability came over her as she found herself tracing their curving path through a sharp right-hand turn into the driveway of the Best Western motel.

LOOKING ACROSS THE forecourt to the well-lit scene on the road outside, she saw that the bomb squad had arrived. Their white van was parked a safe distance from the damaged car, and two uniformed technicians were widening the cordon.

Narrowing her eyes against the glare from the lights, Mweli stepped off the walkway and planted her foot in a deep puddle that lurked on the side of the tarmac. She swore softly as the cold water seeped through the crack in the side of her shoe. Her sock turned cold and squelchy in an instant.

Moving forward more carefully, squelching with each alternate step, Mweli headed to the office for a list of residents and their vehicles, and then made a tour of the motel's parking area.

Mr. Carlos Botha was the owner of the ruined Porsche. But Botha was no longer in his room. Mweli hadn't expected to find him there—life was never so easy. Why he'd fled, and who had sabotaged his car, were questions that she could only hope tomorrow might answer.

For the time being, she could do no more. The bomb squad was still at work, and based on their findings, the case might even be transferred to another department. Organized Crime would be her guess. Headed up by that new hotshot superintendent—what was his name? Ah, yes, David Patel.

As she was heading back to her truck, Mweli saw something that hadn't been there when she left it. A large brown envelope, crumpled and damp, had been placed under her windscreen wiper.

She was about to grasp it when her brain finally caught up with her actions.

Wait.

Who had put it there, and why?

She glanced from side to side, unable to prevent the chills that suddenly prickled her spine at the thought she was being watched. But the roads were quiet. The ruined Porsche was gone now, winched onto the back of a tow truck after it had been photographed from all angles and declared explosive free.

Mweli rummaged in the back of her truck for a pair of gloves. It was unlikely this coarse brown paper would hold any prints, but procedures had to be followed. After stretching them on, she lifted the wiper and removed the envelope. It was unsealed and felt heavy. She peered inside and could not help a hiss of indrawn breath as she stared down at a wad of banknotes.

And then, from in her pocket, she heard the trill of her cell phone.

Mweli nearly dropped the envelope. She placed it hurriedly on her truck's hood and looked to see who was calling.

Number withheld.

"Hello?" She could hear she sounded sharp, stressed.

"Detective." In contrast, the caller's voice was a silken purr. Mweli stared wildly to her left and right, clutching for straws of evidence that would help with an ID.

She saw only the muted lights of the town in front, the blinding crime-scene spotlights behind. Otherwise, darkness. And she was certain she'd never heard this voice before. It was deliberately low and soft. The speaker was a man. She couldn't detect a foreign accent or any other distinguishing traits.

"Forget about the woman," the speaker continued. "She's a nobody. A hired prostitute. Identifying her would only bring shame to Loodts's family. He was a well-respected man." For a moment, the voice took on a wheedling tone before hardening again. "We've left an incentive for you on the windscreen. We hope it will be enough to convince you. We don't want to have to resort to anything further."

"Wait," Mweli began, her voice hoarse, but the caller did not wait.

With a click, he disconnected.

Chapter Fifteen

FOR THAT NIGHT, the best solution Jade could think of was to check into a big hotel in a busy part of town. Safety in numbers, she decided. She still felt uneasy, as if danger was following close behind.

It was nearly midnight by the time they reached central Sandton, but the Central Business District was still humming. There was traffic on the roads, lights on in apartment windows. They followed two large tour buses down Grayston Drive. The buses stopped in front of the Radisson Blu, opposite the Gautrain station.

Jade drove around to the basement parking, and after a jog to the elevator, they arrived at reception second in line, with one German couple in front of them, and a large, noisy group of tourists behind.

The hotel had just two available rooms: one standard room on the fourth floor, and one family room on the tenth, which had two bedrooms. "I'll take the family room," Jade said, handing over her ID. "Name's de Jong."

Botha paid in cash, handing over a slim sheaf of crisp notes. In the pressured rush of checking them in as fast as possible, the receptionist didn't notice that he hadn't supplied his ID.

The hotel was spacious, with a stunning view of Sandton from the window in the elegant lounge area. Everything in the room smelled clean and fresh. The television was enormous and flat-screen; the leather furniture was plush. All in all, this room was about as far removed from the Best Western motel as one could imagine.

Going back to the door, Jade checked that it was properly closed. This was a modern hotel with key cards. She would have preferred one with an old-fashioned security chain on the inside. Sure, an intruder could break a chain, but the sound gave you some warning. What warning would there be if someone got hold of a master key card? Nothing more than the buzz and click of the latch before the door swung soundlessly open, the intruder's footsteps muffled by the thick pile carpet.

That scenario had been one of her recurring nightmares ever since the night when her father's killer had come for her. Alone in the house, she'd woken from a troubled sleep to hear floorboards creaking in the passage. She'd escaped through the window moments before he'd forced the flimsy lock and broken into her bedroom.

As she checked the door, she felt the cell phone in her pocket start to ring. Her heart accelerated in sync with its persistent buzzing. She glanced behind her to make sure Botha wasn't watching, and then took a quick glance at the caller ID.

It was Gillespie on the line.

A call at this hour had to be important. She'd have to phone him back as soon as possible. The rest of Botha's story would have to wait till tomorrow.

"I guess we'll be okay here for tonight," she said. "Let's meet up at eight in the morning. We can talk then and decide what to do. Where to go."

Botha nodded. Jade thought he looked relieved by her decision. He was hollow-eyed with exhaustion, and she wondered just how many sleepless nights had contributed to this.

"Sleep well," he said before closing his bedroom door.

"You, too," Jade said.

She waited a minute in case he came out again, prowling impatiently around the suite. Taking a biscuit from the jar, she crunched down on its chocolatey sweetness, suddenly craving the sugar hit. Then she closed her bedroom door so that he'd think she had gone inside, left the suite and walked swiftly down the corridor to the elevators where she called Gillespie back.

"Jade. Where are you?" He sounded worried.

"I've checked into a hotel in Sandton," she told him.

"What is happening with Botha? I'm worried about you."

"I'm on the run with him."

"On the run?" Gillespie echoed, his voice high.

"The man who was murdered is Mr. Loodts, from Inkomfe. Botha went to the motel to meet him. I happened to hear intruders breaking into Botha's room, so we left in a hurry. They'd wired his car to explode, so I ended up giving him a ride to safety."

Her statement was met by a short pause. If silences could talk, Jade guessed Gillespie's would have sounded shell-shocked. "That's crazy. Absolutely beyond belief. Loodts? Are you sure?"

"Yes. He had his ID on him."

"Jesus, Jade. I . . . I don't know what to say. I think I have to discuss this with you in person," he said eventually. "I need to see you."

"Okay," Jade said. "Tomorrow morning?" She and Botha would have to go to a police station to report the accident. Maybe she could slip away afterward.

"I don't want to wait till then," Gillespie told her. "Tonight would be better."

"Tonight?" Jade echoed, incredulous. It was well after eleven. Her eyes were red and scratchy, and every cell in her body felt depleted from stress. But Gillespie was her client. He called the shots. He paid her the money. Well, he'd promised to, at any rate. If he wanted to see her, she would have to go. "Where are you?"

"At Inkomfe. I've been double-checking our perimeter fences."

Jade's heart sank. Inkomfe was more than an hour's drive from Sandton. Exhaustion wasn't her main problem anymore. Her main problem was what would happen if Botha discovered she was gone.

"If you can," Gillespie said, but his tone told her it was an order, not a request.

So much for a good night's sleep in that sumptuous bed. She took her car key out of her pocket and rode down in the elevator. Ten minutes later she was driving out of Sandton, heading west on streets that were now quiet and empty.

Chapter Sixteen

LATE AS IT was, the guard at Inkomfe's main gate looked alert as he stopped her, searching her car thoroughly. This time, she didn't have the press invitation that had opened doors for her so easily, and she wasn't directed to the same welcoming reception area. Instead, he told her to drive straight up to the closest parking lot and to go through the main security entrance.

The brilliant white walling and space-age décor she remembered from last time had not been installed in this building. The walls here were painted a dull, industrial gray with a yellow stripe at waist level. Steel signs with printed safety warnings were prominently displayed. Other notices directed her to areas whose functions she could only guess at from their Zulu names. Amahhovisi. Behlangana. Inqaba.

One of the guards at the desk escorted her to an office down the corridor where Jade was photographed and fingerprinted.

She saw a printed warning on the wall which read, ATTENTION, ALL VISITORS. NO CELL PHONES PERMITTED IN THE COMPLEX. PLEASE HAND YOUR PHONES, CAMERAS AND ID IN TO RECEPTION FOR SAFEKEEPING.

Safekeeping? Jade hoped they wouldn't ask her for her possessions, but of course they did.

"Your ID, please," the guard said. "And I need your cell phone and any cameras."

"I don't have a camera," Jade said. She handed over her

driver's license and cell phone. Instead of giving it back, he placed the items in a labeled box.

"Wait!" Jade told him. "Can I make a phone call?"

The guard frowned. Clearly she was defying protocol.

"I'll hand it in as soon as I've finished," she said. "Or I can go out to my car and make the call there."

He gave a nod. "All right. Make your call, and then I'll take you to the waiting room."

Praying Gillespie would answer quickly, Jade dialed his number.

"Are you there already?" He sounded surprised. She could hear loud noise in the background—clattering and bangs.

"Yes."

"I'm not there yet. I'm going to be another half hour. Tell them to take you to the waiting room."

Jade bit her lip. Hadn't Gillespie had said he was on-site earlier? Another half hour seemed like a very long time. But she was already here, committed.

She handed her phone to the guard, who gave her an ID tag on a lanyard in exchange. "You must keep this on you at all times," he told her.

The guard led her through a warren of corridors. Up ahead, a steel security gate blocked the way. Quickly, he pressed a code into a keypad, and the gate snapped open. After another couple of turns, he opened a door on the left and showed her to a waiting room. This was not as welcoming a space as the visitors' center had been. Uncomfortable-looking metal benches lined the walls. In the corner, a large urn bubbled. Sachets of coffee and sugar were stacked on a nearby shelf, together with plastic cups and spoons.

The waiting room was chilly, and the neon light was hard on the eyes, but these were minor problems compared to the fact that she was supposed to be in bed and asleep in her luxury hotel suite. Her cover was shaky to begin with. If Botha realized that she was investigating him, her assignment was finished, and she could find herself in worse danger.

Her head snapped around as she heard the faraway blare of a horn from somewhere down the passage. Was it Gillespie arriving earlier than expected?

She retraced her steps after making a couple of wrong turns. The place was a concrete-walled labyrinth. And it didn't help her mood when she arrived at the security gate she had originally come through, only to find it locked.

Realistically, she was still so far from the parking lot that she shouldn't have heard a horn. But there it was again, somewhere within earshot.

"Hello!" she shouted, pounding on the dull metal to no avail and feeling like a prisoner in a holding cell. "Anyone there?"

Her voice reverberated through the empty corridors.

She stomped back toward the waiting room, but on the way saw another passage leading to the left.

Had the sound come from there? Curious, Jade walked down the new hallway and reached another solid door a minute later. She assumed it would be locked like all the others, but tried the handle in any case. It moved smoothly under her grasp, and she nearly fell over in surprise when the door opened.

She found herself standing outside, in a floodlit courtyard. In the distance, Jade saw the taillights of a departing van and heard the third and final blast of its horn, louder this time. It was one of the vehicles she'd seen on her tour, which transported the nuclear waste to its dumping site. Gillespie had mentioned that they traveled at night. This one must be setting off on its journey.

From the left, she heard the rattle of a cart. An elderly black man wearing khaki overalls had come out of a door on the opposite side of the courtyard, pushing a cart piled high with garbage bags.

The man glanced in her direction. When he saw her closing the door, he stopped in his tracks and stared at her open-mouthed, looking her up and down as if he'd seen a ghost.

"Eish," he said. "This I cannot believe. In forty years, I have never seen such a thing. Never, ever."

"Seen what?" Jade said, glancing down at herself with some concern in case she hadn't noticed a bloodstain on her shirt, or mud on her socks or a large tarantula clinging to her cargo pants. The way he was staring, there had to be something very wrong, but although her clothing was a bit scuffed, she couldn't see any blood or spiders.

"I am shocked," the man said, abandoning his cart and walking toward her.

His face was lined, his hair salted with gray, but his eyes looked sharp enough to see straight through her. He wore a battered-looking official card on a lanyard around his neck that identified him as Sbusiso Jabulani. "You came through that door?" he asked.

Jade glanced behind her. "I was waiting in the visitors' room. I heard the truck hooting and thought I'd have a look. I pushed the door, and it opened."

"Forty years I've been working here, and never, ever have I seen that door unlocked. It is supposed to be permanently locked. It always has been. This is a high-security area."

Now that he'd said it, Jade noticed more signs displayed. AUTHORIZED PERSONNEL ONLY. ACCESS RESTRICTED. And on the right-hand side of the courtyard, she saw another windowless building with a solid-looking steel gate. In bright yellow letters on a black background, the sign announced: INQABA MAXIMUM SECURITY STORAGE AREA. LEVEL 4 SECURITY CLEARANCE REQUIRED. CAUTION: DANGEROUS SUBSTANCES WITHIN. PROTECTIVE EQUIPMENT TO BE USED AT ALL TIMES.

"I'm sorry," Jade said. "I didn't know."

"Eish!" Sbusiso said again, shaking his head. "We had a fire drill at ten P.M., and we all had to evacuate this area for two hours. Maybe somebody unlocked the door then."

On the other side of the courtyard was a large rubbish bin. Sbusiso wheeled the cart over to it and began hefting the bin bags into the bin.

"Let me help you," Jade said, picking up a bag.

"I will be in trouble if the boss man finds you out here," Sbusiso cautioned.

"Who's the boss man?"

"Mr. Gillespie."

"He's the person I'm meeting, but he's not here now. He said he'll be back in half an hour, so I'm sure helping you for a few minutes will be fine." Jade hoisted the bag into the bin.

Sbusiso was looking at her more closely. "You are here to see the boss man?"

"Yes."

"At such a time?" His tone suggested amusement, rather than surprise.

"It's urgent."

"What's your name?"

"Jade. I'm doing . . . some freelance work for him."

Sbusiso tapped his nametag in response. "I clean the offices and admin buildings. If Mr. Gillespie is not here now, you can help me if you like. He will probably arrive later than he promised. He is always late. Miss Lisa, who worked here before him, she was the other way around. Always early, and complaining you were late, even if you were on time. That one, she used to complain a lot when she was the boss lady."

"Lisa Marais?" Jade asked. The woman who'd hired Botha before leaving Inkomfe on bad terms to work for Earthforce.

Sbusiso nodded.

"Did you know her well?"

"Lisa is my friend," Sbusiso said. "I still speak to her sometimes."

Jade lifted another bag into the bin. The remaining bags appeared to be full of shredded paper and were surprisingly heavy. "Your job must be hard work," Jade said.

"Hard work, yes. But I am lucky," Sbusiso told her. "I am one of the lucky ones, because I work only in the admin side. I have never worked near the poison. Most of the people who started work with me here are sick or dead."

The cart rattled as he moved it forward.

"How did that happen?" Jade asked, concerned, as they turned to the next bag.

"In the old days, nobody cared about the black workers," Sbusiso said. "My cousin Shadrack, he is at home, dying. He worked here when they were doing the secret nuclear program, building the bombs. He worked in a building called Cheetah. Cheetah was where the bombs were manufactured, and then many years later, taken apart. The bombs were stored in Inqaba, over there." He jerked his thumb in the direction of the high-security building. "And still there is poison in that place today, because they keep the materials there now."

"What happened to Shadrack?" Jade asked.

"Shadrack worked in the red water. They used a lot of

water where the bombs were made, and this water was red in color. Poisonous, from the bombs. He was given boots to wear, but they were not high enough. Every day, the water would splash over his boots. His legs became covered in sores. Those sores are still there today. They have never gone away. And he is sick, sick." Sbusiso shook his head. "He has pains in his bones, he is weak, his stomach is very bad."

"That's terrible," Jade said. Despite the exertion of moving the bags, Sbusiso's story gave her chills.

"His wife worked with the chemicals, the ones that they used to make the bombs. The white doctors wore special suits and gloves, but she did not, and when she asked why, they could not answer her. She was retrenched in 1995." Sbusiso held up his hand, fingers outstretched. "Five years later, she was very sick. She was coughing up blood and had a headache that never went away. And then she died."

Together, they grasped another bag and hefted it into the bin.

"There are others," Sbusiso said. "Maybe fifty others in Atteridgeville, the township near here, who worked on the nuclear program. Some are already dead. But all the ones who are still alive have problems. Many problems with their skin, their stomachs. Cancers, kidney disease, weak hearts, blindness. Every two weeks, another funeral. Somebody else is gone. When we are all gone, who will help us? Who will fight for us so our families can be compensated?"

"Can't anything be done?" Jade asked. "Surely there are employee records that you could use to help? The law's very different today."

But Sbusiso shook his head. "For forty years, I have watched our people fighting for justice, and I have seen them lose. They are told their employee records do not exist, even when the workers themselves have kept the papers and documents

that they were given. All the records were probably shredded. Everything is shredded here for security. But how does
that security help Inkomfe's own workers?"

Jade's thoughts raced furiously. The image of the dead
body sprawled in the flooded motel room flitted through her
mind. "Did you know somebody named Wouter Loodts?" she
asked.

Sbusiso crossed his arms angrily. "That man!" he spat. "He
was the boss when the bombs were made. He was in charge
of the Cheetah building and the Inqaba strong rooms. And
he did nothing when my people asked for safety equipment."

"He's dead," Jade told Sbusiso. It wasn't her place to give
details, but she was interested to see his reaction.

"Did he die from the poison, too?" Sbusiso asked. From his
face, she could see he was not aware of recent events.

When Jade shook her head, Sbusiso's expression tightened again. He placed his callused hand on the last
remaining bag and spoke calmly. "I am not sorry that Mr.
Loodts is dead. He caused a lot of suffering to the workers
here, and to their families. I have decided there are two different sets of rules in life. One is for the rich. The other for
the poor. And the rules for the poor are unfair, because we
are so easily forgotten."

He hefted the bag into the bin. The cart was empty now.

"I'd like to try and help you," Jade said. "In return, could
you tell me more about your friend Lisa?" Assisting Sbusiso
while obtaining background information would be a win-win
situation.

Sbusiso nodded. "I can tell you. But not here, not now. I
have to go back. There are still three more offices to clean."

Jade took down his number and promised to call him
later that morning after his shift was over. Sbusiso leaned

against the cart until it started moving, and then, limping slightly, guided it across the tarmac in the direction he'd come from. She watched him go, feeling troubled by what he'd said and wondering just how hated Loodts had been, and by whom.

Chapter Seventeen

JADE RETURNED TO the waiting room, where she spent twenty more comfortless minutes before at last she heard the clang of the security gate and Gillespie's approaching footsteps.

His tawny brown hair was disheveled, and he'd changed out of the dress shirt he'd been wearing earlier into a black golf shirt and chinos. Even so, he looked a lot smarter than Jade felt. As he walked across to her, she became acutely aware of her own state. Her jacket sleeves were creased because she'd pushed them back before attending to Botha's bleeding wound. She was sure her hair was a mess, and one of the bags she'd just helped to load had left a dusty mark on her pants. Standing up to greet him, she hurriedly brushed the dust away.

"Thanks for coming out here, Jade. You have no idea how much I appreciate your help," Gillespie said. He seemed to be glowing from within, a frenetic energy smoldering in his core. He grasped her hand firmly, and suddenly, looking into his blue eyes, Jade didn't feel quite so disheveled after all.

"This is turning into a nightmare. I can't believe Loodts is dead," Gillespie said. "Or rather, I can believe it, because I have a police connection. I called him just after I spoke to you, and he confirmed it."

They sat down on the hard metal bench.

"Botha wanted to discuss something confidential with Loodts. He hasn't said what. I hope I'll find out tomorrow. I wish I could tell you more, but we've been busy running for our lives," Jade said.

Gillespie shook his head. "This is not good, Jade. Not good at all."

"There was a woman with Loodts," she told him. "I don't know who she was. I don't think the police know either."

Quickly Jade described the woman, and how she had tried to help her after the woman had crashed her car into the pole.

Gillespie listened thoughtfully. "This is getting more and more bizarre. I have no idea who she could be. Do you think she might be a prostitute he picked up?"

"It's possible," Jade said.

"But why were they both dead? What happened?" Gillespie asked, almost to himself. He shook his head. "I trusted Loodts. Perhaps I was wrong to do so. He knew those systems back to front and inside out. Even blindfolded, he could have drawn a diagram to scale of Inkomfe and all the access points to the reactor room."

During the pause that followed, Jade realized how stark the silence was. This room was almost soundproof, a dead-end passage in a concrete maze.

"How serious would it be if information were forced out of him before he was killed?" Jade asked. "How do the systems work?"

Instead of answering immediately, Gillespie stood up and walked over to a large diagram on the wall. Following him, Jade saw that it represented the layout of the entire Inkomfe complex.

"There are many layers of security in every nuclear plant," he told her. "First and foremost, there are physical containment barriers built into the design. The design of the fuel itself, the rods that are used, the piping system—everything is worked out to the most accurate specifications in order to be sealed and contained."

He pointed to a spot on the map. "The reactor building itself—I told you how thick the concrete was?" She nodded. "That can withstand the impact of a jet plane. And then we have the security protocols, which are built around three functions."

He counted them off on his fingers as he spoke. "They are detection, delay and defense. For these to work, we have divided the plant into various areas. The double perimeter fence—the green zone on the map—provides an isolation zone that's continually monitored by cameras and guards. This covers the protected area, shaded in yellow, where all visitors are searched and must be accompanied by an authorized employee. Now you see the red buildings on the map?"

Jade nodded.

"The red security zone covers the plant's priority areas with the highest security. Locked doors are monitored by access control computers, and authorized personnel have to swipe their badges in order to obtain access. If any door in the red zone does not close within two minutes after opening, an alarm will automatically sound. Emergency alarms can also be triggered within the complex, and when this happens, the red zone goes into lockdown. The high-security doors are protected by the access codes."

"I understand," Jade said. She decided not to mention that she had crossed into a red zone earlier, based on the map and Sbusiso's reaction to seeing her. No reason to put Gillespie on edge.

"Alarms sound throughout the protected area if any security is compromised, or if anybody tries to tamper with them.

The guards' patrol schedules cover all areas. Key cards activate only their authorized doors. Botha's job was to streamline all the physical measures into one system. Now we have a very highly qualified team in charge of the three big security initiatives, but ultimately one person takes responsibility and pulls everything together. That was Botha."

He turned to face her. "So to answer your question, it could be extremely serious. Botha left before the final testing of the upgraded systems. I want to be able to say they're fail-safe, but I feel the cards are stacked against us here. If he left even a single loophole, that could be exploited at a critical time."

Jade nodded. She understood the severity of the threat. "How can you find out?" she asked. "Can you check the systems?"

Gillespie nodded. "Of course, although it will take time. Meanwhile, I am personally supervising all security measures here, and I've put extra guards on every shift. But now, Jade, we have another problem to worry about."

There was a new urgency in his voice. She glanced at him. Serious-faced, he met her eyes. "Botha could have killed Loodts. He was there at the time, was he not?"

Jade nodded. "It would have been possible, but he seemed genuinely shocked when he heard about the murder."

But she knew shock could be feigned. The signs of stress Botha had exhibited could have simply been him furiously working out how to string her along while denying his own involvement.

Gillespie rubbed his forehead. "I can't believe I'm having to theorize like this about two people I entrusted with enormous responsibilities. Now that the chips are down, neither of them has turned out to be the man I thought they were."

"I don't know what to say," Jade said. "I don't know enough

about the situation yet. But I'm sure Botha will tell me more tomorrow."

Gillespie stared at Jade for a long moment. Then he shook his head. "Come with me," he said. "I want to show you something. And then I'm going to explain why I'm taking you off this case."

Chapter Eighteen

GILLESPIE DIDN'T GO all the way back to the entrance. He led Jade back through the gate after opening it with a swipe of his card. Then he turned left and unlocked the door to a brightly lit room. Walking in, Jade found herself in a plush office. To her right was a large desk and high-backed leather chair. To her left, four chairs were set around a wooden table in a small meeting area. "Please, take a seat."

Jade sat down at the table while Gillespie walked over to the desk and picked up a folder, then sat opposite her and opened it.

"I don't know you well," he said. "But I think that in different circumstances, I would have liked to get to know you better." His smile was infectious—she couldn't help but return it. "So please forgive me if I share something very personal."

"Go ahead," Jade said, watching his face grow serious as he took something from the folder.

"This is my wife, Andrea. Or rather, this was my wife."

Gillespie passed her a large glossy photograph. Jade stared into the warm brown eyes of a beautiful woman. Her jet-black hair was worn short with a spiky fringe. Her full lips were parted in a smile.

"We were married for five years. The happiest time of my life. I managed a small private security operation in Iraq, and she lived there with me. It was dangerous work, a volatile part of the world. We both knew that. And one day, the worst happened. She and our driver were both caught up in a shooting incident. The car lost control, and both of them were killed instantly."

"Oh, God, how terrible," Jade said. "I'm so sorry."

"It was beyond terrible," Gillespie said. "Beyond anything I've ever known. Jade, I went to pieces after that for a while. I blamed myself for putting Andrea at risk. If she hadn't been in that car, if she had stayed safely at home, then this would never have happened."

"I understand," Jade said gently.

"I left Iraq in February and came back to South Africa. There were too many memories . . . I couldn't stay there any longer. Couldn't run things after what had happened. I returned home, and a couple of months later, when I'd pulled myself together, I started looking for a job. Loodts offered me this position."

Jade nodded sympathetically.

"Anyway," Gillespie continued, "I'm not just telling you this for catharsis. The reason is this: I cannot allow myself to needlessly endanger the lives of anybody I'm responsible for. I've seen the consequences firsthand."

"I'm not—" Jade began, but Gillespie held up his hand.

"No, Jade. I've thought hard about your predicament, and what I've landed you in. You are in danger. So is Botha. I have no idea what's been going on here, but he's clearly gotten himself into something bigger and deadlier than he thought it would be. He has gunmen pursuing him. That puts you at risk as well. And whoever these men are, if they kill him, I cannot ever learn the truth from him."

"I agree with you," Jade said.

"And you . . . if anything happened to you . . ." Gillespie pressed his lips together and shook his head. "You remind me of Andrea in a number of ways. Your independence. Your tough-mindedness and resilience. You are a strong, brave woman, Jade. I refuse to allow myself to take advantage of those qualities."

"But Mr. Gillespie, keeping me out of danger is not going to help you solve your problems. Other lives are at risk, too."

"Yes, they are. And because of that, I've come up with what I think is the best solution, but I'm going to need your help. I want to have Botha arrested."

"What?" Jade stared across the table at him in astonishment.

"With the upgrades we're making to the equipment in the red security zone, the next forty-eight hours are critical for Inkomfe. The reactor room is more vulnerable than usual. We cannot afford to have anything go wrong. If Botha spends that time in a holding cell, it will be safer for us, and also safer for him."

"But . . ." Jade had to stop herself from gaping at him. "Arrested? On what grounds? Are you talking about that malicious-damage-to-property charge?"

"That charge has been withdrawn—I don't know why. It's possible that Botha threatened or intimidated the bar owner. The police can't arrest him without a new charge. There is a detective at the Krugersdorp station who works closely with us at Inkomfe, and is as concerned as we are about this situation. If there were any grounds for Botha's arrest, this detective could do the job immediately."

Jade stared at Gillespie across the desk, feeling a sense of surrealism. "I don't understand. What grounds are we talking about?"

"Well, what has he done?" Gillespie asked, pushing a lined notepad and a pen across the table to her. "You've spent some time with him recently. Did he drive recklessly? You told me that you fled from the Best Western motel at high speed. You could write an affidavit confirming this. Or, given the circumstances, perhaps you would be prepared to do more. Did he threaten or abuse you in any way? Did he coerce you into leaving with him? I see you have a graze on the back of your left hand. Did Botha cause it?"

Jade was quiet for a minute.

Gillespie was clearly desperate. He was asking her to exaggerate, or even fabricate the events of the past day. Getting Botha arrested wouldn't take a wild leap of imagination, since there had already been a warrant out for him. But now that the charges had been dropped, Gillespie had no alternative but to use her to try and get him jailed.

She didn't know what to think.

Putting him in prison would solve her problems, but it wouldn't solve Botha's. There was no easier place to murder somebody than when they were trapped in a police holding cell.

Gillespie was doing this because he cared, because he didn't want to recklessly endanger her, and because he wanted to prevent a catastrophe at Inkomfe during a vulnerable time.

But Botha had genuinely cared about her, too. He'd refused to leave the motel without her, believing she would be in danger if she stayed. Writing an affidavit for his arrest would be throwing him to the lions.

"Jade, while you think of what to write, I'm going to get your check for this job," Gillespie said. "I apologize again for the delay."

He left the room, closing the door quietly behind him.

Jade stared down at the blank page, trying to convince herself that what she was about to do was right. A few untruths would have to be penned, but she'd done worse in the past than lying. She could walk away glad that she had helped Gillespie make Inkomfe a little safer.

She picked up the pen and did a test scribble. The pen worked just fine.

Report of Reckless Driving, she headed the page.

On the night of 20 November, I witnessed Mr. Carlos Botha drive at high speed out of the Best Western motel Krugersdorp. He exceeded the speed limit and drove in a reckless manner that endangered other road users, and which caused him to crash his car . . .

With a sigh, Jade tore the page into pieces. That wasn't working. She'd have to try the other angle.

On the night of 20 November, I was coerced by Mr. Carlos Botha into accompanying him when he left the Best Western motel. He grabbed my arm at one point, pushing me against a wall and causing a deep graze on my hand. Botha intimidated me into . . .

Jade ripped the page up again, with more force this time. Then she wrote on the third blank page:

I'm sorry, Mr. Gillespie. This isn't going to work. The charges are too flimsy. If Botha is arrested, he'll be inside for a maximum of twenty-four hours. Less, if he has a good lawyer. If he's planning anything, he'll still have time to put it into action. And he won't trust me anymore, or anyone else, for that matter. He'll go into hiding, and you'll lose the only link you have to him. Give me another day and let me see what I can do.

She threw the other pieces into the trash bin, stood up and left the meeting room.

From here, there were no locked doors between herself and freedom. She didn't know what to say to Gillespie if she ran into him on his way back with her money, but she didn't see him. However, as she passed one of the other rooms, she heard his voice coming from behind the closed door. She stopped and listened.

"Please," he said in strained tones. "Please help me out. Give me just a little more time. I'll get it to you as soon as possible."

Frowning, Jade walked on, back to the security desk to claim her belongings, wondering what on earth Gillespie could be speaking about.

IT WAS NEARLY a quarter past three in the morning when Jade left Inkomfe, and by the time she reached Sandton, she could see the beginnings of brightness on the horizon. As she drove into the hotel parking garage, she realized that the spot she'd been in earlier was now occupied. She'd have to take the one closest to it and hope that Botha didn't notice her car had moved during the night.

She paced quickly back to the suite and let herself in, breathing out a relieved sigh when she saw the lounge area was dark, and Botha's bedroom door was closed.

Finally a chance to have a shower. After ten minutes under the hottest water she could bear, she climbed into bed and programmed her phone alarm for seven-thirty. She was sure she'd wake before the alarm sounded. Her internal clock was accurate even when she was very tired. Hopefully, three hours of sleep would be enough for whatever the day might bring.

But she didn't get those three hours.

The shrilling of the hotel phone jerked her out of deep slumber. Disoriented, she fumbled for the receiver, picked it up and mumbled, "Hello?"

But there was no recorded voice on the line, telling her the time in a tinny voice. Only an expectant silence.

"Hello?" Jade said again.

The line went dead.

Wide awake now, she sat up. It was a quarter to six. She'd slept for just over an hour. No wonder she felt groggy. Had she made a mistake when programming the wake-up call?

She was sure she hadn't. So had the hotel been trying to contact her?

She dialed reception. "It's Jade de Jong," she said. "My phone just rang, but there was nobody on the line. Do you know anything about it?"

"Just a moment, Mrs. de Jong," the receptionist said.

"Ms.," Jade corrected her, but she was already listening to hold music. The receptionist picked up the call again and said, "I'm sorry. Thandi, the other receptionist on duty, put the call through to you by mistake. A gentleman just called to confirm whether you'd checked in late last night, and to asked if you'd left a package for collection at the front desk. Thandi transferred him to your room instead. I do apologize."

"No worries," Jade said.

A cold knot tightened in her stomach. She and Botha hadn't been well hidden. All it had taken to track them down was patience, a loosely fabricated cover story and some phone calls.

The hunters had found out her name. It hadn't taken them long, either.

This hotel was no longer safe. They needed to get out. Every moment was vital.

Botha must have heard the phone ring. When she knocked on his door after hastily pulling on her clothes, he opened it immediately. She saw he was dressed—half dressed, at any rate. His torso was taut and hard-muscled without a trace of fat, his skin a matte beige.

"Somebody phoned the hotel asking if I was checked in," she told him. "But we got lucky. The switchboard operator made a mistake and put the call through."

"Not good," he said. "We'd better get moving, then."

He walked to the bathroom and returned with his shirt, which she guessed he'd washed and hung up to dry overnight. He slipped it on, put his laptop away and hoisted the backpack onto his shoulder. A minute later, they were running out of the suite.

When the elevator arrived, Jade pushed the button for the second floor. When Botha glanced at her, she explained, "A precaution. I don't want to come face-to-face with them in the lobby."

He nodded.

They got out on the second floor, which was the conferencing and dining level. The aroma of coffee filled the air, and the clinking of cutlery suggested that the first room service breakfasts were being prepared.

They walked down the final flight of stairs, and she cautiously pushed the door open and peered around.

The lobby was empty. The elevator doors were closing.

They jogged across the tiled floor to the basement stairs. Looking back, Jade saw the elevator had stopped on their floor.

They sprinted down to the basement parking and scrambled into the car, and she accelerated out of the garage.

After five minutes of zigzagging, they were on William Nicol Drive, heading north. She felt shaky from nerves and bludgeoned from lack of sleep. This had been a close call, far too close. A simple mistake had saved their lives. Had it not been for the receptionist's error, things would have gone very differently.

"How did they find us?" Botha asked.

"They found out my name," Jade said. "They must have guessed we'd hide out in a hotel, and spent the night calling around."

What could she glean about the criminals from this? They were more patient than she'd guessed, and more intelligent, too. More organized.

She pressed her lips together. Something still wasn't adding up. It was a lot of time for the men following them to have spent chasing a crazy hunch. She needed to think this through. As of now, she had the uneasy feeling that their pursuers had the advantage.

"So . . . no more hotels?" Botha asked.

Jade shook her head. "No. But we need to go somewhere to regroup. Not easy to do while driving around Jo'burg watching our backs."

"I know a place we could go," he said.

"Where's that?"

"It's a townhouse in Honeydew that's being refurbished. The keys are with the caretaker who lives in the complex."

"Who does it belong to?"

"Someone I trust." He didn't say any more.

They made it out to Honeydew in the northwest of Johannesburg by twenty-five past six, as traffic thickened and trickles of cars started to become streams. Jade hadn't been here for years, although she remembered David complaining a few months ago that the precinct had recently experienced a dramatic increase in violent crime. This was partly due to the illegal mining taking place on its outskirts, but also because of the epidemic of development in northern Johannesburg, which had hit the area hard. From upmarket golf estates and townhouse complexes to low-cost housing projects and informal huts and shacks, the influx of new residents made the gathering of crime intelligence impossible. You couldn't spot criminals when everyone was a stranger in town, David had explained.

Luckily, Botha's complex was located next door to the golf estate in a neatly maintained street that was, according to the signage, protected by Scorpion Patrol Neighborhood Security.

On the other side of the main road, they saw a coffee shop rolling up its shutters in preparation for the day. It had a drive-through, which was also about to open. For the sake of coffee, Jade was prepared to risk another few minutes out on Jo'burg's streets.

Looking over her shoulder was becoming exhausting. For a moment, she wished she'd taken Gillespie up on his offer. Written the affidavit and handed Botha over to the police, and told Gillespie she was off the case.

What would she do then? A tropical destination beckoned, somewhere far away. A chalet on the beachfront. Running for miles on the firm, damp sand until her legs ached, swimming in the sea. Fresh fish on the grill, music pumping from a rustic bar nearby where a glass of white wine waited for her. Or a cocktail in a coconut shell.

And then the darkness caught up with her again.

The killers who had called the hotel had asked for her by name. They knew who she was. She'd always have to watch her back, even in paradise. Looking out for pale, muscled arms newly bared to the sun. Cold eyes masked by mirrored shades. Strong fingers that wouldn't hesitate to pull a trigger or clamp around a throat. There were a hundred ways to find somebody who'd fled the country, and a thousand ways for them to die.

Instead, she started thinking about guns.

A weapon would definitely be useful to her now. These guys weren't playing games; this wasn't just intimidation. It was an organized pursuit, a chase meant to end in a kill. Her Glock had been confiscated by the police months ago, and she'd jumped through so many hoops in her efforts to get it back that she was beginning to feel like a circus tiger.

A captive, declawed tiger.

She sometimes wondered if Superintendent David Patel had an active role in frustrating her efforts. He knew about her fruitless attempts to get the weapon back because she'd made the mistake of telling him, thinking he could help. Perhaps he believed she'd land herself in less trouble if she didn't have a gun.

David had always lacked imagination. But she wasn't going to start with the resentful thoughts about him now. The bottom line was, she was weaponless, and she needed a gun.

How could she solve this problem?

A rustling sound caught her attention, and she turned toward Botha again. She was startled to see that, while she'd been staring out of the window at the drive-through, a large pile of high-denomination banknotes had materialized in her car's glove compartment. "What's this for?" she asked.

"It's your payment. Partial payment, rather. I don't have any more cash on me right now."

"Wait a minute. Botha, I never said I'd work for you. I haven't agreed to take on this job."

"This isn't for future services." His voice was soft, and it broke as he was talking. She thought the stress might be starting to catch up with him. You could only go so far on adrenaline.

"What's it for, then?"

"It's for what you've already done. Call it professional services rendered. You've saved my life twice so far, and I think I owe you for that."

"I can't accept this."

"I won't take it back. Please, Jade."

Well, it was the only money she'd received for this job so far, even if the wrong person was handing it to her.

As she tapped the pile of notes with her fingers until it was a perfect oblong in shape, Jade wondered exactly who she *was* working for.

With some difficulty, she folded the thick bundle in half and zipped it into her jacket pocket.

"Thank you," she said, putting the car into gear and heading for the drive-through window, where the attendant was now on duty. "Coffee's on me."

Chapter Nineteen

THE MORNING WAS bright, sunny and clear, thanks to last night's rains. Green grass seemed to have clothed the arid sidewalk strips overnight. Birds chirped and fluttered. A beautiful day, Mweli observed. Pity she was about to spend it holed up in this office, chasing after leads she feared would not be worth the time spent on them. She'd rather be like Chakalaka, snoozing belly-up in the sun.

Her to-do list was getting longer by the minute, with two main cases occupying most of her time: the motel crime scene, and the body dumped in the Robinson Dam. She still had some final calls to make, to confirm the logistics for the dredging operation at the dam tomorrow. Once she'd finished those, it was back to the motel murder investigation. Her first task was to make an inventory of all the personal possessions that had been found in the Best Western room. They had been bagged up at the crime scene and transferred straight to the Randfontein precinct, where they had been locked away in the evidence room.

As she unlocked the evidence room, the shrill of the phone in the office made her jump. Phiri answered it. From what she could hear of the one-sided conversation, another reporter was already on the story. She listened, tightening her lips with satisfaction at Phiri's responses.

No, his boss was not available. No, Phiri was not authorized to speak about the case. Yes, it was under investigation. No, he could not comment about the identity of the murder victim until the next of kin were notified. Yes, his boss's name was Detective Mweli. Yes, she would release more details as soon as she was authorized to do so. Yes, she was the acting station commander. No, the real commander was on long leave due to illness. No, Phiri was not going to give out the cell phone numbers of either the acting commander or the regular commander.

Mweli closed the evidence room door behind her. The room was cool and smelled musty. The cluttered shelves seemed to taunt her with their contents. So many cases, so few convictions.

Easing a pair of gloves onto her plump hands, she placed the bags on the table.

Item one was a wallet containing two credit cards, a driver's license and eight hundred and fifty rand in cash.

Item two was a briefcase. The case was a high-quality item. It had been standing on the table when the bodies were discovered. It contained a silver pen and pencil slotted into special holders, and a zipped-up leather pouch containing an asthma inhaler and a pack of headache tablets with three remaining. The only other item was an empty white plastic document folder with its snap fastener undone.

There was no laptop inside the case, nor had there been any phones on the scene. Mweli was already bracing herself for accusations that the police had pilfered them. And yet, if a criminal had stolen the computer and phone, why had he not bothered to take the cash in Loodts's wallet?

Robbery was clearly not the motive.

And where were the dead woman's possessions? Nothing belonging to her had been found. Not so much as a wallet, never mind the black purse that Ms. de Jong had seen in the SUV.

Which led her to the next item in this investigation: the envelope that had been left under her windshield wiper last night.

It was a sturdy brown envelope, slightly stained with damp. Inside, there were ninety-nine bills. Presumably whoever had left the money under her wiper had spent one of the notes along the way. Buying takeout, perhaps, she surmised in a moment of dark humor.

It was a bribe, and she wasn't going to take it, even though an extra nine thousand, nine hundred rand would come in handy. Nor would she keep some and declare the rest, though she couldn't deny the thought was tempting. She was going to turn this money in, every penny of it, and if somebody wondered whether Mweli had spent the hundredth note on takeaway—well, they could damn well keep on wondering.

"Forget about the woman. She's a nobody. A hired prostitute."

And then the veiled threat of vengeance to come.

Finding out the woman's name would provide her with a starting point for the investigation. These bags did not contain all the evidence. She was certain of it. Had Loodts's killers stolen his secrets as well as his life?

Or were those secrets still hidden somewhere?

Mweli gave the folder a final shake, running her gloved hands inside and opening it up. If it had contained papers, they were gone. But this time, when she opened the plastic flap fully, she saw something she had missed the first time around.

A white label was stuck to the inside of the folder. On it was neatly printed: INKOMFE CLASSIFIED INFORMATION— MEETINGS, MINUTES & MEMOS.

Mweli stared down at the label. The briefcase was neatly ordered, free from clutter and any other folders. Loodts gave her the impression of having been a methodical man who didn't carry unnecessary items around with him. Everything in the briefcase had been neatly closed and secured, apart from the folder. Against the odds, Mweli hoped the classified documents once in that folder had made their way into the hands of someone other than Loodts's killer.

WITH TWO GIANT coffees steaming in the car's cup holders, Jade followed Botha's directions, easing her way through the traffic until she arrived at the main gate of a community development surrounded by high white walls. The caretaker's domestic worker was waiting to hand over the keys and gate buzzer which Botha had called to request a few minutes earlier.

The house was small and neat and bright—typical South African upscale complex living. A paved balcony faced out onto a narrow strip of lawn flanked with flower beds. The architect had even managed to squeeze in a fishpond-sized swimming pool.

They parked outside the garage door, but when Botha opened it, Jade saw that the space was unusable; it was packed with equipment, tarps and tools from the renovations.

The house itself smelled of fresh paint and adhesive. It was small and cozy with the kitchen and open-plan living area downstairs, and glass doors opening onto the patio. Upstairs were two bedrooms with more glass doors and small balconies. On the plus side, she was certain they had not been followed here. On the downside, the front door lock was so flimsy that Jade was fairly sure she could break it just with a strong look.

She'd just have to rely on those high walls and automated main gate.

Botha carried his laptop bag upstairs to the second

bedroom, leaving the main one for Jade. It was freshly carpeted, with a brand-new bathroom.

"Partly furnished" meant a bed but no bedding. Jade opened the sliding door to let in some air, wondering if the house next door was occupied. It was so close by that the residents would surely have few secrets from their neighbors. She saw flowering potted plants on the balcony opposite, in front of closed curtains. Someone was living there, then.

The lack of security concerned her. "We need to assess this place," she told Botha. "Let's get a picture of its strengths and weaknesses. Explore our escape routes for the worst-case scenario of a break-in."

They started with the glass sliding doors that opened onto the postage stamp–sized porch and fishpond swimming pool. The doors didn't appear shatterproof or protected, and their fastening was basic.

"This is a problem," Botha said.

"It's not ideal, but it'll do."

"Why do you say that?" he asked, his tone challenging her.

"Because that latch rattles. If it breaks, it's an early warning system. Like an alarm."

"Speaking of which, I don't see one of those."

"Nope. No alarm."

The downstairs bathroom window had frosted glass but no grille. The builders had obviously decided that the electric-topped wall that surrounded this cluster development would be a sufficient deterrent.

Their safe house wasn't so safe. But then, at least they could be more anonymous here, unlike at a hotel. It might be a cheaply built dwelling with a few serious gaps in its defenses, but it was the best they had for now.

The house felt cool after the oppressive humidity outside.

Her coffee was waiting on the lounge table. Botha stayed outside for a few minutes, speaking quietly on his phone. He disconnected before he walked in. He went to the kitchen, and she heard the tap run before he brought his own coffee into the lounge.

When he did, she saw he'd removed the dressing she'd applied to his forehead last night. The gash had scabbed over. She'd wondered at the time if it needed stitches, but she saw now that her quick patch-up job had proven sufficient.

"You had questions for me last night," he said. "I have answers for you if we manage to stay out of trouble long enough."

Jade was surprised to see a glint of humor in his eyes, and more surprised to find herself smiling in response. "Let's hope we do."

She sat down and took a sip of coffee. Hot, strong, with a hint of sweetness. She could feel the caffeine zinging through her bloodstream, sharpening her thoughts, banishing the last traces of fuzziness. A temporary fix, but an effective one.

"I was hired to work at Inkomfe by the security director at the time, Lisa Marais. She left soon afterward."

"Why did she leave?"

"She'd always clashed with Wouter Loodts. She believed his ideas were old-fashioned, and that he prioritized production efficiency over workers' safety. They used to argue about that all the time, but Loodts is—was—the hands-on manager of Inkomfe's board of directors, which meant he was in charge. He was at least seventy, and scheduled to retire at the end of the year. Overdue, in my opinion. After Loodts employed Ryan Gillespie, Gillespie and Lisa quickly came to despise each other. A few months later, she was forced out, and he took over."

Jade nodded.

"When the nuclear partnership with Russia was announced, Gillespie was immediately concerned about sabotage. He told us he feared that intruders might break in and gain access to the control room, which would give them the capability to destroy the machines or even trigger some sort of meltdown. I suggested some changes that could be made to improve security. Finally, he and Loodts agreed on them, but there were a number of unexpected delays. There seemed to be more and more problems cropping up. We were running worst-case scenarios and trying to troubleshoot."

"And then?"

"I began implementing a major but necessary project, updating the security systems in the strong room and reactor control room."

Jade raised her eyebrows.

"Access to these areas is old-fashioned, still involving security codes. It needed to be upgraded to biometrics."

"I see."

Botha rubbed his eyes—carefully, so as not to aggravate the wound on his forehead. "The project didn't receive the go-ahead."

"Why not?"

He cradled his coffee mug again. "There was disagreement over protocol, which delayed things. Then a meeting got canceled. Then another project was prioritized. I started to get the feeling that there was somebody at Inkomfe who didn't want these changes to be made."

"Who? Loodts? Gillespie?"

Botha nodded. "Lisa and I believed Gillespie was stalling things, though we weren't sure why, because he was the one who'd been so worried in the first place. I stayed in touch with Lisa after she left, and the two of us began to discover

other extremely disturbing facts about Inkomfe's security systems. And then the sabotage took place."

From outside the townhouse, tires squealed and a powerful
engine roared.

Botha stopped talking, and he and Jade turned toward the
window. "Who's that?" Botha asked.

Jade pulled the curtain back just in time to see a black
Land Rover swerve around their car toward the exit gate.
"Probably just a neighbor in a hurry," she said, trying her best
to ignore the fear creeping over her.

Craning her neck, she noticed the flashing lights of a
patrol security vehicle making its way up the pavement in
the opposite direction.

To Jade's surprise, the small car stopped outside their gate.
As the uniformed guard climbed out and headed toward their
front door, she noticed the logo on the black-and-white car
door: SCORPION PATROL NEIGHBORHOOD SECURITY.

She hurried to the entrance as the guard arrived.

"Morning," he said. The walkie-talkie on his belt crackled unintelligibly. "Is this your vehicle parked outside the
garages?"

"Yes," Jade said. "We've just arrived. The garages are full
of building equipment."

"The car's blocking the road. We need clear access here.
Please move it to the visitors lot on the right-hand side of the
entrance gate."

"I will. Can I have ten minutes?" Jade asked. "I'm going out
soon, and I'll park it in the correct place when I come back."

"Ten minutes will be fine, but no longer, please."

The guard climbed back into his miniature car and
drove off.

Jade watched the road for another minute, but the dark

SUV didn't return. All she saw was the security vehicle driving slowly around the complex.

She returned to the living room. Botha was midway through dialing a number, but he locked his screen as soon as she walked in.

"Just a guard telling us to move the car," she said.

"Good to know they're patrolling." Botha put his phone on the table.

"So the worries about sabotage were well founded?" she asked, getting back to the topic at hand.

"Yes. They were. And what happened on Friday could have been far worse."

"How?" Jade glanced uneasily toward the window again.

"You still worried about that SUV?" Botha asked.

"I'd like to make sure it's gone."

He nodded somberly. "Let's take a walk and check out the complex while I explain the problems at Inkomfe."

Jade opened the front door and stepped outside, feeling vulnerable in the bright, clear morning. She wished she knew where their hunters were, and that she had a gun.

Chapter Twenty

JADE AND BOTHA set off along the narrow pedestrian path at a brisk walk, heading toward the complex gate. "It's good to be moving again," he said.

"Do you usually go to the gym? Run?" Jade asked, wondering how he maintained his impressive physique.

"I run occasionally, but my main sport is martial arts," he said.

"Which one?"

"Judo and karate. I'm black belt in judo, third *dan* in karate."

"Wow," Jade said, impressed. She'd always believed martial arts practitioners to be focused, controlled. But Botha had gone off the rails last week, damaging property and assaulting a woman at a bar. It was confusing that there could be such a different side to him. But then, everyone had different sides to them.

"I used to compete," Botha said. "But recently, I haven't made as much time to practice as I should. I promised myself that when my contract at Inkomfe was over, I'd go back to training an hour a day."

"I run most days," Jade said. "I prefer to do it without being chased."

She thought Botha might smile in response to that, but the moment passed. "For now, I guess a five-minute walk will have to do," he said.

They made their way around the small estate, which had

just twenty units divided in half by the main street. There was no sign of the black SUV, and nowhere else in the complex it could have gone.

"About Inkomfe, I believe the most vulnerable part of the plant is not the control room. It's Inqaba, the security strong room," Botha said.

"Why?"

"The strong room holds the dangerous materials. Seven bombs were built back in the 1970s. I'm no expert in nuclear technology, but I believe making them took great ingenuity. At the time, South Africa was under harsh sanctions. They had to manufacture most of the materials here. Others were smuggled in. Now nuclear bombs generally need to be made out of weapons-grade uranium."

"What's that?"

"It's uranium that has been highly enriched through isotope separation. Uranium must be enriched for any nuclear use, but weapons require uranium with at least twenty percent of a special isotope—U-235, if I remember correctly. In apartheid South Africa, the scientists at Inkomfe had to learn how to enrich uranium on-site. They had the raw materials, and they learned to use them. South Africa's nuclear weapons were eighty percent enriched uranium. It was produced in secret and put into the missiles."

"But the missiles were disarmed," Jade said.

"When you disarm a missile, you remove its capacity to be launched in an aerial attack. Disarming it doesn't automatically dispose of all the dangerous materials—in this case, highly enriched uranium."

"So what happened to it?"

They had reached the front gate, and there was no sign of anything untoward. The complex was quiet. Jade guessed that most of the residents had left for work. The patrol vehicle was crawling up the road, sunlight flashing off its windshield.

"The weapons were melted down and formed into ingots," Botha told her. "For a while, these bars were used to manufacture medical isotopes. But a few years ago, scientists switched to a lower grade of uranium—just as effective, but safer. The original stash was hardly touched, since a little of it went a long way. Nearly half a ton is still stored there in the form of small ingots in the maximum-security strong room."

"So why are they a problem? Do they leak radiation?"

"No. But if they were stolen, they would represent a serious risk."

"Why?"

"They are not detectably radioactive—you can't use machines to pinpoint where they are, and you could carry them around in a backpack and probably come to no harm. But while it's not very radioactive, this uranium is incredibly unstable. So much so that if you wanted to cause an explosion that could wipe out an entire city, you'd just have to shape two of the bars in the right way and bang them together with enough force."

Jade frowned. "I see why you wanted to upgrade the strong room's security."

"This is a matter of national security, not just Inkomfe's security. And like I said, our security measures are outdated. Codes can be cracked. Biometrics is far safer."

"And there's no way of getting rid of the uranium? Can't it be melted down again into a less lethal form?" she asked.

"Well, it could." Botha laced his fingers together and stretched his hands above his head. "There is technology that would allow us to do that, but it's very costly. There are other alternatives as well. Last year, the president of the United

States wrote an official letter to our president, explaining that if he was prepared to hand over the enriched uranium bars, the US would replace them with bars of less volatile, lower-grade uranium. It's just as useful for manufacturing, but not as dangerous."

"So I'm guessing he refused the offer."

They turned to walk back.

"He consulted with NECSA— the South African Nuclear Energy Corporation—and NECSA's board refused. They said South Africa was perfectly capable of keeping their uranium bars properly secure, and that they were not prepared to hand them over."

"Why?" Jade asked, puzzled.

"If there's ever another commercial use found for highly enriched uranium, NECSA will be sitting on a gold mine. They're not willing to give them up."

"And Loodts wouldn't update the code system?"

Botha shook his head. "I was hoping to persuade him otherwise at our meeting."

As they walked back, Jade thought about the many motives to kill Wouter Loodts. He didn't sound as if he'd been well liked; Sbusiso had spoken of him with loathing, and she guessed there were many former Inkomfe workers who felt the same way. More recently, Loodts had clashed with Lisa Marais and been instrumental in her leaving. And his micromanaging hadn't endeared him to Botha, either.

"That's everything, basically," Botha said.

"No, it isn't."

"What do you mean?" Botha sounded curious. "What else can I tell you?"

"You said you wanted me to work for you. Doing what?"

"Something that might be impossible. Finding someone's identity."

"Whose?"

"The blonde woman found dead in the motel room with Loodts."

"Her?" Jade blurted out, surprised.

"Yes."

"Why?"

"I think it could be important."

"Her ID wasn't in the room, and the car didn't have license plates."

"I know. That's why I said it might not be possible. But what if there's something out there that can tell us who she is?"

"I'll go back and see what I can find," Jade said. "While I'm out, I'll also stop by the police station and report the accident. I should be back by lunch."

They exchanged phone numbers, and when she left, she saw him outside, talking on his phone again. Botha obviously didn't want her to hear whoever was on the other end of the line.

Botha was still keeping secrets; was he protecting Jade or using her to achieve his own ends? She drove off with a frown.

Chapter Twenty-One

MWELI'S TO-DO LIST didn't look any shorter or simpler when she finally left the evidence room and locked it behind her.

She'd notified Organized Crime about the car bomb and bribe left under her windscreen, and a representative from the department would come through later that morning. She would have liked to have confirmed the ID of the mystery blonde by the time he arrived, but that wouldn't be possible.

The woman's hands had appeared injured, so the detectives had placed evidence bags over them and waited for the pathologist to pull prints. These would then be entered into the system, and if they had a match, Mweli would be the first to know. In, say, four weeks or so.

She sighed heavily. There were only so many favors one could call in from the forensics department; she had to pick her battles with care. And since only criminals with previous convictions had their prints stored in the South African Police Service database, she honestly wasn't hopeful.

The woman had seemingly appeared out of nowhere and gotten herself bludgeoned to death in that damned room. And where the hell was the car? It could have been a treasure trove of trace evidence, but the likelihood of that evidence remaining undisturbed was declining sharply by the minute.

Mweli pressed her lips together as she imagined garage mechanics opening the doors, clearing out all the clothing and possessions inside. From experience, she knew such items tended to disappear. When asked for their whereabouts, heads would be shaken, brows furrowed, hands spread in a gesture of wide-eyed innocence.

Ashveer's Auto. Mweli flipped through the phone directory, and within two minutes, she was speaking to Mr. Ashveer himself. "I'm calling about a car that came in last night," she said.

Ashveer sounded quiet and competent. "Would that be the red Jetta or the white Nissan bakkie from the accident on Piet Kruger Road? Or the black Renault Laguna that lost control after a hijacking?"

"No. This was a silver Land Cruiser. Front-end collision with a pole."

There was a short silence.

"We had no Land Cruisers come in last night. Two vehicles were signed in at around three P.M.: a blue Mercedes-Benz and a white Fiat Uno. Then, at nine P.M., the Jetta and the bakkie were brought in, and the Laguna came around midnight."

Mweli took a moment to absorb this bad news. "So you were open all last night?"

"We're open twenty-four hours to receive vehicles. One of the few places that are. Most of them close at six."

"Please, can you give me the names of the others that were open?"

Ashveer provided her with two names and phone numbers. "They're nowhere near here," he warned. "One's south of Jo'burg, and one's on the other side of Sandton. Otherwise, the car must have been taken somewhere overnight and towed elsewhere in the morning."

"Thank you," Mweli said. She put the phone down gently. Slamming it into the cradle wouldn't help. The stupid thing would only jam up and become unusable until Phiri came in and coaxed it back into working order with his screwdriver.

Two phone calls later, she had established that the Land Cruiser had not been towed to either of the other twenty-four-hour garages.

Where, then, had the wrecked SUV disappeared to?

The tow truck driver could surely answer that, but when she tried the cell phone number on the business card the Best Western manager had given her, she received a recorded message informing her that the number she had dialed didn't exist.

She tried three times. Same message. Either the recipient's cell provider was having a serious glitch this morning, or the driver had mistakenly printed an incorrect number on his card. Neither of these seemed likely, but she didn't want to think about the alternatives.

The card was printed in black capital lettering on plain white. It read *J. Oberholzer*, followed by the phone number. Nothing about towing services. You'd think a tow truck driver might want that information on his card.

Mweli adjusted herself in her chair, hearing its usual squeak of complaint before her thoughts were interrupted by a loud knock at the door.

"Phiri?" she called, suddenly nervous of whom it might be, given the trickery she had been battling lately.

Her fears were dispelled when the detective peeked around the door. "There's an update on the Robinson Dam dredging operation, ma'am. It's all confirmed for tomorrow, eleven A.M."

Mweli dragged her focus back to her other major case. "That's good. We'll need to be on-site with the team."

"I've already briefed the others. I'm heading to the lab now to observe the autopsies from yesterday's motel murder."

"They're doing those so soon?" Mweli asked, surprised. She was well aware of the backlogs, the piles of bodies in refrigeration waiting their turn.

"These have been prioritized because an ex-government minister is involved," Phiri explained.

"Call me as soon as you have any info," she said, relieved that they'd been fast-tracked. "Who's doing them?" she asked as an afterthought when Phiri turned to leave.

"Williams," Phiri said. "We got lucky. They assigned him specially."

Mweli nodded, relieved. At least one thing was going right on this confusing, frustrating morning. Williams was the best, most thorough pathologist they dealt with.

If the bodies held any secrets, Mweli was confident that, under Williams's probing blades, they would be brought to light.

Chapter Twenty-Two

JADE'S FIRST STOP was a nearby shopping mall with a basement parking lot fronted by a gym. It was three-quarters full, and it didn't take her long to find what she needed—her rental was a common make and model. When she'd spotted another, slightly newer white Mazda in the garage, she parked nearby, and after checking to make sure nobody was watching, took a screwdriver from her car's toolkit and removed the other Mazda's rear license plate.

Doing private investigation work meant you were more paranoid than the average person, and with reason. The average person wasn't followed while they went about their daily job. They weren't poisoned by their spouse or murdered by colleagues. You learned to question everything that everybody told you, because people lied for many reasons, and the most dangerous lies were the ones they themselves believed. And you learned the importance of camouflage, of changing your appearance and blending in, to throw hunters off the trail.

Quickly she took both plates off her car. When another shopper passed by, she had to stop and pretend to do post-gym stretches against her hood. When the person walked into the mall, she finished the job and stashed her original plates under the front seat.

Now her car had a different license plate. But it wasn't enough; one unremarkable white Mazda was a lot like another. Same as the guy with a black beanie: Take the beanie off and reveal a weird hairstyle, and that was all people remembered. Maybe she could use Robbie's wisdom to her advantage.

She jogged upstairs to the mall, where she found a stationery store. A quick search and she had what she needed. Five minutes later, the car's new look was complete.

A stick figure family of a woman in gym gear, two young boys, a girl with pigtails and a small dog adorned the bottom left side of the back window. On the right side of the bumper, she'd affixed a sticker that said in pink lettering, *Supermom*, and in the center, another one, with a picture of a dog's head, declared, *My Yorkie Is Smarter Than Our President*.

She scuffed at the edges of the stickers with her nails and rubbed over them with the car key to make them look worn.

The car told a new story now, and with this disguise in place, Jade felt more at ease going out onto Jo'burg's streets.

As she drove into Krugersdorp, she noticed it was trash collection day. She remembered seeing a few of the black plastic garbage bins parked on the curb the previous night. This morning, the streets were lined with them, and the bins were being rummaged through.

Garbage bins contained all sorts of unsavory and even dangerous throwaways. Rotting food, cans with sharp edges, broken glass, dirty diapers. But occasionally hidden among these were items that were still usable or sellable. They could also be treasure troves of recyclable goods.

And so it was commonplace to see the less wealthy appear in the streets on collection day, picking through the trash before the garbage truck came by. The men in this part of Randfontein had fashioned homemade carts with rickety wheels and sides lined with white burlap. She saw two of them working the street, pushing the cart with some difficulty to the next bin.

The cart looked heavy and unwieldy, and Jade was struck by how hard life was for the impoverished people of her country. She wouldn't have wanted to open those bins, much less rummage through them without gloves on. The stench was strong, even in passing. But faced with poverty and starvation, these men risked injury and infection every day as they went about their unpleasant work. Most astonishingly, they did it with a smile. One of the two waved at her cheerfully as he balanced his wobbly cart.

Jade suddenly had an idea.

There had been items missing from the motel room. Loodts's murderers might have dumped some of them in a roadside bin, knowing they would be emptied the next morning.

Might they have abandoned the woman's purse?

She was the only one who'd seen it. She knew what it looked like, and would certainly be able to recognize it again.

She parked the car near one of the makeshift carts and climbed out before greeting the men pushing it. "Hello! Have you seen a black handbag?"

The men proved to be Zimbabwean immigrants whose English was iffy, but after a few moments of confused back-and-forth dialogue combined with pantomime gestures, she had overcome the language barrier sufficiently to be understood.

"We have seen nothing like that," they said. "But you can ask Godfrey and Tshabalala, who are working two streets down."

Jade drove on to the next road, where in the distance she spied another pair of garbage reclaimers hard at work. She introduced herself and asked their names.

This time, when she repeated her question, the response was different.

Silence greeted her words. Then Godfrey, in a torn red overall, exchanged glances with Tshabalala, who wore a white shirt that was more holes than fabric.

Jade realized they had it. But the purse was a valuable item, and they were reluctant to give up something which they believed the owner had thrown away. Especially without compensation.

"It was stolen during a crime," she explained, and now understanding replaced the suspicion in their faces. "There's a reward," she added, reaching for her wallet at the same moment that Tshabalala leaned into the depths of his cart.

Her heart skipped a beat as he pulled out the black canvas purse. Whoever had hidden it must have buried it in the bin, because it looked scuffed and had a suspicious smear of something along its side. He handed it over, and Jade took it gingerly by the handles, noting that the odor of rotten banana clung to it.

This material wouldn't hold prints, so she wasn't contaminating evidence—no more than the bananas had done, anyway. "Was it open when you found it?" she asked.

"No. It was closed," Tshabalala told her.

She unzipped it and peered inside. She saw a matching canvas wallet, the glint of keys, a few papers, pepper spray and a small bag she guessed contained toiletries.

"There was cash in the wallet," Godfrey said reluctantly. "I took it out."

"How much?"

"Three hundred and fifty-three rand," he told her.

"Did you take anything else?"

He shook his head.

"Keep the money," Jade said. "And here's another five hundred for finding it."

The men pocketed the money with grateful smiles, and Jade walked off with the purse.

Back in her car, she high-fived an invisible partner with her right hand, because one of her hunches had finally provided her with some hard evidence.

Then, in the relative privacy of the Mazda, she slid open the black zipper again.

Botha wanted to know who this woman was. Perhaps she could now give him that answer.

The toiletry bag smelled faintly of perfume, and she saw a half-used glass bottle of fragrance inside—Tom Ford's Sahara Noir. She'd received that same fragrance two or three years ago as a gift from Robbie after the completion of a successful job. She'd never worn it; it still sat unopened in her cupboard. Too many bad memories, and in any case, she suspected that it had fallen off the back of a perfume delivery van into his light-fingered grasp.

In a zippered compartment, there was also a pack of cigarettes, a lighter, a plastic vial of headache tablets with one remaining and a transparent box containing a number of other assorted pills whose purpose Jade could only guess at. Certainly this mystery woman had been fond of her medication.

Nothing else. No phone, which was a blow, though she had guessed that it wouldn't have been dumped along with the purse, but destroyed or kept.

And then her final hope: the wallet.

No credit cards inside, to Jade's disappointment. But just as she was about to give up, she noticed a nearly invisible card compartment in the cash pocket. Jade felt another self-five coming on as she eased out a card.

A South African driver's license.

"Who are you?" Jade muttered, squinting at the card.

The license was current—due for renewal the following year, and the photo was indisputably the same woman.

Scarlett Sykes.

"I'm going to find out what happened to you," Jade promised, looking down at Scarlett's blurry photograph.

Apart from that, the purse yielded no other clues, but this was enough. She decided to keep the pepper spray. It wasn't a gun, but at least it was usable. The police could have the rest.

She put the driver's license card back into the wallet and the wallet back into the bag, then locked it away safely in her car's trunk.

It was only a short distance to the Best Western motel.

SOMEBODY HAD SWEPT up the broken glass under the motel's signboard, and the debris was cleared away. Botha's ruined car was gone from the street; only a dark shimmer of oil remained.

In the light of day, the motel looked shabby, peaceful and unassuming. It was difficult to believe that it had been the scene of such a grisly murder.

Jade's first stop was her old room. She arrived at the same time the cleaner was leaving. A short, stocky woman, she was hardly visible behind the wheeled laundry basket piled high with bedding.

Glancing inside, Jade saw that the bed had already been stripped. The pillows, and whatever had been underneath them, had been moved.

"I left a recording machine under the pillow," she said to the cleaner, who looked at her blankly. "A small machine. Silver." Jade showed its approximate shape with her outstretched fingertips.

The cleaner shook her head. "When I came in, the pillows were on the floor," she said. "So was the duvet."

Jade hadn't left them that way. But she'd left the key in the door when she had fled last night. The men who were after them must have come back and searched her room.

She felt a cold fist close around her heart. They would have listened to the recording—and they would have heard themselves on it. They would assume Jade had bugged the room to protect Botha. She was a target now. There was no going back.

She looked into Botha's room. The intruders had indeed forced the lock, which was now loose and rattly, and ransacked the room.

The clothes she'd seen last night, so carefully packed away, were now strewn on the floor, sliced and torn. She'd hoped to bring them back for Botha, but nothing was in wearable condition. One of the cupboard shelves was hanging down, its support splintered. Botha's toiletry bag had been broken and its contents scattered around the bathroom. The pictures had been ripped from the walls, pillows from their pillowcases. The mattress was off its box spring and lying on the tiles.

They had discovered her bug.

It was destroyed now, broken into a pathetic heap of plastic. Jade let out a slow breath.

Deflated, she turned away, trudged back to her car and headed for the Randfontein police station.

Chapter Twenty-Three

WARRANT OFFICER MWELI assessed Jade over the tops of her frameless glasses. Her desk was ordered chaos. Piles of papers and files, a cordless phone and a cell phone, a large plastic bowl containing a higgledy-piggledy assortment of pens, pencils, paper clips and elastic bands, and two framed photos—one of Mweli arm in arm with a round-faced, smiling man, and the other of the ugliest tabby cat Jade had ever seen, glowering yellow-eyed at the camera.

"Nice—er—nice cat," Jade said, by way of an icebreaker. No use in pointing out it resembled the Antichrist.

"His name is Chakalaka." The acting commander didn't smile.

"Ah. Spicy relish. You're fond of it, then?"

"No. I dislike it," Mweli retorted, and Jade wasn't sure if there was dark humor lurking behind that stern expression. But Mweli warmed to her when Jade explained where she had just been, and the evidence she'd found.

"Thank you very much," Mweli said with a grin of relief when Jade handed over the black canvas purse with Scarlett Sykes's ID inside. "This is good investigation work. It could prove critical to the case." She looked as if she might be ready to give a high-five.

"How so?" Jade asked, pleased to be so sincerely complimented.

"Last night, an anonymous caller tried to warn me against even attempting to find out who she is. It was a veiled threat."

"Oh, really?" Jade asked, surprised. "You should have told the caller not to dump crime-scene evidence in garbage bins, then."

"Probably," Mweli agreed. "Now, Ms. de Jong, please update me on last night's situation."

By the time Jade stopped talking, Mweli had filled four notebook pages with her fast, neat handwriting.

"Thank you for coming in. I'll let you know about any important developments," she said, closing the book with a gesture of finality.

Jade wanted to offer her unpaid services as an investigator, but now Mweli was glancing at her watch. "I'm sorry, but I have another meeting now. Somebody from Organized Crime is coming here, in connection with the car bomb last night."

The words "Organized Crime" made Jade tense as her thoughts immediately turned to David. Of course, a police superintendent wouldn't come to this godforsaken part of the world himself . . . He would be far too busy. He'd send one of his subordinates, wouldn't he?

Wouldn't he?

Jade's worst fears were realized when she walked down the shallow concrete stairs and saw David Patel's lanky frame unfold from the unmarked white Ford next to her Mazda.

The man she hated. The man she loved. The man she'd spent far too much time and energy thinking of for the past few months.

She'd made a resolution not to contact him again. Seeing him in the flesh, tall and grim with that trademark frown darkening his otherwise handsome face, felt like a punch to the chest.

He was wearing a red tie that she'd given him—*she'd* given him—some years ago. He looked distracted and preoccupied, running a hand through his spiky black hair before reaching into the back of the car to remove the shabby leather brief-case she'd constantly teased him about needing to replace.

In the end, the briefcase had lasted. It was Jade who'd been replaced.

One mistake on David's part was all it had taken.

He'd been planning to leave his wife, Naisha, but hadn't stopped sleeping with her. Now she was pregnant, and Jade was one of the few people who knew that the baby probably wasn't David's.

Naisha had divulged her plan to a trusted colleague, whose daughter Bhavna had overheard the conversation. A couple of months down the line, a fallout between Naisha and her "friend" had led to the woman losing her job. Angry about her mother's predicament, Bhavna began leaving cryptic notes on David's car in an act of revenge. Jade had investi-gated, confronting Bhavna, who told her everything: Naisha had gotten artificial insemination to use the pregnancy to keep David, and it had worked.

The fury Jade felt toward Naisha was unmatched in her memory. And she was livid with David, too. How could such a high-ranking, experienced detective not pick up on a deception taking place in his own home?

Worst of all, despite the promises she'd made herself, she couldn't tell him.

Because—and this hurt her the most—he would be hap-pier if he never knew.

David glanced up and noticed her; she watched the harried expression on his sharp features tauten into consternation. His icy blue eyes widened when he saw her.

"Jade," he snapped. "What the hell are you doing here?"

She couldn't wipe the scowl from her face. She stood with

her shoulders square, feet slightly apart, hands on hips, as if they were about to engage in hand-to-hand combat.

"You make it sound like I'm stalking you!" she retorted. "I haven't seen you for two months, David. And you know what? They've been two of the happiest months of my—"

"Sorry," he interrupted, holding a hand up. "I'm sorry. I didn't mean it like that, okay? I was just surprised."

"I'm here on business."

"Business?"

"A client of mine was nearly killed by a car bomb last night," she told him, watching his eyes widen at the realization that despite his best efforts to break ties, their jobs had thrown them together again.

"That's your client?" he asked.

"Unfortunately for you," she said.

"Oh, Jesus," David muttered. "Jade, how do you always get yourself into these situations? What's going on?"

With supreme effort of will, she managed to contain her anger. Yelling at David wouldn't help her or Botha survive. Truthfully, she was lucky to have David on the case. She'd get a lot more information from him than she would from Mweli, but not if she carried on like this.

"I've told Mweli everything I know," she responded coolly. "Right now, I'm doing my best to keep my client and myself alive. I have no idea how things ended up this way. It was supposed to be a simple surveillance job. But the more I learn, the better chance I have of surviving this."

His face softened at her words, and she couldn't help but feel a tiny flame of hope flicker inside her, because he still cared. Of course he did.

"You know I'll do whatever I can to help you," he said.

"I'll call you," she told him.

She thought she'd exhausted all of her self-control, but she had to draw deep from her last reserves in order to walk past him and climb calmly into her car. And she did, without losing her temper again, or screaming or hitting him or kissing him.

Without telling him that there was almost no chance the child Naisha was carrying was his.

She drove away from the police station without looking back. By the time she reached the main road, her hands were trembling, and her eyes prickled with tears.

Chapter Twenty-Four

SERGEANT PHIRI HATED autopsies. Not because of the usual reasons; it wasn't the smell, which could be horrific depending on the state in which the corpse was found and the length of time that lapsed before the procedure was done. With the mortuaries so overcrowded, delays could often be substantial.

Nor was he squeamish. The opposite, in fact. He was able to distance himself from the reality of flesh and bone parting under the pathologist's probing blades. He'd never gotten nausea, and although he abided by the sensible rule of not eating beforehand, he'd never been put off from a meal shortly afterward.

Not even one with meat.

What made him uncomfortable was that in the autopsy room, the corpses were stripped of all their dignity. There was no defense against the carving away. No more secrets—in death, everything was revealed.

It helped that the professor conducting these two autopsies, Professor Williams, felt the same way, or so Phiri suspected. They'd never spoken about it. But even though he laughed and joked outside the autopsy room, Williams always went about his work with a quiet reverence for the deceased.

Just that morning, while the two were standing in the lounge finishing their paper cups of coffee, he'd shown Phiri a gleaming set of knives. "I treated myself to some new tools," he said proudly.

Phiri had admired the different lengths and shapes of the steel blades, solid and heavy and razor-sharp, set into ergonomically designed metal handles. "They're beautiful. Didn't they cost a fortune?"

Williams winked at him. "They would have, if I'd ordered them from a medical supplier. These are chef's knives."

"Chef's knives?" Phiri repeated, coughing.

"Same steel, same quality, a tenth of the price. Adding the word *medical* to anything makes it ridiculously expensive. While I was shopping for these, I got the wife a blender and a soup ladle . . . Why are you laughing?"

Phiri wasn't laughing so much as choking on his last gulp of coffee. Finally regaining his breath, he reminded himself never to take a sip of liquid when Williams was about to make a comment, a deadpan utterance that only struck you as hilarious a few moments later.

Coffees done, the two men gowned up and made their way to the autopsy room. And just before entering, Phiri saw the veil of gentle humor that seemed to surround Williams slip aside, replaced by solemnity.

Before he began work on a new corpse, he would stand for a moment, facing the body, his gloved hands clasped together. Phiri sometimes wondered whether he was praying; he didn't seem like an especially religious man. But what else could he be doing?

Photographing her first clothed, and then carefully cutting away the garments, Williams noted down that she was fit, and in her early twenties.

Williams turned his attention to the livid, bloody wound on the right side of her skull. "Undoubtedly, this was what killed her," he told Phiri. "A blow hard enough to cause a depressed fracture of the skull like this would have resulted in immediate unconsciousness, followed shortly by death."

He noted down the air-bag residue present on the woman's face and chest, and said that the damage to her nose had likely been caused by the sudden impact with the air bag, as she hadn't been wearing a seat belt.

Phiri had looked away as the pathologist sliced the skin around her forehead with one of the knives he had so proudly acquired, then peeled her face down to reveal the skull beneath. Then Phiri heard the whining of the electric saw, whose note changed to a shriek as it sliced its way through bone.

"Some bleeding on the brain," Williams noted. "A sizeable hematoma, but no hemorrhaging. This tells me that her heart stopped quite soon. Probably a minute after receiving the fatal head wound."

The weapon found at the crime scene, a baseball bat, had been bagged up and sent for forensic testing, but Williams had acquired an identical bat which was on a shelf in the autopsy room. Williams measured the dimensions of the wound before grasping the bat and placing its rounded tip next to, and then into, the depressed wound. It fit perfectly. There was no doubt; this was what had been used to kill her.

"What about her hands?" Phiri asked. "She had hand injuries. We noticed them at the crime scene."

"We'll get there," Williams said calmly before removing the protective bags on her hands and forearms.

"Now this is interesting," he said after a few minutes of closely examining the woman's limbs. "The skin on all her fingertips has been abraded. If these were inflicted while she was still conscious, there would have been a lot of bleeding."

"She was lying on a flooded floor," Phiri explained. "Her hands were in blood and oil and water."

Williams nodded. "Difficult to tell, then. Was there anything at the scene that could've caused this?"

"Such as?"

"A cheese grater," Williams suggested, and Phiri's eyebrows shot up.

"There was nothing of the sort in the motel room."

"It could have been disposed of after the fact, I suppose."

"How could you tell if it was done while she was still alive?"

"Someone holding her down and running her hands over a sharp, rough surface would have been extremely painful. She would have struggled or have had to be restrained. I can't find any evidence of that. No bruising, no breakage of the skin, no friction marks on her hands or wrists. The damage is very precise. Every fingertip on both hands. I think it far more likely that this occurred after death, and that it may have been done deliberately to prevent her being identified through her fingerprints."

"And?" Phiri asked. Williams's tone had implied there was an *and*.

"She has a broken right wrist and a dislocated right index finger. These aren't from being held down. They look to me like defensive wounds. She was trying to protect herself from the bat."

Phiri nodded soberly.

So far, the woman's body confirmed the initial theory of a domestic dispute; she had been staying in the motel room with Loodts, and things had gone wrong between them. The woman had used the bat to fight Loodts off, then fled. But she'd crashed her car into the motel sign and then decided to go back into the room, where an angry Loodts was waiting to finish the job. He had grated away her fingertips and disposed of the tool somewhere before meeting his own accidental death.

Which was just about plausible, as long as you didn't ask why he hadn't disposed of the bat as well. And why would an ex-government minister carry a cheese grater around with him in the first place? Phiri couldn't think of a single reason.

The media was going to have a field day with this one.

Williams noted that there were no signs that the woman had engaged in sexual intercourse in the hours before her death. No other evidence was forthcoming from her body, but Williams told Phiri her bloodwork showed traces of diazepam metabolites as well as alprazolam.

"In English, doc?" Phiri asked.

"She took prescription tranquilizers. Valium and Xanax. The levels of both are high, pointing toward recent use and also a possible dependency."

Phiri nodded, unsurprised, as Williams completed his notes.

Next it was Loodts himself who submitted to the slow exploration of the blades.

Williams unzipped the body bag to commence his work, photographing, examining and carefully removing Loodts's chinos and collared shirt, now stiff and stained with blood. Phiri noted that, especially in comparison to the woman's toned frame, Loodts's body lacked muscle and was overweight. His pale belly bulged, and the excess fat around his jaw gave his face a rounded appearance.

His hair was short and his hairline receding, so it was easy to see the bloodied mark on his left temple.

If this had been a domestic dispute, then Loodts must

have slipped and fallen on the treacherous floor, coming down headfirst onto the corner of the wooden desk. An unlucky accident, but under the circumstances, surely not impossible?

Phiri watched as Williams examined the wound, swabbing at the bloodstains before bagging the swabs, using forceps to probe the broken skin. "Splinter," the pathologist murmured.

Phiri could barely see the tiny fragment of wood. "From the desk? Or the bat?"

One meant a simple explanation, an unlucky accident, a case neatly closed.

The other meant a whole lot of trouble.

"Impossible to say. It'll have to be analyzed with samples from each item."

Phiri let out a breath he only now realized he'd been holding. Nothing would be resolved today, then. They would have to wait until the lab results came back. That would take longer than a week. Probably closer to a month.

And then the pathologist made a surprised sound. "Look here," he said.

With his initial examination of the body completed, he removed the protective bags the police had placed over each of Loodts's hands at the crime scene.

He pointed to Loodts's left hand, and then to his right, and Phiri felt his heart quicken as he saw.

There were abrasions on the inside of each of Loodts's wrists.

"What you were saying about wrist restraints—would that apply here?"

"It might. I would have expected a breakage in the skin or actual bruising, unless a soft restraint was deliberately used."

"Maybe a sex toy?" Phiri hazarded as he envisioned his

afternoon media briefing turning from acrimonious to down-right embarrassing.

"Possibly. At this stage, we can't rule it out. No other marks on his body, though."

Mystified, Phiri watched as Williams turned his attention to the corpse's fingers. "What are you looking for?"

"Ah, found it. I'll show you in a minute."

So Phiri waited, his questions unanswered, while Williams set up the x-ray machine and took multiple images of each hand.

It was only when the results were displayed against the backlight that Phiri could see, in dull black and white, the damage that Williams's sensitive eyes and grasp had picked up.

There were hairline fractures in three of the fingers on Loodts's left hand, and two on his right. Only now did Phiri notice the small grazes on the skin that correlated to the injury points. "Could he have held a bat with those fractures?"

"It would have been just about impossible, for two reasons. First, the damage would have been extremely painful. And second, if he'd wielded a bat with enough force to cause the woman's head injury, these fractures would have been dis-placed. As it is, they are clean, almost unnoticeable breaks. No disturbance around them. I can say with certainty that Loodts didn't hold anything after these injuries occurred. Not even a cheese grater."

And just like that, the domestic violence theory was out. In its place was something much, much worse.

This was evidence of torture.

Chapter Twenty-Five

JADE DROVE AWAY from the police station feeling contaminated by her own emotions, as if she were covered in a tangible layer of anger and resentment. She wanted to hide for a few quiet hours and lick the wounds which her encounter with David had reopened.

But there were important things to be done; this was no time for self-pity. Especially not with her phone ringing as she reached the main road.

She didn't recognize the incoming number, but when she answered, Gillespie was on the other end of the line. "Jade, I must apologize." His voice sounded muted and slightly nasal.

"There's no need to," she reassured him. "No need at all."

"I put you in an impossible situation last night. What I asked of you was completely unfair. You made the ethical choice by walking away. I can only say that I'm sorry, and that I acted out of desperation."

"I understand."

"I hope you had some rest after you left."

"I didn't. I had to run from the hotel, because the people chasing us almost caught up."

Gillespie's shout of "What?" crackled through her headset. "Are you serious? Jade, this is . . . I don't know what to say." Shock and concern reverberated through his words.

"Somebody called the hotel and asked if we were checked in. It must've been a lucky guess."

"But you escaped?"

"Yes. We got away just in time, and we've found another place to stay. A private residence." A thought flashed through her mind. "You didn't tell anyone we were in Sandton, did you?"

"No. Did you say you were staying there? I don't recall you mentioning it. But it's been a catastrophic few hours."

"What do you mean?" Jade asked, bracing herself for yet more bad news.

"I was at work until four A.M., and when I finally left to go find some food, I was mugged."

"Mugged?" Jade repeated. She could hear the shock in her own voice now. This explained why he sounded so unlike himself. "Are you all right? What happened?"

"I'm okay, I think. I was in the parking lot of the Grand West Casino. Just about the only place that's open for food at that hour. I remember thinking that it might not be the wisest choice, and hoping no one would assume I had any cash on me. Which I did, as it happens." He snuffed out a laugh. "Your cash, unfortunately. Two thugs jumped me as I climbed out of the Merc. They hit me a few times, grabbed my wallet and my phone and pushed me to the ground. By the time I'd stopped my nose from bleeding and was coherent enough to call security, they were gone."

"Did you see their car?"

"They were on foot when they attacked me. I presume they had a car somewhere, but I never saw it. The parking lot was pretty full. People going in and out."

Jade paused, then said, "Are you sure it was random?"

There was silence on the other end of the line.

Eventually, Gillespie said, "Now that you ask, I'm not sure. I assumed it was, but now I don't know. Do you want to meet up? I'm worried the same people might be coming after both of us—if so, the more information we share, the safer we'll be."

"Where are you now?"

"I'm at the Grand West Mall, next door to the casino complex where we first met. Apparently my credit cards will take a couple of days to replace, but at least I have a phone, even if it's a cheap spare I was going to give to one of the guards."

"I'm not far away. I can be there in ten minutes."

"There's a diner just inside entrance three. You need to drive into the basement parking to access it. Do you want to join me there?"

Jade suddenly realized she was starving. "I'll see you soon," she said.

On her way, she fueled up at the same gas station she'd used before. One of the large Inkomfe vans was pulling out of the station as she arrived, heading in the direction of the research center. It looked dusty, as if it were returning from a long trip.

Jade took a shortcut through the industrial complex. This time, no delivery trucks were blocking her way, but when she drove past the big warehouse, she was disappointed to see that all its gates were shut tight.

Winding down her car window, she found herself smiling as she heard hammering coming from inside. Hopefully the shady slot machine technologists were hard at work reducing the odds, or increasing them. If she ever saw those machines being taken out of the warehouse, she'd simply have to follow the truck and see where they were installed. Maybe she could put some money in and see what came out.

A minute later, she drove into the basement lot Gillespie had described, noticing a sleek gold Mercedes near the entrance that she guessed was his.

Gillespie was slouched at a table in the half-empty diner, cradling a teacup. His left eye was swollen, a deep bruise already starting to form under it. The left side of his mouth was split, and he had a graze on his cheek. His sandy hair was tousled, and he was wearing a different shirt—long-sleeved and navy blue with creases that signaled it had just been taken out of its packaging.

"I'm so sorry," Jade said.

Gillespie tried to smile, winced and gave a small nod. "Hurts to do anything. I've even been battling to drink this tea."

"You need a straw," Jade said. "I'll get you one and order us some food."

She fetched him a drinking straw from the counter and ordered plain scrambled eggs for him and an egg-and-cheese croissant for herself, plus a large coffee. The only cash she had on her was from Botha, and it struck her as strange to pay for Gillespie's breakfast with it, so she used her credit card.

"Did you tell the police?" she asked Gillespie when she sat down again.

"No. Casino security called management. There was nothing to tell the police. I didn't see the men well enough—it was still dark, and as I said, they ambushed me. They were dark-skinned and wearing black, I think. Average height. Strong." He raised a hand to his bruised cheekbone. "I'm willing to bet they've done this before, but I didn't get a proper look at their faces, didn't see a vehicle . . . I don't want to waste police time, Jade."

Jade looked at him with concern. The note of resignation in his voice worried her.

Gillespie sipped at his tea, angling the straw into the undamaged side of his mouth. "This is better. Thank you. You're a lifesaver," he said.

Their food arrived. Jade poured chili sauce liberally over her croissant. "Did they say anything?" she asked.

"What do you mean?"

"The men who attacked you. Do you remember them speaking or shouting at you at all?"

"Oh, my God," Gillespie said. He paused for a few seconds. "This feels so surreal. Now that you mention it, I vaguely recall them yelling. I didn't even tell the security guards that. It was like it hadn't happened until now. I don't understand this at all."

"It happens. The brain sometimes gets overwhelmed in those situations and omits certain memories until you're reminded of them, or are ready to deal with them."

"How bizarre. Well, I can attest to the truth in that."

"What were they yelling?"

"It was . . . it might have been . . . 'Get away'? 'Keep away'? I think that's right, because I thought, *How crazy. I'm trying my best to get away from them, so why are they telling me to?*"

"That does sound like a targeted message. I wonder what they were warning you away from."

Gillespie tried a small forkful of eggs, chewing slowly before washing them down with another sip of tea. His hands were shaking. "I have no idea. What's the point of a threat if the person doesn't know what the hell it's for?"

He gave a small, humorless laugh, then patted his pockets, and his good eye widened. "Oh, for God's sake. I've just remembered I left the card in the clothing shop."

"Card?"

"A woman in Markham very kindly paid for this new shirt, because the one I was wearing was covered in blood. I wrote her bank details down on a business card so I could reimburse her. And I left it in the store. I can see it now—I put it on a shelf in the changing room and forgot to pick it up. Hell, Jade, all of this has seriously rattled me. Can you please excuse me for five minutes? I need to get that card."

"Do you want me to come with you?"

"No, no. Please eat your breakfast." With a frustrated sigh, Gillespie clambered to his feet and limped out of the restaurant, turning left before heading purposefully along the walkway.

He was back ten minutes later, by which time Jade had cleaned her plate after making serious inroads into the bottle of hot sauce and was working on her second coffee.

His hands were trembling even worse than before. "I thought it was gone. They'd cleaned the change rooms and thrown it away. You should have seen me and two sales assistants on our knees, scrambling through the trash cans until we found it."

"Mr. Gillespie, I think you need to go home," Jade said, watching him carefully. "You're in shock. After a traumatic experience like the one you've had, you need to take some time off, or it could affect your decision making."

But Gillespie jutted his chin forward, an act of stubbornness she hadn't expected. "I can't leave now," he argued. "This attack has made me more determined to protect Inkomfe, not less. I know I'm being threatened, and that this was an attempt at intimidation. But I won't let them win or allow the lives of innocent people to be endangered. All I need is an hour to pull myself together."

"Then you're back to work?"

"I have to run a few errands. Then I'm back at headquarters for the day."

His phone started ringing, and he glanced down at the incoming number before rejecting the call and telling her,

"I'm going to add so many new layers of security that no one without authorization will ever make it into the plant again, much less the reactor room."

Jade nodded.

"After that, I'll be taking a holiday, spending a week somewhere on the beach," he said with a half-smile. "Maybe even a month." Even with a face half-covered in bruises, he exuded charm.

"All right. Good."

"Personally I'd like for you to drive back to wherever you're staying, pack your things, tell Botha he's on his own and leave. Pardon the card game analogy, but I have an instinct for when to fold, and I believe you've overplayed your hand." Gillespie rested his chin on his hand, perhaps from fatigue. "But at the same time, I can see that you're very good at your job. Perhaps you'll discover something important about Botha, or even prevent a bigger catastrophe."

"Not if I stay here," Jade said, unhooking her bag's strap from its position over her knee and standing up. "I have to get going. I'll keep in touch."

Gillespie's phone began to ring again as she left. She paused at the café door and looked back. This time, he took the call, and as she left, she heard him shouting.

Chapter Twenty-Six

BEFORE HEADING BACK to the townhouse, Jade wanted to speak to Lisa Marais, the former Inkomfe security director. She wondered why Gillespie had been so focused on Botha, when it seemed Lisa would have a far bigger motive for the sabotage. Wouldn't it be easier to trace Lisa, who was now an activist at Earthforce, and find out who she'd been speaking to since her departure, and where she'd been on the night of the break-in?

Well, perhaps she could glean some information now. Earthforce had its headquarters in nearby Roodepoort. She pulled up the company website, the first result of her search.

The front page was up-to-date and filled with news. The latest article was on a visit from Russian environmental activist Dmitri Petrov, who was currently hosting talks around South Africa about the risks associated with nuclear power. "With his military and investigative background, Petrov has succeeded in exposing corruption and incompetency at the highest level," the caption explained. Petrov's photo showed him staring, unsmiling, at the camera; he was a tough-looking man with a solid jaw and short, dark hair. She could imagine him rappelling onto rooftops and breaking down doors to uncover evidence; he looked the type.

She bookmarked the page for when she had more time to read, then called to make an appointment with Lisa Marais.

Earthforce's headquarters weren't nearly as impressive as its website. Its offices were above a strip mall in a dilapidated part of the city. One of the ground-level shops was a fish and chips kiosk, which Jade glanced into on the way to the stairs. The aroma of frying fish and vinegary potatoes filled the air, but she had a feeling the food might smell better than it tasted.

The offices themselves were small, shabby, crowded and busy. Reams of paperwork covered every surface. The walls of the tiny waiting room were filled with posters, some advertising the perils of nuclear power and the threat of global warming, others featuring beautiful, unspoiled landscapes and seascapes. Appropriate for a company whose main objective was to mobilize society around environmental issues.

In pride of place was a poster advertising Petrov's talks. Looking more closely at the dates, Jade saw that she'd missed all three. The last one had been on Thursday evening in Bloemfontein.

When she'd called earlier, Jade had spoken with a consultant named Bongani. His voice had been smooth, deep and lightly laced with an African accent whose specifics she couldn't identify. It reminded her of rich espresso with a side of brandy. When he hurried into the waiting room five minutes after she'd arrived, she saw he was a serious-looking young man wearing gold-framed spectacles.

"How can I help you?" he asked, walking with her through reception and into his office, where he removed a pile of documents from the second chair. The smell of fish and chips was stronger here, thanks to the room's only window being directly above the shop.

Jade decided honesty might get her better results. "I'm a private investigator, obtaining background information for an assignment. I need to get in touch with Lisa Marais. She works here, if my information is correct?"

Bongani nodded, but his initial warmth was swiftly replaced by cautious reserve. "I assumed you were a journalist," he said.

"No. I'm not a journalist." She hoped her words would reassure Bongani, but instead he looked more troubled.

"Lisa does work for our organization, but she's not based here," he told her. "She's—er—currently on leave."

"Is there any way I can reach her? Perhaps you could give me her phone number?"

Bongani's eyes, guarded by his gold-rimmed glasses, wouldn't meet her stare. His gaze rested on the papers covering his desk, which were being disturbed by a draft. He glanced toward the open window, then at the framed certificates on his wall, and finally, hopefully, in the direction of the half-open door.

"What I can do," he eventually said in his measured baritone, "is take your number and ask her to call you when I'm in touch with her again." He shuffled the biggest stack of papers into a tidier pile and placed a polished stone paperweight on top of them.

Jade had to stifle a sigh of annoyance. Unhelpful as he was being, Bongani would completely stonewall her if she tried to pressure him. She had no idea why he was so reluctant to assist. Was he protecting Lisa? Could he know, or suspect, that she might be involved in the sabotage?

She smiled as if having Bongani ask Lisa to call her at some nebulous and unspecified future date was the greatest news she'd had all day. "Thank you," she said. "I'd really appreciate that. And while I'm here, I'd also like to know more about Earthforce and the issues that you tackle here."

Listening to that honey-rich voice for another few minutes wouldn't be a hardship, either.

Bongani leaned forward and rested his elbows on the desk. "Earthforce has been running for fifteen years, focusing on just about everything relating to the environment. I've been here for five of those, and during that time we've tackled important issues and exposed quite a few destructive practices. We're funded by private individuals, some government funding—although never enough—as well as the occasional corporate sponsorship or donation. But there's often a conflict of interest with the corporations." He made a wry face.

"I can imagine there would be," Jade agreed. "Your organization must have a big problem with the proposed nuclear power plants."

"They're a potential disaster in so many ways," Bongani said.

"Why is that?"

He smiled again. "How much time do you have?"

Jade laughed. "I'm sure you have a pile of work, and I don't want to impose for too long. How about a detailed overview?"

"Okay," Bongani said thoughtfully. He made the word sound like an introduction to a vintage merlot tasting. "Let's start with the actual construction of the plants. The 'strategic nuclear partnership,' as they're calling it. I'm calling it an expensive disaster. It will cost forty to fifty billion dollars to build eight nuclear reactors here in South Africa."

"But isn't that worthwhile if they're built safely?" Jade asked. She remembered David the last time she'd seen him, throwing his hands up in frustration over the repeated power cuts delaying his work. He'd sworn repeatedly in that conversation. She didn't want to know what his language had been like in the past few months, with rolling blackouts having all but crippled the country. She guessed his words could have turned the air blue.

"Nuclear technology is risky, even when it's properly implemented," Bongani said. "And I doubt it will be done correctly here. You have only to look at Russia's track record. They can't even keep their own house in order."

"Chernobyl?"

He nodded. "Do you know that all the damage caused by the Chernobyl reactor explosion in 1986 was the result of just a couple of kilograms of radioactive materials entering the environment? That's how little it took. Exposure to radioactive substances can be compared to a cellular explosion that happens inside you and keeps on happening, bombarding all your body cells with its shrapnel. The cells that die aren't the problem, as long as there aren't too many of them. It's the cells that survive that become the problem, causing cancers and birth defects down the line."

"That's frightening."

"The effects of Chernobyl were extremely widespread. Even as far as North Wales, mandatory radiation checks on sheep farms were only lifted in 2012. From the disaster until then, all sheep had to be tested, and many of them were banned from sale or slaughter due to dangerously high levels. It took twenty-six years for the levels to drop enough for restrictions to be removed."

"I can't believe it." Jade said.

"We think we can control the technology, but we're like children playing with fire," Bongani said sadly. "Last year there were thirty-nine separate incidents at Russia's nuclear power stations."

Jade repeated incredulously, "Thirty-nine?"

"Thirty-nine incidents at ten plants. Of course, many of those plants are technical dinosaurs. They were only built to last thirty years and should have been decommissioned years ago, but they've been patched up and kept running because it's too expensive to close them down."

Bongani adjusted his glasses, taking in Jade's surprise. She hadn't realized that nuclear power stations had a finite life span, or how much it would cost to close them down.

"That aside," he continued, "the incidents in Russia were caused mostly because of mismanagement, defects in equipment and design errors. Not exactly confidence inspiring."

"Definitely not," Jade agreed.

"Even at a plant that is built to the highest standards, there's a risk of accidents. And we do not believe that South Africans, with or without Russian assistance, are capable of building or maintaining plants that are safe."

"Would proper safety standards be difficult to enforce?"

Bongani considered the question. "If there was proper transparency surrounding the process, it might be possible to ensure that happened. But there won't be transparency. There never, ever has been with nuclear energy in South Africa. The apartheid mentality is still alive and well in that regard. It's secretive, it's corrupt and it's not going to provide the benefits we need."

Jade nodded. The clearer the picture became, the bleaker the canvas was.

And Bongani wasn't finished yet. "Putting the risk of accidents and leakages aside, there are two other dangerous problems associated with nuclear power—waste and fuel."

"Why are these dangerous?"

"Nuclear waste is a huge issue because we haven't worked out how to dispose of it. Nobody in the world has figured that out. It's extremely toxic to humans and the environment, and it remains that way for up to ten thousand years. Coping with such a long-term scenario is beyond our power.

And then there's the issue of the fuel. Fueling a nuclear power station contributes substantially to radioactive contamination of the environment."

"In what way?" Jade asked.

"You probably know that the Witwatersrand basin, where we are located, is the biggest gold-mining basin in the world."

"Yes, of course."

"What you might not know is that it's also the world's biggest uranium-mining basin."

"Really?" Jade asked, surprised.

"The two occur together in these mineral-rich rocks. You can't mine one without bringing the other to the surface. What this means is that even the tailings from the gold mines have high levels of uranium and radionuclides, unstable particles that can cause radioactive contamination. Water can be contaminated, and usually is, but the dust from our mine dumps and tailings is even more of a threat because it can drift on the wind for thousands of miles. Dust from the West Rand mines has been found in Tasmania and Australia, almost on the other side of the world."

"That's incredible."

"Incredible, but true. So there's already uranium contamination from gold mining, and now with the prospect of nuclear power plants, there could be more. Uranium is fuel for a nuclear plant, and uranium mining has started up again here in a big way. New mines are being opened, and old dumps are being remined to extract more uranium ore from the tailings. When the old dumps were first created, there was stringent dust control in place, and over time, vegetation grew again in the areas nearby. Reopening these without the same restraints is causing a new level of pollution and posing a real health risk to people living nearby. We're talking about poorer communities in particular, people who use the soil for subsistence farming, and who wash and cook with river water because they have no other available water source, even if the water is contaminated—radioactive in some cases—and unsafe to use."

"I can see why you're fighting so hard," Jade conceded.

Bongani nodded solemnly. "It's a massive concern for us, and we're trying our best to make South Africa aware."

With his overview concluded, Jade thanked him again for his time, and left. Bongani had given her a lot to think about. Certainly nuclear power was not the utopian answer to South Africa's problems that Gillespie had described. If the stations were well built and stringently managed . . . if the process of mining the uranium was carefully regulated and the dust controlled, then perhaps it was possible, but she couldn't help agreeing with Bongani's perception that as it stood, the solution was likely to be fraught with problems.

That wasn't what interested her the most, though.

As soon as she'd changed the subject to the work at Earthforce, Bongani's gaze had met hers. Focused, strong and genuine, his body language had matched the compelling charm of his voice. The only time he'd been evasive was when they were discussing Lisa. That disconnect told Jade more than simple words.

Bongani knew something more about Lisa Marais . . . Jade was sure of it.

Chapter Twenty-Seven

JADE WONDERED WHETHER it was coincidence that Earthforce's offices were a stone's throw from the main road leading to Inkomfe. Since she was so close by, she decided to speak to Sbusiso, the jaded worker she'd met last night while waiting for Gillespie.

When she called Sbusiso, he told her he had just finished his shift and was walking to gate one's pedestrian entrance.

"You're still there?" Jade asked, surprised. "You work very long hours."

"We were outside for two hours because of the fire drill," Sbusiso said. "My job still had to be done. All the offices had to be cleaned, and the trash taken out. I am finished now, and from tomorrow I am on day shift for a week."

She offered to meet him at the gate in ten minutes. He told her not to hurry; it was a long walk.

With her car's new rear plate and bumper stickers, Jade felt that she'd taken all the reasonable precautions she could have. Even so, she felt adrenaline flood through her when she checked her mirrors and saw a big black SUV barreling up behind her.

"Just some asshole," she reassured herself through gritted teeth, steering as far to the side as she could to let the driver pass.

Her hands grew cold when the car's speed bled off as it drew level with her, and the passenger turned to stare at her through his open window. Gripping the wheel, she glanced at him, but he'd already turned away, and her only impression was that he looked tough and was wearing a black leather jacket and wraparound mirrored glasses.

Then the SUV accelerated past, and she breathed a shaky sigh of relief. Just some asshole.

Nothing to worry about.

A few minutes later, Inkomfe's bulky cooling towers and concrete buildings loomed into view, and she saw Sbusiso waiting outside gate one.

ATTERIDGEVILLE UP CLOSE was different from how Jade had thought it would be. There was more energy to the place than she'd first supposed. She passed a bustling shopping mall with rows of minibus taxis in a line outside. Some smart-looking houses had been built close to the mall, which seemed to be the township's central hub.

As Sbusiso directed her toward the outskirts, the energy ebbed, and the houses became smaller, interspersed with simple shacks made from corrugated iron, wooden boards and a hodgepodge of assorted building blocks.

This was where Sbusiso lived, down the road from the nuclear research center, in a place that bordered on nothing but a few faraway mine dumps. Perhaps there had once been farms here, but the surrounding land now looked uncared for and barren. The stunted trees were withered and only sparse grasses grew. Jade thought she could see a fine layer of dust in the air, eddied by the gusting wind. She shivered as she remembered what she'd learned about the contaminated mine dumps. Was that why this area looked like such a wasteland? Was it the insidious effect of the toxic dust and water, carrying their radioactive load?

She pulled over to the side of the road and walked with

Sbusiso to his house. It was not a shack, but a government-supplied Reconstruction and Development Program house, painted cream to distinguish it from its khaki neighbors.

Jade hesitated and glanced at Sbusiso when she saw the thin, frail and obviously ill older man seated under a small tree near the front door. His face was gaunt; the skin on the back of his hands was deeply scarred and ulcerated. In spite of the day's warmth, he had a blanket wrapped around his shoulders. In front of him on a rickety plastic table was a large, well-worn envelope.

"This is my cousin Shadrack," Sbusiso told her. "He lives nearby. He is one of the people who became sick from working at Inkomfe. In this envelope are all the papers and documents from the workers proving that they were employed, and that they became sick."

Jade greeted Shadrack and shook hands with him. His hand felt cold, and his voice was soft and husky when he returned her greeting. She felt an immense sadness for this man who'd had so little in life, who had worked so hard for such meager rewards, and was now burdened with ruined health.

"I'm so sorry," she said, but Shadrack shook his head.

"You do not have to be sorry," he said. "I have lived longer than any of the other men who worked in my section. And even though I am sick now, it came more slowly."

He said it in a way that prompted Jade to ask, "Do you know why?"

Shadrack nodded. "When I started getting ill, I consulted a *sangoma*, a witch doctor. He told me to make a tea each day with the African potato. The real *inkomfe*. He told me it has powerful health benefits. So each and every day, I have drunk that tea."

"I've heard of it," Jade said.

"I believe that the tea has helped me to fight this illness. I grow the potato plants behind the house. It is not easy." He made a face. "On this land, nothing wants to grow. But I brought good soil in from farther away to improve it."

"There is no time now to chatter about farming," Sbusiso chided him gently. "There are more important things to discuss."

Sbusiso pulled up a chair, and they all sat together under the tree, shaded from the worst of the heat, with their elbows leaning on the rickety table. Jade took a quick look through the contents of the envelope. The employee records were old, but indisputably official-looking. Jade was sure that in the right hands, this information could be used to get compensation for the workers.

"You asked about my friend Miss Lisa."

Jade nodded.

"She started working at Inkomfe about five years ago. She was a tall woman, as thin as a stick, with curly gray hair. She used to go outside behind her office to smoke. She smoked a lot. Forty cigarettes a day, she told me. Her office was close to our staff kitchen, so I used to see her there most days."

Shadrack grumbled in his soft voice something about cigarettes killing people faster than the red water from the bombs, and again Sbusiso reprimanded him. "We cannot get sidetracked. This lady is busy. See how she is sitting on the edge of her seat? She has not even put her car keys down. She has no time to spare."

Hastily Jade scooted back on her chair and placed her keys on the table. "No, no, I have time."

"Good," Sbusiso continued. "We used to talk, Miss Lisa and me. She with her cigarette, I with my tea. I told her what

I told you, about the poisonous water and the sicknesses, the sores and infections, the cancers. She was shocked to hear this. I could see she was sad, very sad. And she was worried. I said to her, 'What is it with you people? Do you never learn? For years those bombs were stored in that strong room, and now the poisonous ingots are still kept there. Why do you not get rid of them? But no, instead, you want to build power stations that will use more poison and make more people sick.'"

"What did she say?" Jade asked.

"She tried to tell me that the power stations would be safe." Sbusiso laughed. "I asked her how she could believe that."

"Did she have an answer?"

"She told me that she was working very hard to make Inkomfe safer. She was fighting with lots of people. She did not like Mr. Loodts."

"Because he was in charge back when the bombs were built?" Jade asked.

Sbusiso nodded. "She was angry about what he had done. She told me Mr. Loodts did not listen. He had his own ways of doing things and did not want to change them."

Jade nodded. "Who else was she fighting with?"

"Miss Lisa fought with everyone. She wanted to change the world. She told me it was making her very unpopular."

Jade laughed, as much at the words as at Sbusiso's cynical expression. "Anything else you remember?"

Sbusiso lowered his voice. "There was something just before she left. She said she had made a big mistake. She was trying to find out information about somebody she worked with, but she would not tell me more. She said she was going to take what she had to Mr. Loodts, but that she did not know if he would listen, because he had closed his ears to her."

"Really?" Jade said, shocked. She wondered what the mistake was and whom Lisa had been looking into. "Was that all she said?"

"She began to speak less openly. She said that we should not discuss these things at Inkomfe, that it might not be safe. I told her that finally she was starting to understand." Sbusiso tipped his chair back against the tree trunk and folded his arms, looking satisfied.

"So then she quit her job. Did you see her again?" Jade asked.

Sbusiso nodded. "She kept her promise and did not forget us. Three weeks ago, she met me at the Florida Mall. I showed her these papers, and she made copies to take to her new work. She said they could help us there."

Jade nodded. It made sense that Earthforce would want to assist the workers with their legal struggle. "I'll follow up with them and find out what is happening."

"Thank you."

"The last time you saw Lisa, did you ask her about the information she was trying to find?"

"She was in a hurry, like you, sitting on the front of her chair, looking at her watch often. She said she already had lots of facts, but she was collecting more, and soon something was going to happen that would force Mr. Loodts to see reason and change his thinking. But she did not have time to tell me everything. She said that she would send me a copy of the information she had to keep safe, just in case."

"Have you received anything?"

"Not yet," Sbusiso said.

"Can you give me her details?"

"I can tell you where she lives." Sbusiso shuffled the papers together again. "I also have her phone number."

Sbusiso wrote these down on Jade's notepad, then walked back into the house with the papers.

When he returned, she thanked him for his time and said goodbye. But before she left, Shadrack held up a hand and spoke to Sbusiso in a low voice.

"Do you have a garden?" Sbusiso asked her.

"Yes, I do," Jade said. "I live in a rented cottage with a garden." She didn't tell the men that it had been neglected because she was better at killing plants than nurturing them. It seemed selfish to have unpolluted land with fertile soil that was going to waste while the people here strived so hard to coax life from depleted and toxic ground.

"Take this." Shadrack fumbled in his coat pocket and produced a small, clear plastic bag. Inside it was a handful of dark, glossy seeds.

"These are the African potato plant; the real *inkomfe*," he told her. "They are not difficult to grow. Plant them anywhere there is sunshine, and water them well. I hope these seeds bring you good health and long life. Thank you for coming here."

Chapter Twenty-Eight

LISA MARAIS'S ADDRESS was in Florida Lake, which was in the West Rand and not too far away. To Jade's annoyance, she discovered the whole of Florida and part of Roodepoort were currently being load shed. Traffic was snarled up at the nonfunctional lights, and it would take too long to drive the whole way through. Instead, she messaged David to ask him if he could go there later.

She escaped the traffic to find supplies at a small shopping center with a working generator. She selected water, snacks and two toothbrushes from the shelves. On impulse, she made a detour to the clothing shop next door and picked up a few essentials for herself and Botha, choosing darkly colored garments. They were more practical for running and hiding at night, though she hoped they wouldn't be doing that.

Back in the standstill traffic, she turned on her speakerphone and called Bongani at Earthforce. "It's me again," she told him. "Jade de Jong—we met earlier today."

"Ms. de Jong." Bongani's soothing tones filled the car. "How can I help you?"

"I have an important question. A friend of Lisa's has asked me to follow up on a case that Earthforce is handling. It's regarding the workers who helped build the nuclear weapons at Inkomfe and are now suffering from health issues. Do you know about this, and has there been any progress?"

"Ah, yes," Bongani said. "We have been struggling with

that case. It is not easy. There is so little paperwork available; the records at Inkomfe were destroyed, and we ran into difficulties trying to obtain information from the person who'd been in charge of Inkomfe at the time."

"Mr. Loodts?" Jade asked.

"Um." Bongani hesitated. "I'm afraid I can't mention names."

Jade took this as confirmation.

"Anyway," Bongani continued, "we've just managed to escalate it all the way to the district attorney, and she has promised that she will investigate and take action. Lisa—" He stopped himself. "I will arrange a meeting with the original applicants and update them. I have all the contact details in the file. I'll call them tomorrow, I promise."

"Thank you," Jade said. And then, on impulse, she asked, "Bongani, is Lisa in hiding?"

There was a short silence before Bongani said, "Ms. de Jong, I have to go now."

A quiet click, and the line went dead.

THE SUBURB OF Florida was built around a lake, and Swan Street, where Lisa Marais lived, was one of the roads that fronted the park, with a distant view of the waters beyond. David supposed the street name should have clued him in, although these days, developers liked to name their suburbs after whatever it was that had been destroyed in the construction.

He had no idea whether there were, in fact, any swans here. But the area was tranquil. The redbrick houses and apartments gave it a seventies feel, which was emphasized by the lack of security. Unusually, there didn't seem to be much in the way of high walls and electric fences in this part of Jo'burg. Was there no crime here? he wondered, briefly toying with the idea of requesting a transfer to Florida Lake.

He stopped the car on the corner of Swan and Lakeview, where there was a designated parking area. It was an attractive part of the world, and he'd been neglecting his gym in recent weeks. A walk would do him good. He needed some air in his lungs that didn't stink of crime scene or secondhand smoke.

It was a rarity to find himself in a middle-income neighborhood that actually looked clean. He'd become used to grime, graffiti, litter. Used to the pall of smog that seemed to hang over Jo'burg permanently, with smoke belching from factory pipes and blue-black fumes billowing from car exhausts. Metro Police were too busy trying to enforce the new e-toll rules to worry about emissions, it seemed, and so every year, the roads became filthier.

Perhaps it was the presence of the park and the lake that made this place seem lighter and brighter.

He set off along the quiet sidewalk, enjoying the unaccustomed warmth of the sun on his face.

The only other people he could see were a couple and their son walking their dog in the park. The golden spaniel scampered ahead on a winding route, nose down as it sniffed out scents. The couple strolled hand in hand while the boy, who looked to be about David's son Kevin's age, sprinted after the dog.

A family outing. He couldn't remember the last time he and Naisha had done such a thing. Perhaps after the baby was born . . .

Try as he might, David couldn't superimpose his and his wife's faces onto the soft-focus vision of family unity. Naisha disliked walking. David was usually too busy. And Kevin wanted a dog, but pets were not allowed in the townhouse complex where they now lived.

He strode down the paved pathway, becoming accustomed

to the suburban tranquility as he counted down the house numbers from fifty to forty, thirty to twenty. David was making a bet with himself on whether number fourteen would have a tree in its garden. And then he frowned as he noticed a glitch in the serene continuity of groomed hedges.

Up ahead, a section of scorched grass fronted a tumbledown wall. Bricks spilled from its top onto the sidewalk, where they lay scattered haphazardly.

David slowed his pace as he approached, feeling his heart sink lower with each stride. "Damn it," he muttered.

A suburb that resembled a modest Stepford, and he was looking at the only vacant house in the neighborhood.

Number fourteen was not only vacant, it was a burned-out shell.

The walls were blackened and crumbling. Shards of broken glass jutted like teeth from the window frames; the grass near the house was scorched and blackened, with burned streaks stretching through the greenery right up to the damaged wall.

Nobody was living here. With its roof missing, it wasn't even home to squatters. Lisa Marais must have moved elsewhere and failed to update her address.

But then David looked again. He had missed something. During this time of year, with the rains just starting, grass grew long and wild in three or four weeks. Those burned strips shouldn't still be there.

Scrambling over the broken fence, he walked all the way up to the building. Insects buzzed, and a grasshopper whirred past his face. The borders where the burning started were sharply delineated. Life, then no life. He breathed in and smelled the acrid, unmistakable tang of smoke.

This was not an old ruin, but a recent disaster zone.

Meaning the neighbors knew something.

Chapter Twenty-Nine

WHEN JADE RETURNED to the safe house, Botha was
gone.

She parked in the visitors' lot, walked down the paved
road with her bags, unlocked the townhouse's front door and
paused to listen.

"Botha?" she called softly. There was no reply. She frowned.
Perhaps he was asleep on the bed upstairs, but she doubted it.
The place felt empty.

She locked the door behind her and took the bags to
the kitchen. It didn't take long to search the small house,
look onto the tiny back garden and discover that Botha was
indeed gone.

She dialed his number. But his phone was turned off.

Jade let out a frustrated sigh. She paced the thirty square
feet of lawn, wondering what to do now. She'd genuinely
believed that he'd stay here in safe hiding. Unless he had
been lured out . . . or had never been in danger at all.

She didn't want to just sit around, waiting for Botha to
come back or answer his phone. She decided to use the time
to find out something about his backstory.

Gillespie had told Jade that Botha had trashed a Sandton bar on the night of the sabotage. She remembered its
name—Lorenzo's. Botha's behavior there seemed discordant
with what she knew of him so far. She needed to know what
had happened that night.

Forty-five minutes later, she parked the Mazda in the

paved lot behind a cluster of bars and restaurants that looked
to be the wealthy Jo'burger's party destination. Lorenzo's was
nested between a Mexican restaurant called Margaritas and
a steakhouse called Fillet Signature Cut. Across the street
was an upscale-looking nightclub. Lorenzo's was a small
place, subtly lit apart from a glittering crystal chandelier cen-
terpiece. It featured a large bar area and a small restaurant
beyond. With its leather and polished wood décor, it was
classier than she had expected, and certainly stood out from
its neighbors.

The black-clad manageress who came over to help said
that the owner, Lorenzo Rizzo, would be back in ten minutes.

"No problem. I'll wait," Jade said. "I've come to ask a few
questions about the incident that took place early on Friday
morning."

"Oh, I see." The woman brushed back a strand of perfectly
dyed chestnut hair that had come loose from its fashionably
high ponytail. "Lorenzo was the only one working front of
house at the time. The waiters left at midnight, after the restaurant closed, and I was at our Bedfordview branch."

"What time did it happen?"

"Around one-thirty A.M."

"What damage was done?"

"The chandelier was smashed." The manageress pointed
in the direction of the shimmering crystal feature. "This new
one was installed yesterday. About ten glasses were broken,
and a barstool was damaged. Oh, and some bottles as well."
She pointed to the display of brandies and whiskeys behind
the bar.

"What exactly happened?"

"Lorenzo said a customer named Botha got into a fight.
He was very drunk. He tried to hit another customer with

a barstool, missed, destroyed the chandelier and the other items and also injured the other customer's partner."

"Did the police arrive?"

"Lorenzo took photos of the damage and reported it the next morning. The police came around later that day to have a look. The other customer didn't want to get involved, Lorenzo said."

"Why's that?"

The manageress shrugged. "Maybe he just didn't want the hassle. Could also be that he didn't want people to know where he was at that time . . . You know, there are so many possible reasons. Lorenzo didn't push it."

"How did he know it was Botha?"

"Lorenzo photographed his driver's license and confiscated his car keys. After it happened, he threw Botha out and said he didn't care how he got home, whether he called a friend, took a cab, but he wasn't letting him endanger anyone on the road when he was so drunk. He came back later in the day to collect the keys, apparently. Then yesterday, Lorenzo told me that Botha had agreed to pay all damages in return for him consenting to drop the charges."

"Were there any other witnesses?"

"I don't think so. From what Lorenzo said, it was just Botha and the other two."

The manageress's face changed as she looked over Jade's shoulder. Turning, Jade saw a man walk in. He was six feet tall, solidly muscular in build, with dark eyes and a mop of dark hair held back from his brow by a pair of wraparound shades pushed up onto his head.

"What's going on here, Kim?" Turning to Jade, he addressed her in a strong Italian accent. "I'm the owner. Can I help you?"

"Jade de Jong. I'm a private investigator. I came to ask questions about the incident here last Thursday night. Kim's been very helpful."

"Kim's not authorized to talk about that." Lorenzo frowned at the unfortunate manageress, who began stammering out that she'd hardly said anything. Turning back to Jade, he asked, "Who hired you to investigate?"

A question she hadn't expected.

"I can't answer that. I'm sorry," Jade said.

"Let me get this straight. You walk in here asking questions about an incident that I've withdrawn charges on, and you refuse to tell me who you're working for?"

"I'm working for the police," she said quickly.

"Which officers?"

"Superintendent David Patel." Jade felt her face grow hot. She had not expected Lorenzo to be on the attack.

"Unless you have written authorization from Superintendent Patel, I'm not answering any questions, and you're not to, either, Kim. I don't want people interfering. Charges were dropped. Is there anything else I can do for you?"

"No. Thank you for your time."

Jade left hurriedly.

On the way back to the townhouse, she puzzled over what had just happened. There were two possible scenarios that made sense to her.

In the first one, Botha had persuaded Lorenzo to drop the charges after he'd agreed to pay damages.

Jade liked that scenario a lot. She was hoping it was the real one.

Because the second scenario was that there had been no other customer, and no injured woman, and that this had all been prearranged between Botha and Lorenzo.

Why? That was easy to answer.

It gave Botha an unbreakable alibi during the attempted sabotage at Inkomfe.

The problem was that if the second scenario was the real one, Lorenzo might call Botha and tell him Jade had been asking questions. And Jade wasn't supposed to know about this. Gillespie had told her, but Botha had never mentioned it.

She'd better start thinking, and fast, of what to say to Botha if he asked what the hell she'd been doing at Lorenzo's.

Chapter Thirty

THIS TIME, BOTHA was back at the townhouse when Jade arrived. It was as if he'd never been gone—the spare key was hanging on the hook inside the door, and he was in the garden on his phone. As soon as he saw her, he disconnected and walked into the house.

She *had* to get hold of his phone.

"Where were you?" she asked.

"I could ask you the same," Botha said. His face was all hard angles, and his dark eyes were unreadable.

"I came back earlier. You were gone."

"I had to go somewhere."

"You called a cab?"

"No. I went in a minibus taxi. Fast and anonymous. Safest form of transport for a man on the run."

"Oh," Jade said. "Where did you go?"

"I'll tell you that if you tell me where you were just now."

He stared at her, unsmiling. A challenge. She had a sick feeling that he already knew where she'd been.

"How can we work together if I can't trust you?" she asked.

"I think maybe I'm the one who should be saying that."

Jade let out a deep breath. "I told you where I was going. To do research. I found out the identity of the murdered woman."

"Who is she?" Botha still sounded suspicious.

"Scarlett Sykes."

He blinked. "Only a name? What else?"

"It's a murder investigation," Jade reminded him.

"Detective Mweli has to notify the next of kin. I can't go interfering at this stage. She told me she'd keep in touch."

Botha gave a small nod without looking at her.

"I brought some food," Jade told him.

"I'm not hungry right now, but thanks."

"I also picked up a change of clothes for us. I'm going to shower."

Jade walked upstairs to the bathroom and turned the shower on. Then she tiptoed back to the top of the stairs and listened.

Botha was on the phone again.

"The story's holding," she heard him say. Then a pause. "No, still nothing from her. We'll have to assume the worst. And I found out something else today . . ."

He lowered his voice and she couldn't hear any more. But maybe she didn't need to.

Jade stepped back into the bathroom and showered. When she got out, Botha wasn't on his phone anymore, but she heard the faint tap of computer keys.

She was trembling with exhaustion. The previous night's lack of sleep was taking its toll. She needed to have her wits about her, but right then, her eyes were begging to close so she could regroup.

The bed had a mattress, and with the afternoon sun streaming through the glass windows, the room was pleasantly warm. She'd better rest up, because who knew what the evening might bring? She pulled on a fresh shirt, programmed her phone alarm for five thirty, lay down and was deeply asleep within a few seconds.

She woke five minutes before the alarm and turned it off. She felt much better—her thinking was clearer now. There was no sign of Botha downstairs, but his bedroom door was closed. Perhaps he was also catching up on rest.

Jade went into the garden. The afternoon was starting to cool and the shadows were lengthening as the sun set in a clear-aired, cloudless sky.

Standing in the shade of the wall, she called David. He didn't answer, so she left a message updating him on her day's investigation.

He called back a few minutes later, sounding stressed. "I'll try to be quick about this. I went to Lisa Marais's place just now, and it's a ruin. The retired woman who lives next door told me the house burned down last week. It was a massive blaze; it started around midnight and all the neighbors were evacuated."

"Do they know the cause of the fire?"

"They don't. They suspect arson, but there was another small fire in the house last year caused by a cigarette, according to my rather nosy source. Lisa was a chain-smoker."

"Was Lisa there at the time?"

"That's the strange thing. The neighbor said she didn't see her there when the fire happened, and she hasn't been home since. She hasn't even been around to take a look or pick through the wreckage."

"There's something weird going on with Lisa," Jade said. "It seems as if nobody's heard from her recently. The consultant at Earthforce was very evasive when I asked where she was. And she was supposed to send notes to a worker at Inkomfe, but he said they haven't arrived."

"Pity she never got to send those notes just because her house burned down." David's voice dripped with cynicism. "They could have been important."

"It seems like they were. Did her neighbor say anything else?"

"She was in and out at odd hours over the past few weeks. Leaving early, coming home very late, going out in the middle of the night. And the neighbor said she saw a silver Land Cruiser driving slowly past Lisa's house a couple of times. She actually reported the car to the neighborhood watch. But then, she's probably the kind of person who'd report an ice cream van to the neighborhood watch if it went past too slowly."

"A silver Land Cruiser?" Jade felt her pulse accelerate, remembering the car that had crashed into the steel pole. Perhaps it was a coincidence, but if it wasn't, then Lisa might have known the blonde woman. Either that, or . . .

There was another scenario brewing in the back of Jade's mind. Her subconscious was telling her something, but frustratingly, she couldn't seem to grasp it. Perhaps it would come to her later.

"Did you get my message?" she asked.

"Yes," David sighed heavily. "This whole thing is looking messier and messier. Do you want me to try and make arrangements at a safe house for you? I'm worried, Jade. I spoke to Mweli just now, and she told me Loodts was tortured. The autopsy showed several of his fingers were broken."

Torture? Jade glanced nervously at the flimsy sliding door. "Thanks for the offer. But you barely have the resources to provide safe houses for people who really need them," she said reluctantly.

"I know, I know."

"Where we are will have to do. Oh, hell. Hold on."

"What?" David sounded as jumpy as she felt.

"Nothing. A light just went on in Botha's bedroom. I'm outside. I don't want him to know I'm talking to you."

"The less he knows, the better," David agreed.

"Gillespie's been trying to convince me to walk away from this. He told me to fold my hand, if I remember his words correctly," she said.

"Gillespie's right. Jade, if Botha's planning something, he's going to use you until you become an inconvenience, and then he's going to take you out. Has it not occurred to you that he could be manipulating you?"

"Of course it has. But . . ." Jade leaned against the garden wall, feeling its residual warmth on her back as the sun set. "Wait, David. Say that again."

"Say what?"

"What you just said."

"Botha could be using you?"

"No. What you said before that."

"He'll play along until you become an inconvenience?"

Jade straightened up. "Yes." The idea had become clear to her now, chilling in its totality.

"You think that's what he's doing?"

"No. But it might be why Scarlett Sykes died. Maybe she was working with the criminals, not with Loodts. If so, they could have terminated her because she made a bad mistake. She crashed the car when she was leaving the motel. That could have compromised the entire operation. Maybe it wasn't her first error. So they decided to dispose of her. Kill her, contaminate the scene, damage her finger-prints, leave her body to confuse the cops."

"That's a possibility. I'm going to be speaking to Loodts's personal assistant tomorrow morning. I'll ask her if Loodts knew Scarlett Sykes. Personal assistants usually know every last detail, don't they?"

Jade laughed. "In my experience, they do."

"And in the meantime, watch out. Botha doesn't know you were hired to investigate him. Make sure you keep it that way."

"I will," Jade promised, wishing she'd never gone to Lorenzo's.

Chapter Thirty-One

JADE WALKED BACK into the house, her mind racing. It seemed that with every turn this case took, disturbing new information landed in her lap.

Botha was sitting on one of the couches eating a cheese-and-tomato sandwich. He was wearing the black T-shirt she'd bought him, which fit well.

Jade kicked her shoes off and curled her legs up underneath her on the other couch, balancing her notepad on her knee.

"Thanks for the clothes and food. I appreciate it," he said.

"Pleasure." She saw an empty Greek salad container next to Botha's sandwich wrapper. He'd put the other salad and sandwich on the table for her.

"You write in a paper notebook," Botha observed. He seemed to be in a better mood now, or maybe he was trying to make up for his attitude earlier. In fact, she thought he was perhaps even attempting a smile. "Retro."

"Let's see how far you get with that battery guzzler during load shedding," Jade retorted, staring pointedly at Botha's laptop, which was recharging on the coffee table. "I need notes I can read any time. I can drop my notebook down a flight of stairs and pick it up at the bottom, and nothing will be lost or damaged."

"Sorry," he said. "I was just teasing you. It's a sensible choice for what you do."

Jade glanced at him. He was smiling now. It warmed

his face and made her want to smile back, but she resisted. Instead, she slowly flipped through the book's pages until she reached a fresh one. Instead of focusing on Botha, she tried to scan the information, trying to discern coherent patterns within the disturbing tangle of facts.

Her efforts were cut short as the lights went out and the house was plunged into darkness.

"Shit," Jade muttered. She glanced out of the window. No other lights in sight. The suburb was being load shed. A moment later, from somewhere nearby, she heard the noisy rattle of a diesel generator starting up. Some lucky person was about to enjoy hot dinner and television tonight, even if it meant deafening all the neighbors.

Botha reached over to the coffee table for his phone. He turned on its flashlight, and the bright beam cut through the darkness. "Power's out for the next few hours, I guess," he said, packing up his laptop. "I'm going upstairs."

"See you later," Jade said.

As she sat in the darkness and bit into her hummus-and-salad sandwich, Jade remembered she'd bought a bottle of Tabasco, which was still in the shopping bag. She was damned if she was going to eat supper without it. Tabasco made everything taste better.

In the dark, it took a moment to locate it among the extra water bottles, and another moment to get its plastic seal open. Then she unscrewed the lid and shook it over her food. She didn't need light to tell her when to stop shaking the bottle. When there was no such thing as too much, life became easier.

She was on her way back to the lounge when she heard the noise.

It was a quiet, almost furtive scraping sound. If she had

been farther away, she wouldn't have heard it over the nearby generator's thrumming.

Jade paused, looking in the direction of the noise, even though there was only blackness to be seen.

There it was again. Scrape, scrape. Coming from down the corridor.

Jade put her plate down on the coffee table. Then she tip-toed over to the short passageway and listened again.

The noise was coming from the sliding doors that opened onto the patio. The weakest spot in the house's defenses. It sounded . . .

. . . like somebody trying to break in.

No, her mind screamed at her. *No, no, impossible, it must be a bug banging against the window, it must be the sound of a scraping branch, it must be, it must be, because there is no way anybody could have found us here.*

But it was not an innocent noise. It was too regular. Too discreet. She took another step toward it, heart in her mouth, and then she was sure as she heard the distinctive sound of wood splintering.

The door was about to give.

Chapter Thirty-Two

JADE SPRINTED UPSTAIRS. Botha must have heard her running footsteps, because by the time she arrived at his door, he was already on his feet and cramming his possessions into his bag. On the bed, his phone sent a beam of light to the ceiling, casting an eerie glow on everything around.

"What's going on?" he asked. His voice was all hard edges, the way she felt inside.

"Someone's breaking in through the sliding door," Jade whispered. "I don't know how the hell they found us here, but they did."

The window in Botha's room overlooked the front of the house. She peered out. In the deep gloom, she could just make out a man's tall figure near the garage, waiting.

They had all the exits blocked.

"There's no way out," she muttered. There was nowhere she and Botha could run now. Screaming would only tell the invaders exactly which room they were in. Even if they called for help, there was no way it could arrive fast enough.

Jade felt a terrible calm descend. She glanced at Botha and saw the same expression in his eyes. Even as the killers forced their way in, he was not panicking. Instead, she could see him thinking desperately, running through every option in his mind until the choices narrowed down to the final, inevitable one: to stand and fight.

A martial arts–trained body was a dangerous weapon, but

against men with guns, there was no way he could get close enough to use it.

Unless she could somehow provide a diversion. Or unless . . .

Jade thought again about her bedroom. Those big glass doors overlooking the neighbors.

And suddenly she had a plan.

"My room," she said. "The balcony."

She could hear footsteps inside now. The invaders were being quiet, but not stealthy. They must have known their quarry was trapped upstairs.

She wrenched the sliding doors open while Botha closed and locked the bedroom and jammed the bed against it. It might not slow their pursuers down for long, but every second counted.

She grabbed her bag and followed him out.

"We have to jump across," she whispered, pointing to the balcony of the neighboring house, with its darkened windows beyond.

The balconies had looked so close together in sunny daylight. Now the gap seemed to have widened; the drop below was an abyss. It was crazy, suicidal, to think about clambering over that narrow, unsteady rail and leaping across empty space to an equally narrow and treacherous landing point.

But not as suicidal as staying put. She could hear footsteps on the stairs.

With feline grace, Botha climbed over the waist-high railing, bracing his feet with some difficulty on the narrow ridge that protruded beyond. He tensed, then sprang, awkwardly but high. Jade gasped as he straddled the void. His feet thudded into the railing opposite. He grabbed the top of the rail with both arms and then in one lithe movement boosted himself over.

"It's okay," he told Jade. "It's a long way, but I'll get you. I won't let you fall."

She flung her bag across first, and he caught it. She didn't dare to look down. Adrenaline coursed through her as she scrambled over the rail, hating it that her legs were shaking with fright. God, how had Botha done this when there was literally only an inch of brick to push from beyond the rails?

But she had to take that leap of faith, because there were only seconds to spare.

Jade launched herself at the opposite rail. The jump was good. Her fear gave her the wings to leap high and wide.

It was not her fault that as she pushed off, the concrete rim sheared away from the edge, taking with it the impetus from her effort. She knew that she was going to miss any chance of landing on the opposite shelf. Darkness raced past her; she stretched her arms as far as they would go.

She hit the railing with her wrists. She made a desperate grab for the top, missed, slipped and had time only to wonder where she would land after falling twenty feet in darkness.

And then Botha managed to catch her right arm, his grip solid as rock, his steely fingers clamped onto her skin. Jade scrambled furiously with her leg, found a foothold even as he dragged her upward. She clawed at the top of the railing with her left hand, muscles screaming. He shifted his grip, and then she was over, just about falling on top of him as they staggered backward.

Over the roaring of blood in her ears, she could hear the bedroom door give way as their pursuers kicked it open.

Botha wrapped his hands around the padded straps of his laptop bag, lowered his head and, holding the bag in front of him, charged at the balcony door.

The shattering of glass filled the night. Sharp, bright

crumbs of safety glass scattered onto the tiles as he forced his way in with Jade close behind. They sprinted downstairs through a pitch-black house that was a mirror image of their own. It was a furnished home, but thankfully, the occupants must have gone out to eat on load shedding night.

"Left!" Jade shouted. The turn took them to the downstairs sliding door. Botha unhooked it, pushed it open, and then they were out of the gate and running for their lives toward visitors' parking, with Jade expecting at any moment to feel the punch of a bullet in her back.

"Give me the keys!" Botha yelled.

"But you . . ."

"Jade, I'm fast. Let me." He stood between her and the driver's door, his chest heaving, his face tight with tension.

She just about threw the keys at him before scrambling into the passenger side.

The engine screamed, and the Mazda shot backward like a bullet.

"Down! Down!" she ordered, ducking as she saw a figure sprint toward them from the direction of the townhouse. She had no clue how Botha would manage to drive while flattened in his seat, but she was sure the man was holding a gun.

Her suspicions were confirmed a moment later as two shots split the air.

"Go!" Jade shouted.

She was almost thrown on top of Botha as the car jounced over the curb into the paved roadway and, tires wailing, whipped around to the right and down the drive. They were going as fast as they could. But would it be fast enough to outrun the men behind them?

They flew over a speed bump so fast the car was briefly airborne. They were out, they'd made it, but before the gate could close again, she saw the SUV's headlights blaze behind her.

She could have wept with frustration and fear. They were seriously outclassed; their pursuers were in a bigger, faster car.

They didn't have Carlos Botha at the wheel, though.

He hadn't been exaggerating about his driving. He slewed the car expertly onto the double lane main road, zigzagging through a cluster of cars that had jammed up at a darkened intersection where the lights weren't working. Behind her, she heard a blare of horns as the SUV tried to follow. Brakes screeched. Hopefully the traffic had slowed it down.

"Watch out!" To her terror, a group of vehicles ahead was traveling so slowly, it appeared to be standing still.

Botha didn't touch the brakes as he slalomed the Mazda between them. Tires wailed, and the car went into a skid.

Jade's feet were braced against the boards, and her hands were clamped onto the dashboard. She wanted to close her eyes, but was unable to stop watching the horror unfolding in front of her.

But the skid was not unplanned—it was a controlled maneuver. The car righted itself just in time to dart between the last two vehicles.

Then they were off. The speedometer hit triple figures as Botha accelerated, flying down the straight before powering through the curve ahead. She really thought he would lose the car then. Another skid now would kill them. There wasn't even a tiny margin for error here: On one side of the road was a jagged, rocky outcrop, and on the other, a dented crash barrier was all that lay between them and a steep drop.

Their headlights flashed off the battered rails as they shrieked through the bend, and Jade's fingernail bent painfully back against the dashboard.

And then somehow, miraculously, they were through, the road unrolling in front of them. In a different suburb, one that had power. Streetlights ahead, their path slicing through the darkness.

"Have we lost them?" Botha yelled, and Jade abandoned her death grip on the dashboard to look.

Nothing there—yet.

"They haven't caught up. Can't see anybody behind us."

"So where to?" Botha asked. Jade glanced over and saw that his face looked hollow from stress; the dim glow from the dashboard illuminated the shadows under his eyes, and his strongly defined cheekbones.

They approached a crossroad. Three choices, then. Go left, go right, or go straight on. Straight on meant they would be visible for miles. Now her bumper stickers were a liability. They made the car recognizable even from a distance.

Left or right gave them a fifty-fifty chance, which weren't great odds. Their future seemed to be entirely in the hands of fate. That was the way Jade had felt as the car had screeched through the bends. Left or right? Neither option was safe. Neither would keep them alive for long.

She should toss a coin, but it wasn't a coin she was thinking of now. It was a slot machine, like the ones she'd seen being welded in the secrecy of that warehouse. Press the button, see what comes up. Would it be the jackpot, or a near hit? That depended on how the machine was rigged, didn't it? So how could she tip the odds in their favor?

Suddenly Jade knew the answer.

"Turn!" she shouted, and felt the seat belt bite into her chest as the car slowed suddenly.

"Turn where?"

"Go back. Make a U-turn. Put your lights on high beam and drive back around those bends."

It was the only option that gave them a fighting chance, the single action their pursuers would not be expecting of them.

"Got it," Botha said.

He swung the car in a neat turn across the double lanes and switched the headlights to high beam. The bright lights would effectively blind oncoming cars, making it impossible for the drivers to recognize the Mazda until it was driving past them, and maybe not even then.

They sped back up the hill. As they rounded the bend, Jade saw a cluster of headlights approaching. A few slower-moving ones, and one large, high-set pair weaving aggressively between the others. The hunters, impatient to corner their quarry. A couple of the oncoming cars flashed their own lights angrily at Jade and Botha.

And then the group was past, and they were driving back up the main road toward the intersection from which they'd fled just a minute earlier.

"I think we did it," Jade said. Her voice sounded as if she'd swallowed helium. Even now, their pursuers would be making the same choice that she'd been faced with earlier. Left, right or straight.

She hoped they wouldn't think to double back.

"How did they find us?" she asked Botha. "You said that house was safe."

"It was completely safe."

"Who does it belong to?"

"Me. I bought it as an investment a while ago. It's not even in my name yet. Transfer hasn't gone through. Nobody could have known we were there."

"Somebody sold you out. Do you think it could have been the caretaker?"

"How would he have done that?"

"I have no idea! I'm just theorizing, given that the place was broken into and we were a few seconds away from death by bullet."

"There must be a logical reason," Botha countered.

"Well, I can only think of one."

"What's that?"

"Somehow they've managed to plant a tracking device on you," Jade said. "Something simple, like a SIM card device with a battery, that enables them to locate you."

"So why aren't they following us right now?"

"There must be a delay in the interface. Probably due to crappy network coverage in this area, compounded by the load shedding."

"Network coverage can affect that?"

"Of course. I use devices like that from time to time. They're not expensive, but they're also not as reliable as they say on the box, especially in areas with poor signal. It's easy to pinpoint someone if you have time, and they stay in one place. It's much harder when they're on the move, like we are now."

Jade checked the wing mirror, but saw nobody behind them. Hopefully the deception had bought them enough time.

"So what do we do?" Botha asked. "Keep driving all night?"

The thought was tempting.

"We need to get somewhere out of cell phone range and hide there while we search your clothing and belongings."

"You have anywhere in mind?"

"Actually," Jade told him, "I do. I know where there's a dead zone. It might not be the most comfortable place to spend a night, but it's about as safe as we're going to get."

Chapter Thirty-Three

SCARLETT SYKES'S SISTER Abigail lived on the outskirts of Roodepoort, in an area where forlorn-looking mine dumps and small, semiderelict farms were being invaded by high-density, cheaply built townhouse complexes.

Abigail was the closest next of kin that Mweli had been able to track down. When she'd phoned, Abigail had asked why Mweli was calling. Mweli had refused to be drawn out, apart from saying it was a very serious matter concerning her younger sister, and it was necessary to give her the news in person.

So basically, she'd prepared Abigail for the worst.

She dressed in a dark pantsuit with a white blouse. It was what she always wore when breaking bad news to relatives—and as one of the few female detectives in the police service, Mweli felt she'd put on this outfit too many times. She placed her jacket on the passenger seat and drove out to Randfontein with a heavy heart. This was her responsibility: to break the news, and if necessary, to spend time with the bereaved so somebody was there for them. So she could answer their shocked questions, reassure them or listen while they spoke of the dead. In this case, listening would be important, because Abigail might know what her sister had been involved in and with whom.

Abigail's apartment was on the second floor, accessible from a narrow stairway. Mweli knocked on the flimsy door, and Abigail snatched it open as if she'd been waiting behind it.

Mweli could see the resemblance. Abigail, too, was blonde, with similar features. She was plumper than her sister; her hair was longer, and she wore it back in a frizzy ponytail.

"Please come in," she said, welcoming Mweli into the small living area—kitchen, lounge and dining room combined in a space with just enough room to swing a cat. Furniture was crammed in, everything decorated in a bohemian style. Colorful drapes and curtains, bright antimacassars over the upholstered chairs, framed drawings and paintings covering the walls. Sketches of animals plus landscapes and seascapes in strong, bright colors.

Abigail gestured to the nearest chair. "Detective, if this is bad news, please give it to me straightaway."

Mweli nodded, appreciating the directness of her words and the appeal in her blue eyes. Neither of them sat. Abigail faced Mweli, twining her fingers together nervously.

"I'm afraid your sister Scarlett was found murdered yesterday."

Abigail's hands flew to her mouth. "Oh, shit. This is what I feared. Oh, hell. I . . ." She blinked rapidly. Mweli reached into the pocket of her too-tight suit jacket and passed her a pack of tissues.

"Thank you." Abigail collapsed down onto the chair behind her, ripping the tissue pack open. "What happened?"

Mweli took a seat opposite. She sat quietly, her gaze fixed on the coffee table where she saw a nearly empty glass of wine. In a quiet voice, she summarized the scenario, giving the barest outline and sparing the grimmer details.

She listened to Abigail's gasps and sobs, which quieted as she collected herself. Then her hand closed around the wineglass, and she downed the remainder in a gulp. "Do you want . . . do you want anything to drink? I thought from your phone call I might need the wine, and now I need more."

"Nothing for me, thank you."

Abigail reached behind her, grasped a bottle of merlot from the mantelpiece and upended it into her glass until it was brimful.

"I can't say I didn't see this coming," she told Mweli. She was more together than Mweli had expected. A strong woman who clearly knew her sister had been on a destructive path. "For years, I guess I've been expecting something like this to happen."

"Why is that?" Mweli asked.

Abigail gulped down the wine. "Bad choices," she said.

"In what way?"

"Every way." She gave a tight smile. "She's been in rehab a few times over the years. For drugs and other things. Most recently prescription medications. Tranquilizers and the like. She also has a criminal record for stealing cash from somewhere she worked. She didn't get jail time, only community service, but it's a record nonetheless."

Mweli nodded, thinking of the woman's damaged fingertips. Somebody had known about that record and taken care to remove the evidence of her identity. "Did she relapse after her last time in rehab?"

Abigail nodded sadly. "Of course. People don't change, do they? I sent her money a few times—I don't know what she used it for. I didn't really try to stay in touch, but every so often she'd call me up to tell me about her life, her crazy boyfriends . . . I wish now I'd listened better, done more. I should have forced her to come and stay with me, tried to get her into rehab again."

"I don't suppose you had the chance."

"But I did, just a few weeks ago. She phoned me in tears—she'd had a fight with a new boyfriend. I didn't know him, but from what she said, he was her usual type. Dangerous, she told me. He'd gone out of town, and she wanted me to come and fetch her."

"You went?"

Abigail nodded. "In the middle of the night, I drove into a run-down part of Jo'burg and found her. She was crying, terrified. Paranoid, I think. She kept saying he was going to find her and kill her, that she'd gotten herself in too deep." Abigail twisted her fingers together again as she remembered. "She spent the night here in my flat. We didn't really speak. She was exhausted, and I didn't want to ask her too much."

"In case she told you the truth?"

Mweli's suggestion was met with a shaky smile. "Exactly. That was my one opportunity, and I missed it. I should have gotten her help. She seemed to have money then, lots of it. I don't know how she'd earned it—she didn't say, and that worried me. She looked harder. Quieter. She gave me a wad of hundreds as a thank-you. She wanted to fly down to Durban, to get away and make a clean break. But wouldn't you know it, just as we were about to leave for the airport, her phone rang. She spoke for a few minutes, and a little while later, a big silver SUV pulled up outside, and that was it. She was gone. Back to him."

"I'm sorry," Mweli said.

Sympathetic as she was, there was always a part of her that was on the alert for false notes in the response of grief, or suspicious behavior in the questions that were asked. Random as the crime might seem, murders were often set up by spouses or close relatives.

But Abigail was not a suspect in this particular case, and her words rang true.

This visit had also been useful for Mweli; there was one aspect of Abigail's story that provided a promising lead. This boyfriend with the silver SUV, the one who had spelled trouble. "Do you know the boyfriend's name?" she asked.

Abigail shook her head. "Scarlett never mentioned his name. Perhaps she did that on purpose. I don't think he wanted people to know."

"You went to pick her up. Do you remember the address?"

"Scarlett didn't really give me an address. She just told me where she was and how to get there. Which exit to take, which way to turn. I think I remember that okay, and also what the place looked like. I'll write down what I remember, and I can draw you a sketch of the front of the building."

Noticing Mweli's surprised expression, she explained, "This is what I do for a living. I'm an art lecturer at the University of Johannesburg."

Mweli nodded. "The paintings?" she asked, looking at the walls.

"All mine," Abigail said. She fetched a notepad and sketchpad from another room and sat back down on the couch, her wine forgotten as she applied herself to her task.

The directions and sketch were done in a few minutes. She put them in a large white envelope and handed them over.

"Thank you," Mweli said, struggling out of the chair's cushioned embrace. "Once again, my condolences. Do you have somebody who could come and stay with you for a while?"

Abigail nodded. "My fiancé lives here with me. He'll be home in the next half hour."

"That's good. We'll contact you if any progress is made on

this case, and I'll let you know as soon as Scarlett's body is released."

Swallowing hard, Abigail thanked her, and a minute later, Mweli was making her way down the stairs and out into the fresh night air.

In her car, she ripped open another pack of tissues and blew her nose noisily. This part of the job never got any easier. It was beyond question the worst thing she ever had to do. She would go home now, with a box of chicken nuggets and chips, and watch two *Deadliest Catch* episodes back-to-back. She could only hope that Captain Sig's icy blue Nordic eyes would distract her from the tear-filled ones of the woman she'd left behind.

Chakalaka would sleep on her bed tonight, she was sure. He'd leap on when the light was off and curl up in the crook of her legs, purring loudly, turning himself into a miniature furnace as he pinned the covers down, making her legs hot and sweaty and meaning she couldn't move for fear of upsetting the stupid cat.

It was funny how he did this whenever she'd had a really bad day.

Uncomfortable as his presence was, it was also comforting, and she always felt better in the morning. Somehow it was as if Chakalaka knew what to do.

Chapter Thirty-Four

JADE AND BOTHA reached the highway, and she directed him onto the M2, heading into Johannesburg. Driving toward an unlikely refuge—a place she'd hoped she would never have to visit again.

It was more than a year ago that she'd been called by her connection. "Jade," he'd said, his voice sharp and assured.

"Robbie." Her heart sank when she heard his voice. She wouldn't have answered the call if she'd known it was him, but Robbie changed his phone numbers frequently. Plus they hadn't spoken for months. She hadn't had any reason to suspect it was him calling.

What did he want? Was he going to try and draw her into another of his deadly ventures? She knew Robbie believed she owed him, even though it was her opinion the debt had been more than paid.

"I called to say goodbye," he'd told her, and her mind had spun with confusion. "Or rather, *au revoir*," he'd said into her silence.

"What do you mean?"

"Well, baby, I'm going up into Nigeria for a while. Things have developed there. There are opportunities we need to take advantage of."

Jade had no idea what those opportunities might be but knew better than to ask any more questions. "I hope it works out for you," she'd said hesitantly. "Be careful."

"You know me." He'd laughed. "I'm never careful. I prefer

to be lucky. Who knows how long we'll be gone? Maybe a few months, maybe longer. I put a key for the warehouse into your mailbox."

"The warehouse?"

"Yeah, you know. Where we were doing business. I thought it might be handy for you. There's a piece of equipment in the safe that you could use one day if you needed to."

He'd laughed.

Shivers crawled down Jade's spine. She'd understood what Robbie was referring to. He'd once dealt in illegal firearms, but had given it up as being too risky and not profitable enough. But he hadn't sold all his stock, and now one of his weapons was in that safe.

At the time, she'd been in possession of her Glock, a Glock which, ironically, she'd bought from Robbie. She hadn't envisioned herself ever needing another firearm.

"Thanks," she'd said, trying to shrug away the crawling sensation under her skin when she thought of Robbie stopping outside her house, checking to see if her car was there, confidently slotting the key into her mailbox.

Sometimes you needed to forget your past. You didn't want it calling you up and dropping by to give you access to its warehouse.

Even so, the good news was that Robbie was leaving the country for a while. With the life he led, he might never come back. The thought troubled her, but also filled her with relief. Robbie had been her accomplice when she'd murdered the man who had killed her father. He knew her secrets, which made her uneasy.

Sometimes she wondered what would have happened if she'd gone into business with him. He'd asked her to, more than once. No investment needed, just the contribution of her skills from time to time in exchange for generous amounts of cash. She'd always refused. The money was tempting, of course. Who wouldn't want to spend eleven months of the year on a palm-fringed beach in exchange for one month of work?

The problem was, that month of work would stain her soul so deeply not even the tropical sun could bleach it clean again. She knew which skills Robbie wanted her to use. There were always people who wanted someone else killed and were prepared to pay top dollar for it. Especially here in South Africa, with its high crime rate and overworked police force. Even if you were caught, chances were that you would walk free. Murderers had. Many still did.

She'd told him no, which was perhaps why Robbie hadn't asked her to accompany him on this new business venture in Nigeria. At any rate, the key had been in her mailbox when she'd returned home. She'd toyed with the idea of throwing it away, but good sense had prevailed. Who knew if she might need the warehouse for something urgent one day? Or what if Robbie demanded the key back on his return?

Eventually she'd strung it onto her key ring and forgotten about it. Just another item, in between the long key for her security gate and the beaded charm, now scratched and chipped, that David had given her. Now it might finally come in handy.

THE AREA WHERE Jade directed Botha was even more run-down than she remembered. The concrete arch of the highway bridge was patterned with graffiti and papered with advertisements for penis enlargements and witch doctors who promised everything from better job prospects to finding love. The pages were yellowed and peeling, drifting down from the walls to add to the flotsam of litter on the sidewalks.

At this hour, the industrial suburb was quiet. Traffic had come and gone, and she saw only the occasional other vehicle as they sped along the dark roads.

Was it this one?

She strained her eyes in the gloom. No, the next one.

"Here," she said.

"Here?" Botha echoed as he pulled into the driveway she was pointing to. The car jounced over uneven paving. The tall steel gate was closed. She saw that it was locked from the outside by a thick chain and a huge padlock covered in rust. The headlights shone onto a cracked expanse of tarmac and the large warehouse beyond.

Jade climbed out of the car, and after killing the engine, Botha did the same. From far off came the noise of traffic on the highway, and from closer by she could hear the clanging of machinery and the hissing of compressed air. No sounds came from the building they were facing. Grass had pushed through some of the cracks in the paving—the only sign of anything living.

"This place is abandoned," Botha said.

"Yep."

The gate and the fence were crowned with thick, sharp coils of barbed wire. At some earlier stage, somebody had tried to deface the steel bars with graffiti. Now only faint traces of red paint remained.

"What was it?"

"Officially, an auto parts business. It made a pretty nice front for dealing in other things."

Like guns.

She never thought she would have needed that kind of help from Robbie again. But she knew—never say never.

Robbie might have said that, his dark eyes glinting, the skull-and-crossbones earring in his ear catching the light as he shook his dreadlocked head and grinned at her.

She fitted the key into the lock. It didn't want to go in, and then it didn't want to turn. The rusty padlock resisted her efforts, but after a while, she felt it give. It didn't so much spring open as unwillingly come apart, freeing the chain it had held.

Botha helped her with the gate, which screamed on its hinges. They brought the car in and refastened the lock carefully from the inside.

"If you drive around the side, you'll find a place to park," Jade said.

She jogged ahead of him around the right-hand corner of the warehouse. Here was the parking area, a spacious garage whose walls and roof were reinforced with galvanized steel.

The air outside was tinged with smoke and melted plastic, smells wafting through from a factory elsewhere. Inside, everything was stale and dusty, flavored with a hint of old oil.

Where was that light switch? She didn't know if Robbie had arranged for someone to keep paying the bills while he was away. She found the switch and flipped it, and a fluorescent bulb high above flickered into reluctant life.

Its neon glow shone onto the space she remembered. The workshop had been a hive of activity in the past. Its walls had resounded with the sound of drilling and hammering, the hiss of the welder and the shriek of metal on metal.

Now it was quiet. A layer of dust had settled on the floor and every other surface, even the handle of the steel door that led through to the office.

The thick-walled, solid-roofed office.

"They were serious about cars here," Botha said, his voice brightening as he gazed around at the shelves of neatly stacked spare parts, paints and tools now covered in dust. In the middle of the large space were several hydraulic lifts and pits, long unused. "Looks like they did more than just sell spares."

"I think it was a chop shop," Jade observed. "Repurposing stolen cars or hijacked ones. It's why there's no signal anywhere inside. Nothing can be tracked here."

She left him staring at the deserted workspace and walked through a doorway, finding a security door before the office. It was locked, but she remembered how to open it. Robbie had reached under this shelf—pressed something . . .

With a buzz so loud she jumped, the steel door sprang open.

The spacious office housed a mahogany desk, a tall director's chair, a leather four-seater couch. A bar fridge hummed softly in the corner. A kettle stood on the dining table with a giant tin of Robbie's chosen brand of coffee, a revolting chicory blend.

The tin was almost completely full. Jade guessed that not many visitors asked for coffee. She'd certainly told Robbie numerous times he was useless at making it and had poor taste in brews. He'd refused to listen to her constructive criticism or buy a halfway decent bean. Their disagreement on the subject had become a standing joke. Almost a point of pride for him, a reason not to change.

Men.

At any rate, she owed him now, bad coffee or not. Once the metal gate was locked and bolted from the inside, this was the safest possible place she could be.

Botha stood in the doorway, taking in the surprisingly luxurious ambience.

"We have to check your laptop bag," she told him. "And your clothes."

"Let's do it." He pulled off his shirt, unbuttoned his jeans. Stripped down to his boxers.

His body was matte beige, his muscles taut. Six-pack on the stomach and strong, lean definition in his arms and legs.

Forcing herself to look away, she picked up his jacket, which was still warm to the touch. She checked the pockets carefully for anything that might have been stuck on or inserted into a cuff or a seam.

There was nothing.

"I can't find anything in my jeans or shoes," he said.

She checked his laptop bag carefully while he dressed again.

Within minutes, Jade was convinced that Botha was not carrying a tracking device on him. This was good news and bad. How, then, had their hunters had caught up with them so easily? Jade needed to find that gun.

There was only one place to hide a safe in this room—behind the wooden cupboard that stood against the wall opposite the entrance.

Botha helped her wrestle it aside. Behind it was a small, square metal door. The safe was here, as Robbie had promised.

Just one problem. The safe door was firmly locked, and she had no idea where the key might be.

Botha had filled the kettle from the small sink in the corner of the room. "Coffee?" he offered.

He prized the plastic lid off the jar, and Jade wrinkled her nose as the harsh, unpleasant aroma filtered out. Yuck—unpalatable even before adding boiling water.

"You know what? I think I'll pass," she told him.

Where would Robbie have hidden the safe key? Long and narrow, it could be concealed just about anywhere with a piece of double-sided tape. "Anywhere" including in one of the hundreds of dusty boxes of spare parts in the warehouse. But Robbie liked to keep his secrets close. Something this important would be hidden in his office.

Botha helped her search. They went about the job method-ically, tackling the couch first. She looked underneath it, felt around all the legs, then removed the cushions one by one and stuck her fingers down the back gaps. She unzipped the cushions' leather covers and pulled them out. Felt them care-fully all over. They were soft, with nothing hidden in their padded innards.

She checked the sparsely lined shelves. A few books on mechanics, a couple on guns, one or two paperback thrill-ers with eighties-themed covers featuring grim men with oversized jaws and bulging muscles and wide-eyed, gormless-looking women with huge, frizzy hair. Plots as anachronistic as their cover art.

She flipped carefully through each book in turn, check-ing the spines of the hardcovers in case a key was slotted in there. A book was always a good hiding place. People's eyes passed over them—they became part of the décor and were seldom stolen.

Her efforts were unrewarded. No key in the books or con-cealed behind them on the shelves. Or in the spare roll of toilet tissue in the bathroom or in the empty mirrored cabinet.

Botha moved to the fridge, and Jade set about searching the desk and the chair with the same careful methodology. Nothing was taped onto these objects or hidden in the cush-ions or drawers.

Now what? Was there a hiding place she hadn't yet thought of? Or, more likely, had Robbie taken the key with him? Perhaps he'd had second thoughts, or there were other items of value in the safe.

Discouraged, she walked over to the couch. Botha sat down on its left. He took a sip of his coffee and put the cup down—quite decisively, she noticed.

She sat down on the right, slipped her shoes off, put her feet up. It had been a stressful day, and she was starving. Robbie's hospitality hadn't extended as far as a packet of crackers or instant noodles. She shuddered at the thought that she might end up drinking that vile brew simply because there was nothing else available.

"How's your police detective?" Botha asked her suddenly.

Jade shrugged.

"Managed to speak to him?" Botha asked. Perhaps he was testing her story.

"I saw him yesterday," she said. "In passing, at the Randfontein police station."

"And how was it?"

"Acrimonious."

Botha laughed, then stifled it when Jade made a face. "Sorry," he said.

"That's okay."

"I wasn't laughing at you. I was more laughing because I know the feeling. A few years back, with a married woman who ended up breaking my heart. Or so I thought she had at the time."

"David's wife is pregnant," Jade responded, and Botha's smile vanished.

"Well, that's a complication," he admitted.

"The baby's due any day."

"Congratulations to him?"

"It probably isn't his."

Botha frowned slightly and said nothing.

Jade found she couldn't stop talking. It was a relief to be sharing the burden of knowledge that had been weighing heavy on her heart for months. "He made a mistake. They were about to split up, but he slept with his wife while they were officially separated. He doesn't know she went to a fertility clinic afterward. She used a sperm donor to impregnate herself. To trap him in the marriage. I found out about it from a reliable source: Naisha's best friend's daughter overheard them planning it."

Botha made a sympathetic sound.

"So now David's back with her. And I don't know what to do. She hasn't told him, I know that. And she never will, so he's about to go through the rest of his life believing that child is his. It's like she cheated on him to get him back. I hate her for it. I hate her so much that . . . that I'm not sure what to do anymore."

Jade blinked fast, her vision blurring again. She realized her fingernails were cutting painfully into her palms. With effort, she unclenched her hands.

Botha got up and stood behind her. "Breathe, Jade," he told her. "Just breathe."

She took a deep breath. It was shaky going in, better on the way out. Then it caught again as he touched her.

His hands cupped her upper arms, his fingers warm and strong. His thumbs sank into her shoulder muscles, forcing the tightness out of them. His fingertips pushed into the muscles on either side of her spine. She hadn't known how tense she was, how many knots he was releasing in her back. He was expert at this, with a healing touch.

It was what she needed.

"To be honest," he said after a minute, pinpointing a knot deep in her back and loosening it so skillfully that she nearly groaned with relief, "I've never been in a situation that screams, 'Get out' quite as loudly as yours is doing."

She laughed softly. "Thanks," she said sarcastically, then focused on her breathing again. Took the air in and out, slow and steady, and with every exhalation she felt a little of the resentment, the bitterness, the hatred leaving her.

"You can't fix this," he said. "You won't get him back, not from that situation. So you just have to walk away."

It felt cathartic to have somebody else tell her the truth she'd fought so desperately and for so long not to face. But now that she was confronting it, it didn't seem as ugly as she had feared. It was sad, it was inevitable, it was still unfair and hateful, but it was bearable. She found she had the strength to think about leaving David Patel forever, and to accept that reality.

"You're right," she conceded.

"You know what they say—some people come into your life for a reason, others for a season, and only a few for a lifetime."

"I suppose so," she said after a while.

His hands moved to her head. His fingers teased their way through her hair, and she let herself relax into them as he massaged her scalp, pressing gently into her temples and her forehead.

It was shocking that Carlos Botha was touching her in a way that showed more intuition of her body than David ever had. David had never done this to her. She thought there had always been an invisible barrier between them that he was too fearful to break through. Sure, they had made love in the past. Sometimes it had been good, other times great, but she'd never felt that David had attempted to know her completely. It was as if being with her was breaking one of his own rules, which forced him right back into a self-made prison of guilt.

She closed her eyes and abandoned herself to the blissful ministrations of this near-stranger while the comfort of his words washed over her, soothing away the jagged edges of loneliness that had wounded her for far too long.

She knew what she was doing was dangerous. Allowing Botha to touch her was heading down a road she shouldn't go. But right then, she couldn't find the willpower to tell him to stop.

It was only when his hands slipped under the collar of her top, warm fingertips stroking her skin, that she knew she couldn't let this continue.

"Thanks," she said. Her voice sounded husky, and she had to clear her throat.

His fingers trailed over her bare shoulders before he removed his hands and arranged her shirt back in place. "No problem," he said.

He sounded the same as he always did. He took the seat opposite hers on the couch and stared at her with a half-smile. "Going to be a long night," he added, and she nodded in agreement before realizing what he really meant. When she did, she felt her face grow warm.

She wrapped her jacket around herself, lay down and pretended to sleep. She hadn't thought she'd manage to relax in the circumstances, but before she knew it, she was blinking in the harsh overhead light, thinking that only an hour had passed when, in fact, morning had arrived.

Chapter Thirty-Five

BACK AT THE police station that evening, David saw that a small pile of reports from various passport control centers in South Africa had been placed on his desk while he was out. Everyone was working hard to try to locate Rashid Hamdan. What would really help David were fingerprints. Hamdan had been fingerprinted in the past, but though every person entering the country had to stand in front of a scanner that measured body temperature, South African passport control didn't take prints. The threat of Ebola coming into the country was taken far more seriously than that of terrorism.

Even so, in the past twelve hours, three individuals on flights arriving from Middle Eastern countries whose features vaguely resembled those of the man in the outdated photo had been detained and questioned. All were subsequently released and sent on their way. Passport control was trying their best, but they couldn't manufacture a Rashid Hamdan out of an entirely innocent Mufasa, a Persian carpet salesman; or Dangor, who imported hairdressing supplies; or Motan, who was visiting South Africa for the first time as the drummer of a rock band.

Hamdan could be traveling under any name, any nationality. His hair could be brown or blond or shaved completely. David needed more information. If the FBI's reliable source could find out why Hamdan was here, it would help him. Was he looking to buy or sell commodities? To launder money? A profit scheme?

At least their efforts had been recorded, and he could send these reports on to the commander and reassure him that he had been seen to be trying his best.

Putting the reports aside, he picked up the phone and called Naisha, gritting his teeth as he waited for her to answer.

Their relationship was uneasy at the moment, "uneasy" being a euphemism for "gone to shit." Not that Naisha would ever describe it in those terms. In fact, she'd had a discussion with him the other day about swearing within earshot of ten-year-old Kevin.

"I really don't think it's necessary to use profanity in front of our child," she'd snapped when he'd let out a heartfelt oath in front of the television after seeing that information from a sensitive case had been leaked to the media.

"I'm not using it in front of him. He's in his room," David had argued, already knowing he was on the losing side of this one. Hands laced over her swollen belly, feet up on a stool, Naisha was glaring at him.

"His room is just down the hall, and the door is open. This is a small house, David. You're supposed to be a role model, not somebody who curses like a sailor in the presence of their son."

"Naisha, I'm a police detective who's just seen a leak on television that has ruined a major corruption case. I think I'm justified in venting some frustration. If you knew the work stress I was under right now . . ." David attempted weakly, but she held up a manicured finger.

"I work for Home Affairs. In security, no less. You think I don't know about job stress? Do you have any idea what the pressure is like in my department? But I don't use that as an excuse to come home and use vile language around my child. Now please go to the kitchen and make me a cup of tea."

His temporary banishment had ended the discussion, if you could call it that.

Naisha. He knew she was expecting a baby and all, but he still found her behavior utterly unreasonable most of the time. She clearly wanted him in her life. She'd said as much when she'd broken the devastating news that she was pregnant. David had struggled to conceal not only shock but also bitter disappointment. Having tried his best to forget their one unwise night together during their separation, he'd been about to officially propose a divorce. Now, with a second child on the way, Naisha made it clear that was out of the question.

He couldn't do it. Couldn't leave her, knowing that he would be neglecting his fatherly duties. And he did love Naisha in his way. The problem was that he loved Jade in a totally different way. Was that why Naisha was so controlling, so peevish, so moody, so *nasty* toward him? Was it jealousy?

He was trying his best to be a good husband. He made dinner every Sunday night, even if it was only boiled eggs or peanut butter sandwiches. There was nothing wrong with peanut butter sandwiches, was there? They were very nice with apricot jelly, and surely healthier than his traditional staple as a single man had been: greasy chicken pies from the kiosk at the nearby gas station.

As part of his newly minted resolution to be a better partner, and so that she wouldn't start getting paranoid about where he was and what he was doing, he called Naisha daily to tell her what time he was going to be home.

Now he steeled himself for the moment his wife would pick up.

"Hello?"

"Naisha." Glancing at his watch, he realized with a start it was already after seven P.M. Where had the time gone? "Sorry

I'm only calling you now. I've been held up at work, and I'll probably be another hour or so."

"Again?" The accusation in her voice came through clearly. "Another late night?"

"A couple of new cases have come in, grown wings and flown straight to the top of the urgent pile."

Flown straight to the top of the urgent pile. He'd thought that was quite witty. He hadn't exactly anticipated a belly laugh, but he'd hoped the banter would lighten things up, break some of the tension that seemed to crackle down the line every time he and his wife spoke.

It didn't, of course.

Naisha sighed. "Whatever, David. Come home when you come home."

Maybe it hadn't been so funny after all.

"I'm tired, so I'll be in bed. Or at the hospital," she added.

David nearly dropped the phone.

"At the hospital?" he squawked, causing a passing detective to glance curiously into his office. "What's wrong? Are you okay?"

"I'm pregnant, in case you've forgotten."

"Is the baby on its way?" Suddenly his caseload didn't matter so much. Even Jade's predicament could wait.

"Not yet. But I've been having slight pains. You don't need to worry about it."

"Of course I do! Do you need to go to the hospital now? Naisha, listen, I'll be back in half an hour to drive you there."

"I know how busy you are." Her words speared him like shards of ice. "So I've made an alternate plan. My mother flew up from Durban this morning. I've set up a spare bed in Kevin's room for her. She'll stay for the next few weeks and help with the baby when it arrives."

"I . . ." David stopped himself. He had only one thing in common with his mother-in-law, Ada—they each loathed the other. And she was in his home for an indefinite period, without so much as a by-your-leave? The last time she'd stayed, her disapproving gaze had constantly followed him around, seemingly powered by its own gimlet-fueled force. And she loved hot curries, which meant vindaloo was on the menu for the foreseeable future, annihilating David's digestive system.

He reflexively glanced at his top drawer, remembering the packet of antacids he kept there, but he'd already used them all. He'd need to stop at a gas station shop on the way home and stock up. Hell, maybe while he was there, he could save his stomach and buy a couple of goddamn pies.

"Well, that's great," he managed to choke out. "I'm so glad you're going to be spending some time with your mother. It'll be . . . lovely to see Ada again." He closed his eyes briefly in anticipation of a thunderbolt from on high—the liars' punishment. "And you'll call me, won't you, if you think the baby's going to arrive?"

"Mm," she responded noncommittally.

"I'll see you later," he concluded.

He replaced the receiver quietly. Then he yelled, "Fuck it all." His words reverberated off the opposite wall, which was decorated with two dog-eared crime prevention posters and the latest staff memos.

The passing detective, coming the other way now, glanced in his door again. "Everything all right, Sup?" he asked.

"Fine," David snapped. He felt marginally better after screaming his anger out. Perhaps he could sit here every evening and yell profanities at the wall. It sure beat passing sambals around the dining room table with Ada.

He let out a deep sigh. Then he pulled the topmost case file toward him.

Where to start with the motel murder? There were so many possible angles.

There was the now-dead Mr. Loodts and his murky history at Inkomfe. There was Gillespie, who controlled security there, and there was Lisa Marais, the ex-employee turned environmental activist. All of these people deserved close scrutiny. But first he was going to focus on the person who worried him the most.

David didn't trust Carlos Botha. His gut told him there was more to the man.

And he was deeply uneasy that Jade was on the run with Botha. It could prove very dangerous for her, and David had a bad feeling that danger might not only be from the assassins pursuing them.

"Carlos Botha," he said aloud.

He didn't have much information on the man, but there was enough to look him up in the system, probe his background.

"Right," David said under his breath, turning to the flickering screen. "Mr. Botha. Let's see who you really are."

Chapter Thirty-Six

JADE AWOKE TO find the small office window bright with the first light of morning. Botha was nowhere in sight. How many hours of sleep did this man survive on? She felt cold, tired and stiff. She was in dire need of strong coffee, but she'd have to make do with a glass of water, and she thought there might be a dried fruit bar in her bag.

With a jolt, she realized that her bag was still in the car. She'd locked it, and the key was in the pocket of her jeans, but even so, the Mazda didn't have an alarm, and wasn't exactly a challenge to break into. She wasn't worried about anyone getting into this fortress from outside, but she *was* paranoid about Botha checking up on her.

Where was he?

Listening intently, she heard footsteps coming from the warehouse.

She padded quietly across the room and down the narrow corridor, then peered out the doorway.

Morning light flooded in through the warehouse's east-facing windows. The glass was opaque with dust; the light streaming in turned the smooth concrete flooring to gold.

Botha, dressed only in the spare pair of track sweatpants she'd bought him, was standing on the warehouse floor in the open space between the farthest rows of shelves, which was slightly larger than a boxing ring.

His pose was balanced, his arms held at chest height with muscles taut. The posture looked both natural and relaxed.

She watched his shoulders rise and fall, the only sign of movement. Then he exploded into action. Limbs became weapons, feinting and stabbing with the speed of a predator on attack. He never pulled a punch, seeming to have no reservations about hitting the edge of his capacity. He launched himself straight upward with one foot and punched the other into a vicious kick. The ball of the foot went into a perfect, brutal arc that would have connected with the jaw, or maybe the throat. Crushing the larynx, shattering jawbone.

She watched Carlos Botha transform from a reserved, self-contained security expert into a finely tuned killing machine.

This didn't look like classic karate to her—she had seen that practice before. Perhaps the key difference was discipline, because she suspected a karate sensei might frown at the amount of focused aggression driving this workout. It was as if Carlos Botha was unleashing a terrifying anger out on an invisible opponent, anger she hadn't known he possessed.

She watched for another fifteen minutes before the workout was over. He slowed, rested for a moment with his hands on his thighs. She could see his chest heaving, and the gleam of sunlight off his sweat-dampened forehead.

Quickly, so he wouldn't know she'd been checking up on him, she went back into the lounge. After a minute, she heard him approach. He headed straight for the small bathroom next to the office.

Jade hurried across the warehouse to the garage and opened the side door. There was the car. Still locked, safe and sound. But where was her bag? It wasn't on the backseat where she'd left it. Worst-case scenarios unfolded in her mind as she yanked the back door open, breathing a sigh of relief when she saw that it had fallen onto the carpet in front of the seat.

She lifted it out, but as she did so, a small plastic bag fell out of the side compartment, and tiny black objects scattered onto the garage floor.

Oh, hell. The gift that Shadrack had given her when she'd met up with him and Sbusiso yesterday, the seeds of the African potato plant. The real Inkomfe, Shadrack had said. She'd better clean them up before Botha noticed them.

She knelt down and carefully picked up the shiny seeds, placing them back in the bag. Maybe one day she would plant them in the garden of her rented cottage. It seemed a shame not to, since Shadrack had been kind enough to give them to her. She had a knack for killing anything she planted, though, so perhaps she could ask somebody else to do it for her.

A few of the seeds had rolled under the car. She was tempted to leave them there, since they were out of sight, but they were a gift. And it was better to be thorough.

She bent lower, groping in the blackness under the car but finding only dust. With a sigh, she sat up and pulled her cell phone out of her pocket. With its flashlight activated, she leaned down again.

And that was when she saw it.

Jade's breath caught. The few rogue seeds were forgotten; her attention was fixed on the white oval piece of plastic attached to the underside of the Mazda.

Completely out of sight until now.

With shaking fingers, she took hold of the object and wrenched it free. It came away reluctantly; it had been affixed with strong double-sided tape to the plastic belly pan just behind the front wheels.

"Oh, Christ," Jade whispered, staring down at the device. She knew it well—it was a model she had used herself in the past. It was a GPS tracking device. The plastic shell contained a SIM card and battery. It was waterproof, simple and reliable, and usually lasted about three days before needing to be recharged.

Suddenly everything that had happened in the past forty-eight hours made sense. Especially how their pursuers had managed to catch up with them whenever they had thought themselves to be safe, even if it had taken time, plus trial and error. The device was badly positioned—it would only have been able to pick up a sporadic signal under the car, but if you were a patient hunter, that was enough.

She had been leading the gunmen to Botha.

But when and where had this device been planted? Jade's thoughts raced as she replayed where she'd been since their escape from the motel, and who she'd seen.

She surely hadn't been followed to that disastrous meeting with Lorenzo, so it must have been done when she was with Gillespie. She should have been more careful, and realized their pursuers might have posted a lookout near Inkomfe. If they'd recognized her, then her attempts to disguise her car would have been futile.

That meant it was thanks to her complicity with Gillespie that the killers had been able to track Botha again. Last night, she and Botha had escaped with seconds to spare. It could so easily have turned deadly. And it had been her fault. All hers.

A soft footfall sounded behind her and Botha's voice cut into her confusion. "What are you doing?"

Jade's own body language betrayed her. She started at his sudden appearance, and as she spun around, her instinctive reaction was to hide the device from him.

She stopped herself, but it was too late. He saw instantly what she'd been trying to do. His surprised expression quickly hardened into an angry suspicion, which her stammered, "I—I was about to show this to you," did nothing to dispel.

Chapter Thirty-Seven

"GIVE THAT TO me," Botha ordered, pointing to the device.

Warily Jade handed it over. Although his voice gave nothing away, she sensed he was smoldering. She had no way of predicting what he'd do next. He was an unknown entity, and she was intensely aware of how little of himself he'd revealed.

What would she have done if she'd found out she'd been double-crossed this way? There'd been trust between them, fragile and short-lived. Now it was gone. If his anger erupted into violence, she'd have to try to fight him off, even though she didn't rate her chances against his training and raw, aggressive strength. What could she use? She had her bag and car keys. There was the pepper spray she'd taken from Scarlett Sykes's purse. If she could get to it or use her keys to do damage, then she would be able to sprint outside and head for the gate. Botha was wearing only his jeans, which must have been hastily pulled on, and he was barefoot. That surely meant she had a chance.

He was beside her lightning fast, his hand clamping over her wrist as fear boiled inside her. She could feel heat radiating from him. "No running away."

"I'm not running," Jade told him through gritted teeth. She stood frozen in his grasp, her mind racing, wondering if his tightly clenched fingers could feel the hammering of her pulse. This was a risk she should have considered more seriously. Of course he would figure out who she really was.

She had no plan for what to do if this happened. She hadn't discussed her whereabouts with anyone. Only one person in the world knew where she was right now, and that person had her trapped in a viselike grip.

She'd never thought she would want to see Robbie again, but at that moment she prayed he might walk into his abandoned garage.

Abruptly Botha let go of her arm just as she had begun to gasp in pain from his pincerlike grasp. He put the device down on the car roof, turned to the door leading to the warehouse and slammed it shut so hard it rattled in its frame. Using the side of his hand, he punched it with incredible force. If it had been plywood, it would have splintered. As it was, the metal door simply shook.

He was breathing hard, in time with her own breaths. He pinned her with his glare, poised to chase her if she ran.

"Okay. Okay. Let me explain!" she shouted.

"What is there to explain? You're working for somebody else. Who? Gillespie?"

"I am not." Jade couldn't afford to back down now. Her instincts were warning her not to show weakness; Carlos Botha was a key player in this case, and she was the only person who could find out anything about him, even if she was working on her own now. "I haven't been paid a cent by anyone except you, and I've been fighting just as hard as you to stay alive."

"Then what the hell is that?" Botha's finger stabbed in the direction of the device.

"It's a tracker."

"And you knew it was there?"

"I had no idea. I came to get my bag and dropped something. I only found it just now, when I was looking under the car. Damn it, Botha, if I'd wanted to tell anyone where you were, I could have just made a call. And if I was working with the people who are trying to kill us, then why would I have gotten us out at the Best Western? And at the Radisson in Sandton?"

There was a pause. With the main garage door closed, the room was quiet except for the ragged rhythm of their breathing.

"Who put it there?" He spoke through clenched teeth.

"I don't know," Jade said. She still felt dizzy from the shock of finding the tracker and realizing when it must have been planted.

"You're not telling the truth."

"I am."

"Tell me this, then. Where did you go the night we were at the Radisson?"

Jade stood very still, trying not to let her face betray the speed at which her mind was racing.

"You weren't in your room that night," Botha said. "I knocked. You didn't answer. I checked, and you weren't inside. I went down to the garage, and your car wasn't there. You didn't say anything about it the next day. Where were you?"

He was facing her directly, and even though he wasn't much taller than her, she found his physical presence over-powering. The channeled rage in his demeanor, the brute strength within his streamlined frame.

Jade grasped desperately for the right response, but nothing came to her. Silence filled the garage, thick as smoke, an unspoken admission of her guilt.

"You were asking questions at Lorenzo's today," Botha said, and Jade's stomach twisted with dread. "How did you even know about Lorenzo's? I didn't tell you, so who did?"

She couldn't meet his gaze, but stared narrow-eyed at the exit door beyond him, her only means of escape.

"Who hired you?" Botha asked her, his voice now dangerously soft. "Loodts? Gillespie? Someone else from Inkomfe? I've been expecting them to try to plant somebody close to me. I just hadn't thought it was you. But it's my job to pick up on these things, Jade. It's what I do."

She thought his job was security systems. Maybe she'd been wrong.

"Why would you be expecting someone from Inkomfe to track you?" Jade finally snapped, but Botha was not to be deflected.

"It's Gillespie, isn't it?"

She pressed her lips together.

"Isn't it?" Botha shouted, leaning toward her. His voice hammered her. His eyes were blazing, his fists tightly clenched, but Jade wouldn't give an inch. Drawing on the reserves of steel-hard toughness that she'd developed over years of working with the corrupt and the untruthful, with thieves and abusers and killers, she glared back at him. She met his anger with her own resistance, willing him to hit her, to see how far it got him.

She wouldn't give up a name, not even if he split her lip. She wouldn't give it up if he blackened her eye or broke her jaw. If he landed a blow, she would ride the pain and use her limited combat skills to fight back. As soon as she saw his hand move, she would knee him in the groin, hard, and then kick him in the face as he doubled over. And then . . .

"Jade," Botha said again, and her eyes widened at the unexpected gentleness in his voice. She saw that his tension had abated. His fists had unclenched, his eyes had relaxed. "Fighting with you is going to get me nowhere. I don't want to do it. I—hell. We barely escaped with our lives last night. I don't know what you were hired to do, but I do know I owe you big time. I need you on my side. But you might already have chosen a different side."

She hadn't prepared herself for this approach. His unexpected honesty disarmed her more effectively than a punch in the face could have done.

She took a deep breath, thinking of their survival, and for the first time ever, she made the decision to betray the identity of the person who'd hired her.

"Gillespie asked me to trace you," she said softly.

Chapter Thirty-Eight

JADE AND BOTHA stood facing each other in the small garage. It was suffocatingly warm, the morning sun blazing onto the corrugated iron that protected them from outside cell signals.

"Let's talk in the office," Botha said. "Can we bring that thing in without it broadcasting?"

Jade nodded. "The whole building is a dead zone."

They walked back into the office, which was blessedly cooler. She was still trembling from their earlier confrontation. She laced her fingers together so Botha wouldn't see.

"Gillespie hired you to find me?" Botha asked. He pulled on the gray shirt Jade had bought him and sat down at one end of the couch. She took the other.

"Yes."

"So you traced me. And then?"

"Gillespie wanted to know what you were doing. He said I had to talk to you if necessary to get information."

Botha nodded. "Did he tell you why?"

"There was a sabotage incident at Inkomfe early on Friday morning. He suspected Lisa might be involved, and she'd been the one who hired you before she left Inkomfe. You'd also gone AWOL from work. He couldn't reach you, so he wanted someone to check up on you."

Botha was watching her closely. "Why did he suspect Lisa?"

"He said she quit her job on bad terms and made an

unusual transition to environmental activism. I can't fault him for wanting to check on you. It's what people do. There *was* attempted sabotage at Inkomfe. And something is clearly going on. Loodts was murdered, you're being hunted and Gillespie was beaten up when he left work yesterday morning."

"Gillespie? Beaten up?"

Jade nodded. "He really was hurt. I met him at the Grand West Mall. I think somebody saw me arrive there, and planted the bug on the car to trace me back to you. When I asked Gillespie about what happened to him, he said he thought it was a warning."

To her surprise, Botha gave a humorless laugh. "I'm sure it was."

"For what?"

She hadn't expected Botha to tell her straight out, and he didn't. Instead, he answered her question with his own. "You said I was the only one who'd paid you. Is that true?"

"Yes, it is. Gillespie was supposed to pay me, but he hasn't so far."

"Gillespie has a habit of not paying people. Or shorting them."

"Why?" Jade asked, surprised.

"Because he spends all his money elsewhere," Botha said, with no warmth in his smile.

And then the blare of a horn came from outside.

"What the hell?" Botha asked.

They hurried to the large window, where they saw a red Subaru was parked outside the warehouse gate.

"Did they follow us?" Behind her, Botha's voice was sharp. "I thought that tracker didn't work here."

"It doesn't," she retorted. She was certain of it. And in any case, this wasn't the same type of car. Their pursuers had used big, heavy SUVs, and she hadn't recalled them honking the horn, either. They'd arrived in silence.

This low-slung sports car was different. The spoiler hadn't come standard. It was an add-on, something that the boys in the southern suburbs of Johannesburg liked to flaunt. As they watched, the horn blared again.

Decision time.

"I'm going out to talk to the driver," Jade said.

"No! You're crazy. Don't go out there; you'll be shot."

"Whoever's honking isn't here for me or for you. They're here for the owner of this place. They've seen the gate's padlocked from the inside, so they know somebody's here, and they're going to stay out there making noise until they get answers."

"How sure are you?"

"One hundred percent," she said confidently, although it was really about ninety.

"I'm coming with you." Botha reached for his shoes.

They were halfway across the parking lot when the door of the souped-up vehicle swung open. A tall, lean black man climbed out. His head was shaven, and it gleamed in the morning light. He wore a studded jacket, blue jeans and expensive-looking boots. "Hey," he called.

"Hey," Jade responded. She stopped by the gate. Botha stood half a pace behind her, his arms folded, looking every inch the tough, silent bodyguard.

"You open for business?"

She shook her head. It was an innocent enough question. But Robbie's businesses had never been innocent.

Sure enough, the man's next question was, "Robbie there?"

"No. I don't know where he is."

"Funny, 'cause I heard he was back in town."

Jade remembered her wish for him to appear just a few minutes earlier and suppressed a laugh. But this was bad news for her; Robbie never brought good things with him.

She shook her head in response.

"Who are you?" the man asked. There was a hint of a threat in the question. She wondered if he would have been more aggressive without Botha there—it was probably the silent, muscular presence behind her that commanded this stranger's respect.

"I came here to get something."

"You got a key?" His voice was sharp.

"Security let me in," she lied.

"Never seen security here before," the man said.

Jade shrugged.

"I want a cell number," the guy said. "For Robbie, I mean."

"The one I have won't help you. He told me it was getting disconnected," Jade said.

"I don't care. An old number's better than no number."

Jade took her phone out of her jeans pocket and read him the last number she had for Robbie.

He punched it into his phone. Without speaking to her again, he got into his car and roared off. She noticed that he was already making a call.

"We've got an hour, maybe," she told Botha when they were back in the garage. "That guy's going to be back with his friends."

"Who is he?"

"One of many people Robbie's screwed over."

"Screwed over how?"

Jade shrugged. "Robbie never specialized in doing business honestly."

Botha nodded. "We need to get going, then. But I'd like

to make you a counteroffer to Gillespie's, Jade. Work only for me. No more running, just fighting back. Your job—our job—is to find those hit men. Have them arrested, whatever. I want to be able to sleep at night, and I'm sure you do, too."

Jade stared at Botha, wishing she could be sure of his intentions. "The tracking device could be useful to draw them in," she said eventually.

Botha picked it up and examined it closely. "You said it's not accurate? That the signal comes and goes?"

"In my experience, yes."

"We could help it along a bit." With his fingertip, he loosened the SIM card. "Now it's disconnected. Signal is gone. Damn this unreliable GPS." When he glanced up, she was surprised to see wicked humor in his expression. He eased the card back into its slot once more. "And there you are. Signal's back again. Now all we need is a plan."

"Coffee to help you brainstorm?" she asked jokingly.

"I think I'll pass. Never tasted such disgusting coffee," Botha said.

Disgusting coffee . . .

"Of course!" Jade laughed out loud, causing Botha to stare at her in surprise.

"What's up?" he asked.

"I think I've worked something out," she told him.

She picked up the coffee tin and carried it to the sink. She upended it there, letting the thousands of granules stream out into the stainless-steel bowl until it was empty and only a trace of acrid dust floated up.

She looked inside the can.

Stuck to the bottom with a piece of duct tape was a long, narrow key.

She peeled the tape away. The shaft of the key felt cold

and sticky to her touch. She grinned in triumph. Robbie and his warped sense of humor. Had he known she'd find it? Or had he been laughing at the thought that she never would?

She slotted the key into the safe's keyhole and swung the heavy door open.

Inside was the gun.

Not her first choice of firearm. It wouldn't even have been her second choice. It was a large, heavy Desert Eagle in a leather holster. This weighed three times what her Glock 19 had. But it sure as hell would have stopping power.

The gun smelled faintly of oil. The magazine was full: eight bullets. She had no idea how accurate the gun's aim was. She was unfamiliar with this weapon. But she had eight chances to get to know it better.

Jade relocked the safe and taped the key back in the bottom of the coffee tin. Then she scooped a few giant handfuls of grounds out of the sink and dumped them back in the container. She replaced the lid, turned on the tap and let the remainder wash away. "I want to do one more thing before we go," she said.

"What's that?" Botha asked.

"Come into the warehouse, and I'll show you."

Gun in hand, Jade walked the length of the warehouse past the hydraulic lifts and the pits; the oil smell was stronger here. Past the rows of shelves. She could see Botha's footprints in the dust. Two sets there and back. In the center of the floor, on the far side, was the trodden evidence of his workout. The large circle of footprints had stamped the dust away, allowing the industrial gray floor paint to gleam.

She stood in the middle of the circle and turned her back to the window. She raised the barrel and focused on the office wall. The gun was heavy; it felt unwieldy and awkward in her grasp. The serial numbers had been filed off. No proof of this weapon's history, or where Robbie had obtained it, or how long it had spent in the safe. Jade didn't want to know. For now, she was lucky to have something usable.

The back wall was about twenty paces away. Botha had already drawn a large X on the bricks and stood near it.

She only had eight bullets, but she'd rather waste a couple now than have a misfire or a wide shot when her life depended on it.

The middle of the X was at about his chest height. Center mass. With a gun like this, heavy and powerful, that would be the most sensible place to aim. A head shot would be too risky.

Jade exhaled. She didn't give herself much time to aim, because it wasn't likely that she would have any in an emergency. She simply squeezed the trigger and felt the weapon kick, slamming painfully back into the heel of her hand as the noise of the explosion filled the warehouse.

Dust billowed out where the bullet hit the wall, and fragments of brick tumbled to the floor. When they cleared, she saw the shot was a few inches too high. She'd overcompensated for the gun's heaviness.

"One more," she yelled, hoping Botha could hear her, because she couldn't hear herself over the ringing in her ears. He waved, indicating understanding, and she fired again.

This time she was more familiar with its weight, even though nothing could help with the vicious, bone-bruising recoil. When the dust had cleared and she'd picked up the shells, she followed Botha's footprints back across the warehouse floor.

The second bullet had hit a half-inch from the intersection of the lines in the X.

At that range, this was more than good enough. She'd familiarized herself with its action. And the experiment had taught her that the gun was reliable.

As if Robbie would have kept a faulty or damaged weapon in his possession. There would never be a reason to doubt him on that score. Guns weren't toys or status symbols to him. They were tools that served to do a job.

"That was very good shooting," Botha said. "Exceptional, in fact."

"Thanks," she told him.

"You practice often?"

"Every week or two, usually. Unfortunately, my gun was confiscated a few months ago. It was registered," she added hurriedly, seeing his sidelong glance. "There was a quibble about documentation. Now police red tape is delaying its return."

"Why do you shoot so often?" He sounded genuinely interested.

"Because I choose to carry a weapon," Jade told him. "I need to have it with the line of work I'm in. My father was a police detective who taught me to shoot. He always told me that if I owned a gun, it was my responsibility to make sure I was skilled at using it."

"Sounds like sensible advice," Botha agreed. "But what did your mother think?"

"I never knew my mother. She died when I was very young. But based on what I know of her, I think she would have approved of that decision."

She wasn't about to tell Botha any more. She hadn't told anyone that she kept a photo of her mother in the cottage and looked at it every day. And when she did, she always wondered how the gentle-looking woman smiling into the camera had spent part of her life working as a contract killer.

Who had she murdered, and why? What had driven her to do it? Jade would never know. These secrets were hidden somewhere behind her mother's serene features and sparkling green eyes. But she had passed at least one of her traits on to Jade, a talent that had proved to be a blessing and a curse. The ability to kill.

She thought about that as she holstered the gun.

Killing in self-defense was something most people could do if their lives were threatened, especially if they were trained in handling a firearm. Killing in cold blood was another matter. Even if you knew the man you were aiming the weapon at was a murderer himself, an evil psychopath who deserved to die, many couldn't pull that trigger.

And there were only a few who could sight and aim with a steady hand, fire calmly and send a bullet straight into the bastard's brain.

THEY WALKED BACK to the office. There wasn't much to pack, but she wanted to leave the place as tidy as they had found it.

"Tell me about your parents," Jade said to Botha as she plumped up the couch cushions. He had found a broom in the bathroom and was sweeping the floor.

"You don't want to know," he said. He smiled, but there wasn't much humor in it.

"Well, now that you've put it like that, I *really* want to know," Jade said, and saw his expression warm slightly.

"I never really knew my dad. He was a career soldier—a mercenary. Spent most of his life out of the country. When I was twelve, he got into a fight with a civilian, ended up killing the guy and went to prison, where he died a year later. Another fight, I believe. My mother took on various jobs to try and keep us afloat, including working as an escort at one stage. She wasn't home much. Not that home was a great place to be."

"I can imagine," Jade said.

"She remarried when I was fourteen. I think it was to one of her clients, although she never said. He wasn't a nice guy. I left home at sixteen and hardly saw her after that, which I'll always regret, because a year or so later, they got into an accident on a drive down to Durban for the holidays. He was speeding, lost control, collided with a tree. They were both killed instantly."

"I'm sorry," Jade said softly.

Botha shrugged. "You make decisions, you live with them. I decided I was never going to be like either of them. Not like my dad, not like my stepfather. I got myself an education. I practiced martial arts. I like the discipline. The calmness of it, I suppose you could say. Focused energy."

"I saw you this morning," Jade said.

"Like you, I believe in continuously sharpening one's skills," Botha said. "Especially since it takes years of hard work to achieve them in the first place."

Jade put the mug back on the shelf and hung the dishcloth on the hook where she'd found it. Botha shouldered his laptop bag. It was time to go.

Before they reached the door, he turned to her and said, "May I?"

She blinked in surprise as he took her hands in his own. She felt his fingers brushing over the ridges of callus on her palm and the heel of her hand. Hundreds of hours of practice at the shooting range had formed them, and they had been there for years. Even a couple of months away from the range hadn't been able to rid her skin of the thickened scars it carried, the protection it had developed to cushion the repetitive kick of her firearm.

"That's a lot of shooting," he observed. "No wonder you're so accurate."

Jade nodded.

"You can feel the difference between the left and right," he said. "But your left is slightly callused, too."

"I shoot with it sometimes," Jade told him. "If one hand is injured or I can't use it for some reason, I need to be able to shoot with the other. So I do a session with my left hand every so often. I'm not nearly as accurate, but I'm working on it."

"Ambidexterity's hard to achieve."

"Yes, it is."

Botha let go of her hands, and Jade took one last look into the office before closing up.

There was something creepy that had settled over the room, not because it had been abandoned, but because it was as if it was waiting. In limbo. A leather-furnished hideaway that would remain untouched until its owner's return. Robbie might walk in, turn on the kettle and make himself a cup of that abysmal coffee, then slouch down onto the couch—and just like that, the place would have its heart back again.

Or perhaps not.

Maybe Robbie was dead. Maybe the place would wait forever.

Chapter Thirty-Nine

DAVID PACED HIS office. Back and forth, back and forth. He gripped his cell phone in his fist, wishing he could use it as a weapon to break through the distance and the silence that existed between him and Jade. Simply making a call on it was futile. His attempts had rung straight through to her voice mail.

Carlos Botha.

His background alone would have aroused David's suspicion. A broken home, a troubled childhood. A highly intelligent renegade who'd turned his back on society's norms and chosen a different, more dangerous path.

Wait a minute. This sounded awfully familiar. Was it Botha he was researching, or Jade?

Stop it, David told himself.

Jade was not the spider who'd spun this complex web of deception. But she could well end up being the fly caught in it.

The sheets of paper, the online links, the information David had obtained by calling in favors from contacts who owed him, assisted by two of his sergeants, represented a full twelve hours of work. Hours he should have been spending on cases that were bigger priorities. Instead, he had single-mindedly, obsessively hunted down every available scrap of information on this man. David's fourth cup of coffee in as many hours stood forgotten on his desk as he collated the facts.

Botha had begun his career in intelligence, working for two private military organizations. Read: mercenary groups. Groups that specialized in brutal killing for money in godforsaken places, even though they liked to justify their actions by claiming they kept the peace.

Botha had then gone back to civilian life, becoming a security systems specialist, but as David well knew, a leopard couldn't easily change its spots. He interviewed one of Botha's ex-employers, who said that Botha had been hired by the company's former director just before she had resigned, and that certain major software had been stolen from the company while Botha was working there—software for a blueprint that was about to be patented. Botha had left straight afterward, and the previous director had secured the patent for the lucrative blueprint.

The man stammered as he told the story, and reading between the lines, David guessed that the previous director had, in fact, written most of the software before being forced out of her job. But even so, it was company property, and Botha had stolen it. The fact it was a Robin Hood–type of maneuver didn't make it right. It was clear that Botha was prepared to take money in exchange for breaking the law.

Like somebody else you know? the little voice in David's head asked.

David ordered the voice to shut up.

To cover all angles, he had requested the case file on the sabotage at Inkomfe, and now he was going to call in another favor.

He had obtained Botha's cell phone number and was hoping to view a list of the recent calls he had made.

This information was kept confidential by the service

providers, and a subpoena usually had to be issued before the records could be made available. But David had a contact who worked for Botha's cell phone provider. His name was Fanie. He was an ex-police reservist who now worked in data management and had access to all his company's online systems and call information. He understood the pressure of police work and the fact that obtaining a subpoena took time, and was generally willing to bend a few rules in order to help out. Of course, if these phone records were found to contain important information and David needed to use them in a case, he would request them again through the official channels.

"How are things going?" David asked when Fanie answered his call.

"Work's slow," Fanie replied. His voice was muffled. David suspected he usually went to the restroom for privacy during their calls, but he'd never been bold enough to ask. He'd heard running water once or twice, and other sounds, too. Maybe he went outside and stood near a fountain.

Maybe not.

"You mean the systems are behaving?"

"Of course. I've been managing them for seventeen months now. And I'm telling you, I'm on fire. I'm the reason you and everyone else in the country are still making calls."

"My connection dropped twice yesterday."

"There was a faulty tower. You know, like the old Monty Python comedy series? 'Fawlty Towers'? That's what happens here, all the fuckin' time. Comedy of errors."

There it was, that trickling sound in the background. "Why was it faulty?"

"Ask my predecessor. He used to watch online porn at

work instead of fixing stuff. Bypassed the firewalls to do it. He was hopeless at maintenance, but man, was he a genius at hacking."

David heard a toilet flush in the background. He was sure of it. "Left to go and work for Eskom, did he?" David asked, and Fanie snorted.

"So anyway," Fanie continued, "send me the number you need. I'll get the info to you."

They said goodbye and disconnected.

Checking his watch, David saw it was time to leave for his meeting with Loodts's personal assistant, Tina Strauss. Strauss had worked for Loodts for fifteen years, so David was hopeful she had useful information.

They met up at Strauss's home in Centurion. Her apartment was well-kept, with a wide view of the lake. She looked to be in her forties, with neatly styled platinum hair and an immaculate French manicure.

"I am very shaken by Mr. Loodts's death," Strauss explained. "We became good friends over the years. I hope I can help you, Detective, although my life is somewhat in chaos at the moment."

She showed him into the neat dining room. Not so much as a teaspoon was out of place. At the table, her laptop stood open, a work planner beside it, and a full jug of freshly squeezed orange juice off to the side. If this was chaos, David wondered what order looked like.

He sat down and gratefully accepted a glass of orange juice with ice and a sprig of mint. "I'm sorry if any of the questions I'm about to ask are upsetting to you," he began, and Strauss tightened her lips.

"I'll do whatever I can to help," she promised.

"Firstly, the crime scene. You might have read that Mr.

Loodts's body was found along with the body of a young blonde woman."

Strauss gave a tiny nod. "I did read that, yes."

"Her name was Scarlett Sykes. Do you know if Mr. Loodts had any personal or business association with her?"

"No, he did not. Not to my knowledge, not at all. He never mentioned that name, and I never saw any correspondence from her, or put through any phone calls."

David wrote a note on his pad. It looked as if Jade's hunch was right, and Scarlett had been working with the criminals. He guessed that having a young blonde woman on the team must certainly have opened doors. Loodts surely hadn't suspected her. He moved on to the next subject: Carlos Botha.

"What is your impression of Mr. Carlos Botha?" David asked.

"I don't know him very well," Strauss admitted. "He's a difficult man to assess. Quiet, always polite, but I always got the impression there was a lot he thought but didn't say. I'm an Afrikaans speaker, but I think the English expression would be *self-contained*."

"Yes, I think I know what you mean," David said.

"He's very fit. Good-looking," Strauss observed, with a slight smile. Thinking of Jade on the run with Botha, those words made David want to fling his glass at the spotless, cream-colored wall and watch it shatter onto the tasteful white tiles below.

He resisted the urge with a concentrated effort.

"Their interactions," he asked, getting back on track, "how often did they meet or speak that you knew of? Was there any conflict between them? I'm especially interested in the last month or two."

"In the last month or two, they met more often," Strauss

said. "I also overheard . . ." Her voice trailed off, and she looked embarrassed.

"Any information will be extremely valuable right now," David encouraged her.

"I overheard Mr. Loodts having a huge argument with Mr. Botha. That would have been, oh, maybe three weeks ago. I have no idea what it was about. It wasn't uncommon for them to argue, but this was worse than usual. I actually left my office and came back when Mr. Botha had gone."

Another note went on the lined page, and David moved onto his third topic. "What was Mr. Loodts's relationship with Ryan Gillespie?"

Strauss pursed her pink-lipsticked mouth. "Mr. Loodts has known Mr. Gillespie for a long time. Mr. Gillespie's father used to be in charge at Inkomfe years ago, when it was still called Mamba. I know that Mr. Loodts trusted Mr. Gillespie because of that existing family connection."

"Now," David said, moving on to the nitty-gritty of the meeting, "I was given a folder found in Mr. Loodts's briefcase at the crime scene. It was labeled 'Inkomfe Classified Information: Minutes, Meetings & Memos.' Do you know anything about this folder, or what it might have contained?"

"Mr. Loodts always printed out the latest minutes and meeting agendas. His eyesight made it difficult for him to read on a laptop screen. He had a meeting at Inkomfe that very morning with Mr. Gillespie."

"Just the two of them?"

Strauss nodded. "They had private meetings every month to discuss top-level issues, and at those meetings they changed the door codes for the strong room and one of the entrances into the reactor room. They were the only two who were authorized to open those particular doors."

David couldn't believe what he was hearing. For a moment, he was unable to breathe. "So you're saying Mr. Loodts had hard copies of the access codes in his possession?"

Strauss nodded apologetically. "He usually locked them in a briefcase after the meeting, then stored them in the safe at his home. He believed that hard copies were safer than sending information online."

"The briefcase was unlocked when we found his body. And there were no papers inside."

David had no desire to mention to Strauss that Loodts had in all likelihood been tortured before his death. The motive for that was becoming clearer.

"Please," Strauss implored, "you must notify Mr. Gillespie about this immediately. It is essential that he knows so that he can take steps. If those codes were to fall into the wrong hands, it would lay Inkomfe wide open to the threat of sabotage."

David's head was spinning as he drove back to headquarters.

It was possible that Loodts had been tortured to give up the codes and had directed his killer, or killers, to open the briefcase and take the pages where they were written.

David needed to speak to Gillespie right away.

But to his surprise, when he got back to Jo'burg Central police station, he was told that he had a visitor.

Ryan Gillespie was in the reception area, waiting for him.

He was surprised to see Gillespie, and impressed by his physical presence—tall, broad-shouldered, good-looking and well-dressed. However, Gillespie's handsome mouth was swollen and scabbed on the left side, and he was hiding a recently blackened eye under a pair of sunglasses, which he removed when he was inside the office.

"Thank you so much for everything you've been doing,"

Gillespie said. Even lopsided, his smile was warm and genuine. "I thought it might be helpful if I met with you to answer any questions and give you some background."

"You have a very serious situation here," David told him as they sat down on opposite sides of the small, rickety meeting table. "The security codes for your doors have fallen into the wrong hands."

Quickly he updated Gillespie. "This points to an insider job. Somebody knew that Loodts had come from that meeting, and that he had that information with him."

Frown lines appeared on Gillespie's brow.

"This is extremely worrying," he said. "Superintendent, I think this crisis has its roots in problems that go back a long way."

"Tell me," David said.

"I'll give you a brief history. When I first joined Inkomfe, I was impressed by Lisa Marais, who was head of security at the time. But as we worked together, I was forced to revise my opinions."

"Why's that?"

"She was extremely stubborn. She had no concept of how to handle people, and she clashed frequently with her colleagues. The more responsibility I took on, the more aggressive she became toward me. She started working against me. It became destructive. It delayed the rollout of the new systems."

"Go on," David encouraged him.

Gillespie laced his fingers together. David noticed that they were trembling slightly. "She conducted a personal smear campaign against me . . . a character assassination, I suppose you could call it. She compiled a dossier of information that could have been very damaging if it was taken out of context. Luckily, Mr. Loodts had worked with my father, and he was prepared to give me the benefit of the doubt. Lisa became angry, and she resigned."

"What was in the dossier?" David asked curiously.

"It's embarrassing to have to admit." Gillespie looked down at his clasped fingers. "She followed me during non-working hours. She took photographs of me doing what I do to relax."

David wondered what that was. Prostitutes? Bondage? Worse? He was expecting a lurid confession and found himself slightly disappointed when Gillespie said, "I enjoy going to casinos in my off time. I think Lisa assumed that would damage my reputation in Mr. Loodts's eyes, because he wasn't in favor of gambling. But luckily, her attempt was unsuccessful."

David nodded.

"It was humiliating nonetheless to have my private life dragged up like that, and I think Lisa was furious when her attempt didn't work. Unfortunately, it backfired. It discredited her in the eyes of everyone who knew her."

"Go on."

"I thought that nobody would take her seriously after that, but I was wrong. I should have checked more carefully on whom she was speaking to before she left. I didn't realize that she had been meeting with Botha outside of work. He must have believed her stories and bought into whatever she was planning."

"Oh, really?" David felt his pulse accelerate.

"I don't know whose idea this sabotage could have been. Lisa was a rational woman. But note, Detective, that I say 'was.'"

"What do you mean?" David felt his guts plummet into

his shoes. It was a sick feeling that had everything to do with Jade.

"I have tried," Gillespie said softly. "Believe me, in the past few days, I have tried very hard to get in touch with her. She was a difficult person, but even when we fought, even after she resigned, she would answer her phone, even if she ended up slamming it down after swearing at me. I went to her house this morning and saw it was burned down. Detective, I fear the worst has happened."

"What do you think happened to Lisa?" David's mouth had gone dry.

"I think she got in over her head, and in her quest for revenge, she became involved with people whose goal is to destroy Inkomfe."

"Who?" David asked through cold lips, but Gillespie shrugged.

"It must be somebody who wants to make a point by causing a catastrophe and endangering the lives of thousands of innocents. They are going to get rid of whoever they need to along the way. And I am sick with worry that I won't be in time to stop them."

Chapter Forty

WARRANT OFFICER MWELI had seen enough dead bodies in the past week to last her a lifetime. What the hell was happening in this quiet suburb of Randfontein? Corpses were turning up in the most unexpected and unwanted places. And this latest looked to be the most macabre of the lot.

Finally the dredging operation was underway. She was standing at the edge of a large body of water in a fenced-off area of Randfontein that was sandwiched between two gold mines—one still operational, the other now closed.

The Robinson Dam was a polluted place, full of acidic mine water. This was a problem that had been plaguing Johannesburg in recent times and had not yet been properly addressed. After speaking to an expert, Mweli had learned that it was caused by contaminated water from abandoned mines that was no longer being properly managed and treated, leaching into the wider environment. Normal water had a pH of seven. Acidic mine water could be anywhere from three on the scale to as low as minus three. Mweli hadn't known you could have negative pH values, but apparently, given sufficient contamination, you could.

This dam was not one of those, though. Its pH was somewhere between one and two. The expert had told her about the few organisms that could survive in such a lethally acidic environment. Extremophiles, he'd called them. Enjoying the rotten-smelling water, living happily in and around its slime-coated surface.

Nothing else could survive. The dam was dead—a toxic body of water awaiting a treatment that it had not received.

And now, in its depths, there was a dead body.

She shifted from foot to foot, breathing in the unpleasant stink of the polluted water and watching as the backhoe hauled up a massive bundle of detritus, cradled in the giant shovel bucket that had scraped the dam's base. As the machine hummed and cranked and hissed, gouts of mud splashed down from its edges, further disturbing the discolored surface.

Then the winch operator guided its thick metal arm back toward the land, and downward until it rested on the dam wall. Liquid mud dripped from the arm and gushed out of the vents in the steel cradle.

Was there anything in there? It was impossible to tell amid the rotted remains of what had once been vegetation, the stagnant water and the dark, slimy mud. Mweli already had her protective boots on, but even wearing them, she was reluctant to go closer. She didn't want to tread in that stuff. Foot covers or no, she had the feeling that once she touched that stinking residue, the stench would never leave her.

"Let's do this," the pathologist standing next to her said, picking up his equipment bag. He was fully suited up in protective gear, including goggles and a white face mask. "Just don't expect to get this guy a name anytime soon, okay?"

Mweli frowned, not understanding. She followed him cautiously along the dam wall, nervous of slipping and landing butt-first. Carefully she maneuvered her weight over the uneven ground.

By the time she neared the metal bucket, the pathologist had already begun his work. He was laying a sheet of plastic all around the base. Then, using a small spade, he gently dug at the bucket's corrupted contents.

Standing a safe distance away, Mweli stared at what the man had uncovered and felt her stomach do a slow, uneasy spiral. She swallowed hard, tasting acid in the back of her throat, aware that the Wimpy breakfast she'd had two hours ago—a light meal of just one egg, a slice of bacon and toast—was threatening to make a hasty reappearance.

She supposed this expert with his knowledge of acidic mine water had been ready for what he saw. Mweli hadn't been.

The body was all but rotted to slime.

There were no facial features to speak of; they had been eaten away. The eyes were empty sockets. Teeth, pitted and eroded into stubs, stood out in a mirthless, mud-stained grin.

It was impossible to tell where decayed flesh ended and corroded rags of clothing began—if, indeed, the corpse had been clothed at all. Only the occasional bone surfaced in response to the pathologist's careful probing.

The bright sunlight above them made the sight appear all the more gruesome. It seemed to mock these half-eaten bones, dragged from their corrosive resting place.

"We're not going to get much," the pathologist said, sounding apologetic. "I'll extract what I can from here; we can't take these contents back to the lab." He gestured at the brimming bucket. "I'll put the bones together as best I can, but you're not going to get an ID from this. I might be able to tell you a gender. Depends on what condition the pelvic bones are in—oh, and we do have a clump of hair. Caucasian hair, from the looks of things. I'll try to measure it. Beyond that . . ." He pressed his lips together. "I could probably estimate height to within a few inches. Problem is that the corpse doesn't have feet left, or ankles. From the knees down, it's gone, and I can't find hands, either. We can dredge again . . ." He shrugged. "Looks like the feet must have been tied to weights to prevent the corpse surfacing, so they're down there somewhere. Far down in the slime."

Height to within a few inches. Mweli shook her head. She realized sweat was streaming from her forehead. She was breathing hard, swallowing frequently. Her armpits were soaked, and the sun was making her dizzy.

Hurriedly she turned away from the water, which was still pocked by tiny ripples. She gazed out over the grassy, treed overgrowth beyond.

They wouldn't be able to identify this corpse from this dredge alone. Despite the pathologist's expertise, the dam had done its work, and those damaged bones might keep their secrets forever.

But she was a detective, and she would find another way.

There was a witness who said he'd seen a car; he showed them where he thought it had parked. He described what he'd seen in the half-darkness, how the body had been lifted out of the car and carried swiftly to the bank of the dam.

The killer had driven here, gotten the body out. It had clearly been premeditated.

What had he been thinking? Mweli decided to go with *he* as the killer, because that had been the witness's impression, and also because lifting a dead body required a fair amount of raw physical strength. More likely a man, then.

He'd been confident. Practiced. He had clearly thought this through—dumping a corpse in wastewater so acidic the body would quickly become unidentifiable.

Driving a car into a fenced area and carrying the body up to the dam wall was a brazen act. It indicated a certain amount of arrogance, perhaps even hubris.

Pride could sometimes be a man's downfall.

Had he been careless? Left just one tiny clue behind?

"Phiri!" Mweli called, and despite her nausea, she was surprised by how strong her voice came out. "Bring the team here. We're going to comb this area flat. Search it until we find some evidence. I don't care how long we spend on this. I'm not leaving without something." She spread her hands as if to encompass the whole of this large, treed area. "Anything that can tell us who this killer was."

Walking away from the beslimed dredging apparatus, Mweli slipped and angled her way down the steep bank, stopping to pick up a pair of gloves and an evidence bag before heading for the grassy field beyond.

She started with the car tracks, planning to trace them to the place where the vehicle had stopped. Lifting a body from a car would not have been an easy thing to do. It would have required pulling, fumbling, maneuvering. Perhaps one of the victim's possessions had fallen out, unnoticed, in the darkness.

First prize would be finding a driver's license, although even Mweli acknowledged that was somewhat optimistic.

She felt better now that she was breathing in fresh air. In front of her was nature, a vista of grasses and stunted karee trees. Relatively unspoiled, give or take the occasional discarded chocolate wrapper and cool drink can near the trodden pedestrian path that wound its way from the gap in the eastern fence to the gap in the western fence a ten-minute walk away.

She followed the tire tracks carefully, imagining the car driving through here in the darkness. It must have been a high-riding vehicle, an SUV or a truck. The ground was uneven, and there were small rocks and other hazards hidden in the grass that could easily have damaged a lower-slung car. She stumbled over a termite mound as she walked. It was ankle-high, camouflaged by the greenery.

Glancing up, she saw Phiri and another detective combing the stretch of grass between where the body had been dumped and the area the car had been parked.

Something flashed in the sunlight, but bending to check, she found it was only a shiny candy wrapper. She straightened up with some difficulty. Her legs were already beginning to ache from scrambling through this rough terrain. She was going to have to get back into shape. Really, she should be walking this distance daily, from the eastern fence to the western one and back again. Doing that was something to think about—a goal to set for next year, perhaps.

Or even next week?

And then Mweli's head shot up as she heard Phiri shout and saw him wave his arms. The young detective was standing near the edge of the trees

Pointing down at the grass, he called. "Come quick!"

Mweli's legs forgot their tiredness as she broke into a run.

Chapter Forty-One

AS SHE AND Botha drove away from the warehouse, Jade felt lighter. Perhaps it was that she had a gun now, which gave her a fairer chance of fighting back. Or perhaps it was that she knew they couldn't be tracked any longer. The device sat on the dashboard, its SIM card dislodged. The sun was high in the sky, it was a beautiful day, and Jo'burg was a huge city with thousands of cars on its roads. The odds of their hunters finding them by chance? They'd have better success looking for a specific grain of sand at the beach.

"Are you hungry?" Botha asked.

"Starving," Jade said.

"Do you think there's time amidst all this running for our life to stop somewhere for a quick breakfast?"

"I'm sure there is."

They found a diner near the Turffontein racecourse. It looked like a greasy spoon, which suited Jade, because right then she was hungry enough to scarf down every fried dish on the menu and call for more. And it was busy. There were some gray-haired men clustered around a table together, speaking earnestly in Portuguese accents, and a couple of short, fit-looking jockeys in jodhpurs and riding boots sitting outside. They were drinking black coffee and eating plain scrambled eggs without toast, and as she passed them, she heard one of them complaining bitterly to the other about his love life.

"You're twice the man her ex is," she heard the other jockey reassure his friend, and Jade suppressed a smile.

She and Botha sat at a corner table inside. They ordered large coffees and three-egg omelets with cheese and tomato and mushroom and green pepper, plus a double helping of toast and butter on the side.

"Are you a vegetarian?" Jade asked him curiously.

"Nope." He shook his head. "I eat meat. Just not often. And you?"

"I'm the same," she said.

She watched the street, enjoying the sight of the traffic passing by, the Mazda safely parked in the courtyard behind the eatery. Looking at the sheet glass, she saw the faint reflection of herself and Botha.

A bystander might think the two of them were a couple: sitting close together, talking in low voices. But a bystander would be wrong. Impressions could deceive.

The Desert Eagle was too big and unwieldy to be carried concealed on her hip, so Jade had moved the holster under her shirt, strapping it around the small of her back. With a jacket covering it and her bag slung over her shoulder, nobody would guess she was toting a weapon that measured nearly eleven inches in length from the tip of its muzzle to the back of its well-worn grip. And if it meant she had to keep immaculate posture while she sat waiting for her food—well, that was a small price to pay.

"How are we going to get rid of these guys?" Botha asked.

If Jade had been sitting with Robbie, she knew how they would have strategized, and it would have involved the gun. They would have conspired to take out the boss. That was all that would be needed. He would be the interface with the client. Remove him, and the others could run for the hills and forget they were ever brought on board.

But she wasn't sitting with Robbie. And she couldn't very well tell Botha about the darker side of her past.

"There are several ways we could do it," she said. "But I think we should start with the simplest option."

"What's that?"

"We hand the device over to my police detective," she said, noting Botha's wry smile. "The car, too, if he needs it. Let him set up a sting operation somewhere suitable. He can arrest the gunmen, and we won't have to worry about anything."

After some thought, Botha nodded. "That sounds sensible," he said.

"If David's too busy, then we can make Plan B and Plan C. All we'll need is a quiet location to draw them in."

Botha nodded, his face grim.

David sounded stressed when Jade got hold of him and explained the situation.

"What the hell?" he asked the moment she'd finished talking. "Who put that tracking device under your car? And when?"

"I think it was done yesterday morning when I met Gillespie at the mall near Inkomfe," she said. "I have no idea who did it, though."

There was a short silence. "So what do you want?"

"If it's activated, it will draw in the hit men in and allow you to arrest them. Would you have a chance to put an operation together today? It's urgent, because the battery life is limited. I know it's very short notice. If not, don't worry. I can always—"

"No!" David shouted. "You cannot always. I don't even want to know what you were about to say. I'll handle this today with my team. If we draw in the suspects, we'll make arrests, and hopefully one of them will turn state witness so we can figure out who hired them. Until then, I want you and Botha somewhere safe." He paused. "Come to the police station. I'm not there right now, but I'm going to ask my captain to book you into a residential hotel nearby—one I know is secure. You can brief him, and he'll drive you through to the Faircity Mapungubwe Hotel, where you are both to stay for your own safety until I give you permission to leave, which will be tomorrow at the earliest. Promise me you'll listen to me on this."

"Yes, David," Jade replied meekly.

But her fingers were crossed behind her back as she said it, just in case.

Chapter Forty-Two

ON HEARING PHIRI'S shout, Mweli broke into a run, stamping through the overgrowth, clutching at her pockets to prevent her belongings and loose change from spilling out and tainting any evidence in the grass. Behind her, the backhoe clanked and rattled as the operator turned the machine away from the stinking dam.

"What've you got?" she shouted. She dropped back to a walk as she approached. She was wheezing—dear God, was she unfit. Things had to change. Starting tomorrow, she decided, she was joining a gym. "What . . . do . . . you have . . . there?" she repeated.

Phiri was bent over, bagging the evidence carefully. He straightened up and turned to Mweli. "I've got this," he said.

In the plastic bag was an ordinary-looking key. A plain metal door key on a small, round key ring. "Is that all?" Mweli asked. "There's nothing else near it?" The disappointment hit. All this cardiovascular exertion, and for what? Just to stare down at some nameless, untraceable piece of metal?

Looking at the faint tracks and drawing an invisible line from where the body had been found back to the taped-off area where the car had parked, Mweli was certain that this had been dropped on the way to the dam. Either by the man carrying the body, or else fallen from one of the pockets of the corpse.

But an unmarked key like this? They could do nothing with it.

"You didn't find a wallet or anything?" she asked.

"We don't need to, ma'am." Was there a note of exasperation in Phiri's voice? "Here," he said to the sergeant holding the bag. "Turn it over. Look at the other side."

Mweli stared down, her eyes widening.

Now she saw what Phiri was so cheerful about. The other side of the metal disk had been engraved, and now she realized that the disk itself looked familiar.

In tiny, worn letters, the logo read, *Best Western*. And there was a number under it. *19*.

The motel again? Her mind racing, Mweli ran through the ways her two murder cases could possibly be connected. She wondered if her legs could survive another sprint through the long grass—this time, in the direction of her truck.

SHE HADN'T THOUGHT she'd be driving through the Best Western's entrance again so soon. She had made the journey in record time and power-walked her way into the reception area. Holy hell, it was dark in here. Even without load shedding, the place seemed to be a few lightbulbs short, and as the big-haired receptionist slowly scooted her chair away from her computer game with a resigned expression, Mweli uncharitably decided this applied to the staff as well as the surroundings.

"Good day, ma'am." The receptionist's teased style was so frizzy she looked like she'd lost an argument with a power socket. "What can I do for you now?"

"This key," Mweli said, holding out the bag. "We found it at another crime scene."

She waited for the receptionist's puzzled frown to indicate this news had sunk in. "Oh. So you're returning it?"

Resisting the urge to roll her eyes, Mweli explained, "No.

It's police evidence now. What I need to know is who was staying in that room at the time."

"Mr. Carlos Botha," the receptionist said, frowning down at the bookings calendar, and Mweli's heart jumped into her mouth. "But he damaged the lock when he left, so that key isn't usable anymore."

Mweli's excitement ebbed as she remembered whom she was dealing with. "No, no. Not the most recent guest. This would have been a week or two ago."

"Oh," the receptionist said. Light dawned—for her at least, if not in the gloomy room. "Yes, the previous guest never returned her key."

"Who was she?"

"Lisa Marais."

Mweli felt her heart quicken. "Do you know why she was here?"

She hadn't expected any usable information, but to her amazement, the receptionist said, "Her house burned down, and she wanted somewhere out of the way to stay. She was concerned about being followed. She was quite paranoid, actually. She wanted a room at the back of the motel so her car would be out of sight. She said she was going to be here for a few days, but I only saw her the one time when she came to the front desk to post a package, and I think she only stayed two nights. She was quite rude. She complained about the lack of Wi-Fi in the rooms. Maybe she was just stressed out, but you know, guests forget that we're people, too." She gave a martyred sigh.

"Do you have any details on the package?"

"She wanted it sent Speed Services, so I wrote everything down in the book, and she paid with a credit card. I can look it up if you'd like."

If you'd like?

"I would appreciate that," Mweli said, drawing on hitherto undiscovered reserves of patience.

The receptionist took a dog-eared book out of a drawer and paged through it slowly. "Here it is," she said. "It weighed a hundred and fifty grams, so it went in the lightest bag, and it cost sixty-five rand."

"Who did it go to?"

"I unfortunately don't write that information down. Only the sender and the amount."

"And you say you never saw Lisa after that?"

The receptionist's brow furrowed as she considered the question. "No," she said eventually. "No, I never saw her again."

Chapter Forty-Three

BACK IN THE car after breakfast, Jade and Botha drove into town before exiting the highway and zigzagging through the streets of Newtown—freshly paved, with clean, bright sidewalks, street art and newly renovated buildings—before plunging into the crowded inner city.

Aware of the possibility of smash-and-grab crime, Jade opened her window an inch. Having the window open would make it more difficult for the glass to shatter if it was hit by a brick or a spark plug. Under stress, things could break more easily, which Jade supposed was true for humans as well.

The inner city of Jo'burg had been through more than a life's worth of changes in the last thirty years. Originally, its city center had been crammed into one of the only non-gold-bearing areas. A cramped high-rise business district, surrounded by mines. From the start, the Central Business Distict had been characterized by overcrowding and traffic jams that had grown worse over the years. It was no surprise that businesses eventually began to move out of town and into the new office developments that were springing up in the suburbs.

Today fewer formal businesses remained, but there was no less energy in the streets. It had just changed in character, as Jo'burg's poorer classes had claimed the city center for their own.

With her window open a crack, sounds and smells filtered in. The throbbing beat of R&B music from a hair salon with

a hand-painted sign above the door. The aroma of food cooking, rich and spicy, from the hawkers' stands that lined the
roads. Shrieks of laughter from a group of brightly dressed
women as they bustled their way across the tarmac carrying
clear plastic bags crammed with clothing. The whiff of rot
from a rusty garbage bin that stood on the street corner, followed by a breeze of fragrance from a kiosk selling soaps and
bath products.

When they arrived at Jo'burg Central police station, one
of David's captains was waiting for them in the parking lot.
Jade and Botha climbed out of the Mazda, and Jade showed the
detective the tracking device and explained how to reinsert
the SIM card so that it would start receiving a signal again.

"Please try not to get any bullet holes in the car," she said
as they left the Mazda in the basement parking and climbed
into the detective's unmarked. "It's a rental."

"We'll try our best," the detective replied gravely.

It took less than five minutes to drive to the hotel, and
Jade was impressed when the captain showed them into the
chic, African-themed lobby of the four-star establishment.

"Who's paying for this?" Botha asked Jade in a low voice as
the captain conversed with the receptionist.

"I imagine David will end up paying, if his department
doesn't have budget," Jade said, wishing that he wasn't so
stubborn when it came to her safety.

Botha wasn't prepared to go along with that.

"I'll pay," he insisted, stepping forward. "We can't burden
the police with it. What do you have available? Is the penthouse suitable for two people?"

The answer to that was yes, and after signing them in,
the porter showed Jade and Botha up to the luxury suite
on the top floor.

The spacious living area contained a dining room table, a lounge and a fully equipped kitchen. There were two doors on the right-hand side that Jade supposed led to en-suite bedrooms, and at the far end of the lounge was a large window.

Walking over to it, Jade saw western Jo'burg spread out beneath her; no other high-rises nearby were so tall. She gazed down over flat roofs, onto the bustling streets far below. The clustered city thinned out into treed suburbia that stretched to the horizon, giving her a faraway view.

She sat down at the dining room table, looking out over the breathtaking vista, and Botha poured them some water from the bar fridge. Jade felt as if she'd been whisked away on an unexpected vacation. She told herself she needed to be careful, because they were not out of danger yet, nor was David. With your head up in the clouds, it was easy to forget about those laying snares at your feet.

"You never finished telling me about Gillespie," Jade said.

"What do you want to know?" Botha handed her the glass.

"You said he makes a habit of not paying people, that he spends the money. On what? And how do you know?"

Botha nodded. "To explain, I'm going to have to give you more background."

"Okay."

"Lisa was in charge of security at Inkomfe when Gillespie blazed in like a comet, apparently. His father had a history with the place and had been a trusted employee, plus Gillespie had overseas experience. He was charming and capable and he had vision. But Lisa hated Gillespie's guts and believed he was useless. Now Lisa was a dedicated manager, and her work was her life. She had zero people skills; she was tall and skinny and gray-haired, a real sergeant major of a woman, but there was never a time when she didn't put Inkomfe first.

Her conflict with Gillespie turned into a personal vendetta, and in the process she lost all credibility. Before she left, Lisa sourced and hired me. It was one of the last decisions she made as a manager. She said I needed to be on-site to make up for Gillespie's incompetence, and because she wanted a reliable pair of eyes and ears there."

"How did you feel about coming into that situation?"

Botha shrugged. "It's what I do, Jade. I assess setups like that and compile evidence on individuals who aren't doing their jobs and aren't working in the company's best interests. That's what Lisa briefed me to do when she sourced me. I've also done industrial espionage assignments for IT companies as well as stealing intellectual property back for people who've been screwed over and forced to leave. I suppose Lisa felt that Inkomfe's security was her intellectual property and that Gillespie had stolen it."

"What did you find?"

"I found a whole lot of evidence of mismanagement. Systems were being changed to make them more vulnerable. Employees were becoming disempowered. I compiled a dossier of what was wrong as well as an urgent list of recommendations of what needed to be done to make Inkomfe safer and get the security back to standard."

"Then what happened?"

"Lisa had left by then, but she was continuing to investigate Gillespie's personal life. We were staying in touch and speaking frequently. She contacted me one night, told me she'd gotten something on Gillespie. Something big. The information she had discovered wouldn't just hurt Gillespie, it would destroy him."

"So you met up?"

"We met the following night at Grand West Casino. She

called at about eight. I was leaving work and went straight there."

"What did she show you?"

Botha let out a long breath. "She gave me a big pair of sunglasses, and we snuck into the *salon privé*. Gillespie was sitting at one of the high-stakes blackjack tables."

"Oh," Jade said. Her interactions with Gillespie were suddenly making sense.

"He'd been there for four hours, she said, and he would stay for the night, like he always did. So I said, 'Okay, let's see if he does.' We sat outside the casino and ordered a couple of drinks. We stayed there until four thirty A.M. From time to time, I went in to check, and he was still there, at one table or another. Blackjack, roulette, craps. And while we drank, Lisa told me what else she'd found."

"What was that?"

"She said she'd researched his family history. Gillespie Senior had become an alcoholic who drank a bottle of vodka a day. I knew he'd died years ago, but I hadn't known the circumstances. Lisa told me he'd crashed on the way home one night. Wrapped his Mercedes around a tree."

Jade tilted her water glass, watching the condensation trickle down. A compulsive gambler whose father had been an addict. She should have guessed from Gillespie's delays, his meeting points near casinos, his excessive use of gambling terminology. But the man had indeed been charming and had hidden his problem well. Like most serious addicts, he was an accomplished liar who knew how to put just the right spin on his fabrications.

"It all made perfect sense. Gillespie's constant absences and lateness. The times he hadn't had cash on him for emergencies and had to borrow from us. And other things, too.

One of the last projects that Lisa worked on before she left was a clock-in system based on biometrics. Gillespie delayed its implementation and prioritized something else. Then he exempted management from it. That way, nobody knew that most of the time, instead of driving around the center and checking perimeter fences, he was at Grand West or Silverstar or Montecasino."

"Did Gillespie know Lisa was following him?"

"She said she was being careful, but that he might have seen her once or twice. She didn't care, she said. She had left Inkomfe. What could he do?"

"What indeed," Jade agreed cynically as she thought of Lisa's house, torched to the ground, and Lisa herself, who had been missing since then.

"She said there was more information coming. Facts about his previous job in the Middle East. He'd gotten himself into very big trouble there. Lisa had done some research and called a few contacts. She said she'd get it to me when it was ready. And I asked her for something else."

"What?"

"I asked her to find out where Gillespie's money was coming from. Management salaries are good, don't get me wrong, but Gillespie was playing for enormous stakes, and any gambler is bound to lose more than they win; that's how the house advantage works. My feeling was that he'd gotten himself deeply into debt. That his financial situation was becoming a crisis."

"And did you tell Loodts?"

"I took all the evidence of Gillespie's incompetency to him and presented it at a meeting three weeks ago. I told him Lisa and I had researched the situation and found the facts. But he wouldn't hear a word against Gillespie."

Jade raised her eyebrows as Botha set his glass down on the table hard and repeated, "Not a single word. He said that I was to keep out of this, and that he would investigate it his own way, in his own time. I could see that he didn't believe me; he thought Lisa had influenced me and that the accusations were fabricated. After logical argument and then shouting didn't work, I stormed out of his office. He yelled after me that I'd just put the nails in the coffin of my career."

"And then the attempted sabotage took place?"

"Yes. After that, Loodts agreed to meet me again. I think he realized that he'd been wrong. But our meeting never took place, because he was murdered before I could speak to him."

Jade nodded, but inside she felt sick when she remembered Loodts's body in the bloodied motel room, and David telling her there had been signs of torture.

The situation at Inkomfe had reached the boiling point. A meltdown was approaching. Somebody had set these events in motion. Someone with a strong enough motive to take down a company, even commit murder.

Ambition, greed, desperation or revenge. She wondered which had been the driving force, and for whom.

Chapter Forty-Four

IT WAS THREE thirty P.M. when Mweli left the police station after updating her case notes. Finally, she had the chance to follow the directions Abigail Sykes had given her the night before. She wanted to check out the place Scarlett Sykes had stayed with her boyfriend, now her suspected murderer. Mweli had intended to take another officer with her for backup, but after the dredging operation, nobody was available. Phiri and one of the other detectives had been called to the scene of an attempted robbery, her sergeant was stuck in traffic outside Pretoria High Court and the two constables had to man the office.

So she went on her own. Taking a quick drive past couldn't hurt. She wouldn't do anything risky and would only go in to ask questions if she deemed it safe. She made sure that Phiri knew where she was going before she left.

Finally, before she walked out, she checked that her service pistol was fully loaded and holstered it on her hip, noting to her surprise that she was able to pull the belt buckle one hole tighter than she had the time before. It must have been the activity of the past few days, she decided, combined with all the clean living in the form of meat-free meals. At any rate, it was incentivizing her to take another step toward health. Maybe one day every week where she cut out the Coke and drank only water? Soda-Free Sunday? She'd have to strategize later.

Mweli put the directions on the passenger seat, fastened

her seat belt and headed off, hoping that she'd be there and back before the afternoon traffic became too heavy. She had a lot more work to do before her day was over.

With her attention focused on the map and the road ahead, she didn't notice the big black SUV that eased its way into the line of cars behind her as she headed onto the main road. Although she glanced into her rearview mirror regularly, she didn't spot it. The driver was careful to stay a few cars behind, to camouflage himself behind bigger trucks, and to change lanes frequently to stay out of her line of vision.

As she drove, Mweli puzzled over the case. It made sense that Scarlett Sykes was working with the criminals. Perhaps that was why Loodts's life had ended in that motel room. Even the most suspicious person would tend to be trusting of a young blonde in need of help. She could imagine how it might have gone down.

"*Mr. Loodts? I have important information about the sabotage . . . I think my boyfriend was involved in it. I've taken some photos of what I saw, and recorded a phone call I heard. Who's my boyfriend? I'm scared—I'd rather tell you face-to-face. Yes, of course we can meet urgently. I live in Randfontein. No, I'm scared to give anyone my home address. Can you check into the Best Western motel? It's close by, and safe. We can meet there, and I'll show you what I have.*"

Using her as bait, the criminals could very easily have overpowered him.

And then her usefulness had ended—or more likely, she'd made a mistake and become a liability. Crashing the car into the motel's signpost was enough, Mweli supposed. It had attracted attention far earlier than the murder would have done otherwise. And it explained why the tow truck driver and the wrecked car had been so difficult to trace. He hadn't been a real tow truck driver, and had simply moved the vehicle somewhere it wouldn't be found.

Here she was. This was the point where Abigail's map began. Now she needed to start focusing carefully. She was prepared to take a few wrong turns along the way, because Abigail would have made her journey at night, frightened and stressed. In the daytime, things looked different. You saw side roads that could easily be missed in the dark, and distances seemed shorter in sunlight. But even so, the map was pretty clear. It was definitely somewhere in this run-down industrial suburb.

When the driver of the black SUV saw where Mweli was headed, he pulled over and made a quick phone call. He asked a question and received instructions. The instructions were very clear. There was no room for doubt in what he was being told to do. When he disconnected, he accelerated, catching up with the detective, this time not caring if she saw his grille close and threatening in her mirror.

Mweli glanced down at her map again. She was in the right area for sure, but she'd turned too early. This road led to a cul-de-sac. She'd have to go back. Slowing down, she glanced in her mirror and drew in her breath sharply as she saw the idiot who'd nearly rear-ended her. Well, she needed to turn around anyway. Let him pass; she would pull over.

It was only as the car accelerated past her before swerving to block her way that Mweli realized with a sickening lurch of her stomach that he could be going nowhere because there was nothing ahead except a concrete crash barrier.

And now the door was opening, and there he was, gun in hand, a Kevlar vest strapped over his black shirt. With cold fingers she fumbled for her service pistol, wishing that she'd spent more time on the shooting range in recent months because it felt awkward, its grip almost slipping out of her damp palm. She opened the window and shouted, "Police! Put your weapon down!" Her voice sounded squeaky with stress, and of course he didn't obey. A shot split the air, and Mweli jumped so hard her head nearly hit the roof as a star-shaped crack appeared in the windscreen and the bullet thudded into the passenger seat. Another shot split the air above her head as she ducked down.

Before she knew it, she was firing back, leaning out of the window, supporting the gun with her left hand as she aimed with her right, muscle memory flooding back and lending her arms a steadiness she hadn't expected.

When you are threatened, you shoot to kill.

Bullets pumped out of her pistol. One, two, three, four. The man dove for cover, but staggered, clutching his thigh, as he reached the safety of his car door. He tried to fire again, but the shot went wide, and her next one hit him in the neck. He stumbled and fell. Mweli climbed out of the car on cotton-wool legs. He was still holding the gun, and she didn't trust him. At the same time, she found she couldn't shoot again.

"Put your weapon down!" she cried.

But the man didn't put it down. His fingers remained curled around it even when he succumbed to his injuries and collapsed, his forehead thumping onto the pitted tarmac.

"Dead . . . he's dead. Oh, my God, he's dead." Mweli climbed into her car again and collapsed on the seat. One of the criminals . . . she'd killed him. It was the first time she'd fired her weapon at an attacker, and she could only pray it would be the last. She was shaking all over, so badly that she stalled the car twice as she reversed away from the SUV and drove back down the road, parking at the intersection with her hazard lights on while she got on the radio and made her calls.

When the paramedics arrived fifteen minutes later, they had to prize the gun out of the man's tightly clenched fingers before declaring him officially deceased at the scene.

Chapter Forty-Five

Working with his task team, it took David just two hours to formulate their sting operation. He felt more motivated than he'd been in a long time. He was thrilled—amped—that he could strike a blow against organized crime while saving Jade from danger. This assignment, code-named Operation Zebra because they were currently on a wildlife theme, meant far more to him than he would ever admit. It was a deeply personal endeavor.

He needed to make sure that he didn't allow his emotional involvement to cloud his judgment or lead to any errors. This had to go like clockwork, start to finish. He wanted it to appear in police textbooks one day as an example of how to do things right.

His preparations were interrupted by two important phone calls.

The first was from a still-breathless Officer Mweli. She had been investigating the premises where Scarlett Sykes's boyfriend had operated. While approaching the warehouse, she had been ambushed by an armed criminal who had fired shots at her. Returning fire, Mweli had killed the criminal. In the car, which had been reported stolen a few days earlier, Mweli had discovered another firearm as well as a pack of commercial explosives in the trunk. It was possible that these explosives were the same type that had been used to blow up Botha's Porsche.

"Excellent news!" David had shouted over the phone. "Well done."

"He didn't have any ID on him," Mweli said, "but we're running his prints through the system as a priority. Hopefully this is one of the gang who was involved in the incident at the Best Western."

One less for him and his team to worry about later. David felt triumph surge inside him, briefly overcoming the nervousness that clawed at his stomach whenever he thought about the sting operation ahead.

After finishing his conversation with Mweli, he turned back to his planning meeting, for which he'd printed out a map of the area they were going to use and drawn a diagram on a whiteboard.

"Thembi, you're going to be in charge of coordinating the backup vehicles. We need two plainclothes detectives per vehicle. Two vehicles following us, a third waiting at the rendezvous point. We have no idea what their strategy will be, but so far the modus operandi seems to be aggressive pursuit during hours of darkness. We will put the plan into action after nightfall, but in order to give the team better visibility, the garage we draw them into will be lit. Even though it will be dark out on the roads, the criminals will be looking for two people in the car, a man and a woman. So we'll give them those two. I'll drive, and I'm going to ask you to sit beside me, Alberts, wearing a wig."

Smiles all around followed that announcement.

"To add an element of surprise, we will—"

David's phone started ringing again. He snatched it up, hoping that the interruption would be brief.

"Is that Superintendent Patel?" the caller asked. She sounded young, breathless and excited.

"Speaking," David said.

"I'm Yasmin Pillay from the Sandton Sun Hotel. I work

at the reception desk. This might be wrong, but we were all shown an email yesterday from Organized Crime, telling us to be on the lookout for a suspected terrorist sympathizer."

The Rashid Hamdan case. "Yes?" David said, scooting his chair over to the desk and picking his pen up eagerly.

"Well, I think I saw him here. I checked with one of the porters, and he also took a look and said it could definitely be the same person, except his hair was longer and brown, not black."

"When was this?" David pushed the pen into the paper, leaving an inky stain. "What room is he checked into?"

"He's not checked in. He was here for a conference today. I saw him when he arrived, and a red flag kind of popped up. After the conference he went for lunch, so the porter and I went to the restaurant and walked past to get a better look. I wanted to take a photo on my cell phone to show you, but I was worried they might see. He was quite alert. You know, he saw me looking, so I got scared and went back to the desk. I think he's gone now. The lady who organized the conference and luncheon just left."

"Okay. You've done a great job. I'll send someone from our team through to speak to you personally. In the meantime, I need all the details for the woman who arranged this conference."

"Sure. I'll give them to you in a sec. Just hold on."

The minutes he spent on hold seemed endless to David.

Eventually Yasmin came back on the line. "Here we go. Her name is Mrs. Baloyi, and she is the CEO of a company called Gold City Gaming. I've got all her details here. Company address, cell phone number and the confirmation of the bookings."

David scribbled the details down, thanked Yasmin and

replaced the receiver, his mind speeding through the next steps.

"I've got an urgent lead on an FBI case that I need to follow up on immediately," he told his team. "You can start on the preparations we've discussed so far, and we'll finalize the planning for the operation as soon as I'm back in the office."

Chapter Forty-Six

MRS. GRACE BALOYI, CEO of Gold City Gaming, was a large woman in every sense of the word. She stood six feet tall in her gold Louboutins. The shiny black wig she wore added volume to her head, and her black-and-white checked Chanel jacket showed off her massive bosom as well as the breadth of her shoulders. Her voice could have cut glass, and seemingly had no down button on the volume control, but her most impressive feature at that point in time was her anger.

"You are oppressing me, Detective," she roared, resplendent in her rage, the sound filling her spacious Fourways office and reverberating off the walls. She hadn't yet offered him a seat. They were standing in between her huge, glass-topped desk and the mahogany conference table, which had six comfortable-looking chairs.

"We have had a tip-off that the guest you met today at the Sandton Sun may have been the terrorist sympathizer Rashid Hamdan, who is wanted by the FBI," David explained. "Gold City Gaming booked out a small conference room. You were present for an hour in the morning before leaving your guest and his four colleagues there for another two hours."

Baloyi was already shaking her head, although her shiny wig hardly moved.

"Then you joined your guest for lunch on the outdoor patio with two other representatives from Gold City Gaming. I have the booking numbers as well as the names of hotel staff who are prepared to testify about your guest's resemblance to Mr. Hamdan."

"Uh-uh. I don't know anybody of that name." She clasped her hands decisively. David noticed the nails were perfectly manicured in stripes of blue, white and gold.

"He wouldn't have been traveling under his own name. He has a number of passports in different names. He's approximately fifty years old, with brown eyes, about five foot eight in height."

"The overseas guest I had lunch with earlier today did not resemble your description. He was not five foot eight in height!"

"Was he taller or shorter?"

"Yes," Baloyi shot back in a defiant tone.

David sighed. "This is a criminal investigation, and if you purposely obstruct it, you could be charged with defeating the ends of justice."

"Detective Patel!" Baloyi drew herself up to her full height, her lips quivering with fury. "I am a businesswoman who has run Gold City Gaming successfully for four years now. I have a stellar reputation in the industry. We employ a total of two hundred and fifty workers, ninety-five of whom are women and one hundred and eighty of which were previously unskilled. My husband, you may or may not know, is a member of our South African cabinet! He is the Deputy Minister of Small Business Development."

David had known. That fact had given him a headache even before he'd met her. "That's not the point," he insisted. "This isn't about Gold City Gaming, it's about international terrorism."

"I do not do business with terrorists. I do business with companies. I was awarded a tender in October to supply sixty slot machines for Suhail Services, a registered and legitimate company based in the Middle East. These slots have been shipped out of our warehouse and are going to be airfreighted to Iraq."

"Is gambling legal in Iraq?" David asked, surprised, but his question backfired.

"Are you implying that I conduct illegal business deals?" Baloyi flared. "Maybe you should educate yourself better before you come here making unfounded accusations. Yes, gambling is legal in Egypt, Israel, Lebanon and Iraq. Suhail Services has casino operations in Egypt, Lebanon and Iraq. The slot machines are being shipped straight to Iraq. This was an important international tender, and I have spoken with many of the company representatives over the past month."

"What was the name of the representative you met with today?"

"Like I said, there were a few of them."

"The man you had lunch with. You must know his name."

"I am unwilling to disclose it to you. He was here to do business, Detective. Not to cause terrorism. We cannot treat our business visitors like criminals, or they will go and do their deals elsewhere."

David took a deep breath. "I'm going to be forced to arrest you and take you in for formal questioning if you cannot answer me now."

"His name was Peter Smit." Baloyi glowered at him.

He didn't think she was lying, but neither was the information very helpful. It was a common name. Well, that made sense. No point in getting a fake passport made in the name of Ignatius Quisenberry. The whole point was to blend in. And Hamdan might have other passports with him—it was likely he'd have backup plans, especially since he'd met up with a business associate in a public place. Even so, David would put the word out to Passport Control. "Where was he staying?"

"Detective, I have no idea. I was not told what hotel he was booked into, or what transport he used or even what date he arrived. I did not organize this trip! He came here as a courtesy to meet me and to supervise the transit of the gaming machines, which are being air-freighted to Iraq early tomorrow morning from O.R. Tambo Airport. They are already loaded up. All the paperwork is in order."

"Where's he staying tonight?"

Mrs. Baloyi checked her watch, which was silver, studded with Swarovski crystals. "Unfortunately, Mr. Smit has already departed the country. He left our lunch table at two P.M. and went straight to the Gautrain to catch his flight. He told me it was leaving at four thirty P.M. I see the time now is four forty-five. You are fifteen minutes too late."

"You'll receive a subpoena regardless," David snapped, turning away irritably.

"The ANC Women's League will hear of this!" she called after him. "Our police service is working against the country's interests. You are enslaving our entrepreneurs with petty laws and bureaucracy. You are disempowering honest businesses with your talk of terrorists. Trade and commerce are our life-blood, Detective."

Her voice followed him through the glass double doors and into the beautifully marbled reception area. He thought he could still hear her outraged cries echoing in his ears even after he'd climbed into his car.

Chapter Forty-Seven

ENSCONCED IN LUXURY at the hotel that was their safe house, Jade and Botha had nothing to do except wait. David would only be able to start the operation after dark. It was a magnificent afternoon, and the suite's western aspect allowed an incredible view of the sun setting among crimson-lined cumulus clouds.

Jade couldn't enjoy it. She paced the gleaming tiled floor impatiently, wishing she could focus on something and settle down. It was all out of her hands now. Waiting had never been one of her strengths.

Botha, on the other hand, appeared as calm as usual as he sat at the table, typing away on his laptop as if nobody's lives were at stake. Occasionally he glanced up and spent a few moments staring thoughtfully at the red-and-gold splendor beyond the window.

When it was dark, he said to Jade, "Come on. I'm taking you to dinner."

"Dinner?" Jade looked at him blankly. Despite the fact she hadn't eaten since breakfast, food wasn't very high on her list of priorities right then.

"There's a restaurant downstairs. I have a rule in life: When you can't do anything in a situation, worrying won't help. Getting on with things is the best way. Come on."

"Okay," Jade agreed. "Give me fifteen minutes."

She showered quickly, blow-dried her hair and threw on a pair of black jeans and a silver-gray short-sleeved top. Botha was right. The preparations had given her something to do and took her mind off worrying. She locked her gun in the safe, and by the time she stepped out of her bedroom, she already felt better.

"So tell me. Your connection with Robbie, that gangster whose place we used? Were you close?" Botha asked her as they headed down the carpeted corridor toward the elevators.

"Working relationship only," Jade said.

Botha nodded. "So you have a working relationship with a gangster who screws people over and specializes in assassinations."

"Had," Jade corrected him. "We haven't been in touch for years."

The doors opened, and they stepped inside.

"And you're trying to date a police detective." Now the corners of his mouth were curving up.

"Was trying. It's in the past. Like I told you, David ended it."

She spoke in a low voice. In this small space, they were so close she could feel his breath on her cheek.

"You're beautiful," Botha said unexpectedly, and Jade's head snapped around as she stared at him in surprise. "Beautiful, intelligent . . . and a ton of trouble. I'm debating whether David made a smart decision, or he's the dumbest guy I've ever heard of."

Jade scowled. "Probably a smart decision," she muttered, and Botha laughed softly.

"I'm teasing you, Jade."

"Oh." She tried to retain her frown but found it dissolving. She looked down, hiding her smile behind a curtain of hair, but his fingers smoothed it back, pushing it away from her face.

Then the doors slid open, and they walked out, heading

for the double doors opposite, where Jade could hear the clinking of cutlery and smell the rich aroma of cooking meat.

Botha ordered a Meerlust Rubicon, a legendary red wine that Jade had heard of but never tasted. They clinked glasses and toasted to David's success. The wine was rich and smooth, and it went some way toward dissolving the tight knots in her stomach. She put her phone on the white tablecloth, next to the leather-covered menu. She scanned the food options, wishing she was hungrier and wondering what David and his team were doing right then. A successful operation meant they would all be out of danger. She didn't want to think about what the alternative meant.

David called at eight thirty, just as their main courses arrived. She snatched the phone up. "What's happening?" she asked. She couldn't relax until she'd heard his voice in reply.

"We got them," he said. His voice sounded tight with tension, even as she let out a huge breath of relief. "Successful operation. There were two of them. Both armed. They followed us to the rendezvous point, and we drew them in. Only problem was that they started shooting, so we were forced to return fire. One was killed immediately, and the other's been taken to the ICU with two bullets in the head and the chest. The paramedics didn't rate his chances and said if he survives, the head injury would mean brain damage for sure. So we couldn't question them."

"That's a shame," Jade said. It was frustrating to think that they would never know who had hired the men or why. "But at least that's two of them out of circulation."

"Three," David corrected her. "Mweli went to investigate the place where Scarlett Sykes stayed with her boyfriend. She was ambushed along the way by a third man and managed to shoot him dead. There's enough evidence to link him to the motel murders, which means we have sufficient proof that Scarlett Sykes was working with the criminals. So now they're all dead."

"Right," Jade said. Two plus one equaled three, and they had never seen more than three men after them.

It was paranoid of her to suspect there might be a fourth. A mastermind, lurking in the shadows.

"It's been a hectic day," David said. She could tell the stress of the shooting had made him talkative. Her food forgotten, she was glad to provide an ear as he continued, "I can't believe we managed to organize this with so much else happening. We had a tip-off about a suspected terrorist sympathizer who's managed to infiltrate the country."

"A terrorist sympathizer?" Jade asked.

"Name of Rashid Hamdan, but he goes under various other passports. He was hiding out in the Emirates before he came here. Someone saw him at the Sandton Sun and tipped us off. It turns out he was here to do business with Gold City Gaming, and I've just had a lovely discussion with their outraged female CEO."

Jade laughed. "I'm sure she was helpful."

"Absolutely. Very cooperative. She didn't accuse the police at all of trying to interfere in the deal she did with him, selling slot machines to his casino in Iraq."

"Oh, dear. Not still in the country, is he?"

"It seems we're too late, because he's already flown out, and his cargo's packed and ready for air freight. So the upside is that Hamdan was here doing legitimate business and not planning any terrorist activity. The downside is that we lost him. He slipped away, which I'm sure the FBI will be delighted to hear."

"I guess that means some paperwork for you?"

"Yes. Back to the office for me. With the Hamdan case and the operation we've just done, it might even be an all-nighter from here."

"Well, good luck. I'm glad you're okay. Drive safely, hey?"

"I will do." He paused. "I'm . . . I'm so glad I could do this for you, Jade. Take care—rest well, and I'll sign you out in the morning and get my captain to give you a ride wherever you want to go. Oh, and please tell Botha I appreciate him picking up the tab, but it was unnecessary."

"I'll tell him," Jade said, disappointed that David wouldn't be coming through himself in the morning. Though maybe it was a good thing. Somehow, it stung less than it would have a few days ago. Hope could sometimes be crueler than despair, as she had learned at great cost.

She disconnected, feeling her appetite flooding back, suddenly aware of the spicy aroma of her Cape Malay lamb curry. She raised her glass to Botha. "Well, he did it," she said. "The operation worked. The only problem is that the hit men can't be questioned. One's dead, and the other is in ICU with head injuries but probably won't make it."

She drank the wine, enjoying its silken-smooth flavor. Botha refilled their glasses as Jade spooned hot atchar over her curry before digging in.

"What else did David say?" Botha asked. "I heard you mention a terrorist sympathizer."

Jade nodded. "Another case. They had a tip-off that a terrorist sympathizer infiltrated the country. He came here from the Emirates. Name of Hamdan, but he travels with different passports. He was buying casino equipment for his business in Iraq, and he left the country before they could arrest him."

"That doesn't sound good," Botha said.

"No. I feel sorry for David, with this crisis coming right on top of ours. I feel guilty sitting here enjoying wine and food while he's pulling an all-nighter, racked with stress with only bad coffee to see him through. Terrorism is so frightening."

Botha nodded.

Bad as she felt for him, Jade could no longer allow David's predicament to dent her appetite. She finished her curry and had two large glasses of wine. She was surprised that after drinking to David's success, Botha didn't touch his wine again, and ate only sparingly from the Scottish salmon he'd ordered.

They were back in their suite by nine. The day's adrenaline, combined with all the good food and wine, had left Jade craving sleep. Her eyes were heavy, and she was looking forward to an uninterrupted night, knowing she could rest peacefully because the threat had at last been nullified, and they were safe.

She thanked Botha for dinner and went straight to her bedroom.

Just before sleep took her, she thought she heard him outside, speaking softly but urgently on his phone.

Chapter Forty-Eight

WHEN HE'D RETURNED to the office, David found more information in his inbox. The report on the Inkomfe sabotage had been sent to him, and Fanie had sent Botha's cell phone records from his personal email address to David's Gmail account.

David wanted to get to the phone records. Those were what were making him most impatient. But he decided to read through the sabotage report first, to get a picture of what happened and when. If his gut was correct, the timing of Botha's phone calls might well dovetail with the events of Friday morning.

At approximately two a.m. on the morning of the first of November, two men armed with handguns gained access to the Inkomfe Nuclear Research Center, the investigating detective had written in a painstakingly neat hand. *They climbed over the two perimeter fences between the old entrance and gate one with the help of ropes and ladders. The fences were subsequently found to not be electrified, as had been assumed.*

That sentence gave David a headache for a moment. He pressed his fingers into his temples before continuing. *The men were wearing ski masks and black clothing. They were described as being of average height and fit build. They could not be further identified due to the masks and gloves.*

"Okay," David muttered, reading eagerly on.

The men forced their way into the secure visitors' complex, which at that time of night was locked, and crowbarred open the

main security door. *This caused the alarm to go off. By the time
guards arrived, the men had smashed and opened the glass visitors'
door and had made their way into the orange zone, where they
succeeded in forcing open two further doors that led to an auxiliary
control room as well as gaining access to two management offices
along the way.*

David turned the page.

*The offices were unoccupied, but there were two technicians
on duty in the control room. The men forced the technicians
out of the room at gunpoint and smashed a backup computer,
which was not connected to the system. It is believed they were
going to attempt to log in to the system and disable the doors
that lead into the red security zone, gaining access that way.
However, the technicians triggered the main alarm, and Inkomfe went into lockdown mode, with gates to the red security
zone being sealed. Upon hearing the alarm, the staff still inside
the red zone powered down the reactor before taking shelter in
a secure room nearby.*

"So what happened to the masked guys?" David wondered,
reading on.

*Police were called, and security reinforcements arrived, but the
two intruders were nowhere to be found and were not captured on
camera footage leaving the premises. A search was started at three
fifteen a.m., and by eight a.m. the premises were declared to be
secure, and the red zone was opened.*

"The men?" David said aloud, turning another page impatiently. "Any theories on how they got out?"

*It was later discovered that after leaving the control room, the
intruders had broken into a locked storeroom down the passage.
Nothing was missing from this room, but it is thought that they
may have accessed the room, which was not often used, to obtain
security staff uniforms that had been placed there for them at an*

earlier date, and had thus blended in with the personnel on-site, which included a number of extra guards brought in to assist as well as police and detectives. This would have enabled them to leave the premises unnoticed.

"Aha," David said, making a note on his own paper. A clever way of disappearing. It indicated preplanning, and the help of an extremely trustworthy inside source. As did the fact that they were going to use the computers to access the red zone.

With so many security staff on-site and the fact that it was dark, it would then have been easy for them to blend in and to make their escape. It was later confirmed by Mr. Gillespie, who was in charge of security operations, that due to the disruption after the break-in, IDs were not checked upon leaving until approximately five a.m.

"That's a big oversight," David said out loud. Perhaps a forgivable one, though, given the chaos that must have ensued. At any rate, it had allowed the men to escape. He assumed they were men. Of course, one or both could have been a woman, but he was going to go with men for now, given that the physical description had been of men—average height, fit build.

It was interesting, too, that there were no fatalities or injuries reported. The men had been armed but had not used their weapons. They could easily have shot the laboratory techs instead of forcing them out of the control room. In fact, that had proved to be a fatal error in an otherwise flawless plan, because the techs had been able to trigger the alarm that shut down the red security zone before the intruders could hack into the system and open the doors.

Insider knowledge. For sure, this indicated insider knowledge.

Pressing his lips together with frustration that this hadn't been more proactively followed up on by the detective in charge, David turned his attention to Botha's phone records. Perhaps he would strike gold here. He was optimistic as he paged carefully through the printed sheets, but even so, he was unprepared for the bombshell that he discovered.

JADE DREAMED THAT she was trying to follow Carlos Botha through a crowd. It was in town somewhere, with tall, dark buildings looming on each side of the street and cutting out the sun. He was walking ahead of her, not very fast. He was strolling along, looking around casually, but she couldn't keep up with him because other people kept bumping and jostling her. And it was hard to tell which one he was, because his face was in shadow, and it was difficult to make out his features. She kept on losing him, then having to try and find him again in the gloom.

She realized the problem. He was wearing dark glasses that were obscuring his face. Without them, it would be much easier for her to follow him—but how could she tell him to take them off?

She had to catch up with him. She started running, pushing her way through the crowds, but although he didn't seem to be hurrying, he was outpacing her still. And the crowds around her were becoming threatening. They were closing in, bumping her, blocking her off from her goal. A long-fingered hand snatched at her clothing, pulling her back, and she stifled a cry.

Suddenly she needed to get away from these shadowy streets. She was walking into danger—she knew it. She was sure that the strangers around her had concealed weapons in their ragged clothing. What if the next thing that touched her wasn't a grabbing hand, but the cold steel blade of a knife?

And then she saw him. He'd stopped near a doorway and was speaking on his phone. This was her chance. She had to get to him—now or never.

Jade ran through the crowd, sprinted what seemed like an endless distance until she reached the doorway where he was standing. She touched him on the shoulder, and he slowly turned to stare at her with dull, yellowed eyes in a menacing face.

She staggered back a step, discovering she'd been wrong. This wasn't Botha at all; in the gloom and confusion, she'd made a mistake.

And then she realized that this man, now moving toward her with predatory intent, wasn't wearing dark glasses, either—none of the crowd were. Their eyes gleamed faintly in the growing dusk. Putting her hand to her face, she discovered the truth too late.

They weren't wearing the darkened shades.

She was.

JADE SAT UP in bed, breathing hard, the shadows from her dream still crowding her mind. God, she hated those nightmares . . .

And then she nearly screamed aloud as a dark form appeared in the doorway.

"What is it?" she whispered shakily. Her heart was hammering. Her palms felt cold.

"Are you okay? I heard shouting."

It was Botha, which didn't exactly reassure her. The imagery from her nightmare filled her mind, confusing and unsettling. Why had she dreamed that? What was her sub-conscious trying to tell her? What was she missing?

"What time is it?" She felt disoriented.

"It's only half past ten. You've been asleep for an hour."

"I had a bad dream."

"You have them often." It was a statement, not a question. Jade shrugged.

"I've heard you shouting before in your sleep. And crying, too."

Her face went hot. "I'm okay. Really," she said.

He walked quietly over to sit on her bed. His skin was damp, and she thought he must have just come out of the shower. He was wearing the gray boxers she'd bought him and nothing else. A thread of moonlight spilled through the window and shone onto him, turning his tan skin to silver. Suddenly the thin cotton shirt she was wearing felt insub-stantial, and she shivered.

"I have them, too, sometimes," he said. "Nightmares, I mean."

Jade's mouth felt dry. "I know," she told him. "I've heard you, too."

"Come here," he said softly. It was a question, an invita-tion, but she could hear the need in his voice, and it tugged at her core.

He held out his hand.

Jade wanted to say no. She shouldn't. But she found she had no defenses left, and compared to the terrifying imagery of her dream, Botha's reality seemed like the lesser evil.

I'll just let him hold me for a minute, to chase the bad memo-ries away, she told herself, knowing already that this was a lie.

She leaned into his embrace, wrapping her arms around

him even as his own pulled her close. His skin was warm, silken to the touch. She ran her hands over his defined shoulders, along his muscular back while his fingers smoothed her hair and stroked her face. His lips were on hers in a kiss deep enough to allow her to forget the past few days.

"Jade," he whispered.

He leaned in and kissed her again. His eyes were open, but he'd moved out of the beam of light, and try as she might, she could not see the expression in them.

Chapter Forty-Nine

JADE WOKE UP with a start, reaching automatically for the man she'd sensed beside her earlier. She'd fallen asleep in his arms, but now the space beside her was empty except for cool, tangled sheets. She sat up in the darkness, breathing hard. What had woken her?

The silvery thread of moonlight had moved around, illuminating an African-themed tapestry on the wall, the colors dull and muted in the dim light. From the bathroom, she heard the hiss of the shower providing a steady, soothing white noise.

Sleep had allowed her to piece troubling parts of the puzzle together. Her subconscious had been working, and now the events of the past few days seemed suddenly clearer.

Gillespie had planted that tracking device under her car.

It made all the sense in the world now.

Gillespie had seen Lisa Marais following him. He knew Lisa and Botha had stayed in touch. Between them, the evidence they were collating could destroy his career.

But that would mean Gillespie had also hired the hit men. Had the likable head of security been that desperate to keep his secrets? And on a practical note, how had he been able to afford them? Hit men were expensive, and she'd seen how short of cash Gillespie had been after he'd gambled it all away. Maybe he'd paid them with a night's winnings before losing all his money again.

"The timeline makes sense," she said aloud.

Gillespie had asked her where they were staying the night that she drove to Inkomfe. She'd told him a Sandton hotel. Then the hit men had called around, phoned all the Sandton hotels until they had found the right one. But Jade and Botha had escaped just in time, so Gillespie had needed to make a plan B. He, or the hit men, had obtained the tracking device. And then he'd called her again to meet up with him after he'd been beaten up and mugged.

Perhaps he'd told the hit men to beat him up deliberately. But actually, she thought it was more likely he really had been beaten by somebody he'd owed money to. Either way, he'd been able to bring Jade running. If it hadn't been the mugging, Gillespie would have found another way.

She'd changed the number plate and disguised the car, so locating it had taken longer. She remembered Gillespie's excuse for leaving the breakfast table, saying he had lost the business card of the woman who'd bought him his shirt. He'd been away ten minutes, and his hands had been shaking worse than ever when he'd got back.

Most tellingly of all, when she'd left the mall, she'd turned left to go to the parking lot and hadn't passed a Markham or any men's clothing shop along the way. At the time she'd assumed that Gillespie had just been so rattled after the attack that he'd gone in the wrong direction. Now she realized he'd never been going back to the shop. He'd been heading down to the parking garage to help the hit men attach the tracking device that would lead them back to Botha.

She couldn't understand why Loodts had been tortured, though. That was the one discordant note in the symphony. It was the only thing that didn't make sense, but what she had was enough to convince her that the threat wasn't over yet. While Gillespie was alive, Botha was in danger.

She reached for her cell phone but couldn't find it on the bedside table where she'd left it. And then the noise that had awoken her sounded again. Over the soothing hiss of the shower, she heard it ringing faintly from somewhere in the lounge.

Jade scrambled out of bed, pulled on her shirt and tiptoed out of the bedroom, closing the door softly behind her.

Her phone was under one of the couch cushions in the lounge, and she felt cold all over as she pulled the cushion aside and retrieved it. No way had she left it anywhere near here. It had been moved. Botha must have done it, but why? It stopped ringing as she grabbed it.

Blinking down at the screen, she saw it was half past midnight, and to her consternation, she had six missed calls from the same number, one she recognized: David's office landline.

Hurriedly, she called him back. He snatched the phone up as soon as the call connected. "Jade? Is that you?"

"Yes," she said, confused, feeling dread starting to prickle over her spine. "What the hell's going on?"

"Are you okay? Are you safe?"

"I'm fine. Why shouldn't I be? I'm at the hotel."

"Where's Botha?"

"He's in the shower."

"Whatever you do, don't let him endanger you. I'm going to send a team over in the next half hour to arrest him. I can't get anyone there sooner than that. I'll call the hotel's security as soon as we've spoken and get them to place an armed guard outside the door to stop him escaping. In the meantime, I want you out of there. I'm going to come and fetch you myself in ten minutes. Be waiting in the lobby."

"But . . ." Jade's lips felt numb. Her heart was pounding frantically. She felt as if reality as she knew it had been yanked from under her. "David, please explain. Tell me what's going on."

"I called in a favor and got hold of Botha's recent cell phone records. They arrived an hour ago in my inbox, and I've been having a look. He's been calling the Middle East so often in the past few days he might as well have his own goddamned hotline set up. Jade, he's contacted about eight different Iraqi numbers and been contacted by others, and he's been communicating regularly with a cell phone user registered in the Emirates. Including in the early hours of last Friday morning. Phone calls were made to the Emirates cell phone number shortly before and after the sabotage that occurred at Inkomfe. When Botha was supposed to be drunk and trashing a bar in Sandton. Nice alibi. The cell records tell the true story."

"Oh, shit," Jade said. This news was a hammer in the gut, a tub of ice water down the back. Her mind was reeling as she battled to process David's words. All she could remember now was Botha's strange stillness earlier when she'd told him about the tip-off David had received on Hamdan. How he'd stopped drinking his wine and had barely eaten. And the way she'd heard him speaking on the phone, so urgently, as she'd fallen asleep.

"Loodts had Inkomfe's strong room and reactor room access codes with him when he went to the meeting at Crown Street, which Botha would have known about," David continued. "I'm sure that's why he got Loodts to meet him on that particular afternoon. Loodts was tortured before he died, and there were no papers in the briefcase."

"Give me five minutes, and I'll be ready," Jade said.

"Be careful. Please be very careful. Botha must be regarded as extremely dangerous."

"I'll be careful," Jade whispered.

She tiptoed back into the darkened bedroom, adrenaline flooding her. Rummaging through her bag, she pulled on her underwear, black cargo pants, a dark T-shirt, her trainers. She couldn't even brush her hair because her brush was in the bathroom. She found a scrunchie at the bottom of her bag and scooped it back into an untidy ponytail. Then she went cautiously to the safe and opened it. Thank God, there was the gun, still inside. She shoved it into the holster and buckled it behind her.

She turned quickly to go, but in the darkness, she knocked against the table with the kettle and teacups. Her heart jumped into her throat as the cups fell over, clattering onto the table's hard surface, the noise deafening.

She froze, terrified that the sound might have alerted Botha.

But the hissing of the water continued unabated.

Jade let out a shaky breath as new suspicions flooded in.

That convenient soft splashing, concealing any sounds that might have alerted her that Botha was moving around and hiding her phone instead of sleeping next to her. Why would he spend so long in the shower at such a time? Especially since he'd come to her room just a couple of hours ago, his skin damp from the shower.

Jade pulled the gun out of her holster. She tried the bathroom door and found it was unlocked. No time to think about what she was going to do. She held the weapon at the ready, pushed the door wide, and in two strides she was pulling open the frosted glass door of the shower.

Inside, only a stream of cold water spattering onto the white tiled floor.

The cubicle was empty.

Chapter Fifty

"OH, HELL," JADE whispered, staring in dismay at the empty shower stall. She reached in and turned the water off, brushing the cold droplets from her skin. She ran out of the bathroom, still holding her gun, and quickly searched the suite, already knowing it was a pointless exercise. Botha's room was unoccupied; his bed hadn't been slept in at all. A swift hunt through wardrobes and under couches convinced her that he had gone.

With shaking hands, she dialed his cell phone number. She was sure it would be turned off, but to her surprise, it rang. She willed him to answer and give her an explanation for the nightmare that she'd awakened to, for him to tell her that everything was all right.

For him to really be the man she'd believed him to be, instead of the monster whose existence she'd been blind to.

It rang six, seven times, and just as she'd resigned herself to hearing an automated voice mail message, the call was picked up.

There was silence for a moment. Then a man's voice asked, "Who is this?"

It was not Botha who spoke. The voice was not as deep as his. It was strongly accented and filled with suspicion.

Jade stabbed the DISCONNECT button.

Then she shoved her gun back into the holster and her phone into her pocket, picked up her bag and ran out of the penthouse suite, slamming the door behind her.

As she sprinted through the lobby, her phone started ringing again. She dragged it out of her pocket, unreasonable hope lifting her heart that it might be Botha calling her back, but cold logic telling her it was David.

As it turned out, it was neither of the two.

To Jade's surprise, she found herself speaking to Sbusiso.

"I thought I had better tell you," he said.

"Sorry, what was that?" The cell reception was terrible. She could barely make out what he was saying.

"I thought I had better tell you I had a parcel delivered to me today." Jade pressed the cell phone to her ear, willing the connection to improve, and for a few moments, it did. "It was sent to my house while I was at work. My neighbor took it for me. He only just got back from his shift at Spur. It is from Miss Lisa."

"From Lisa?" Jade said. This must be the information she had sent from the motel right before she disappeared.

"I am sorry to phone you so late, but I thought it might be important. It was sent via Speed Services, but I know the post office has been on a go-slow, so even priority packages have been delayed by many days. And maybe my house was difficult to find."

Jade stepped out of the lobby. There was no sign of David yet. The city center was quiet; she heard music coming from far away and watched a minibus taxi bump its way down the road. "Can you open the package and tell me what's inside?" she asked Sbusiso.

"I have opened it. But I cannot tell you much," Sbusiso said. "It is a USB drive, I think they are called. But I do not have a computer here." He sounded regretful. "There is a note with it which says, 'Sbusiso, please keep this for me. It is a backup. If I go missing, please give it to Mr. Carlos Botha.'

And there is a phone number there for Mr. Botha. But I have not phoned it yet."

Headlights approached, fast and bright. Was this David?

No. It was a cab, slowing outside the hotel's entrance while four well-dressed occupants climbed out. They were talking and laughing among themselves as the cab driver unloaded their shopping bags from the trunk, handing them over to the waiting concierge who followed the guests into the lobby.

In a split second, Jade made her decision.

David was frantically busy, and there was no way he'd allow her to follow a hunch that led straight into the path of trouble just after he'd snatched her out of it. If she climbed into his unmarked, she'd be out of action for the rest of the night. And by then, who knew? It might be too late to stop whatever disastrous sequence of events had been set into motion.

"Don't phone Botha yet," she told Sbusiso. "I'll be there in an hour. Please wait up for me."

Sprinting over to the sidewalk, Jade waved her arms and yelled, running after the departing cab until its brake lights flashed red.

A minute later, she was sitting in the backseat, giving the driver rather breathless directions to Atteridgeville.

As they rounded the corner, she passed David's unmarked speeding toward the hotel. She saw him at the wheel, grim-faced, and wished she'd called him earlier to explain, instead of wasting his time when every moment was precious.

But then, he would never have listened to her. David could be ridiculously stubborn. She ducked down in her seat so that he wouldn't notice her. When she straightened up again, he was safely past, and shortly afterward, Jade's cab had reached the highway and was heading west.

Once she was on the highway she sent David a short text message. *I'm okay. Following a lead.*

Then she put her phone on silent. If he called back, she wouldn't answer—not until she had a clearer picture of this situation, which she was hoping Sbusiso's information would provide.

At night, the lack of infrastructure in Atteridgeville became apparent. Much of the township was swathed in darkness, thickened by a hanging veil of smoke. With electricity unavailable for some people and unaffordable for others, those who were not brave or foolish enough to steal it were relying on burning wood, coal fires and paraffin lamps.

"I can't go too much farther into here," the cab driver told her. "We aren't allowed to drive into the settlements at night."

"It's just down here. No, no, damn it, it isn't." At night, the place was unfamiliar to her and so confusingly dark, and she had told him to turn too early.

"I can't carry on," the cab driver said in a tone that brooked no argument. "I'm really sorry, but I'll be in trouble with the control room if I do. You must get out here, or I can take you back to the main road."

From here, she could find the house on foot, but the delay was frustrating. Still, at least she was most of the way there. After paying the driver, she climbed out, breathing in the harsh tinge of smoky air, and watched the cab depart. Then she shouldered her bag and set off on foot down the potholed road, toward the next turning, which she recognized, thanks to the pile of old car tires on the right-hand side of the road. Someone had been sitting on them last time she'd been there, using them as a makeshift chair.

She jogged down the dirt road until she reached Sbusiso's house. "Sbusiso?" she called softly.

The shack was in darkness. No lights went on as she approached.

"Sbusiso?" she said again.

As she reached the front door, it was opened suddenly, causing Jade's heart to jump into her mouth. Sbusiso hustled her inside. "I didn't hear you arrive. I was listening out for a car," he said.

He turned on a lamp. It shone into a space that was neatly arranged. The large single room contained a cooker, a table with two chairs, a bed, a small cupboard and a bookcase which was being used as a storage shelf, piled with pots and plates, cleaning utensils and groceries, with the topmost level stacked with scores of dog-eared paperbacks.

From among the books, Sbusiso carefully lifted down the small package.

He placed it on the table, and Jade took her laptop out of her bag and plugged in the device. As she waited for the machine to power up, she read the note. Lisa's handwriting was small, neat and cramped. It looked like she'd written it in a hurry on a plain piece of notepaper from the motel. And the phone number she had given Sbusiso for Botha was the same one that Jade had tried, just an hour ago, to be met by that unfamiliar voice.

What accent had it been? Mediterranean? Middle Eastern? Had it sounded familiar? She hadn't heard enough to be sure, and she wasn't going to call it again.

The USB drive had loaded. Eagerly, Jade clicked on it, leaning forward to stare intently at the screen.

The notes were concise, if rather erratically laid out. Lisa was obviously not a linear thinker and had been working in a hurry.

Botha, this is a backup for you, the note began. *I know you said no emails, but I'm going to get the receptionist here to post it to somebody I trust, just in case. My house has been burned down, so I'm hiding out in a motel, but I have the feeling I'm being followed. We knew when we started this that we were in over our heads, but I just didn't know how deep. I don't want anything to mess up what happens at Inkomfe on the first of November. That operation goes ahead regardless. Hopefully you can use this info! It's not complete, but it's a start.*

Thank you again and speak soon, I hope.

Lisa.

Jade let out a deep breath. The mention of the first of November troubled her. That was last Friday, when the sabotage had occurred.

She was so sure that Lisa and Botha hadn't been involved, that they were innocent. But she'd been wrong. Lisa's note served as a confession that the two had at least known something about it.

Perplexed, she opened the file and read through the contents carefully.

She read them a second time, involuntarily chewing on one of her nails.

Then she checked to see if her data connection was working.

Out here in the middle of nowhere, she had virtually no phone signal, and there was no way to send an email right now—there wasn't enough bandwidth available.

Jade grimaced in frustration. Lisa had left behind dynamite, the key to everything, and she needed to get it to David immediately. She'd have to call him and explain, but in the meantime, she needed to get to Inkomfe as fast as possible. Much more than the plant was now at risk. She had to get somebody to sound the alarm, to put the red zones into lockdown.

Chapter Fifty-One

QUICKLY JADE SCRIBBLED her own notes on the back of the page Lisa had used, adding David's phone number and work address.

"Please keep this, Sbusiso. I'll tell David you have it, and where you are. He can come and collect it from you. If for any reason he doesn't, will you deliver it to his office? They'll know it's important."

She put the note and USB drive back into the envelope, and Sbusiso replaced it on the top shelf. "What's the quickest way to get to Inkomfe?" she asked him.

"What do you need to do there?" he said with a puzzled frown.

"I need to somehow put the place into lockdown. There's no time to lose. Every minute represents a huge security risk."

Sbusiso nodded, his face stony. "This is exactly what Miss Lisa thought would happen one day," he said. "Let me come with you. I can speak to the security at the turnstile gate. Perhaps they will understand and let us in together. My friend Abel is on shift now. And at this hour, the turnstile is closed, so there will only be him on duty."

"How can we get there fastest?"

"Two streets down, there is a minibus taxi stand." Sbusiso grasped the edge of the table and stood up, putting on his jacket. "Come, Jade. I will walk there with you. One of them, I am sure, will agree to drive us to Inkomfe."

Jade had to contain her seething impatience and allow

herself to walk at Sbusiso's slower pace, instead of sprinting there as she would have done on her own.

On the way, she called David's cell phone, but wasn't surprised when it went straight through to voice mail. She had ditched their meeting, and he was probably on a call as this latest crisis hit the fan.

The taxi stand was nearly empty. The first driver they approached refused to take them. He'd worked double shift and was starting again early tomorrow morning; he was too tired for that route, and no amount of money could change his mind.

The next driver, washing dirt off the battered wheel arches of his minibus, was more agreeable to doubling his income for the day in exchange for a thirty-minute round-trip.

The air was thick with smoke and mist; the headlights cut it with difficulty. The taxi driver sped along the rough surface, the houses and shacks seeming to press toward them on either side of the narrow road. The only place for pedestrians was an uneven pathway on the left-hand side.

Jade had expected to go back the way she had come, but instead, the taxi driver took a right turn before they were out of the township. They were taking a shortcut.

The headlights dipped and bobbed, illuminating the angled roofs and blank windows of dilapidated shacks that became sparser as they drove. The road was terrible and grew increasingly worse until it became nothing more than overgrown track. Jade wondered whether any vehicle, even a taxi, had driven down it in the past few years, but then saw that the grass was crushed in places. People used this road, then, but not often.

She looked ahead, hoping to see the glow of the lighting that signaled Inkomfe's perimeter fencing, but all she saw were the headlights reflecting on grass. Jade winced as the transmission banged against another large rock. She prayed that the taxi wouldn't sustain any permanent damage. If they were stranded here, it would be an endless walk to anywhere.

She tried to call David again. No luck. She'd just have to hope that he would get back to her before her fears materialized.

Then the taxi veered to the right, inched its way up a steep, rocky road and rounded a small cluster of trees. There, to Jade's utter relief, was the main road, with Inkomfe's flood-lights in the distance. Another minute, and the driver was pulling up outside gate one, waiting just long enough for Jade and Sbusiso to scramble out before pulling his vehicle into a tight U-turn and heading back the way he had come.

Jade walked across the paved sidewalk and up to the gate. A narrow, high gap in the double fencing, it was fitted with two steel turnstiles painted in the same dull yellow that she remembered from Inkomfe's interior.

Between the two fences, she saw a small building with its deeply tinted glass windows. This was where the guard would be.

But there seemed to be no guard on duty now. The cubicle's door remained closed, even when Jade shouted hello and grabbed onto the cold steel to rattle the turnstile loudly.

"What's going on?" she asked Sbusiso.

He shrugged, looking worried. "The gate is never left unguarded." But then he cupped a hand to his ear and listened. "You hear that?" he asked.

Jade didn't know what she was listening for. A breeze sent a paper cup tumbling down the tarmac, making a hollow banging noise. A car drove past, perhaps coming from another of Inkomfe's gates. She heard the click and growl as it shifted gears. And then she heard the noise Sbusiso had picked up on: a high, faint droning sound that seemed to come from far away.

"It's the fence alarm," Sbusiso told her.

"Does that mean the perimeter's been breached?" Jade glanced wildly to her left and right, as if she actually might spot somebody breaking through.

Sbusiso shrugged. "It could be the wind. But maybe that is where Abel has gone. When the alarm goes off, guards are called from their stations to check the fence."

"Maybe we should try another gate," Jade said in desperation, but Sbusiso raised his hand.

"You can get through here if you are quick."

"How?" Jade stared at him, frowning.

"While the alarm is sounding, the electricity to the fence is cut. It takes a few seconds after the alarm has stopped to be restored again."

"Oh." Jade looked again at the turnstiles. They were narrow and tall, a formidable barrier to entry, if that was what you were looking for. But see them with different eyes, and they became a ladder, which could be climbed to reach the concrete shelf that topped them. Scramble onto that, and you would then be faced with six electrical wires carrying a shock of ten thousand volts. Enough to kill.

"What about the second turnstile?" she asked. "Same thing?"

"It will be even easier for you. You can open it from inside the guardhouse. There is a red button you press."

"Is there a button to open this one, so I can let you in, too?"

"No. The outer gate requires a magnetic card to be swiped, which only authorized guards carry on them. If Abel comes back, he can let me in."

"On second thought, it will be better if you stay outside," Jade said. Being anywhere near Inkomfe could shortly prove to be very dangerous.

There was no time for delay. She was on her own from here.

Jade grasped the cold steel turnstile and pulled herself up. Hand over hand, like a ladder. The paint felt smooth and slick under her hands. It was difficult to grip, and the blowing wind didn't allow her to hear the faraway sound of the alarm clearly. A few seconds after it stopped, the fence would have its power restored. If she was touching it, then . . .

Jade's foot slipped, and she banged her ankle painfully against the metal. With a curse, she suppressed her fear and focused on the job at hand. This was the hard part. The solid shelf above the turnstile jutted out. It was too wide for her to get her arm over. She'd have to grasp one of the metal supports that held the electric wires in place, supports that were not made to take the full weight of a human being.

She grasped it carefully, testing it. It seemed secure enough. The rim of the shelf was rough. It grazed her skin as she put her weight onto the metal and pulled, kicking her legs hard to try and boost herself up and over.

"Can you still hear the alarm?" she shouted down.

"I think so," Sbusiso said.

And then, with an ugly grinding sound, the metal strut worked loose from its moorings, and she felt the electric fence support start to give.

Praying that the wires weren't electrified, Jade pushed her weight against them, shoved her arm through the bottom two, made a desperate grab for the other side of the concrete rim and got hold of it. She pulled herself onto the rim, cursing the electric wires. They were like a spider web. Her arm was through two of them, her leg through another two, and for all the entanglement they were providing her with, their fragile, bendable nature offered nothing in the way of support.

Grasping the metal strut carefully, pushing down rather than pulling out, she managed to ease her arms and legs into line and stand upright, staring at the fence line stretching far ahead, lit at intervals by the glowing spotlights. She was aware of Sbusiso watching her a long way below. The wind tugged at her hair, teasing a rivulet of sweat down her cheek. She'd have to step over the electric wires with care. They were thigh-high, solid and ropy to the touch, and the concrete on top was uneven. She stepped over. One leg. Now for the other.

"I think the alarm has stopped," Sbusiso shouted up, panic in his voice.

Jade jackknifed her other leg over the fence. Grabbing hold of the steel support, she tried to lower herself down, her legs flailing blindly as she prayed to find the turnstile's steel.

And then the strut gave. It loosened with a hideous ripping sound, and still grabbing it one-handed, Jade felt herself fall downward with it, as the wires it carried bent and stretched.

But the neighboring struts stopped it, leaving her dangling in midair, bouncing gently as she clutched the metal, the wires just a few inches from her upturned face.

Jade let go of the strut and allowed herself to fall.

An endless, whirling second, and then the paving hit her. She buckled at the ankles, rolling forward to break the fall, trying to protect the gun holstered at her back while the bricks scoured her knees and shoulders. She thought suddenly of Botha and his catlike grace. She wasn't Botha. A sharp pain in her foot told her that she hadn't come out of her climb unscathed, but when she tested it, she could at least bear weight on it.

Above her, with a piercing click and a blue flash, the fence began to short out. The power was back on. But she had made it; she was inside.

Chapter Fifty-Two

JADE LIMPED BACK to the turnstile where Sbusiso was waiting anxiously.

"Are you all right?" he asked.

"I'm fine. How do I get to the main buildings?"

"Follow that walkway and turn right after the first warehouse." Sbusiso pointed. "You will need to be careful, because they do not patrol on foot at night, but in carts. If they see you, even from far away, they will know something is wrong."

"It's good if they know something's wrong," Jade said, but Sbusiso shook his head.

"If they catch you, they will lock you in a secure compound and call Mr. Gillespie. Then they will call the police. They will not listen to you if you ask them to sound the alarm. Guards can get into big trouble for sounding the alarm unless there is a real emergency. Locking down the red zone means work gets delayed for up to eight hours."

"Has it always been that way?" Jade asked.

Sbusiso shook his head. "New rules. In the old days, when Miss Lisa worked here, every single employee was allowed to sound the alarm and lock down the red zone. You would never get into trouble for it. Miss Lisa said that we should all be aware of threats, and it was better to be safe. But Mr. Gillespie changed things."

Jade nodded. She could see why he'd done that. Disempowering the guards would have been a necessary step for him to achieve his ends. It didn't help her now, though.

"Okay. I'll be careful. Dial this number, Sbusiso." Jade read out David's cell phone number. "Please keep on calling him. If you get through, tell him he needs to send the flying squad here as soon as he can. And call emergency services. The fire department and the ambulance. Tell them someone's badly injured, and there's a threat of fire. We need them here if the worst happens."

"I'll do it."

Jade turned. Walking gingerly on her injured foot, she opened the guardhouse gate and pressed the red button. Getting through the second turnstile was as easy as pushing it open. She set off, limping slowly up the walkway. She was the intruder now, alone in this concrete-paved conglomeration of buildings housing a noiseless reactor and its deadly fuel.

She needed to orient herself and make a quick decision about which way to go. She struggled to place herself in a mental map of Inkomfe and wasn't sure how to find somewhere she could sound the alarm, or at least alert somebody higher up the chain of command who was authorized to sound it.

And luck was not on her side. There was nowhere to hide in this paved wasteland, with bright spotlights set at intervals. She could only pray that she didn't bump into anyone patrolling until she reached cover, even if it was only the wall of the warehouse in the distance. However, she was still limping far from the buildings when she heard the buzz of an approaching cart. As its headlights grew larger, Jade felt like prey. She knew the game was over.

Unless she could use this to her advantage.

Her heart lifted slightly as she saw there was only one guard inside. He'd seen her. The cart accelerated, driving straight toward her. She raised a hand to shield her eyes against its blinding lights.

"Abel?" she said hopefully as it reached her and slowed.

Nope. No response. Whoever this guard was, he wasn't Abel.

"What are you doing here?" he asked. "Where is your security card?"

He was tall, grim-faced, dark-haired. His own card swung on a lanyard around his neck, and his gun was holstered at his hip. Her absence of a card marked her as a stranger. Too late, she realized she should have asked Sbusiso to borrow his.

"I lost my card," she said. "I ran down to the gate to check that fence there. You see, the wires are broken. See how it's shorting out? I took my jacket off while I was running, and my card must have come with it. Now I'm looking for it."

Reluctantly the guard climbed out of the cart. He stared at her suspiciously.

"My name's Scarlett Sykes," Jade said, holding out her hand in greeting. The pepper spray was concealed inside her palm. She already felt guilty for what she was about to do, but it would potentially save lives.

The guard held out his hand, and as he did so, Jade raised hers and sprayed him full in the face.

With an agonized yell, the guard twisted away and fell to his knees, his eyes tight shut and his hands clutching at his face.

Jade ran to the golf cart, climbed in and floored the accelerator. Her ankle screamed at her, but she ignored the pain, swinging the car in a tight semicircle. The cart rocked as she sped in the direction of the complex. The guard's cries followed her for a while before she drove out of earshot.

She had bought herself a few minutes, at least. The guard's walkie-talkie was in the cart, crackling softly, so he couldn't use it to alert anyone. She needed to trigger the alarm as quickly as she could.

She had no idea how much time she had. She might already be too late, or there might be a few hours left, if she were lucky. She wasn't hopeful, especially after reading Lisa's clear, concise notes. Lisa had discovered everything. Her only downfall was that she'd underestimated Gillespie's cunning.

Gillespie was likely on-site. She guessed he must be in Inqaba, the top-security strong room where the ingots were stored. She triangulated her possible routes to avoid the area altogether. She couldn't risk running into him now; he had proven to be incredibly dangerous.

She decided to head for the only place familiar to her—the one where she'd gone on her guided tour. There had been passages that led to the reactor room, and the glass-walled control room. She had a gun on her. The admin staff and technicians hadn't been armed with anything more than Geiger counters, and she was sure they would be empowered to shut down the red zone, especially if motivated to do so by a furious woman with untidy hair brandishing a Desert Eagle.

In the cart with its conveniently bright headlights, she'd be anonymous until she pulled into the big building.

Minutes felt like hours, even though she was going as fast as she could.

She finally reached the big doors to the main building. She remembered how the guard had opened them on her guided tour, with a simple press of the dashboard button on the golf cart. She tried the same maneuver and they swung open for her as well. Another loophole in the security system, likely another "innovation" introduced by Gillespie. No wonder Lisa Marais had been driven mad with frustration.

She stopped the cart inside the warehouse. Would pressing the button again close the doors? She tried it, and to her relief, they swung shut. At least nobody could follow her in now—unless, of course, they were riding in another of the conveniently programmed security carts.

There was nobody on duty at the reception desk, so Jade hurried over to the elevator and rode it to the bottommost floor.

It opened onto the underground passage she remembered from last time. White walls, eerie silence, freezing air and the feeling of being entombed in concrete. Where the hell *was* everyone?

She suspected that Gillespie was a step ahead of her. He must have cleared the area with a well-timed fire drill or evacuation rehearsal. And she couldn't go much farther before reaching the locked door where he had punched in the code the last time. There might be someone beyond there, but she wouldn't be able to reach them—unless there was some sort of communication system in place, a way of calling the technicians inside. She hadn't noticed a receiver by the door, but it would be worth taking another look.

She half-jogged, half-limped down the passageway, passing a side door which was locked. Then she was at the coded door. The place was deserted, and she couldn't get past this point. And there was no phone receiver nearby. No way of reaching anyone inside, and no button that could be pressed to alert them. Seething with frustration, she punched in a random code, then another.

The door didn't open, but nor did any alarm sound. Jade made several more attempts before realizing it was pointless.

She was trapped inside Inkomfe's concrete heart, so close and yet unable to do what she needed to. Frustrated, Jade punched the door. The solid metal absorbed the blow without as much as a shudder.

She turned away, rubbing her knuckles. She was wasting

time. She'd have to retrace her steps and try another path in. Perhaps she could use the walkie-talkie on the golf cart to communicate with the control room and convince them to shut the plant down.

The elevator had returned to the top floor, and she pressed the button to summon it again. On her way up, she'd take out her gun, she decided. She wanted to have it ready when she stepped back out into the hall upstairs.

But the elevator wasn't empty on its return. There were two people inside, and as Jade froze in her tracks, staring into the muzzle of the Sig Sauer pointed directly at her, she realized that her decision to unholster her own gun had been a sensible one, but she had made it too late.

Chapter Fifty-Three

JADE RAISED HER hands and backed away as the two men stepped out of the elevator.

"What are you doing here?" Gillespie, standing on the right, almost shouted the words out. He was twisting his fingers nervously, and his face looked drawn with tension. He was wearing a pair of dark glasses that hid his blackened eye from view, which meant she couldn't see his expression or make eye contact. Golden stubble frosted his cheeks, camouflaging the graze he'd received during his earlier attack.

"I told you she'd be here." That was the other man speaking, his voice calm.

Jade couldn't believe who she was seeing beside Gillespie, aiming the pistol at her chest with a steady hand. Her mind could not encompass the scale of this treachery, the extent of betrayal. The impossibility of seeing him here made her dizzy. Was this reality or a terrible living nightmare?

"Turn around," he told her. "Keep your hands in the air."

A voice she knew all too well. She turned and felt his left hand pull her shirt up. Expertly he unholstered her Desert Eagle. Frustration boiled inside her as she realized she'd never even had the chance to fire that damned gun at a criminal before it had been taken away from her.

"Down the passage. Keep your hands up."

She walked steadily, listening to the twin sounds of the footsteps behind her. Nowhere to hide now, nowhere to run.

"Face the wall," he told her when she was a few paces away from the door.

Jade pressed her palms against the cold metal and listened to the beep of the keyboard as Gillespie typed in the code.

"Walk on now."

She saw Gillespie use a doorstop to keep the door open. If she remembered correctly, that meant the alarm would go off within a short time. Perhaps that didn't matter now. It might all be part of the plan. She was still light-headed from shock. Her legs didn't seem to belong to her at all.

Her mind was racing. Could she negotiate? Could she somehow bargain with the man holding the guns to save her own life, or was it too late? She should have foreseen this. There had been enough clues, but she had missed them all.

They reached the second door, and again, Gillespie left it open. The windowed control room was up ahead. He opened that door, and they walked inside.

Nobody in the control room, confirming her earlier suspicion of an evacuation drill.

"Stand with your back to the wall over there. Keep your hands in the air."

Her arms were beginning to ache, but she had to comply.

The gunman stepped forward between her and Gillespie.

His dreadlocks were partially covered by a plain black beanie; he was wearing the same uniform as the Inkomfe guards, with what looked to be a functioning ID tag on a lanyard around his neck. All supplied by Gillespie, no doubt, so that he could do his work more easily.

Not Botha, but a man whose history with Jade went back even further. A hit man for hire . . . With his reputation, it was no surprise that Gillespie had ended up sourcing him when he'd looked for a paid killer.

"Robbie," she blurted out.

"You know each other?" Gillespie's voice was tight and high. He checked his watch. Even with her heart banging in her chest and the gun's black muzzle drawing her gaze in, Jade thought that was an odd thing to do. But then, the whole evening had become surreal. If her life was going to end now, at least she'd be in too much shock to worry about it.

"Old business acquaintances," Robbie said. His voice was flat and hard. He stuck his left hand into the pocket of his uniform pants.

From ally to adversary. He was looking at her now as if they'd never done a job together. She stared back pleadingly, but his stony gaze met hers without any concession of their past.

Behind her was a soft hum from the banks of computers. The tiny sounds of fans cooling, of microprocessors crunching away at incoming figures, turning them into streams of data that somehow helped to contain the processor's phenomenal power. But she knew now that the reactor wasn't Gillespie's main target. He'd used the threat of nuclear catastrophe and the vulnerability of the reactor to distract from his own plan, which was to steal Inkomfe's enriched uranium ingots.

Once she was dead, he'd have all the time in the world to do it.

She wondered what kind of nuclear terrorism attack the ingots would be used for. How many would be destroyed instantly by the explosion's fiery blast, and how many would suffer for days or weeks as the radiation destroyed their body's cells, triggering the unstoppable, untreatable sickness?

Jade decided right then to go down fighting.

Gillespie turned as if in response to her resolve. He checked his watch again. "All right," he said. "Kill her."

He turned his gaze to the door. A coward to the last, she thought, who would order somebody's death but didn't have the guts to watch.

She knew Robbie well, but her knowledge only helped her understand how fast she would die. He wouldn't hesitate, he wouldn't miss. He would fire a double tap to be sure of the kill. At this range, it would take her full in the chest. He would only risk a head shot from very close, although once she was down, he might execute a final shot in the head to be sure she died quickly.

The gun's muzzle would follow her. He would be ready for her to try to avoid him, to break left or right, to drop to the floor. Nothing would allow her to escape the twelve bullets that were waiting in that fully loaded magazine.

Unless . . . unless she could plead with him. Would talking work?

She drew a deep breath, ready to find out, but before the words came, Robbie spoke.

"You can't say you don't deserve this," he said in a low voice. His gaze drilled into hers. "It's not like you haven't killed before."

"Robbie, I . . ." she began, tension turning her voice to a cracked whisper.

"This bullet's had your name on for a long time now, even if you didn't know it. Word gets around."

Her hands went numb, her face cold. She could only listen and wait. Every second that Robbie kept talking meant another second of life for her. Miracles happened, right? Perhaps Gillespie would reconsider her fate as he listened to Robbie's weird diatribe.

"You knew it was going to catch up with you one day, didn't you?" A dark humor laced his next words, and she could only nod, because all actions had consequences, and now hers were staring her in the face. The nightmares she'd had. The times she'd woken up filled with guilt and fear, unable to fall back asleep, wondering what important details she'd forgotten, and who was going to come after her wanting retribution or revenge.

The good she'd tried to do and the people she'd tried to help—a vain attempt to compensate for the fact that she had stolen the lives of others. And even if she'd believed they deserved to die, who gave her the right to judge?

"You should have known it would come to this. There was plenty of time to do things differently." Robbie's words sliced into her like steel shards.

"Get on with it!" Gillespie snapped.

Robbie drew in a deep breath, seeming to ignore the man standing behind him. He hadn't taken his eyes off Jade.

"There was plenty of time to do things differently," he repeated, speaking slowly. "But you didn't. You never did. You thought you were untouchable for so long, but now you've finally pissed off the wrong person. Maybe you should pay the people you hire in full, instead of blowing half their fee at the fucking blackjack tables, you lying, cheating, short-paying bastard."

With that, he turned around and drilled two bullets into Gillespie's chest.

Chapter Fifty-Four

THE EXPLOSIONS FILLED the room, crashing in Jade's ears as she dove for the only cover the room had to offer, the nearby chair. She crouched behind it, watching the expression of terminal surprise in the tall sociopath's eyes as he slumped to the floor. Blood welled from the wound, darkening the cream fabric of his shirt and staining the white tiles below. The fingers of one hand briefly twitched, and then he was gone.

So Robbie's words had been for Gillespie, not for her. She was weak with relief at the unexpected reprieve, but she still didn't trust Robbie, not with ten bullets left.

Her ears were still ringing from the blast, and now there was another sound from outside: the shrilling of the emergency siren.

"What the hell is going on?" she yelled at him.

"Gillespie hired me to get rid of some people he said were interfering with the running of the place."

"Who? Lisa Marais? Wouter Loodts?"

Robbie nodded.

"You killed Lisa?" Jade could hear the outrage in her own voice. "She was totally innocent, Robbie. She was working her ass off to make Inkomfe safe, even after being manipulated into leaving."

"I didn't know that." Robbie spread his arms defensively, a gun still in each hand. "And in any case, baby, she was a chain-smoker with a forty-a-day habit. Scarlett and I watched her. It was fucking unbelievable. She literally lit the next one with the last one's butt. All I did was slightly shorten her life expectancy."

"And what's this with Scarlett Sykes? She was your girlfriend."

Robbie shrugged. "She was a messed-up kid who thought she wanted to hang with gangsters."

"So you killed her?"

"Look, I gave her loads of chances. I didn't want her to be involved in any of this. I tried to keep her out of things, even offered to pay for rehab. She didn't take me up on it. She wanted to stay with me and help with jobs, but she was off her head with those fuckin' tranquilizers and other shit. It was just a matter of time before she really screwed up. I told her—two strikes and you're out. I gave her other options. It was like she had a death wish. She refused to help me dump Lisa's body in the Robinson Dam and didn't warn me properly that a witness was watching. Those were two strikes right there, but I gave her another chance. Crashing the car into the motel signpost was number three."

Jade was silent for a moment. The siren's scream filled the room. "What about Loodts? Why did you have to kill him?"

"It was supposed to be set up as a torture scenario. Something to do with secret codes for doors. Gillespie said he had them already, but it had to look like Loodts had been tortured for them. I didn't really torture him, Jade. It was a clean kill. He didn't know what hit him. I twisted his wrists and smashed up his fingers a little after he was dead."

"And me? I was on the run with Botha. You were trying to kill me!"

"Are you dead?" Robbie tilted his chin up, sounding defensive.

Jade pressed her lips together. "He didn't just hire you to kill a few people. He hired you so he could steal enriched uranium ingots from the strong room and sell them to terrorists. How can you justify putting thousands of innocent lives at risk, even for money?"

"What are you talking about?" Robbie frowned in confusion. "My guys and I were hired to kill three people. Lisa Marais, Wouter Loodts and Carlos Botha. We killed Lisa and Loodts. We haven't killed Botha yet. The job got delayed because you helped him get away, and because my guys were all shot dead by cops today. I wasn't hired to steal anything for terrorists. I wouldn't do that."

"But . . ."

Jade thought again about Gillespie's behavior. The way that he'd been checking his watch. How he had cleared the area. Lisa's notes, and what she had written.

Robbie was right. He hadn't been hired for anything else, and yet Gillespie had arranged for him to end up here and triggered the alarm. He had planned to use Robbie, but not in the way Robbie had imagined.

"He's already done it!" Jade shouted. "We need to shut down the red zone and get out of here, Robbie, quick. Do you know how?"

There was only one button it could be. The one marked EMERGENCY, lit up on the console. Jade jabbed at it, and a moment later was rewarded with the louder scream of a new siren.

Robbie was shouting something to her now; with the ringing in her ears, it took her a moment to understand. "Okay, baby. Let's get going!"

He headed for the doorway at a run.

But as he reached it and sprinted out into the corridor,

there was another burst of gunshots, the staccato sound of automatic fire. Bullets stitched themselves along Robbie's body, and he twisted like a marionette, his body arching backward before falling to the ground.

Jade clapped a hand over her mouth in horror.

She was too late. Gillespie might have been murdered, but he'd already set into motion the second, deadlier phase of his plans.

She had only one chance. Robbie had dropped his guns when he fell, and the Desert Eagle had fallen just inside the door. She had to get to it.

But as she lunged forward, a shadow darkened the doorway.

One lone gunman: tall and lean, clothed in black, carrying an AK-47 machine gun. A balaclava covered his face, but she could see his eyes, deep-set and dark in pale skin; they were without mercy.

He stood still, staring into the control room, and his head turned toward Gillespie's fallen body.

This sight gave him pause, and Jade realized that he had not expected to see the sandy-haired man dead on the floor. The gunman was operating under Gillespie's instructions, and Gillespie had never intended for Robbie to leave this place alive. He had been covering his tracks, hoping to walk away in the clear. Dressed in a guard's uniform, Robbie was always going to be disposed of, an Inkomfe employee tragically shot during the break-in.

Shot by the real enemy. The people Gillespie had been dealing with ever since he'd gotten himself indebted for hundreds of thousands of dollars while in Iraq.

Hamdan's men.

Lisa had explained it all. *Hamdan's casinos, Baghdad City, Casino du Liba, Grand Sinai and The Oasis, are not only money-laundering operations. They serve to recruit vulnerable people for terrorism purposes by extending open lines of credit to certain gamblers, allowing them to incur vast debts and then at a later stage demanding payback either in cash or in kind, through facilitating terrorist acts . . . I believe Gillespie was earmarked by Hamdan as one of these individuals who could be useful in the future. He had an open line of credit at Baghdad City . . .*

Upon seeing Gillespie's body, the gunman was debating what to do. Reaching a swift decision, he raised the gun and aimed it at Jade as she leaped for cover behind the chair, knowing it would do nothing to stop the lethal barrage of automatic fire.

And then the gunman hesitated, turned his head. His gun muzzle wavered, and he started to spin around. She realized he must have seen somebody else approaching, but over the screaming of the sirens, she could hear nothing until Carlos Botha launched himself at the masked man in a desperate tackle, and the two of them sprawled to the ground inside the control room.

Chapter Fifty-Five

BOTHA HAD THE element of surprise, and he was swift as a panther. He had the man on the ground and was wrestling his arms down, but the gunman still had his rifle in his hand. Bullets ripped along the wall in Jade's direction, the gun taking on a life of its own in response to the shooter's struggles.

Jade hit the ground, flattening herself until the stutter of shells had ceased. Looking up, she saw Botha had forced the man to drop the machine gun, but the man had pushed it out of arm's reach. Botha had the man's hands pinned down on the floor. His adversary was fighting with all the strength of desperation. He was bigger and heavier than Botha, but he didn't have Botha's raw power.

Botha was going to be able to hold him for now, but threatening the man with a gun would be an easier solution than using brute force. For that matter, a bullet through each wrist would severely hamper his ability to use that AK-47 again.

Jade scooted to the door, keeping her back to the wall and a careful watch on the struggling man. Leaning over, she snagged the gun with her left hand, her fingers wrapping around the grip. The sirens were so loud she couldn't hear her own voice, and it was only sheer luck that made her glance up at the doorway to see that a second masked gunman had arrived and was aiming his weapon at Botha's back.

No time for anything but to shoot.

Left-handed . . . that's why you train with both. For that one time when you need to use it.

Jade raised her left hand and pulled the trigger.

The gun's kick nearly ripped it out of her grasp, but the shot was accurate. It hit the second gunman's chest, and his fire went wide, his clenching trigger finger sending the shots rattling into the computer consoles, shattering their screens. *Double tap . . .* she fired again. Another hit. He folded down in the doorway, on his knees and then on his side, as his machine gun clattered to the ground.

Botha still had the first man's hands behind his back. Straddling him, he climbed to his feet, yanking his wrists viciously higher. Stepping sideways, he aimed a hard kick at the man's head. The gunman's body jackknifed, the tension leaching from his limbs. Botha kicked his head again.

Then he turned to Jade. "You okay?" he shouted.

Jade nodded. "I'm fine. Let's deal with him and get out of here. Emergency services should be on their way."

They needed something to tie him up with, but the only materials on hand were the cables connecting this bank of computers. Jade prayed she wouldn't cause a nuclear meltdown if she unplugged a few of them. Hopefully the alarm had already shut the reactor down. She crawled under the console and yanked out the first cables she could find, passing three to Botha, who used them to hog-truss the still-unconscious gunman.

Holding another cable, Jade stepped over the dead body of the shooter in the doorway. Emotions surged inside her as she looked down at Robbie's slumped form, although she couldn't say whether her regret or relief was stronger. How many times had he been hit? She didn't know. His torso was soaked with blood, and a bloody stream was still oozing from a wound in his thigh.

She bent and threaded the cable around the top of his leg, pulling it tightly into a makeshift tourniquet before knotting it. Tears stung her eyes. There was barely any blood flow for it to contain, and she didn't know why she was taking the time to do it. A token gesture, perhaps. Even in the afterlife, if such a thing existed, she didn't want Robbie thinking she owed him.

As she climbed to her feet, the shrieking of the sirens stopped. Her ears were ringing, and the silence felt louder than the noise had done. The floor was a mess of blood, pooled in places, scuffed and smeared in others, littered with discarded shell casings. The shots to the computer bank had done some damage. A connection was misfiring, flashing sparks. As Botha reached the door, the power tripped, and the area was plunged into darkness. A moment later, with a hiss and a sputter, overhead sprinklers began to spray down.

Botha switched his phone flashlight on, casting a bright beam into the darkness and reflecting off the falling water. She could smell smoke from somewhere. Inkomfe was burning. They needed to get out, and fast.

He grabbed her hand, and they ran down the passage through the chilly downpour, back toward the elevator. With the power gone, it was out of commission, but a door beside it led to a pitch-black stairway. Keeping hold of Botha's hand, Jade limped up the stairs, following his flashlight's dancing beam.

"We need to get to Inqaba," she shouted. "The strong room."

They burst out the door at the top of the stairway and climbed into the security cart. Jade grabbed onto its side as they sped out of the building and down the road.

"Gillespie wasn't interested in sabotaging the plant. He

never was; that was all misdirection. He wanted those ingots. He needed them, because he was in a financial black hole of his own making. He did a deal with a terrorist sympathizer— or rather, he was forced to do the deal in exchange for money. I read Lisa's notes," she told Botha.

She remembered Gillespie mentioning his bonus. He had earned no bonus from his work in Iraq. Lisa's extensive research had proved that while in Iraq, Gillespie's gambling problem had cost him his job, his marriage and his savings, and had plunged him deeply into debt from both moneylenders and the casino. And he had lied. His wife had not been killed in Iraq. That had been another falsehood, told to Jade in order to gain her sympathy and compel her to do what he wanted. His wife had left him while they were in Iraq and traveled to Israel with her new lover, an American security consultant. The two of them had later been killed in a shooting incident there.

Jade was suspicious about that shooting. It could just have been chance bad luck, but Gillespie could easily have set it up. Perhaps a precursor to this whole debacle?

The cart rocked as they rounded a corner.

"I had to do my own research," Botha told her as he whipped the cart around a row of concrete pillars. "Lisa was murdered before she could send the notes to me. We were trying not to communicate too often in the past few weeks. Phone calls and messages leave a record, and even secure emails can be hacked. I worried that Gillespie would get to her, and he did. He hired someone to take her out. So I had to do my own research. I started making some calls to the places he'd worked in Iraq and found out enough to get a picture."

"Why were you trying not to communicate?"

Botha glanced in her direction before focusing again on

the road ahead. "Because we'd already planned the sabotage attempt."

Jade felt as if the breath had been knocked out of her. "That was you?"

Botha nodded. "It was the only way I could get Loodts to listen. Lisa and I discussed it; we looked into every angle. There was just no other way. We had to prove how vulnerable the research center was so that we could force him to make the changes we needed and get Gillespie out of there. At that stage, Lisa knew Gillespie had an agenda. She just wasn't sure what it was. None of us knew the extent of the trouble he'd gotten himself into, or we might have decided to do things differently."

"So you sabotaged Inkomfe?" Jade felt stunned by the news.

"*Attempted* sabotage." Botha gave a tight smile. "Petrov helped me. He's the expert who Lisa brought out to give talks for Earthforce. While he was here, he agreed to do it. I needed someone with military background and knowledge of nuclear plants, and the ability to leave without a trace afterward was a bonus. It was dangerous—more for us than for anyone else, because we'd agreed that no shots would be fired. Our weapons, which I stole from Inkomfe's own stock, weren't even loaded."

"And you both had alibis?"

Botha nodded. "I was falling down drunk and trashing a Sandton bar, courtesy of my karate training partner Lorenzo. Petrov was giving a talk in Bloemfontein, booked to fly back to Johannesburg and Dubai the next day. He drove five hours from Bloemfontein to Inkomfe straight after his talk, did the job and was back in Bloemfontein by morning, ready to check out of his hotel and go to the airport."

"So Petrov is based in Dubai?" Jade asked. Now the many phone calls that Botha had made to the Emirates made sense.

"For the moment, yes."

Botha slowed the cart as they approached the paved yard Jade remembered from the night she'd met Sbusiso. The blaze of the floodlights dazzled her. There were the yellow notice boards with their danger warnings. Thanks to the sirens and the lockdown of the red zone, the yard was empty now, all security staff safely evacuated.

But Inqaba's steel gate, which had been tightly closed the first time she'd seen it, had been left wide open. Beyond it, the storeroom was brilliantly lit. Neon ceiling lights cast their unwavering glare onto the massive iron structure, whose heavy door stood ajar.

The giant strong room was empty. Its numbered yellow shelves bore nothing except the faint dusty outlines of the deadly uranium that had rested there in its ordered piles.

They were too late.

The ingots were gone.

Chapter Fifty-Six

STILL STARING AT the empty strong room, Jade jumped as the noise of a helicopter cut the air. Looking up, she saw that the flying squad had arrived. Two choppers were circling the courtyard. A fire truck and an ambulance were heading at high speed to the reactor room, red lights blazing, and the pair was soon surrounded by a phalanx of security guards, drawn to the strong room by the sound of the chopper.

"Police." Broadcasting over a megaphone as the first chopper descended, David's voice filled the air. "All security guards must stand by and await police orders." The helicopter blades whipped Jade's hair across her eyes, stinging them.

A moment later, David was out, running to her, closely followed by his team. "Jade, are you okay?" He closed his eyes briefly at her nod. "Bring me up to speed," he demanded.

"The ingots are missing. They've been taken already," Jade shouted. "We need to find them. And there's a live gunman hog-tied in the backup control room next to three dead bodies, including Gillespie."

"I'm on it. We already have the main road to the east blocked, with all vehicles being pulled over. I'm going to send both helicopters up again—one going east, one west. I have backup cars arriving in the next few minutes that can help with the search. You said the cargo was in the form of ingots, about the size of a small brick?"

"A silvery, circular, flat brick," Botha said.

"And they're not detectably radioactive? How's that possible?"

Botha answered his question. "Uranium has an extremely long half-life, which means it decays very slowly. Wherever they are, the bars aren't emitting dangerous levels of radiation, but the bad news is they're less trackable. A Geiger counter would only pick them up if the cargo was very close by."

"We'll get a couple counters to the roadblocks immediately. Now, it's a load that you couldn't fit into a car trunk. We're talking a van, a minibus, something bigger, right?" David asked.

"Definitely. A trailer, maybe. Or they could've divided the ingots into several cars."

"Got it." David shouted updates into his walkie-talkie, putting roadblocks at the entrances of all major airports and border crossings, with an alert to all officials on what to look out for.

Then he turned back to Botha. "The other possibility is that they're still hidden here onsite, with plans to be shipped out later. You know Inkomfe well. Can you coordinate a search of this facility, sweeping everything—buildings, vehicles, containers?"

"Will do," Botha said. Striding away, he spoke urgently to the three security personnel on his right, then hurried toward the golf carts with them, speaking into a radio as he did so.

Jade's hair whipped across her face yet again as the helicopters took off. David was already in a golf cart with two other officers, driving purposefully toward the reactor room. Jade guessed that the fire had been contained before it spread. She couldn't see any flames or smoke coming from that part of Inkomfe.

She thought again of Robbie's body, sprawled on the tiles, riddled with bullet holes and lying in a lake of bloody water, not unlike the contaminated scene he'd set up for Loodts and Scarlett. Robbie had never believed he would die. Mind over matter, he'd always said. Better lucky than careful, but luck could run out.

Gillespie's luck had ended—or perhaps he'd never been lucky. Despite his destructive actions, Jade felt sorry for him. A flawed man with a monkey on his back so big and greedy it had stolen his whole life. She'd seen addiction at work before. It overrode the most compelling arguments of logic or conscience. He'd become a pawn, used by people who had taken advantage of his weakness, promised him the money he so urgently needed in exchange for just one carefully planned favor. She remembered him talking about the house in Dainfern, the apartment in Sea Point. Dreams that he perhaps knew, deep down, would never be realized.

Any money from Hamdan would have been placed on red or black, or on the face card in the hope of seeing the ten appear.

This had been a carefully planned operation. Gillespie had used his own initiative to source domestic hit men in conjunction with his overseas contacts.

That was what troubled her the most. She shivered as the early morning wind cut through her thin jacket, carrying with it the coolness from the recent rains. There was nothing for her to do here. David was coordinating his team. Botha was managing the search of the premises. Taking her phone out of her pocket, she called Sbusiso to tell him everything was all right. He sounded relieved to hear her voice, and told her he was with the police, helping to guard the entrances and exits.

So Sbusiso also had a job to do. She was jobless, with nothing to do except to wonder at the folly of a plan with malicious
intent that had been so well coordinated, but failed in its final
step.

Surely they had anticipated this? You couldn't exactly
smuggle ingots of enriched uranium out in your pockets,
or swallow them down. Was the plan to hide them somewhere until the furor abated? To remove them one by one?
That would mean possible months of logistics, patience, and
potential vulnerability.

How would she do it?

Think like a criminal, Robbie had said.

Words from a man whose voice she'd never hear again,
but whose advice would live with her always, because it had
become part of her.

Jade brainstormed. She thought of the ingots, and Gillespie. Of the fire drills Sbusiso had told her about when they
met right after one. Of the suspected terrorist sympathizer
and the angry Gold City Gaming CEO David had mentioned.

Most of all, she recalled that warehouse she'd seen, so conveniently close to Inkomfe, with its stash of slot machines and
its welding operation, and the way the doors were abruptly
closed when she'd tried to look inside.

And Jade finally realized how they were doing it. How
they had already done it.

Chapter Fifty-Seven

"DAVID!" JADE CALLED.

But David was underground now, in the concrete labyrinth leading to the reactor room. Not contactable on his cell phone, and his hands full dealing with the crime scene. She couldn't drag him away from that now. And Botha was spearheading the Inkomfe search. Jade was certain that they'd find nothing on the premises, but even so, he couldn't just abandon what he was doing.

She'd go on her own, then. Sbusiso would let her out. She could call a cab and wait by the side of the road.

A long walk to the gate, he'd said. He wasn't kidding. It would take her ten minutes, at least, to limp the whole way, since the guards had commandeered all the golf carts.

Well, she had no choice.

Jade dialed directory inquiries on her phone as she walked. The lights of gate one still looked very far away as she listened to the automated voice tell her that the call would be answered in five minutes and forty seconds. Where were all the operators? On a midnight tea break?

She heard the rattle of a security cart behind her. Turning to look, she saw to her surprise it was Botha. He was heading straight toward her. She stopped and waited for him to pull up beside her.

"I thought you said you were okay," he said, his voice filled with concern.

"I am."

"You're limping."

"It's nothing. I twisted my foot when I climbed over the fence."

His eyes widened. "Over the fence?"

"By the pedestrian gate. I went up the turnstile and then over the top."

"You sure it's nothing more serious? Come on in." He held his hand out and helped her into the cart. He smoothed his hand over her hair, stroking it through the tousled locks, his palm warm on the nape of her neck. "Where were you headed?"

She lifted her fingers and touched his forearm, feeling the ropy, corded muscle under that soft skin. "I have a hunch. More than a hunch, actually. It's a certainty."

"Tell me."

Jade gave him a brief summary.

When he'd heard the full explanation, Botha was quiet for a few moments, then said, "Let's go."

"Don't you have to search Inkomfe?" Jade asked.

"I've got a very efficient team doing that, and Ismail, who's heading it up, is on top of things. They don't need me there. And I have a car. We can ride together, and you can make your calls on the way."

"I thought your car was blown up."

"I borrowed Lorenzo's car. He's happy to let me use it, as long as I don't drink and drive." Botha grinned briefly as he turned the cart toward the parking lot.

"Is that where you went when you left the hotel suite?"

Botha nodded. "I wanted to comply with the detectives, and to believe that there was no longer any threat. But I didn't believe it. I couldn't sleep. There are a few Inkomfe guards I trust, old-timers who suspected things were going wrong, and Ismail was one. I called him to ask what the situation was. He said Gillespie was on-site with two men that Ismail didn't recognize, and that there was another big fire drill set for eleven P.M. He didn't like any of it, nor did I. I caught a cab to Lorenzo's and spent some time updating him on the situation in case it turned really bad. I left my phone and laptop there, because there's a lot of evidence on them that he could show the police if I didn't come back. Then I borrowed his car and came here."

"After leaving the shower on and hiding my phone," Jade said accusingly.

"I didn't know how dangerous it would be." His tone was apologetic. "I knew I might be killed. So I decided to go quietly without telling you. When I got to Inkomfe, I had no idea where Gillespie could be. Then the fence alarm went off way down on the southern perimeter, so I rushed over to see what was happening. On my way back, I came across a guard who told me he'd just been blinded and had his vehicle hijacked by a woman carrying pepper spray. I knew that was you. He said he thought you'd driven in the direction of the reactor room, so I hot-footed it over there and found you."

"Just in time, too. I—" Jade began, but at that moment her call to directory inquiries was finally answered. Once she and Botha climbed into Lorenzo's BMW and headed for the exit, Jade got all the numbers she needed and started making calls.

Chapter Fifty-Eight

BOTHA SLOWED DOWN well before the police block-
ade outside Inkomfe. He showed his ID and explained where
they were headed. Jade only picked up snippets of the conversation because she was still on the phone. Her first call
had been to O.R. Tambo International Airport's cargo section. She'd been frustrated but not surprised when it had rung
unanswered. At this hour, there must be only a skeleton staff
on duty. It was why she needed to get there in person as soon
as possible.

Her second call was to the Randfontein police station.
She negotiated hard with them to obtain Officer Mweli's
cell phone number and was finally successful. Mweli sounded
sleepy, as if Jade had woken her, and she heard the loud noise
of a cat meowing in the background.

Mweli promised to contact all the necessary people immediately. Jade knew the policewoman would be able to do so
far quicker than she could.

Then there was nothing to do except to watch the road
unroll in front of her as she tried and retried the two phone
numbers she had for the airport's cargo section. Now that
the roadblocks were behind them, Botha was driving faster,
speeding at nearly double the limit. His lights were on high
beam, his focus on the road ahead, but when Jade had finished her calls, he said, "Explain to me again why you suspect
this?"

"I was thinking about how clever Gillespie's scenario was.

He tried to make every aspect look as if someone else had been to blame. He wanted to come out of this without any dirt under his fingernails so that he could stay out of prison and spend the money he was being paid."

"So how did he do that?"

"He had Loodts murdered in a way that it would look as if he'd been tortured for the new strong room door codes. Meanwhile Gillespie had the codes. He could open the doors anytime he wanted to. But because he wanted to point the finger at a different mastermind, Loodts had to die."

Botha nodded. He shifted gears to drive around a bend, engine racing.

"That made me think. If Gillespie could open the doors anytime he wanted to, then he must already have done it. He could have committed the important part of the crime before the fact. Schedule a routine fire drill or emergency drill, clear the area, get Hamdan's helpers in and pack up the bars. If alarms go off while the doors are open—well, it's an emergency drill, and the area is evacuated anyway."

"Makes sense."

"I think he did it the night I drove to Inkomfe. He was late for our meeting even though he'd said he was on-site, and Sbusiso told me there had just been a big emergency drill. I think he packed the bars into one of the trucks that delivers the nuclear waste to the dumping site in the Northern Cape. The trucks leave at night, he said."

"Yes, they do."

"They fuel up at the new industrial complex nearby. It's newly built, and only one warehouse next to the gas station is occupied—I know because I drove through a few days ago. I saw the slot machines being off-loaded there, and I saw them being worked on inside. It amused me, because I thought the machines were being rigged. But they weren't. I think they were being prepared. Hamdan wanted his ingots, and this was a foolproof way of getting them out of the country undetected."

"So you think the bars were off-loaded while the truck fueled up?"

Jade nodded. "Probably just beforehand. Tell the truck to stop by the warehouse door and pay the driver to look away for ten minutes. That's all it would take to get them out of the truck and into the warehouse, if you had a few men working and the right equipment to help. Then the ingots would have to be put in place—carefully, I would think. One per machine, and the machines sealed up again to look like new."

She disconnected the unanswered call and redialed. Eventually somebody would have to pick up the phone.

"Hamdan has gone back to Iraq. He wouldn't have done that unless he'd known the cargo was organized. And freight takes time to book in. It would have had to be checked by customs, loaded up . . . You couldn't do any part of that process in a hurry. That's why I think it's already been done. The only thing I don't know is when the flight is due to leave. It could be any minute. It might already have gone. If the airport would answer their phone, it would help."

Botha's fingers tightened on the gear shift as he sent the car powering forward, eating up the miles as they headed toward O.R. Tambo International Airport.

The call was answered as they arrived at the cargo terminal's entrance. Just as well, because the security officer at the entrance refused to let them through until a flying squad car, dispatched by Mweli, screamed up behind them. Once her captain had shown his ID, the gate was opened.

They met the dispatcher on duty at the front entrance,

a stressed-looking woman carrying a clipboard. "The slot machines went on the air charter flight," she told them. "It took off half an hour ago."

Jade's heart sank. They had tried so hard, all for naught. But then the woman checked again. "No, wait. Sorry. Everything was delayed after an oil spill on the runway. That flight is in the queue now, waiting for takeoff."

"Recall it immediately," the officer ordered. "In fact, ground all flights until further notice. We're officially seizing that cargo for close inspection. The charter plane must return to the terminal at once. Ms. de Jong, you say you saw these machines? Would you know where the ingots were inserted, so we can take a look?"

"I know what parts of the machines were being worked on, and Botha has seen the ingots," Jade said.

Two hours later, in a sealed warehouse, they watched as the first of the slot machines was off-loaded from the shipping pallet. Wrapped in plastic and padding, it looked as good as new, fresh from the assembly line. It was only when the technician opened the machine's backing and shined a light inside that its modifications were revealed. A metal cage had been welded to the inside, into which one carefully wrapped bar had been placed. Through the transparent packaging, Jade could see its silvery shine. A deadly material that had been moments away from being flown out of the country, to people who would use it in the most destructive way to achieve their ends.

It took a few more hours for Jade and Botha to finish up their part of the investigation, write the necessary affidavits, and wait for a truck to be dispatched to collect the precious cargo once again. With Inkomfe shut down for repairs and the strong room's codes breached, the ingots were transported to Koeberg nuclear power station in the Western Cape to be temporarily stored in their top-security area.

Jade could only hope they would be safe there.

Her eyes were red and scratchy as she walked out of the cargo area, blinking in the hot noonday sun. "Thanks for your help," she told Botha. "You saved my life."

"Likewise."

They were standing close to each other, but not touching. Not because she didn't want to. She wanted to hug him tightly, feeling those broad shoulders and his strong arms around her in turn. There was nothing stopping her. No hitches that she could foresee. No pregnant wives to contend with. Perhaps that was why she suddenly felt unsure.

"What are you going to do now?" Botha asked her.

She shrugged. "Get some sleep, I guess."

"Where?"

Jade found herself smiling reluctantly. "At this stage, just about anywhere sounds good. Why do you ask?"

"Because I was thinking I've always slept well in the sun. A beach in Phuket sounds good. Or maybe Jamaica, or the Yucatán Peninsula. I'm not going back to Inkomfe. I'm going to take long leave until my next job starts in mid-February, and I'd love for you to join me. We're at the airport now. We could go book a flight and be on it by tonight."

Now Jade was smiling for real. "Okay," she said. "Let's do it."

Chapter Fifty-Nine

JADE STRETCHED OUT her legs, feeling the edges of the towel dig into the soft sand. Her skin was browner than it had been two months ago, its dark tan contrasting with the brightness of her ice-blue bikini. Her feet were toughened from daily running on the sand, and her body was used to the feel of the salt water, the buoyancy as the waves carried her out deep enough that the breakers became swells, and she felt one with the body of the ocean.

Their chalet was right on the beachfront, a five-minute walk from the nearest restaurant—a seafood grill—and a sea-shell's throw from a tropical bar that served icy white wine and cocktails in coconut shells.

It had been an amazing eight weeks, the longest holiday she'd ever had. Botha had left the previous week to start a six-month contract updating security systems in a plant in Namibia. They'd already made plans to meet up again as soon as he had some time off.

Without him there, a little of the magic seemed to have gone from this tropical paradise. Jade was glad to be flying back tomorrow. Perhaps it was her own guilt or paranoia, but she'd found herself looking over her shoulder for the last day, imagining that she was being followed by unfriendly eyes. Maybe she could never escape the consequences of what she'd already done.

Best to get back home. There were plenty of jobs to do, legitimate stuff that would keep her busy and bring in honest money. She'd had several inquiries while she'd been away, and now her phone was buzzing again with an incoming message.

Jade turned onto her front and shaded her phone with one hand so she could read it. The number was unfamiliar to her. But as she scanned the words, her eyes widened, and the warmth of the sun seemed to leach away.

I've always said it was better to be lucky, the message read, *and I was. No vital organs hit, and thanks to the uniform and staff ID Gillespie kindly gave me, I spent two weeks in the ICU and another two in a private ward as Moses Nhlapo, c/o Inkomfe's medical insurance. Those surgeons are excellent, baby. The scars are already healing. And thanks for the tourniquet—I think you applied it? They said it helped a lot.*

Anyway, I've been doing some research, and I have a tip-off. Rashid Hamdan is traveling to Istanbul next week to attend a conference. I know where he's staying, and I've got an insider there who can help. Best of all, I've got a shitload of money coming our way once we do this job. Serious moolah. We'll split it fifty-fifty. You'll be set up for the next few years. No more following cheating husbands for a while.

I assume you're in on the deal to take out the murdering sonofabitch? I won't accept no for an answer. I didn't just take one bullet for you, I took three. I think you owe me, so let's use Hamdan to square up the account, then go our separate ways. I'll wait to hear from you ASAP.

Robbie
P.S. Nice bikini.

Acknowledgments

Every writer needs a special somebody who can offer criticism worded so tactfully that it sounds like praise. I'm incredibly fortunate that my loving partner, Dion, is that special somebody. He's also really good with dispensing sympathy, pouring wine, buying chocolates, and other essential support services a writer needs. Dion, words cannot express my love and gratitude.

I'd like to thank my wonderful agent Stephany Evans from FinePrint Literary Management for all the amazing work she's done on my behalf, as well as Bronwen Hruska, Juliet Grames, Amara Hoshijo, and the incredible team at Soho Press, who took a chance on the first Jade de Jong thriller and who are the reason that it's a series today.